# Guardians of the Four

## The Helyan Series – Part One

S.M.Tidball

Second Edition



Cover design by: daniellefine.com

ISBN: 979-8-6349-3191-3

# DEDICATION

For my family, whose encouragement and support
has been unwavering.

# PROLOGUE

The flight deck of the *Nakomo* blazed with white light, forcing Brother Finnian to duck away, shielding his eyes. He grabbed the back of the pilot's seat and prepared himself for the shockwave, but even his tightest grip didn't stop him from being thrown to the floor. Pain ripped through his elbow and up into his neck, reopening the deep gash in his shoulder. He ignored it all, his thoughts in turmoil.

His decision to order the *Nakomo* to retreat had been a testing one, but if he hadn't, they'd all be dead – and there'd been too much loss already. That didn't alter the fact that he'd left people behind on the transporter, and for a moment he allowed the guilt to ripple in his chest before he forced it deep inside. His mission was to save the woman, he only hoped he hadn't been too late.

The blinding light dissipated, and he looked out at black space – the remains of the transporter no more than sparking debris blinking into nothing. He thanked the Gods for keeping the *Nakomo* safe then turned his attention towards the cabin.

"Report." He wasted no time on pleasantries.

Brother Noah looked up and shook his head. "We were too late," he said before returning his attention to the shattered body of the man on the cabin floor. Finnian stepped around him, his thoughts refocused on the woman. She was so still that for a moment he feared she, too, was dead, and that he had been too late, but then her eyes opened and fixed on him. He knelt next to her, holding her hand.

"You came," she said in barely a whisper.

"Of course."

"You're hurt," she added, her eyes drawn to his shoulder.

"It's nothing."

"I don't believe you. You always were a bad liar." She smiled weakly then blinked slowly and turned her head. "What does it say?" she asked the other man kneeling next to her.

Brother Benjamin studied the medi-scanner a moment longer before flicking a glance towards Finnian.

"What?" she said. "I saw that look. What's going on? Is she all right?" She tried to sit up, gasped with pain, and then laid back on the cold floor of the cabin, her head resting on the makeshift pillow made from Benjamin's rolled up robes.

Benjamin looked to Finnian for guidance, receiving a brief nod in response. "Your baby's showing signs of distress," Benjamin said. "I fear we'll lose her if we don't act soon."

"Then do what you need to. What are you wait—" The woman's words were cut off by a cry of pain. "Save her," she continued through gritted teeth. "She's all that matters – you know that, Finnian."

"We're not equipped to do surgery here," Benjamin protested. "To attempt to now would put you both in great danger."

"I hear you, Brother, now hear me; my life is of no importance, but the baby—" She coughed, blood trickling from blue-tinged lips. "Do what you need to make sure she's safe. Whatever you need," she reiterated. Neither man responded. "Please," she implored, looking directly at Finnian, her gaze so intensely passionate that after a moment he nodded.

"Of course," he replied.

The woman smiled again and mouthed the words 'thank you' before closing her eyes. Her breathing faltered and he held his own breath, but after a couple of seconds her eyes opened. With difficulty, she lifted her hand to his cheek. "I need you to promise me something, Finnian..."

"Please, Mia, save your energy."

"No, you don't undertsa—" Another wave a pain surged through her. "I need you to promise me you'll look after her."

"I…" He paused, confused by her request.

"You know what's at stake. I need you and the Brotherhood to look after my child. You – at the monastery. No one else; nowhere else. Do you understand?"

"Mia, we can't take in a baby, let alone a girl. People will talk, they'll be suspicious."

"It doesn't matter. No one messes with the Brotherhood's Warrior Caste – not even the Royal Earth Force. She'll be safe with—" She cried out in agony, and Finnian wished so badly that he could take the pain for her.

"I hate to interrupt," Benjamin urged, looking at the medi-scanner again, "but if we're going to do this, we have to do it now."

"Wait! Not until he promises," Mia sobbed, her eyes fixed on Finnian again. For the first time in his life he was lost; he had no idea what to say. His word was his bond, but what would the Primus say? "Promise me," she pushed, but he was torn. Whatever he decided there and then, the Brotherhood would have to honour. But what if… A pained sob broke his thoughts.

"Okay, I promise." His words came out in a tumbled rush before he could measure them.

"I need more than that."

"I promise to you, and the Gods, that the Brotherhood will take in your child, and that we'll look after her – at the monastery – and protect her with our lives. She will be family."

Mia smiled sadly. "Thank you. You have no idea what this means to me – to know she'll be safe. I'm ready now," she said, but then her expression changed as she remembered something. "When she's old enough, you must give her this." She pulled a small, brushed-bronze medallion from her neck and placed it carefully in Finnian's hand. "I cannot tell you how vital it is she gets it. Lives will depend on it, do you understand?" He nodded, even though he didn't, and brushed damp hair from her eyes. "And something else… my pocket…"

Finnian reached into the pocket she'd indicated, pulling out what appeared to be a ripped-out page from a large ancient manuscript. Most of it was covered in swirls and patterns he didn't recognise, but along the bottom there was something written in a different hand. Even though the paper was stained with blood, he could make out three distinct words: Family, Honour, Courage. He had no idea what they meant.

"I'll make sure she gets them both."

"I know you will. You're a good man, Finnian."

The baby was blue and silent when Benjamin pulled her from Mia's womb, and for a tense moment Finnian was cold with fear. He'd never felt as helpless as he did right at that moment, nor had he ever experienced such an overwhelming wave of relief when the first screams filled the cabin.

Benjamin wrapped the child in a towel and tried to pass her to Mia, but she was so weak she was scared to take her. Finnian leant forward and helped, supporting Mia's arms with his own, and for a moment he was saddened that he would never hold a child of his own like that.

"Have you chosen a name?" Benjamin asked.

"Shae," Mia said, smiling. "Her father chose it." With difficulty, she turned her head to look at the man lying on the floor further down the cabin. Tear-tracks marked her pale face. "Take her," she said, her voice failing. "Tell her, her father and I loved her with all our hearts."

# 1

Angel Ridge – what a shithole. At least that was my first impression as I followed Ash and Francis through the large marketplace, roughly carved from the hard, black rock of the asteroid's interior. I stepped carefully to avoid garbage and crap, the smell of decay biting at the back of my throat.

Occasional wafts of stale air brushed my skin, and I was grateful I'd chosen not to wear a jacket. Even in a T-Shirt I was hot, the back of my neck uncomfortably clammy.

As we passed through the crowd, I got the distinct impression the locals weren't happy to see us. Those that could, gave us a wide berth, while those that couldn't shuffled past avoiding eye contact. Some even disappeared into shops, closing doors swiftly behind them before peering back out at us through grimy windows.

Others, however, were more confrontational.

"Hey, pretty lady." The man was short, overweight, and smelled like decomposing anko-root. He stared openly at my chest, his leer revealing black teeth and rotting green gums. "You wanna party, Missy Miss?"

"You know what?" I replied. "I'd rather boil my head in a bucket of acid."

The man lost his drunken smirk, producing a nine-inch, double-edged hunting knife instead. I wasn't impressed.

I took a large step forward and grabbed his knife hand, swinging it to the side, while bringing my knee upwards. I wasn't even putting in that much effort, but it was enough. I knew the moment my knee connected with his groin because he let out a slow, choked howl. As he doubled over in agony, I swung my knee forward again. That time it connected with his face, and a satisfying crunch told me I'd broken his nose.

The man fell backwards onto the ground, unconscious.

"Already making friends I see," said Francis, scratching at his bald head, but unfortunately Ash wasn't quite so indifferent.

"One of these days you're going to pick a fight with the wrong person, Shae," he said, deep frown-lines crossing his forehead.

"Me? Never," I joked. "Besides, that's what I have you for, isn't it? To save me from trouble?"

"Hmm," he mused, but after a moment he added, "Maybe the Primus shouldn't have let you come; Angel Ridge is a dangerous place."

"I know."

"Do you? Even the Royal Earth Force gives this place a miss – that should tell you something."

I noticed his left hand resting on the gold medal at the centre of his belt, awarded to him by the Primus on his ascent to Ninth Degree – a position he adopted when he wasn't happy.

"Ash," I said, sighing with mock weariness. "You're my brother, and I love that you worry about me, but we have this conversation every time the Primus lets me go off-world."

"I know, but..." He pointed towards a faded logo daubed in grey paint on the wall.

"ARRO? Here?" I marvelled, looking around me with

renewed awareness.

"The asteroid is a cesspool of criminals, gun-thugs and mercs – just the kind of place a terrorist group like the Anti-Royalist Rebel Opposition would recruit from." He ran his fingers through short, light-brown hair, the reflection of the chem-lights flickering in his grey eyes as he shook his head. "I know you're not going to change after twenty-nine years, but just be careful okay? You know it would kill me if anything happened to you… and then Finnian would kill me for letting something happen to you."

"Okay, okay," I conceded, too hot to get into another debate about my safety. I pulled a band from my wrist and scraped my damp hair into a ponytail.

"Hate to break up the party," Francis whispered, "but I think we should move." I followed his gaze towards one of the shop fronts, taking note of the small group of men who'd gathered together. My eyes flicked between gun-belts and hands as I counted the number of weapons.

"Agreed," said Ash, lifting the hem of his full-length, dark-blue robes to step easily over the fat, smelly man, still unconscious on the floor.

The Warrior Caste was admired and feared in equal measure, so I was surprised the Primus had ordered the monks to wear their official robes to a place overtly hostile to any kind of authority. I'd thought the sun and rune symbol embroidered in gold on the monk's chests would be like a red-rag to the locals – but perhaps the blatant show of discipline and strength was exactly what the Primus had intended.

"So who's in charge of Angel Ridge?" I asked idly as we walked.

"A particularly dangerous man called Dax," Ash replied, distaste clear in his voice. "Ex-military – dishonourably discharged. At best he's an ARRO sympathiser, at worst he's part of an active cell, but we've never been able to pin anything on him. Oh, and he's also got no morals or honour."

"Sounds like a charmer. We nearly there yet?"

"Not quite," replied Francis, pointing at a rusted metal cage suspended by fraying cables.

Ash raised an apprehensive eyebrow.

"It's this or the stairs," Francis said. "I'm sure you remember just how far down the next level is... but it's your choice," he added, grinning.

"Come on, Ash, where's your sense of adventure?" I teased.

"Being held hostage by my sense of personal survival," he replied, but it was followed by his trademark lopsided grin.

Francis had to yank the handle several times to open the corroded lift door and my bravado wavered. As I stepped in, the whole cage shuddered and dropped slightly. I braced myself against the sides, glaring at Francis for laughing.

"You don't flinch when some random bloke pulls a knife on you, but you go all weak at the knees over a little shake. Where's your sense of adventure?" he mocked.

"That was funny – you're a funny man," I replied sarcastically.

"Come here, I'll protect you," he said, pulling me into a vice-like hug.

"Get off me, you big jerk," I protested into his broad chest, his laugh rumbling in my ear. He let me go and I punched him on the shoulder.

"Ouch!"

"Serves you right for being annoying."

The lift jerked and juddered as it dropped the considerable distance towards Level 3. A power outage killed the lights and we ground to a standstill, completely encased in smooth, black rock. I fidgeted and opened my mouth to speak, but before I had the chance to say anything, the chem-lights flickered back into life and the cage continued on its precarious journey. I was relieved when I saw the pale glow from our destination in the shaft below.

The relief was premature.

The cage slowed to a stop with a painful screech that pierced my skull, but it was the smell that literally took my breath away. I'd thought Level 2 was bad, but I wasn't prepared for the stomach-churning blend of raw sewage and rotting refuse.

"You'll acclimatise to the smell in no time," said Ash, laughing.

"I'll take your word for it," I replied, gagging, my voice almost drowned out by the combination of music, laughter, and shouting. It took a moment for my brain to adjust and separate the sounds and their origins.

The lift had brought us to the crossroads of two large tunnels. Where Level 2 had been light and cavernous, Level 3 was dark, dank and claustrophobic. The chem-lights were old and weak, and they flickered intermittently, but they were adequate – as long as you didn't want to see too far. On the wall opposite, a zigzagged black arrow, superimposed over a grey diamond, was barely visible beneath the grime, and I wondered how many of the locals had ties to the rebels.

I stepped over a stream of dark liquid that ran along the gutter, trying not to think about what it was, but my foot slipped and I put my hand out to stop myself falling. My fingers sank into the festering green slime that covered the clammy tunnel walls, and I swore loudly.

Francis took us down the East tunnel, passed crude stalls covered with an assortment of illegal or stolen goods. Most of the tables looked like they'd been cobbled together with whatever material the trader could beg, borrow or steal. Humans and Others – the colloquial term for any mixed-species being – hustled potential customers, but no one approached us. I wasn't sure whether it was the Brotherhood uniform or the uncompromising, focussed look on Ash's face that discouraged people.

Most of the stalls were fairly standard, but one caught my attention – not because it was piled high with weapons and explosives, but because each piece was branded with the small eagle-head and wings emblem of the Royal Earth Force, Fleet Division. I veered towards the table, but Ash took my arm and led me away.

"You'd think the REF would be more careful with their munitions," he whispered. "How could they let this lot get their hands on them?"

"I don't know, but we can't just leave them here," I said.

"I have to agree with Shae on this one, Ash," added Francis. "We have to do something."

"Normally I'd agree with both of you, but…" He paused, his grey eyes narrowing. "Look, our mission takes priority, but let's not rule anything out just yet. Depending on how things go, we may, may," he reiterated, "be able to come back. Francis?"

"Agreed," Francis replied, but I hesitated. I knew he was right, but it didn't alter the fact that alarm bells were going off in the back of my mind.

"Shae?"

"Agreed," I said reluctantly.

The seller, a skinny guy with bright red hair, glanced up from his data-pad, but after no more than a curious glance in our direction, he went back to whatever he'd been doing. Francis and I were reluctant to leave, but Ash pushed us on.

A few minutes later we reached our destination: Finnegan's Bar – one of the few structures on Level 3. Standing in the doorway was a Rhinorian; his large body, and tree-trunk sized limbs, taking up the entire space.

Rhinorians were as dumb as a box of rocks, but their impressive strength, and their ability to follow simple orders, made them perfect as thugs-for-hire – or in his case, a bouncer.

"Stop," the Rhinorian grunted, holding one hand up in

front of me, and for a second I thought it weird that it was actually bigger than my head. He jabbed a stubby finger at a sign to the right of the entrance that read, 'No Weapons Allowed,' in bold black writing, and in several different languages. Underneath, in smaller letters, was written, 'Failure to comply may result in death.'

Ash had made us leave our weapons on the *Nakomo*. He'd said three strangers would cause enough interest, but three armed strangers would be like inviting trouble. He was probably right, but I never felt comfortable without them.

"No weapons," I said, taking a step towards the entrance.

"Stop," the Rhinorian grunted again, studying me with beady eyes, black and glassy in his round, wrinkled face. He motioned for me to lift my arms.

"Come on," I moaned. "You've got to be kidding me."

The Rhinorian grunted again, making a bizarre flapping motion with his thick, grey arms, and I had to suppress the urge to laugh. I lifted mine in compliance, and he patted me down with enough force to almost knock me off balance. He followed the same ritual with the monks, and when he was satisfied, he wrinkled his stubby nose and stepped away from the door. As I passed him, he grinned broadly and rumbled, "Enjoy."

The bar was simple enough, I'd been in worse, and from a security perspective, it was ideal: one large open space with no side rooms or private lounges where threats could remain undetected.

A weary-looking, plump waitress with a tray of drinks steered her way around tables that looked as filthy as the floor – which was tacky under my boots. It wasn't busy, but there were a few groups occupying the u-shaped booths that ran the full length of both side walls. None of them seemed overly interested in our arrival.

Four Santians sat at one of the back booths. Like the

Rhinorians, the Santians were a humanoid species, but that's about the extent of things they had in common. Their home-world was a Category 3 planet: a rock world with extremely high temperatures, few water resources, and even less vegetation.

I thought them oddly beautiful. Their skin – shades of light brown, beige, and taupe to help camouflage against predators – seemed darker and richer under the chem-lights. I glanced over and noticed the distinct lack of body hair, and even though I knew to expect it, it still freaked me out that they didn't even have eyelashes or eyebrows.

I noticed one of the Santians watching me, and when he blinked his third eyelids across bright, amber eyes, I looked away, suddenly aware that I'd been staring.

The bar was at the far end of the room, but I managed to navigate past the few patrons without much trouble. I picked a barstool that wasn't quite as grimy as the others and sat. I had my back to everyone, but there was an aging mirror behind the liquor bottles so I could see most of the room in its reflection. Ash leant casually against the metal bar, facing the main door.

I breathed in the heavy scent of sour beer and herbacco, something that would've normally turned my stomach, but after the stench of the tunnels, it was surprisingly pleasant.

The only other exit from the room was a door to my left marked, 'Toilets,' in several languages. Francis disappeared through it to assess an alternative exfil route.

A huge Human barman approached, intricate black-ink tribal tattoos covering his arms and shoulders. I noticed the wide, rough scar that ran along his jawbone, punctuating his dark beard, and decided he probably wasn't someone you'd want to mess with out of choice.

"The name's Beck," he grunted, eying us suspiciously. "Welcome to my bar. What can I get you?"

"Three beers," I replied. "And none of that watered down Teki-piss you've got on tap," I added as he moved towards one of the pumps. "Make it bottled – and open them on the bar so I can see they haven't been tampered with."

Beck stopped what he was doing, and in a split second was leant over the bar, his face only a fraction from mine. I didn't flinch, but I regretted leaving my weapons on the *Nakomo.*

"What's the matter, little girl? You don't trust me? Me? In my own bar?" he bellowed.

"Hell no. I'm not an idiot. Of course I don't trust you," I replied, my voice calm and measured.

In the mirror's reflection, I noticed a few customers turn in our direction, probably in anticipation of a fight.

Beck stared into my eyes a moment longer, as if he were trying to see something in them, then his own eyes crinkled, his lips broke into a wide grin, and he let out a booming laugh.

"Quite right, too. I wouldn't trust me either," he said, clapping me hard on the shoulder. He bent down and retrieved three bottles from under the bar, which he opened in full view. "I like you," he said as he passed me one of the beers. "You've got balls."

"Thanks… I think."

Beck handed a second bottle to Ash. "Not sure about you, though. Don't get the Brotherhood around here much."

"Just passing through," Ash replied politely, taking the beer.

"Nobody just passes through Angel Ridge," he replied sceptically, but when Ash didn't bite, he turned his attention back to me. "What about you?"

"What about me?"

"We don't get many like you around here either." He winked, smiling again.

"Oh, umm, just passing through," I replied pathetically.

"Interesting company you keep." He flicked his eyes

towards Ash. "I bet there's an interesting story there." Beck leant on the bar again so his face was near to mine, his muscular, tattooed arms folded on the countertop. He looked straight into my eyes and after a moment I rearranged my position on the stool, giving me an excuse to look away and break the contact. I think I even blushed.

His attention was unexpected, and although it wasn't entirely unwelcome, I wasn't quite sure how to handle it. When the Primus allowed me to go off-world, it was on the condition that I remained in the company of at least one monk at all times. I'm sure he has his reasons, but a permanent chaperone certainly complicated my relationships with the opposite sex. As a result, I wasn't particularly experienced – romantically or sexually.

I was much more in control when I thought I might have to fight Beck.

My stomach fluttered nervously and I welcomed the distraction as Francis reappeared. The barman drifted away to serve another customer, who'd been trying to get his attention for some time.

"You see these get opened?" Francis asked. I nodded and he took a deep swig.

"What's the situation?" Ash asked.

"The corridor takes you out to a side alley. Take a right and there's an access panel to a maintenance shaft. Twenty metres left and there's a ladder that leads to Level 2. It'll be some climb, but safer than going back into the main tunnels if things turn bad."

"Okay then," said Ash. "That's our alternate exfil route. If all goes to plan, we go back the way we came. If that exit becomes impractical, we take the back door and head for the ladder. Francis, if we get separated use whichever route is safer and we'll meet back at the shuttle." Francis nodded. "Shae, you stick with me."

"Sure."

"Whatever happens," he reiterated.

"Jeez, I heard you, Ash."

"Good, because it's not a request."

Ash glanced around the room before nodding his head towards the booth nearest to the rear exit. He and Francis sat at each end of the u-shaped bench so they could get out quickly if needed. Stuck in the middle, the high seatbacks blocked my view of everything except what was straight in front of me. I felt trapped and uneasy.

Ash looked at the com-pad on his wrist. "What time's your guy getting here?" he asked.

"We agreed on eighteen-hundred so he's got another ten minutes," Francis replied. "And he's not, 'my guy.' I've never met the man."

"Then why, exactly, are we here?" I asked. I'd been on an off-world supply-run with Brother Thomas when the Primus had held the initial briefing back at the monastery. In fact, I'd only just got back in time to convince him to let me tag along – something I was beginning to regret.

"You remember Trayan, the leader of the east coast farming community on Calay 3?" Francis said.

"Nope."

"Sure you do. He's the guy who borrowed money from the Khan Brothers to buy medicine for his kid, then couldn't pay it back because of a poor crop yield. Brother Benjamin and I stepped in to mediate, remember?"

I stared at him blankly. "Must've missed that exciting mission brief," I confessed. "But I do know how the Khans operate."

My face flushed with anger. We dealt with scum like them all the time, but the Khans were always one step ahead of us – and the military. The REF did their best, but even their resources and reach were limited, which was why the Brotherhood of the Virtuous Sun created their Warrior division in the first place: to protect the unprotected. It's the Warrior Caste's manifesto. We lived by it. We died by it.

My fingertips slipped underneath the sleeve of my T-shirt and traced the outline of the tattoo on my upper right arm. The black-ink Sun and Rune insignia, with the words 'Protect the Unprotected' in delicate ancient script underneath, was the tangible symbol of a Warrior's honour, integrity and respect. Everything criminals like the Khans lacked.

Francis's voice brought me back to the conversation. "During my last follow-up visit, Freya, Trayan's wife, told me her brother had turned up late one night completely drunk, talking about his life being in danger because of something he'd overhead. Apparently, Nyan wasn't making much sense, but Freya heard him mention something about the assassination of an important person."

"Who?"

"She doesn't know. When he'd sobered up in the morning, she tried to get him to say more, but he claimed he didn't know what she was talking about. He said she was talking dangerous rubbish; the kind of rubbish that would get you killed if the wrong person heard about it."

"So why didn't she contact the REF?"

"There was nothing to substantiate the information, and Nyan is… well, let's just say he's not the most credible of witnesses. Freya asked for my help, so I agreed to take it to the Primus – who felt we should follow it up, just to be on the safe side. After quite a lot of persuasion, Nyan agreed to—"

A couple of metal chairs upended and two men launched into a full-on fist fight, the rest of the group jeering them on. In the moment it took the three of us to rise from our seats, Beck had vaulted the bar and taken out one of them with a Sky-Orb bat. I was impressed.

The party concerned continued to mill around, reluctant to leave until Beck put two fingers in his mouth to produce a high-pitched whistle. The main doors opened and the Rhinorian filled the space they left. After a couple of nervous glances at the bouncer, the group made the wise decision to move on.

Beck turned and started back towards the bar, but then he detoured towards our table instead. "Sorry about that folks. I hope you weren't disturbed." He didn't take his eyes from me, and when he smiled, I couldn't help but smile back.

"Was there something else?" asked Ash pointedly.

"Umm, sure, can I get you guys any more drinks?"

"No thank you." The words were clearly dismissive.

I picked at a piece of stuffing escaping from the cracked seat while I waited for Beck to move out of earshot. "So, let me get this straight," I said. "We're here to meet an alcoholic thief, who may, possibly, have information about a supposed assassination attempt?"

"Yes," said Francis.

"And the Primus actually agreed to this?"

"Yes."

"He does appreciate it could be nothing more than the ramblings of a drunk?"

Francis sighed. "Yes, Shae."

"Great," I grumbled.

"You didn't have to come."

"I know, but it wouldn't be so much fun without me, would it?" I pulled him towards me so I could kiss the top of his bald head.

"Yeah, well, maybe," he conceded, his face breaking into a wide grin, but it disappeared just as quickly. "He's here."

I raised myself so I could see over the back of the booth. A remarkably average-looking man stood just inside the entrance, fidgeting and wiping his forehead on his jacket sleeve. When he made no attempt to approach, Francis rose from his seat and went to greet him.

Whatever he said to the man must've worked because Nyan's shoulders lowered and his face lost some of its panic. Francis led him towards our table, but just before they reached us, he intercepted the waitress and asked her for another round of drinks.

Ash stood so Nyan could scoot around the bench to sit next to me, and then he re-seated himself, hemming Nyan in.

The smell of alcohol was bitter on the man's breath, and I couldn't help thinking we were wasting our time. I wondered whether Ash would let us ditch the drunk to go and deal with the stolen Fleet weapons – at least our trip to the Ridge wouldn't have been wasted.

"Nyan," Francis said to get the man's attention. "This is Brother Asher, and this is Shae." Nyan looked between us, his gaze eventually lingering on me.

"You're not Brotherhood," he grunted. "Why are you here? What's going on? Is this a trick?"

"Shae is Brotherhood, Nyan," Francis said quickly. "She may not be a monk, but as far as we're concerned, she is one of us." Francis's deep, confident tone left no room for discussion. "This isn't a trap, I give you my word."

"Yeah, if you say so." He didn't sound convinced. "Listen, man, I know you said I was safe with you guys, but…" he raised himself so he could see over the high back of the booth, "I'm scared, and I mean shit-scared." His hands trembled on the chipped table, and when the waitress arrived with our beers, he looked set to climb his way out from the booth.

"Freya is concerned about you," Francis said, opening the discussion as soon as the waitress had moved away.

"She fuckin' should be," Nyan replied too loudly. "How many times do I have to tell you my life's in danger?"

"Why do you think that?"

"I can't tell you, man." He was agitated again. "They'll kill me… and Freya, too, if she doesn't keep her trap shut."

I was paying way more attention.

# 2

Nyan couldn't sit still, and if he hadn't been wedged between Ash and me, he would've bolted. His gaze was unfocussed, and his eyes flicked rapidly, as if he was working through something. We sat in silence, letting him think, but I could tell Ash was getting impatient.

"Tell us what has happened. Who's trying to kill you?" Francis pushed, but still nothing.

"Think about it, Nyan." Ash spoke for the first time. "You've already taken the biggest step by meeting us."

The drunk hung his head, shaking it from side to side, his whole body trembling as his internal conversation continued. Periodically he slurred disconnected sentences, but it was difficult to understand what he was talking about.

Unexpectedly he looked up. His eyes were clearer, the violent shaking had calmed, and it was obvious he'd settled whatever debate he'd been having in his head.

"Okay. I'll tell you everything – as long as you promise to protect Freya." Nyan looked pleadingly at Francis. "My life's over, man, I've accepted that now – but she's a good girl. She's kind and caring, and deserves better than family like me. Promise me you'll keep her safe and I'll tell you everything I know."

"The Brotherhood will do everything in its power to keep Freya and her family safe," replied Francis. Not quite what Nyan asked for, but he didn't seem to notice the difference.

"Here goes nothing then... I guess it's no secret that I steal stuff – just enough to get by, you know? I'm not a bad guy," he paused, "not a really bad guy. I don't carry a weapon, and I try not to hurt anyone. I'm not good with conflict, see. Fuckin' ironic, isn't it?" He was starting to relax, ramble even.

"It's all right," I said. "We're not here to judge you."

"Really?" He wiped the sweat off his forehead with his sleeve and I got another hit of stale whisky. "I'd heard about that worker's strike on the Planet of Souls – the grave diggers from the rich quarter – anyway, I thought, 'what the fuck.' If no one's going to be there, I might as well take a quick look. See what I can see, right? If those people are retarded enough to bury their loved ones with treasures, they deserve to be robbed. Besides, I figured I wouldn't be doing no one no harm. It's not like they need that shit, is it?" He paused, looking intently at the peeling label on his beer bottle.

"What happened?" asked Ash.

"Security was busy controlling the pickets so they didn't notice me slip by; I guess they had their hands full. I worked my way around to one of the older areas – been there a couple of hours when I heard voices. Scared me shitless, I can tell you. Thought it might've been Security, maybe other looters, so I hid behind one of the mausoleums. The voices didn't get any closer so I went to take a look." Nyan closed his eyes for a moment and took a deep, faltering breath. "Biggest fuckin' mistake of my life. If I'd left then, none of this would be happening." He rubbed his eyes as tears began to well.

"Please, carry on," I urged.

"I could only see shadowy shapes, but there were a fair few people there, and it certainly wasn't Security – or diggers. Someone wasn't happy; I couldn't hear what he was saying, but I could tell by his tone he was fucked-off big time. After a bit, the wind must've changed in my direction or something because I could pick up bits of the conversation. Not whole sentences, mind, just bits and… I can't do this," Nyan spluttered. "Please, let me go. We can pretend this never happened."

"It's all right." I had my hand on his shoulder, practically pinning him to his seat. He looked so terrified, so lost, I pitied him.

"We have somewhere we can take you, somewhere you'll be safe," said Ash.

"No!" He almost choked. "There isn't anywhere safe for me. Not now. You don't fuckin' understand."

"Then help us understand. What happened on the Planet of Souls?" he coaxed.

"Like I said, I could only hear bits, and none of it made sense. I heard them talking about taking out someone of great importance. Don't know who." He shrugged his shoulders apologetically. "But whatever they're planning, it's going to be big. They said it was going to be something everyone would be talking about for decades. I heard a place, too, GalaxyBase4, and somewhere called Frampton Edge." Nyan shrugged again. "No idea where that is. You guys?"

I didn't have a clue. Ash and Francis both shook their heads.

"Can you tell us where on the Planet of Souls the group met?" Francis asked.

"Not exactly. I'd moved around a lot, searching for tombs with the most potential." He looked ashamed, but then the hint of a memory caught in his eyes. "Wait a minute. The mausoleum I hid behind… there was a name on it…" Nyan banged his fists against his head, muttering.

"It was double-barrelled, I remember that."

"Try to picture the grave," Ash suggested.

"What the fuck do you think I'm trying to do? It was something Huntley. Barrington-Huntley? Yes, that's it: Timothy Barrington-Huntley. I remember because it reminded me of Bartington Huntley. You know? The Sky-Orb player for the Tamon Tigers?" We looked at him blankly. "Jeez, you guys must live under a rock. Anyway, the group was just south of that. I tried to leave but they must've seen me, or heard me. There was shouting from everywhere, and then they came after me. The guy, the one who'd been arguing earlier, gave everyone the order to take me out, so I bolted. I got no clue how I got away, but I've been in hiding ever since."

"You've done the right thing, meeting us," said Ash.

"Like you can do shit," replied Nyan. He wasn't sarcastic, just resigned somehow. "I was dumb as a fuckin' Rhinorian not to get the hell out of there as soon as—" A noise stopped him mid-sentence.

"Don't move," I ordered before rising so I could see over the back of the booth. Ash shifted around the bench to shield Nyan.

A skinny guy with red hair steered through the main floor, but in his haste, he careered off tables and chairs, almost dropping the data-pad he carried. He stumbled and bounced off an Other, causing him to spill his beer down his already matted pelt, but he didn't stop to apologise. He skidded around the side of the bar without slowing and came to an abrupt stop at Beck's elbow.

Beck scowled at him and said something that caused the man to glance towards our table, but he was no more interested in us then than he'd been back in the tunnel. As their conversation continued, the man got more desperate, looking back towards the entrance every few seconds.

The Other, whose drink he'd spilled, towered over the bar, angrily waving his empty tankard and banging a claw on the countertop. Beck apologised, refilled the mug, and handed it back with a manufactured smile. As the Other walked back to his seat, still grumbling, the two men dropped down behind the bar. After the briefest of moments, the barman reappeared alone and continued serving patrons as if nothing had happened.

Ash relaxed and moved back to his original position at the end of the bench.

"Wasn't that the guy—" I began.

"I believe it was," Ash agreed. "But there's nothing we can do about it at the moment. Our priority is to get Nyan somewhere safe. If you'll come?" he added to the thief.

"Sure. Whatever, man. I guess I got nowhere else to go."

"Good, then I suggest we leave immediately."

We stood to head out, but Nyan was reluctant to follow. "Wait. I lied!" he blurted. "I'm sorry. I was scared, and I didn't know if I could trust you." We sat back down. "I know you're trying to help, but you can't. Not against these guys. See, I lied – well, not so much 'lied' as didn't tell you everything. It's just that I recognised his voice; the guy who was arguing – the fucker who wants me dead. That's why I know you can't help me. Not in the long run."

"It's okay," said Ash. "We... what now?" he added, frustrated by another distraction.

I looked over the booth again and watched the Rhinorian backing into the room, his thick arms raised. He was followed by an REF Fleet trooper, whose latest issue TK70 plasma rifle was pointed directly at his chest.

I counted three more troopers entering through the front door, and another one appeared behind us from the rear, all kitted out in standard assault gear: combat fatigues under full body armour.

Beck, who'd been talking to a customer in one of the booths on the opposite side from us, started to edge his way back towards the bar, but the troopers quickly took up flanking positions, cutting him off.

"This isn't our fight," Ash whispered. "Nyan is our only concern."

We stood to leave, but then something even more unexpected happened.

The main doors opened again and a Full-Wing Fleet Captain strode in, his immaculate uniform a stark contrast against the battle-gear worn by his squad. I wondered whether the lack of body army, combined with the fact that his two Sentinel plasma pistols were still holstered, was naïvety, bravery, or just plain arrogance. Storming through Angel Ridge with an armed tactical unit would, if nothing else, paint a big fat ARRO target on his back. Factoring in the way he'd marched into the bar, I was favouring arrogance.

He squared his broad shoulders, surveying the room, and I was struck by how young he was to hold the rank of Full-Wing Captain.

He raised a hand in the air. "Listen up," he shouted above the objections and indignant complaints. There was a slight decrease in volume, but not much, so he pulled a Sentinel from its holster and shot one pulse into the ceiling. A shower of rocks spilled to the floor and he had their attention.

"Hey, that was unnecessary," said Beck, taking a step forward, but a trooper turned her weapon on him and he retreated, holding up his hands in compliance.

Ignoring the interruption, the Fleet Officer continued. "My name is Captain Marcos. I'm here about stolen Fleet weapons, and stolen Fleet weapons only. I'm not interested in anything else. Am I clear?" A few people mumbled, a few nodded, but most were silent. "The person I'm looking for entered this bar a few minutes ago, and hasn't been seen leaving. My troopers are going to move you together and Lieutenant Grainger here will check your identity. If you're not the person we're looking for, you'll be allowed to leave without further delay. This will go as easy or as hard as you make it. Do you understand?" That time there were a few more nods. "Good. I'm glad you appreciate the situation."

Ash caught my eye and raised both eyebrows. I had to laugh because I knew what he meant. Without doubt, it was arrogance.

The troopers started to work their way around the bar, herding customers into a line on the other side of the room. Lieutenant Grainger produced an Ident tablet and began checking the group nearest to the door. Once she was satisfied with their identification, she gestured to one of the other troopers who escorted the person out of the bar.

Ash turned to Nyan. "You do what we tell you to do, okay? You don't argue. You don't question. You just do it. What we say," he reiterated. "Not the troopers." Nyan nodded but looked terrified again.

Ash, Francis and I moved off the bench and positioned ourselves at the opening to the horseshoe booth. Nyan remained seated, as ordered.

One of the troopers approached – a young guy who looked not long out of training. The name Roberts was printed on his immaculate breastplate.

"Sirs, Miss, you need to move to the other side of the bar," he said.

The lights flickered and I automatically looked up.

"As you can see, we're representatives of the Brotherhood of the Virtuous Sun, and therefore do not fall under your jurisdiction, Roberts." Ash spoke with quiet authority. "We're not bound by your orders, and request permission to take our leave without further interruption."

Roberts hesitated, on the brink of uncertainty. "One moment," he said tapping his earpiece to open a com-link – presumably to Lieutenant Grainger, who mirrored the action on the other side of the room. They had a brief discussion then she passed the Ident tablet to another trooper and headed over to where the Captain was interrogating the Rhinorian. She spoke discreetly in his ear, and he looked intrigued before heading over.

"Roberts," he said, his voice strong and confident. "Report to Grainger. I'll deal with things here."

"Yes, sir," replied the trooper, disappearing quickly.

Marcos studied Ash, taking in the Brotherhood robes and the Ninth-Degree medal fixed to his belt. His eyes flicked to Francis's Eighth Degree medal, but when he got to me, confusion swept briefly across his face. He looked at me for a second longer before tilting his head so he could see Nyan. Abruptly he turned his attention back to Ash, the higher ranked monk, as protocol dictated.

"Jared Marcos," he said holding out his hand.

Ash hesitated for a fraction of a second, then he extended his arm and the two men shook firmly. "Brother Asher," he said. "Brother Francis and Shae." He didn't mention Nyan.

Ash was just over six foot, but next to the Captain, even he looked short. I was loath to admit it, but Marcos was definitely imposing.

"It's an honour to meet such high-ranking Warrior Caste monks." Marcos seemed genuine. "However, I'm intrigued to find you…" he looked around the bar with obvious distaste, "here."

"And yet, here you are also," stated Ash. "A Full-Wing Captain on a low-level retrieval operation?"

"Touché!" Marcos grinned broadly. "Just stretching my legs. I'm sure you understand."

"Captain, as I've already said to your trooper, we request permission to take our leave without further interruption." Marcos's eyes narrowed. "It's only out of respect that we've waited this long to depart, but our business is pressing and I insist we be allowed to leave without further delay."

"What is your business?"

"I'm afraid that's classified."

"Really?" Marcos looked intrigued again, and not like

someone who was about to give up any time soon.

"I'm sure you're aware of the Constantine Agreement, Captain?" Ash pushed.

"Of course. It's required reading at the Academy."

"Then you know the Brotherhood is not regulated by REF rules, and has special dispensation in situations like this. I repeat, it's only out of courtesy we've not invoked our rights under section Delta 7 of the Agreement."

"Hmm." Marcos took in a deep breath and puffed it out slowly. "Seems we have a problem then. You see, I'm looking for an enemy of the Crowns, and said enemy was seen fleeing into this bar. The three of you had a perfect view of what happened, and that makes you material witnesses. Correct me if I'm wrong, but section Delta 7, subsection fifteen, allows a high ranking military official – that would be me – to hold members of the Brotherhood – that would be you – for interrogation, if he believes they have evidence that may prove beneficial in an ongoing, high threat-level investigation." He smiled smugly. "I don't think I got it word for word, but you get the idea."

Pretentious arse.

I thought Ash would be angry, but he actually smiled. I think he was even impressed. Ash could be extremely intimidating, and most officers weren't that well versed in the Agreement.

"Besides," Marcos continued, "you may be Brotherhood, but she sure as hell isn't."

The arrogance of the man! Who was he to say whether I was Brotherhood or not? But perhaps that was too harsh; he was right after all – I didn't look like Brotherhood. I wasn't a monk, and I didn't wear robes, but I was still annoyed, and I was sure Marcos knew he'd riled me.

He hailed Granger over, who was back on Ident duty. "Please don't take offence, Brothers, but wearing robes and quoting the Constantine Agreement doesn't guarantee you are who you say you are. I hope you understand."

Before she started, Grainger spoke briefly to Marcos. "I've just heard from Team Two, sir. They found a false panel behind the stall hiding a load more of our munitions. They've removed the lot and are taking them back to the Warrior."

"Understood. Carry on."

Grainger held the Ident tablet out to Ash and I hoped he would object, just to annoy Marcos, but he complied without hesitation. A moment later the tablet produced his file. The top left corner displayed an up-to-date picture, while the top right showed his name and rank within the Brotherhood. The rest of the screen, which would normally show an individual's personal information, was blank, and across the middle a red banner flashed the words: 'Brotherhood of the Virtuous Sun – Information Restricted'. Satisfied, Grainger moved on to Francis, whose result was the same.

The lights flickered and went out for a couple of seconds. When they came back on, the Lieutenant pushed the pad in front of me and I noticed Marcos watching. My file appeared instantly. In the top left-hand corner was my photograph, and in the top right was my name: Shae. Just Shae – nothing else. Underneath, a bright red banner flashed the words: 'Brotherhood of the Virtuous Sun – Information Restricted'.

The look on the Captain's face was priceless – at least it was until the lights went out again.

"This happens all the time down here," Beck said when they didn't come straight back on. "I've got an independent genny, should kick-in in about thirty seconds."

The sudden lack of lights spooked Nyan, so when the generator started up, I turned to calm him. Grainger indicated that she was receiving a communication through her earpiece and walked away a couple of paces.

"Captain, this man is why we're here," Ash explained. "And he's the reason we need to leave. I'm afraid I'm not at liberty to tell you any more than that."

Marcos looked over Francis's shoulder at Nyan, who was still cowering in the booth. "Understood. We'll finish our search of the building then escort you back to your ship."

"We appreciate the offer," I replied, wondering if I was warming towards him, "but time's of the essence, and the Brotherhood is more than capable of looking after itself. Plus, we're more of a target with you than without you."

"Is that so?" Marcos looked amused, and I decided I definitely wasn't warming to him.

"Yes, that is so," I replied, squaring up to him. "Look, Captain, I believe you said you weren't interested in anything but stolen Fleet weapons; I promise this man has nothing to do with them. Let us get on with our business, and you can get on with yours. You seem like a man of your word, or am I overestimating you?"

"Well you're certainly spirited, I'll give you that… but you make a fair point. Agreed."

"The man you're looking for isn't here. He was long gone by the time you even arrived," I said. "He came through the bar, spoke briefly to Beck there, and then disappeared behind the bar. I'm guessing you'll find some kind of hidden escape hatch. That's all we know."

"Now that wasn't so difficult, was it?" he said. "You should go before I change my mind. If we should meet again—"

"Sir, we have a situation," Grainger interrupted. "Team Three say there's an armed gang descending on the hangar where the Warrior's docked. They say it could be ARRO, or it could just be local gun-thugs, either way they can handle it for the moment but would like permission to engage if necessary."

"If, and only if, they're shot at first," agreed Marcos.

"Something else, Captain…" She relayed information as she received it. "Team Two are taking fire… they have casualties… Sir, Team Three are now taking heavy weapons fire in the hangar and have engaged to protect the Warrior."

"Tell Team Three to defend the ship at all costs. Tell Team Two to get back to the hangar ASAP and take up defensive positions."

"Team Two wants to know about us, sir. About you."

"Tell Team Two to comply with their orders. Team One will make its own way back."

"Aye, sir... Sir, they believe we have hostiles inbound and suggest we move out immediately." Grainger had barely finished talking when the front door of the bar swung open and a trooper backed through, slamming and locking it behind him.

"Captain, we've got a problem," he said without looking away from the entrance, his TK70 raised, his finger on the trigger.

"Report," Marcos ordered.

"Sir, there's a group of approximately thirty armed hostiles descending on our location from both the North and South tunnels," replied the newest trooper.

Marcos turned to Grainger. "Give me an update on the Warrior."

"Taking minor damage, sir. Both teams have wounded. Westenra's dead."

A flash of anger crossed Marcos's face. "Tell them to hold their position and to defend the Warrior unless their safety, or the integrity of the ship, is jeopardised further. If that happens, they're to take off and return to the *Defender*. They're not to wait for us."

"Just a thought," said Beck, "but you might want to lock the back door."

"Already done, Captain," said one of the other troopers, "but it won't hold for long. If they want in, they're coming in."

"Well, it looks like your business has become our business after all, Captain," said Ash.

"Yes, well… that certainly wasn't my intention," Marcos replied before turning his attention to Beck, who sat at a booth table on the opposite side of the bar. "It seems current events have taken priority," he called over. "Do you have an escape route – yes or no?"

"Yes." Beck didn't bother trying to negotiate a deal for himself. "It's behind the bar like she said. If—"

The rest of his words were drowned out by the explosion that rocked through the bar. Half the wall on the right-hand side blew in, with one of the troopers taking the full force of the blast. The room, already dull from the emergency lighting, instantly filled with debris and dust.

Rough hands pulled me off the floor as dark shadows pushed through the gaping hole in the wall. Muzzle flashes were no more than hazy lights in the smoke.

Through the ringing in my ears I heard the unmistakable sound of TK70's returning fire, but between the dust and the grit in my eyes, it was impossible to tell what was happening. My hand automatically fell to my thigh but came up empty.

Ash pulled Nyan from the bench before we ducked between the booth and the rear exit door.

"We need Beck," I yelled above the racket. "He's the only one who knows exactly where that hidden exit is." Dust stung the back of my throat and I hacked to clear it.

"Okay, here's what we do," shouted Marcos. "We get Beck, fall back behind the bar, and then get the hell out of here."

"Great plan," I said as a barrage of gunshots peppered the wall behind us, showering down more debris.

The dust began to settle and I could just make out an Other get a choke hold around a trooper's throat before he yanked hard to the right, breaking his neck. My stomach lurched and bile burnt the back of my throat.

The Other let go of the trooper's body, then turned and thumped one of the hostiles standing next to him. I scanned the rest of the bar and saw they were all fighting each other. "Why?" I asked, not needing to expand.

"I guess if you put a load of armed, angry troublemakers in confined quarters, they were bound to implode at some point," Francis replied. "Ash, their lack of self-control will work in our favour."

"Agreed. Shae, stay here. Protect Nyan until one of us gets back with Beck. As soon as you have him, leave. Don't wait."

"But—"

"Don't wait," he reiterated. "Nyan is our priority. Understand?"

"Yes," I replied. "Good hunting," I added as he and Francis disappeared into the fight.

"Protect the civilians," Marcos ordered Grainger before he followed.

Civilians my arse. I was better trained than she was.

Keeping Nyan safe was my main concern, but part of me wanted to be with Ash and Francis, watching their backs, protecting them. I hated it when they fought without me, and I always had a knot in my stomach until they came back.

"Keep down," I yelled to Nyan as a metal chair flew over our heads, smashing against the wall. He dripped with sweat, and shook uncontrollably, so I put my arm on his shoulder. I wasn't sure whether it was to comfort him, or to stop him from doing something stupid.

I glanced around the side of the booth, frustrated that I wasn't part of the fight. I watched Marcos disappear behind the Rhinorian, who, still cuffed, was knocking people around with his sheer size and strength until a plasma shot to the head finally brought him down.

Francis was engaged in unarmed combat, Brotherhood style. He and Ash were both experts in Tok-ma – an unarmed combat style mixing ancient martial arts with a modern brawl twist. Highly effective; totally deadly.

The stench in the bar was overpowering. On top of the general sweaty, unwashed odour from the amassed pack, the air was thick with sulphur from the explosives and the smell of burnt skin from the plasma weapons. I made a mental note to breathe through my mouth and…

A gasp made me spin around.

# 3

A chunky woman with more than a few Rhinorian genes dragged Grainger away from the booth by her hair. I reached out, managing to grab a boot, but I was caught off balance and tumbled away from the protection of the booth. Grainger's foot was ripped from my fingers.

The Lieutenant lay on the floor in front of the bar, pinned down by the woman who sat on her stomach, landing punch after punch to her head. I checked the bar to see if any of the others had seen her situation, but I could only see Francis and he had his hands full.

"Grainger's in trouble," I said to Nyan. "I need to help her, but I also need you to stay down, stay safe." I held his face in both my hands so I had his complete attention. "Do you understand?"

"Yes," he replied. "I'll be okay. I won't move." I hesitated, still looking in his eyes. "Save her!" It was the first time since I'd met him that he seemed definite about anything.

"Okay, I'll be right back. Stay down."

"I promise," was the last thing I heard him say as I left.

I covered the distance to Grainger in a matter of

seconds, relieved to see her choking because it meant she was still alive. I raised my foot and landed a well-aimed kick hard to the side of her attacker's head. She fell sideways, off Grainger, but was still conscious. I bent down and grabbed the front of her jacket, lifting her shoulders and head off the ground before smashing them back down with all the force I could muster. The woman's head cracked against the concrete floor and she stopped moving.

Grainger coughed and spluttered, but her eyes were closed. I slapped her cheek, trying to rouse her, and she half-opened her eyes – but there was no focus. I took her wrist to drag her back to the booth but stumbled as I was grabbed from behind. I swung my arm up hard around the back of my assailant's knees, taking his legs out from underneath him. As he fell, I heard his head smack on the ground. I smashed my elbow down onto his windpipe. After that he was too busy trying to breath to worry about me.

Through the dust, I saw Marcos wrestling with a local, but I also saw something else. "Captain, behind you!" I yelled. He looked over his shoulder, seeing the approaching danger, but he had his hands full.

I searched the floor for any kind of weapon, locating Grainger's gun. The skeletal Other was just about to bring his knife down into Marcos's back when I took him out with one shot. I thought I saw a flicker of a smile on the Captain's face before he mouthed, 'thanks.'

I returned my attention to Grainger, grateful to see her more alert, but then I heard a unique sound. I froze, listening carefully above the shouts and gunfire that echoed off the walls.

Nothing.

I'd just convinced myself that I'd been imagining things when I heard it again; the distinctive, high-pitched popping noise of an H'toka pistol – the unique weapon used by a small clandestine group of assassins.

In the corner, diagonally opposite from us, a cloaked figure climbed on top of a booth table. The hooded man seemed calm, almost oblivious to the fighting going on around him. What the hell was an Agent of Death doing…?

"Nyan." His name came out as a whisper. I spun around to see him standing in full view, watching me. "Get down," I screamed, launching myself towards him. I saw the look of confusion on his face at the same time I heard the distinctive 'pop'. Nyan's head whipped back and he began to fall. "No!" I yelled, catching the front of his clothes.

My heart stopped and my stomach turned. A dark circular mark punctuated the middle of Nyan's forehead, and just one small drop of blood trickled from the hole.

Still holding Nyan with one hand, I turned and aimed Grainger's gun towards the cloaked figure, but he'd already gone. My eyes were wide and my breathing, which had stopped for a long while, was back in fast ragged breaths. I lowered Nyan gently onto the table before closing his eyes with my fingertips. His legs draped lifelessly over the edge, his arms splayed out to the sides.

Why didn't he do what he'd promised? Why hadn't he remained hidden? Questions swam around my head, repeating themselves over and over again, banging off the sides of my skull.

Nyan had been my responsibility and I'd failed. I felt sick.

I was oblivious to the fight still raging around me, going back over what had happened in my head, replaying all the events. I was so caught up double-guessing myself that I didn't notice the Other, but through my daze I heard someone yell my name and I turned just in time.

The knife sliced into my left arm about half way between my elbow and shoulder. The blade was sharp and my skin and muscles gave little resistance. I didn't feel pain so much as a burning sensation that radiated outwards from the wound.

The force of the attack pushed the knife all the way through my arm, right up to the hilt, and for a moment I was face-to-face with my attacker until Ash appeared out of nowhere, tackling him away from me. It only seemed like a couple of seconds later that he re-appeared, propping up Grainger, his grey eyes flashing with concern.

"Nyan…" I turned to point at his body, gasping at the resulting bolt of pain.

"I saw," said Ash as he pulled us all down behind the booth. "Is there anything you can do?"

"No."

"Are you sure?"

"There's grey-matter all over the booth. Not even I can fix that," I replied, my voice hollow. "Why didn't he stay hidden? Why did he stand up? I told him not to." Francis appeared, his face bloodied and his robes ripped.

"We'll talk about it later, we need to get out of here first," Ash said.

"We need to get that knife out first," corrected Francis.

I glanced down at the handle. It looked like bone, and I didn't want to think where or who it had come from, or how hygienic it was. The point, and about an inch of the blade, protruded from the back of my arm.

"All right, but don't tell me when you're going to do it." I looked away and prepared myself for the inevitable pain, but Marcos suddenly arrived with Beck and I knew Francis couldn't remove it with people watching.

Marcos looked like crap. A wide cut in his eyebrow oozed blood down his cheek, and from the looks of the boot-print bruise already appearing, he'd taken a pretty good stamp on the side of the head at some point.

"You okay?" he asked, looking between Nyan and my arm.

"We're in the middle of a war-zone, the one person I was supposed to protect is dead, and I have a knife sticking through my arm that hurts like a son-of-a-bitch… but yeah,

I'm peachy."

"Well that's okay then," he replied, with equal sarcasm. He moved away to check on Grainger, yanking Beck with him.

"Francis, get that knife out," Ash whispered. "I'll keep the others occupied so they don't see anything. Be quick."

Francis moved so that his body shielded mine and ripped the bottom of his robe into several strips. "This is going to hurt," he said. "On three..."

When he pulled the knife out, a cruel pain shot up my arm, through my neck, and into my brain. The wound was surprisingly neat, no tearing or ragged edges, but the second the knife was removed, a shimmering silver glow with a pale blue tint radiated from the thin line of the cut. It spread slowly outwards from the injury, tinting the flesh around it in the same silver-blue. Francis quickly bandaged the wound and we waited, watching. The skin above and below the material began to luminesce.

"Damn." I sighed.

"No problem," Francis said, tearing a longer strip from his robes. He wound the new bandage around my arm beginning at my shoulder and finishing at my elbow. "That should do it. I don't think it'll spread any further than that, but keep an eye on it. How does it feel?"

"Still hurts, but now I've got that tingly sensation that drives me nuts."

Francis laughed and indicated to Ash that we were ready to move out.

Staying low, we headed the short distance towards the bar in crocodile formation. Part of a table clattered over our heads and everyone froze, but the focus of the mob seemed to be exclusively aimed towards each other. I think they were too busy beating the crap out of their neighbours to care about us anymore. We managed to make it behind the bar without further trouble.

"Out the way," Beck grunted, indicating to a barely

visible rectangle on the floor. He put his hand behind some of the bottles on the shelf directly under the bar and the floor panel dropped a little before sliding out of the way to reveal a metal ladder.

Francis was closest so Marcos held out one of his Sentinels. "Would you mind?" the Captain asked.

"Not in the least," Francis replied, taking the gun before descending the ladder. "All clear," he yelled up after a moment.

Ash stepped into the hole, climbing down until his shoulders were floor level. He held out his hand to Grainger, who painfully lowered herself in.

"Take care of her," said Marcos. Ash nodded before starting down the ladder, carefully supporting Grainger as they went. Beck followed, leaving me behind the bar with Marcos. "After you," he said, waiting until I was half in before adding, "Close the hatch after you."

"What about you?" I asked, trying to read his face.

"Campbell, Rivers and Walker are dead, and Grainger's hanging on by her teeth, but Roberts and Harrison are still out there. I'm not leaving without my people."

I understood; I also knew I could better the odds. I couldn't change the fact I'd lost Nyan, but maybe by helping Marcos I could redeem myself slightly.

"Fair enough," I said getting back out of the hole. "You take the left side, I'll take the right."

"What? Absolutely not!"

"You're seriously going to argue with me?"

"I order you to go down the ladder."

I laughed because it was funny he actually thought I would obey him. "Haven't we already established that, contrary to your opinion, I am Brotherhood. You can't order me to do anything. Besides, I don't think you're in a position to negotiate. I suggest you quit complaining and we go find your troopers."

"Fine," he conceded. "We'll discuss this later."

"Whatever."

"How's the arm? Is it going to be a problem?"

"Hurts like hell, but I'm good. Thanks… for asking." I took a quick peek over the bar. Roberts was still alive and fighting, but I couldn't see the other trooper. "Change of plan. I can see Roberts on the left and I can't remember what Harrison looks like, so I'll take the left, you take the right."

Francis stuck his head up through the hole in the floor. "What's the delay?"

"We're going after my troopers," Marcos explained. "Guard the hatch. Any trouble, seal it up."

"Be quick," Francis replied.

I didn't need to be told twice. I heard Marcos close behind me, but I focused on my own mission. I ducked and weaved, fighting off locals until I got to Roberts, who was trying to fight two assailants at the same time. I was surprised he still looked in relatively good condition.

Picking up a metal table leg, I smacked one of the men across the head, cracking his skull and spraying an arc of blood across the floor. Roberts dispatched the other with two bricks. I grabbed his shoulder to get his attention, ducking to avoid a blow to the head – thankfully he recognised me before attempting another shot. As I told him we had to get behind the bar, he swung the brick again, but that time it was aimed at someone approaching from my left. He hit them centre face and their nose split open adding more blood to the stained floor.

"Follow me and keep low," I said before taking out a hostile with a particularly impressive Tok-ma manoeuvre.

Francis was crouched by the hatch when we got behind the bar. "Good to see you back," he said, giving me a relieved smile.

"Good to be back," I joked. "Go," I added to Roberts, pointing at the floor. "You too, Francis. Give me the Sentinel, I'll wait for Marcos."

I rested my back against the bar and closed my eyes for a moment's respite, but as soon as I did, my mind started replaying the seconds leading up to Nyan's death. My eyes snapped open and I looked over the bar to take my mind off it.

Marcos hauled the last trooper along the floor, attempting to fend off various attacks. I primed the Sentinel, took a few steadying breaths, and then stood. It was the same type of weapon I carried so it felt comfortable in my hands, and I laid down a suppressing fire, being careful to avoid Marcos. After all, it wouldn't have been good if he'd managed to survive that far, only for me to put a hole in him in the closing moments.

It was a couple of seconds before the Captain realised where the support was coming from, immediately using it to his advantage. It was only a few seconds longer before everyone else realised. Fortunately, not many of those who were left standing had guns, but those who did fired them in my direction, shattering the old mirror and bottles behind the bar. Glass and liquor sprayed everywhere, and I ducked as low as I could while still returning fire.

Marcos slid around the side of the bar towing the trooper. "We've got company," he yelled.

"I'll keep them off. Get him down the hatch," I shouted back, and for the first time he didn't argue, stuffing the groaning trooper into the hole.

An Other appeared at the entrance to the bar and I fired instinctively, taking her out. A plasma shot hit a couple of spirit bottles that were still intact, igniting the liquid that sprayed in the face of a man who'd tried to vault the bar. He pitched back screaming.

I fell into the hole, only just managing to grab the side of the ladder before my feet found their footing on one of the rungs. The fire had caught hold and began to swirl dangerously above my head. I felt the heat rising as I hit the illuminated pad to my left and the reinforced hatch slid shut. The heat and noise abated.

I placed my feet on either side of the ladder, released my grip, and slid to the bottom.

The tunnel was impressive – easily big enough to stand up in, and wide enough for three people to walk side by side. It wasn't that well-lit, but the air quality wasn't too bad. In fact, it was good to breathe air that wasn't full of dust and debris.

"The Warrior's docked in Hangar Six on this level," Marcos said. "I suggest we stick together and fall back collectively."

"Your Warrior's already taking fire, Captain," countered Ash. "Chances are we wouldn't make it within twenty metres."

"Have you got a better idea?"

"Our shuttle's docked on Level 2, and with luck the locals haven't associated us with Fleet." Ash did a quick mental count. "There are eight of us so it'll be a tight fit, but I can't imagine anyone will object at this point. Beck, can we get to Hangar Four from here without being seen?"

"Mostly. I can get you to within about fifty metres, but after that you're wide open."

"Captain, what do you think?" I asked, trying to push for a decision.

He rubbed his chin and thought for a moment. "Agreed."

"Good," said Francis. "I suggest I take a quick look at the wounded and then we move. This poor guy isn't going anywhere until I stabilise him." He leant over Harrison, removing the body armour constricting his breathing.

"Sir, I'll contact the Warrior and tell them to return to the Defender," Grainger croaked.

"Wait," replied Marcos. "What's their current situation?"

"Unchanged, sir. They're holding their own. No further casualties."

"Good." He sounded relieved. "If the locals think we're

going to head for the Warrior, they'll get suspicious if it takes off now. Tell them to wait fifteen minutes and then fire up the engines. We'll rendezvous with them on the Defender."

Francis continued to work on the injured trooper, but without medical supplies things didn't look good. "We're ready to move out," he said after a couple of minutes, "but I'm not happy with Harrison's condition. We need to get him to the *Nakomo* ASAP."

Ash and Grainger took the lead with Beck behind them. Francis and Roberts carried Harrison between them on a makeshift stretcher, while the Captain and I took up the rear. Marcos looked at my bandaged arm with a frown.

"A touch excessive, isn't it?" he asked, raising a quizzical eyebrow. I wasn't sure if he was joking or not so I just smiled and thought better about making a sarcastic reply. "And don't think I've forgotten about your insubordination behind the bar earlier," he added.

"Insubordination, my arse!" I snorted. He shot me a look, but I didn't know him well enough to recognise what it meant.

"Seriously though, you got one of my troopers out of there alive, so… well, thank you."

"You're welcome," I replied, wondering how hard it had been for him to say that.

We walked in silence for a long while before eventually gathering around the bottom of another metal ladder. "This is the only way up," said Beck, pointing. "And it's going to be a long, hard climb." He looked purposely at Harrison, laid out on the ground. The trooper wasn't moving – his lips blue, his skin greying.

I beckoned Ash away from the rest of the group and we huddled, talking in hushed voices so that no one else could hear us.

"I know what you're going to say," said Ash, but I said it anyway.

"He's not going to make it, and I can't let him die just to keep my secret."

"I know… and I agree." He sighed. "We all knew it would come to this eventually."

"I've been thinking though. They're definitely going to know something's up if I heal him completely, but what if I fix him just enough to get him out of danger? When we get back to the shuttle, Francis can do the rest with the medical supplies we have on board, and no one will be any the wiser."

"It's risky, but I don't think we have a choice. Follow my lead," said Ash as we returned to the rest of the group. "Captain, would you mind going up first to check for danger?" Marcos glanced at Harrison, but Ash didn't give him the chance to object. "Grainger can go after you, then Beck and Roberts. Brother Francis with Harrison next, Shae and I will bring up the rear. Everyone agree?"

The troopers looked to their captain.

"Sure. You heard the man. Let's move," Marcos said, but his eyes narrowed.

When Roberts was the only Fleet person left, Francis and Ash made a show of checking on Harrison, discussing loudly their surprise at how much better he looked. Roberts knelt next to the wounded trooper to see for himself, but I could tell by the deep crease in his forehead that he wasn't convinced.

"I know it doesn't look it right now, but I think Harrison's going to be just fine," Francis said. "I'm going to do a couple more checks and then we'll be right behind you."

Roberts didn't move, so I held out my hand and pulled him off the floor. "Don't look so worried," I said. "Injuries often look worse than they are, and Brother Francis is very good." Roberts looked sceptical but I ushered him to the ladder, keeping an eye on him until he was a murky shadow.

Francis watched the shaft to make sure nobody came

back down, while I knelt next to Harrison's prone body. I lifted his T-shirt up to his neck revealing a distorted torso with several broken ribs pressing against bruised flesh.

I centred myself and tried to clear my thoughts. Taking a few deep, steadying breaths, I placed my hands on his chest. I don't know how it works, I just know that if I think really hard about fixing what's broken, it just… happens. I closed my eyes, let out a deep, slow breath, and felt the familiar tingling sensation start to build in my stomach.

I opened my eyes and the same silver-blue light that my arm had produced when Francis removed the knife, radiated from my whole body. The tingling in my tummy spread to my chest before a pulse flowed down my arms, collecting briefly at my hands. Thin, dancing strands of shimmering energy arced to Harrison's chest with a small flash. His skin began to glow like mine, and within seconds the tunnel was lit by the silver-blue light emanating from the two of us.

Harrison's body shook but I remained focussed. His breathing evened out, and I felt the strength returning to his heart. I watched skin smooth as his ribs reset in his chest, changing from purple and blue to pale pink. I could've continued – I could've completely healed him so that not even a scratch remained, but I'd done enough to save him. I pulled my hands away and the light dissipated.

Harrison opened his eyes. "What…? Where…?"

"Welcome back, Trooper. You gave us quite the scare," I said, smiling down at him.

When it was my turn, I started up the ladder. Just as I thought my legs couldn't make another rung, I reached the top to find Harrison lying on the floor, joking with his fellow troopers. Captain Marcos stood over him, hands on his hips, a deep crease between his eyebrows.

"Obviously, I overestimated the extent of his injuries," Francis told him. "I think your trooper's going to be just fine… as long as we can get out of here without any further trouble." Marcos didn't look completely persuaded, but Francis's explanation sounded credible, and without knowing the truth, what else would've been plausible?

After a moment to allow Ash and me to catch our breath, we were off again, but I was extremely grateful when Beck assured us that our destination wasn't far.

"We're here," he said not long later. "This door opens on to one of the shopping areas, and Hangar Four's entrance is about fifty metres straight ahead. Trouble is, you won't know what's waiting for you until you're out there, so I suggest you lose the tactical gear. Fleet uniforms will attract too much of the wrong sort of attention."

"I agree, and I also suggest we leave in two groups," added Ash. "Francis and I will go first with Harrison and Grainger. Hopefully it will look like we're simply tending to the sick and injured. When we get to the *Nakomo*, I'll inform Shae over our com-channel, and the four of you can head out. By the time you get there, the shuttle should be ready to depart."

"You three can head out," Beck corrected. "I'm not going."

"Huh?" I replied, genuinely surprised. "Why would you stay after what's happened?"

"Because everything I've got is here. Besides, where else would have me?" Beck gave me the same dazzling smile he'd first given me back in the bar.

"But your bar's toast; literally."

He grinned. "The bar ain't everything I've got. Anyway," his smile slipped, "I need to speak to Jovan's mate."

"Who?"

"My bouncer, Jovan – the Rhinorian. I need to tell his mate what happened. Least I can do. Don't worry that pretty little head of yours, I guarantee I won't say anything about helping the law. I value my life way too much for that. I know what it's like here, give it a week and this'll all be forgotten. They'll have found something else to fight over, trust me."

"Well, if you're sure. Thanks for everything, Beck," I said, but he simply shrugged. "I mean it. You gave help when we needed it, and that's not something the Brotherhood takes lightly." I held out my hand to him but he wrapped his tattooed arms firmly around my waist, lifting me clear off the ground. As he put me down, he moved his hands to my backside and gave it a cheeky grope. I heard someone object and assumed it was Ash, the keeper of my virtue, so I was surprised when it turned out to be Marcos.

Beck laughed, shrugging his shoulders boyishly. "Hey, can't blame a guy for taking the opportunity."

"We should leave," Marcos growled, glaring at him. "I'm sick of this dump."

Francis picked up Harrison while Beck punched numbers into a keypad, and as the suction on the rubber seals released, the door opened with a gentle slurp. The first group left with as much confidence as they could muster, and I took a peek outside as the door closed shut behind them. The knot in my stomach, the one I got when I was separated from my brothers, began to grow.

Roberts took off his assault gear and piled it next to the wall as the Captain removed his jacket. Marcos wore the same black T-shirt with Fleet insignia as the rest of his troops, but I noticed that his was more fitted. As he paced, I saw his muscles flexing below the material and I realised I was staring.

What was I thinking? I didn't even like the guy. He was a conceited, egotistical, superior, big-headed pig. I snuck another look.

I was relieved when Ash's voice came through my earpiece.

"The others made it to the shuttle," I said. "They had a few interested glances, but nothing more serious."

"Our turn." Marcos wasn't hanging around. He lifted

the back of his T-shirt and pushed his remaining Sentinel into the waistband of his trousers.

"This is it then," said Beck with mock melancholy. "I bid you all farewell and good journey. Feel free to never come back." He aimed that last bit squarely at the Captain. "Except you," he added, turning to me. "You can come back any time you want."

"Take care of—" I started, but Marcos shoved me through the door and out into the marketplace.

In the brighter lights of Level 2 we were an identical dark grey colour, our faces and clothes smeared with dust, sweat, and drying blood. Marcos and Roberts were covered in bruises, gashes and scrapes, but not me. Apart from the bandage on my arm, I didn't have an injury in sight. The lesions and bruises I'd received during the fight had healed almost as soon as they'd been inflicted – even the knife wound on my arm would've repaired itself.

We were almost to the hangar when two men approached. Marcos tensed and his arm twisted behind his back, moving his shirt out of the way so he could grip the Sentinel. I don't know why, but I had a feeling the new arrivals weren't going to cause us trouble, and the last thing we needed was for the Captain to overreact.

I acted quickly, nestling into his side so I could move my arm around his back into an embrace. My hand rested gently over his, stopping him from drawing the Sentinel, and I had to go up on my toes to whisper, "Be cool," into his ear. As he relaxed, I felt his hand loosen on the weapon.

He tilted his head down towards mine, and I could see in his eyes that he understood. He lifted his free arm, wrapping it around my shoulders, his breath warm on my temple. We were nothing more than a couple hugging.

It felt odd. I know I'd made the first move, and I know it was just an act, but even after all the chaos we'd been through, right there, right then, I felt safe with him.

As I'd suspected, the two men were simply trying to sell

us something. I didn't even hear what bargain of the millennium they were trying to flog, but Roberts declined their offer and they ambled off, targeting a couple who were walking through the concourse. I expected Marcos to release me immediately, but it was a few heartbeats before I felt him move his arm and I gently pulled away. We continued to the hangar without further incident.

The *Nakomo* was old and she wasn't very big, but she was ours, and she did us proud, so I was annoyed when I caught Roberts looking at her in disgust.

"She may not be a Warrior," I said, "but she's going to get your sorry backside off this rock." He blushed as he scuttled up the rear ramp.

As expected, it was cramped on board, especially as Harrison was strapped in horizontally across several seats. The med-kit lay open next to the trooper, but he was conscious and alert. I went straight up front to the flight area where Francis was communicating with the control tower.

"Angel Ridge Control, this is the *Nakomo*. We're ready to leave on your final authorisation."

"*Nakomo* this is Control. That's a negative on your last. Stand down your engines."

"Please repeat, Control. We're ready to depart on your authorisation."

Ash stood beside me, listening to the conversation.

"*Nakomo*, this is Control. I repeat, your request for take-off has been denied. Stand down your engines."

"Please clarify, Control."

"There's been trouble on Level 3 and Management has put a lockdown on all departures while they locate the perpetrators. You're going nowhere, *Nakomo*. Might as well sit tight and put your feet up."

"This is Brother Asher, Ninth Degree representative of the Brotherhood of the Virtuous Sun. To whom am I speaking?"

"Prout, Edgar Prout." I heard an uncertainty creep into his voice that hadn't been there before.

"Well, Mr Prout, if you check your records, you'll see that the *Nakomo* was given special dispensation to land so we could undertake vital Brotherhood business. That business is now concluded and we're ready to leave. I'll give you a moment to verify this."

There was silence for a couple of minutes, during which time Marcos appeared in the already cramped flight area.

"Why haven't we left yet?" he asked impatiently and I wanted to punch him.

"*Nakomo*, this is Control," said Prout with a slight waver to his voice. I held my finger in front of my lips to stop Marcos from saying anything further. "I can confirm what you've said, but I'm unable to authorise your departure during a lockdown."

Ash cleared his throat. "Mr Prout, we have wounded on board who need urgent medical attention. If you cannot authorise our leave, please connect me to Mr Dax immediately. He may be difficult to track down, given the trouble he's trying to manage, but I'm sure he won't mind taking a break from that to deal with a call from you." He was goading the man. The com-link fell silent.

"*Nakomo*, this is Control. You're clear for take-off. Apologies for any delay."

"Thank you, Control. *Nakomo* out."

# 4

I left Francis flying the shuttle and went to check on Harrison, but Ash was already seeing to him. The shuttle was cramped and there were no seats left, but I found a small area of floor next to Roberts and slid down to sit by his side. I rested my head against the cool wall, listening to the rhythmic hum of the engines, and within seconds I was asleep.

"Shae, wake up. We're here." Ash sounded far away, but I forced my eyes open, stretching my back and rubbing the stiffness out of my neck before making my way forward to the flight area. Marcos obviously had the same idea because we bottle-necked at the entrance, but he stood back, gesturing for me to go before him. He tried to hide it but he winced as he lifted his arm, and for a nanosecond I wished I could heal it for him – heal all their injuries – but that would've given my secret away for sure.

I covered my mouth and yawned deeply before stretching my arms above my head, my fingertips brushing the low ceiling.

"Hey, Francis," I said, putting a hand on his shoulder. "You okay?"

He turned and smiled and I was shocked by the bloodshot eye and deep purple bruise spreading across his face. "I'm okay," he said. "I… hold on, we're being hailed."

"This is the Royal Earth Force Cruiser, *Defender*." The disembodied voice was curt. "You're entering a no-fly zone. Identify yourself immediately."

"*Defender*, this is Brotherhood shuttle, *Nakomo*." Francis paused with a wicked grin on his face. "Taxi service to stranded captains, waifs, and stray troopers." Ash and I laughed. Marcos didn't.

"*Nakomo*, hold your position until we authorise approach."

"Why have they locked weapons on us?" I demanded, watching the blinking warning sign on the console.

"Standard protocol until they confirm you are who you say you are," Marcos replied casually.

"*Nakomo*, we demand to speak to Captain Marcos immediately."

"Friendly bunch, aren't they?" said Francis as he motioned toward a com-pad on the wall just to the Captain's right.

"*Defender*, this is Captain Jared Marcos, authorisation Delta-Seven-Zero-Niner-Bravo. Approve approach and issue docking codes without delay."

"Of course, Captain."

"We have wounded. Have a med-team on standby in the hangar."

"Aye, sir. Oh, and welcome back, sir."

Marcos disconnected the com-link without replying. "Keep me appraised," he ordered Francis before walking away.

I was seething. Who the hell did he think he was, treating Francis like his own private pilot? I was about to rant when Francis said, "Well, would you look at that?"

I followed his gaze through the *Nakomo's* streaky panoramic window. I had no idea the *Defender* was

Vanguard Class, one of the newest, fastest and deadliest Cruisers in the REF fleet. There were only a few finished, and the *Defender* looked straight off the line – not a scratch on her. I glanced back at the young captain and wondered what he'd done to be given the Chair of such a prestigious ship.

The *Defender* was sleek and smooth, and even though I knew nothing about spaceships – other than they got you from one point to another – I was impressed.

We approached from the port side and I lost count of the number of plasma cannons mounted around the hull. Strikefighter bays ran half the length of the ship, and an imposing communications array sat on top of the long body between four Starflower railguns. As Francis brought us around the stern, the *Nakomo* was dwarfed by colossal FTL engines, which were nothing like anything I'd seen before.

We headed towards the middle of three hangars.

"Beauty, isn't she?" Marcos made me jump. He had his hands on either side of the entrance frame, casually leaning forward so that he practically spoke right in my ear.

"We're coming in to land," Francis said over the internal com-system. "If you have a chair, lucky you, please strap yourself in. If you don't, take a seat on the floor."

I returned to the main cabin and made sure I sat as far away from Marcos as possible.

The landing, as always, was perfect – except for a slight judder as the skids touched. "Not bad for an old tub, is she?" I teased Roberts.

"Not bad at all," he replied, blushing again.

A symphony of moaning suspension, hissing hydraulics, and the knocking of cooling metal filled the air before the rear hatch groaned open and the cabin filled with fresh, properly circulated air.

The medics tried to board immediately, but when they saw there wasn't enough space to swing a cantooa, they backed out, letting the rest of us off first.

The hangar was vast and I stumbled down the *Nakomo's* ramp, wide-eyed and open-mouthed. A Warrior was parked in the next bay with small arms damage, and I assumed it was the one that had been at Angel Ridge. I couldn't believe engineers and technicians were already buzzing around it, mending and replacing bits. Boxes marked with spare-part codes were stacked next to the ship waiting to be opened.

It was all so clean, so… perfect.

I looked at the *Nakomo* and she was definitely the poor relation, but I would take that battered, tub-of-rust over any of Marcos's shiny new toys any day. As if she knew what I was thinking, the *Nakomo's* suspension gave another deep groan in appreciation.

I moved out of the way so the medics could fly past with Harrison strapped to a gurney, but as they went passed, he urged the team to stop.

"Thank you," he croaked.

"For what?" I replied.

"For…" He looked confused. "I'm not really sure. I just felt like I needed to say it."

"There's really nothing to thank me for. I'm just glad we all got out of there."

"You can say that again." He rested his head back on the gurney and the medical team saw that as an indication to set off.

When I turned back to the *Nakomo*, I noticed Marcos watching me – until a man approached him and he looked away. The newcomer wore the uniform insignia of Chief Medical Officer, and whilst he was almost as tall as Marcos, he wasn't as broad. His hair, greying at the temples, was the only thing that betrayed his older years.

"Captain," the Doctor said with a note of authority that only he – as the single person on board who could remove Marcos from command – could get away with. "As you're well aware, it's protocol that all returning wounded… no matter how bad they are," he added as Marcos tried to interrupt, "are examined and cleared by my staff. If, as you say, your wounds are superficial, you'll be cleared in minutes, but…" He reached forward and Marcos grunted in pain. "Broken ribs, just as I suspected."

Marcos opened his mouth to growl something, but it looked like he was distracted by a call. He stepped away, talking too quietly for me to hear.

I thought the doctor was turning to leave the hangar, but instead he strode the few steps to where I stood with Ash and Francis. He gave each of us a visual once over.

"Doctor Anderson, Chief Medical Officer," he said, holding out his hand. "Forgive me for being blunt, but you fellows look like you could do with some medical assistance. I'd be happy if you'd let my team take a look at you."

"That's a kind offer, Doctor," replied Ash, "but we're good. Besides, we should be on our way. We need to return to our monastery and debrief our Primus on today's unfortunate events."

"Brother Asher, you must let our doctors look at your injuries," said Marcos, wading into the discussion, his com-call over. "In fact, I insist you stay the night. I'll even get my engineers to refuel your shuttle and give it a health-check so it's ready for you first thing in the morning. It's been a hell of an evening – what's a few more hours?" Ash shook his head, but Marcos wasn't budging. "Look, I dragged you into our business this evening. It's the least we can do."

I started to wonder whether our welfare was his true reason for wanting us to stay, or whether there was something else driving his insistency. Eventually Ash must've thought it was a sound idea, or at least the diplomatic choice, because he gave in and thanked Marcos for his generous offer.

"Excellent," Anderson boomed, way too upbeat for that point in the evening. "I'll expect to see you all in Med-bay within fifteen minutes. Fifteen minutes. And that includes you, Captain. Not a minute longer or I'll come get you myself."

I believed he probably would, too.

We excused ourselves and returned to the *Nakomo* to retrieve our ready-bags – small backpacks containing a change of clothes and toiletries. When we were alone, I said, "There's no way I'll be able to show a med-tech my arm. There's not a mark on it."

Ash grabbed a jacket out of a storage locker and passed it to me. "Put this on."

"Really?" I said sceptically. "This is your big plan?"

"You look unhurt. If they ask you whether you have any injuries, just tell them you haven't. They can hardly force you to be examined. You're not Fleet."

"What if I get caught out?"

"Then we deal with it."

Marcos was waiting for us when we left the *Nakomo*. I'd hoped he'd gone on ahead, leaving some minion to escort us to Med-bay, but no such luck. He ushered us to a set of doors which opened automatically as he stepped up to them.

"Welcome back, Captain Marcos," said an electronic female voice.

"Thank you, Grace."

"Grace?"

"She's the ship's central operating computer," he explained. "Every Fleet ship has a sponsor – typically a female civilian – who is seen by the crew as a kind of charm, bestowing good luck and protection on a vessel and all serve on her." He stepped aside to let me into a lift. "Level fourteen," he said before continuing his story. "It's tradition that the sponsor chooses the name of the ship's computer. The *Defender's* sponsor, Abigail Pritchard, daughter of Admiral Pritchard, chose Grace after her grandmother."

"That's kinda nice."

"We were lucky with Grace." He smiled, shaking his head. "You wouldn't believe some of the names sponsors come up with."

The lift – a nice, secure lift, unlike the one on Angel Ridge – pinged. "Level Fourteen," Grace said.

"This is us," added Marcos.

We walked along a lengthy corridor with windows down the left side, plants and paintings down the other. Every so often there was a door with a room number and title printed in bold, block lettering; occasionally there was an accompanying name. All of it looked… perfect.

At the centre of an approaching group was quite possibly one of the most beautiful women I'd ever seen. It looked like she was authorising various things on data-pads because as she passed each pad back, that person peeled away from the group. By the time she reached us, there was only one other person left. Her uniform insignia bore the rank of Commander.

"Captain," she said. "It's good to have you back in one piece." Her almond-shaped, amber eyes mirrored the smile she gave him, but the inflection in her voice suggested she wanted to add, 'but protocol says you should never have gone in the first place.'

"Commander, these are Brothers Asher and Francis, and their…" he struggled to find the right word, "companion, Shae." I let it go; I was too tired to argue with him. "Everyone, this is Commander Tel'an, my First Officer."

Tel'an was, I'm guessing, half Human, half Santian, and the result was stunning. As she held out her hand to shake mine, I noticed that her skin had the same marble effect as Santians, but the colouring was much paler – more coffee and cream. The slit irises in her eyes were long and thin under the bright hall lights, but I didn't see any sign of a third lid, and they were framed by dark lashes. She also had matching brown hair that was pulled into an elaborate and perfect knot on top of her head; not a strand out of place.

"I can't tell you how much we appreciate your support today." Tel'an spoke with the barest hint of the smooth, soft, Santian accent.

"It's not like we had much choice," I replied. I knew she was trying to be gracious, but had everyone forgotten that Fleet got us caught up in that mess, and Nyan had died as a result.

No. Nyan had died because he hadn't stayed down like he'd promised.

No. Nyan had died because I left him. Because I'd failed to protect him. I felt weary all of a sudden.

"I'm sorry," I said quickly, my cheeks warming with embarrassment. "That was rude. Please forgive me."

"There's really nothing to forgive. Although I think we should get you all to Med-bay before Doctor Anderson sends out a search party. Ensign Normstrung will take you. I'm afraid I need to steal the Captain away for a while." She turned to Marcos. "I've cleared it with Doc. He said it's all right as long as I get you there tonight – or he'll rule you medically unfit to command."

"He can try." Marcos laughed, and it was nice to see him genuinely amused.

As Marcos and Tel'an headed back the way we'd come, Ensign Normstrung took us further down the corridor. A few hallways later, he deposited us in Med-bay and made his excuses before heading off to undertake other duties.

"Ah, there you are," boomed the Chief Medical Officer. "I was about to send out a search party." I suppressed a smile.

"Here as ordered, Doctor Anderson," said Francis.

"Please, call me Doc, everyone else does."

I noticed Harrison sleeping in the far corner, and Grainger was going through a series of tests on one of the med-beds. She looked up and beckoned me over.

"Hey, I'm glad I got to see you. I wanted to thank you for what you did. I wouldn't be here if you hadn't come after me." Her eyes were wide and shining.

Words stuck in my throat. Bubbling to the surface were anger and pain: anger that she was alive and Nyan was dead; pain because it was my fault, not hers. It had been my decision to go after her and leave Nyan, and I couldn't blame her for my incompetence. The anger dissipated.

"You're welcome." I said genuinely. "Any time."

"I might hold you to that. Roberts says you're, quote, 'one kick-arse fighter'. Says you saved his life, and with an injured arm as well." She looked impressed.

"Really?" asked the med-tech. "We'll need to take a look at that."

"Roberts was exaggerating; it's no more than a scratch. Brother Asher's already dealt with it so no point messing further. Where is Roberts anyway?" I tried to change the subject.

"Discharged. He was going back to the hangar to see if you'd left. I think he's taken quite the shine to you." Grainger's eyes sparkled wickedly.

I was glad he'd been released because it meant he wasn't too badly injured, and also that he wasn't there to insist about my wound.

"I can take a look at that arm," said the med-tech catching me by surprise. "Won't take but a minute."

"Honestly, I'm okay," I replied, waving my arm around a bit and prodding it to prove I wasn't in pain.

"All right, if you say so." The med-tech gave Grainger one last injection and then some orders about coming back the next day for a check-up. "That's you done. No duties for a few days and then light duties until you're completely healed."

"Thanks," Grainger said, sliding gingerly off the bed. "And thanks again," she said to me. "Maybe I'll see you around?" She left, waving to the others as she went.

Ash and Francis were both having injuries seen to, but as I ambled over to them, I was collared by Doc Anderson.

"Let's have a look at you, little lady," he said. Normally I would've baulked at being called that, but weirdly it didn't sound patronising coming from him.

"Oh, it's all right," I said breezily. "I've already been seen to."

"You have? That was quick. By whom?"

I had to think fast. The med-tech who'd seen to Grainger was right at the other end of the room arranging some instruments, but fortunately for me she looked up in our direction.

"That med-tech gave me the all-clear," I lied, but I smiled and waved at her enthusiastically and she returned the gesture. Doc seemed satisfied.

The medical bay of the *Defender* was clearly as advanced as the ship itself. There were surgical displays on all the med-beds, and hi-tech instruments lay sealed on sterile trays ready for use. Lights flashed and things beeped, and I was surprised they could remember what everything was for. By the time the technicians had finished with my brothers, there wasn't much left for me to heal.

Just as we were all signed off by Doc Anderson, Ensign Normstrung reappeared. "Brothers, Miss, if you would please follow me, I'll take you to your quarters. Captain Marcos has given orders that you're issued the best VIP suites we have."

I threw my bag over my shoulder, grateful that Ash had agreed we could stay. All I wanted was a hot shower and a soft bed.

Normstrung took us along a series of corridors and lifts, each one almost identical, and I was amazed that anyone could find their way around the ship without getting lost. We stopped in one of the beautifully pristine, but totally indistinguishable, corridors.

"Brother Asher, these will be your quarters. Brother Francis these will be yours." He pointed to two doors opposite each other. "Miss Shae—"

"Just Shae," I corrected.

"I'm sorry?"

"It's not Miss Shae. It's just Shae. On its own."

"Of course. Shae, you'll be just down the passageway on the same side as Brother Asher."

"Thank you," said Ash. "Francis, Shae, can you bear a quick de-brief before bed?" Francis nodded.

"Can I shower first?" I asked. "I feel like I'm wearing half of Angel Ridge."

Ash laughed. "Sure. See you in thirty."

After showing me to my room, Normstrung programmed a control pad inside the door to recognise my thumbprint for access. Before he left, he said, "If you need anything, just ask Grace – the ship's computer."

My quarters were huge and opulent. The lounge area led to a bedroom and then to a bathroom, which was so big you could probably fit my entire living quarters back at the monastery into it alone. Everything was of the best quality; the furniture, the fabrics, the bed linen – even the bathroom had a display of the most expensive toiletries in the Four Sectors.

I dropped my faded ready-bag on the bed and it looked out of place amongst all the luxury. I looked in the full-length mirror against one of the walls and I looked out of place.

After turning on the shower to heat up, I carefully removed each piece of clothing, trying not to drop too much dust and dirt on the floor. I untied the filthy bandage from my arm, and as expected, there wasn't a single mark on my skin.

I wiped the fogged-up mirror above the sink with a plush hand towel and looked at myself closely with bloodshot eyes. My hair was grey and matted, and I had to tug painfully at the band holding it in a ponytail. My pale skin was ghostly underneath smeared dust and blood, but lighter lines tracked down my cheeks where sweat and tears from the smoke had washed away some of the dirt.

I stepped into the shower and it was sheer bliss. The hot water ran over my head and down my body, pooling in a dirty puddle at my feet before draining away. I washed every part of me, and then I washed again. Once the water ran clear, and I was convinced I was totally clean, I turned the temperature up and just stood there, eyes closed, letting the steaming water warm me to my insides. After a bit, I forced myself to turn it off and get out, wrapping myself in a luxurious bath towel.

When I got to Ash's room, Francis was already there. Like me, they'd both showered and changed into plain, dark-blue fatigues. Thanks to the med-techs, their wounds were almost non-existent, but Francis still had a nasty-looking bloodshot eye and I automatically put my hand out to heal it. He pulled away.

"Appreciate it, but best not," he said. "Perhaps tomorrow after we leave?"

"Sure, of course." I understood.

He pulled an armchair opposite the couch Ash and I had sunk into, but before he sat, he poured us all a glass of water. I had no idea how thirsty I was until I started drinking.

"We're all tired," started Ash, "so I'll make this quick. Each of us will run through our account of what happened during the fight, so we'll be straight when we meet with the Primus tomorrow. Okay?" Francis and I nodded. "We were all together up until the explosion, and then again once we were in the tunnel, so I suggest we concentrate on the bit in the middle."

Ash talked about heading into the fight to help find Beck, engaging various locals, and hearing the 'pop' of the H'toka. At that point Francis began to ask a question about the Agents of Death, but Ash said that would be something to discuss at the end when we'd heard all accounts.

He continued, explaining that he'd seen me save

Grainger and then try to save Nyan. He'd collected Grainger from the floor in front of the bar on the way back to me. That was his account.

When he got to the bit about Grainger and Nyan my gut twisted. My heartbeat increased, and I felt heat rising in my skin. Beads of sweat formed on my forehead and I wiped them away with the sleeve of my top. Like Francis, I tried to interrupt, tried to explain, but Ash held up a hand to indicate I would have my turn.

Francis went next, but his account was very similar to Ash's: the search for Beck, the fighting, and the 'pop'. The first thing he saw after that was Nyan lying dead on the booth table and the knife sticking out of my arm.

Then it was my turn.

I'm far more emotional than my brothers, and my account of events was not so focussed or clear. I started somewhere in the middle and Ash had to take me back to the beginning with a few calming words. I told them about keeping Nyan down and calm, and then about Grainger being dragged away. My voice started to speed up and my breathing became shallow and uneven. Francis poured me some more water, and when I put my hand around the glass to take it, he placed his other hand gently over the top and held it there for a couple of seconds. My breathing settled and I carried on.

I explained my dilemma: stay with Nyan and let Grainger die, or save Grainger and leave Nyan for a moment. I told them I spoke to Nyan and he seemed in control, that he told me to save Grainger, that he'd promised to stay hidden behind the booth. I'd heard the H'toka 'pop' just as they had, but neither of them had seen the hooded figure and they were interested in that additional piece of the puzzle. I told them I'd tried to save Nyan, but he'd taken the H'toka bullet straight to the forehead.

I apologised again and again for not following orders,

for not staying with Nyan. For letting him die.

Ash moved along the couch and put his arm around me. It was a tight, protective hug, because as always, when I hurt, he hurt.

"Shae, you can't blame yourself," He said. "It was a series of unforeseeable events that led to Nyan's death. We can play the 'what if…' game forever and still not come up with a satisfactory answer – because in the end, Nyan is dead. We need to accept that. You need to accept that. You made a decision to save someone's life based on the information you had at the time. You couldn't have done more than that. We don't know what made Nyan stand up, and we never will. You're not responsible for his actions. Whatever the outcome with Nyan, Grainger is alive because of you. Remember that."

I understood what he was saying and the guilt lessened, but it was still there, right in the pit of my stomach.

"So, are we agreeing that Nyan was killed by an Agent of Death?" asked Francis. Ash and I both nodded. "We're actually saying someone hired the Agents of Death – the Assassin Elite – to take out a petty thief? A nobody?" he clarified.

"I believe so," said Ash. "It certainly adds credence to his story. I think our unfortunate friend actually stumbled onto something – the assassination of someone so influential that their death would have a major impact on society. As we've heard of nothing so far, it could be argued that the assassination is yet to happen – which means there may still be time to stop it."

"How? We have so little to go on," I said.

"That's a question for tomorrow," he replied. "There's nothing more we can do tonight. I suggest we sleep well and return to the monastery first thing to brief the Primus."

When I got back to my suite, I went straight to the bedroom and slumped on the end of the bed – which was big enough to fit all three of us comfortably. I kicked off my boots and lay back, closing my eyes, but all I saw was Nyan – the look of shock on his face just before he died, and the blankness of his eyes after he was dead.

I got up and paced for a bit before trying to sleep again, but every time I did I was hit by a replay of what had happened, over and over again. After about half an hour I gave up and pulled my boots back on. "Grace, is there a bar nearby?"

"Thank you for your query," she replied. "There's an Officer and VIP Bar on Level 3. Do you require directions?"

I thought about all the similar looking hallways and doors. "What do you think?" I replied.

# 5

The opaque glass doors were branded 'The Queen's Tap – Officer and VIP Bar' in fancy letterings, and they slid open automatically as I stepped towards them. Warm, light, and airy, with pleasant music playing in the background, the bar was the complete antithesis of Finnegan's, and like everywhere else on the ship, it was spotless.

I breathed in the delicious smell of warm bar snacks mixed with the soft aroma of perfume.

A few people looked around as I entered, and I wondered whether news of our arrival on the *Nakomo* had spread. I suspected it probably had by the interested glances followed by hushed conversations.

I approached the bar and sat on a green padded stool over to one side, away from everyone else. The barman, a distinguished-looking older gentleman, put down the glass he polished and came straight over.

"Good evening, Miss Shae," he said politely.

"I'm sorry, have we met?"

"Met? No. But it doesn't take long for gossip to spread around the ship. I'm afraid your arrival on board is just about common knowledge."

"I see," I replied, noticing that people averted their gaze when I caught them looking in our direction.

"I'm Malcolm, by the way. What can I get you to drink?"

I thought for a moment. "I don't normally drink anything other than beer, but maybe today's events warrant something stronger. I'll take a vodka on the rocks please, Malcolm. Earth vodka, not Santian – I have my limits." The barman laughed and poured me a glass. He left me alone after that, appearing only to place another drink in front of me when my glass was empty.

I looked out of the window as a Warrior passed, and when I turned back, I caught the eye of a humanoid Other sitting further down the bar. I absentmindedly wondered what job would most benefit from her four arms – maybe medical, or engineering. I imagined she would be good at multitasking.

I smiled respectfully at her; she smiled back.

After a couple more drinks I began to feel suitably numb. A yawn surprised me and I thought about returning to my suite, but then the image on Nyan dead on the booth table filled my mind and I decided to stay for one more glass.

"Excuse me," said Marcos quietly. "Is this seat taken?"

"That depends, Captain," I replied unenthusiastically, not taking my eyes of the glass I swilled in front of me.

"Depends on what? And please, call me Jared."

"Well, Jared," I downed the remaining contents of my glass, "it just so happens this seat is reserved."

"Reserved for whom?" He sounded surprised.

I sighed heavily and waved my empty glass at Malcolm. "For a drinker, not a talker. Which are you?"

"Umm… a drinker?" I didn't believe him, but I indicated he could sit anyway. "Malcolm," he continued as the barman headed our way. "Good to see you this evening." They shook hands.

"You, too, Captain. Sounds like you had a bit of excitement today."

"That we did." He didn't elaborate further.

"Is it true the crew of the *Makani* took down the ARRO cell responsible for the bombings on GalaxyBase3?"

"That's what I've heard."

"Twenty-seven people dead last reports said. Travesty if you ask me."

"It should never have happened, but the *Makani* did good. About time we got a win against the rebels. Two Fire Whiskies when you're ready."

Two? I presumed they weren't both for him so I finally turned to look at Marcos, and my breath caught.

Washed and clean, Marcos wore another pristine uniform. His mid-brown, military-short haircut was slightly damp, and his tanned skin glowed from the shower I was certain he'd just had.

I must've missed it at Finnegan's, probably because of the dim lighting, but Jared had the most remarkable eyes. The outside of the iris was intense blue, almost sapphire, but the middle, towards the pupil, was an extremely pale, ice-silver blue, not dissimilar to the colour I glowed when I was healing. He also had a small black dot in the iris of his left eye, just below the pupil. I know because I found myself staring, and I had to remind myself that he was still an arse no matter how attractive he was.

"I'm impressed," I said, referring to his choice of liquor, not the fact that he was stunning. "You really know how to party."

"Life and soul." His genuine smile reached his eyes. "Or so I've been told," he added after a short pause. The boot-stamp bruise on his face had almost disappeared, but the cut in his eyebrow was still raw, and he had an old, faded scar that sloped above his left eye. The knock of glasses being put on the bar in front of us pulled my gaze away. Malcolm slopped strong amber liquid into the two glasses and began to turn away.

"On second thoughts, leave the bottle," Jared said. "I have a feeling we're going to need it."

Malcolm left the unusual, ship's-decanter shaped bottle on the bar. I idly traced my fingertips over the flames embossed against opaque black glass, the name raised in jagged red lettering above. I picked up one of the shot glasses and waited for Jared to do the same.

"To King," I said.

"To Queen," he replied. We chinked glasses and both swallowed the contents in one go. My throat burned. Tears welled in the corners of my eyes, and my stomach felt like someone had punched me.

"Damn, that's good stuff," I wheezed.

"Sure hits the spot," Jared said, putting his hand to his mouth to stifle a cough. His fingers brushed against deep pink lips, full and soft. At least, I'm pretty sure they were soft. "Another?" he asked, pouring without waiting for an answer. "To the *Makani*," he said.

"The *Makani*," I replied, and we both slammed back the shot. That one didn't burn as much – perhaps I'd become anesthetised. Jared poured two more, but neither of us picked one up.

I looked at him and he was a little fuzzy around the edges, but I put that down to the Fire Whisky, and the several other vodkas I'd had before he'd arrived. After a minute of silence, I wondered if he was waiting for me to say something, but I was captivated by his lips – his full, soft, temptingly-kissable lips. I felt myself lean towards him and had to pull up short before I did something stupid. I hoped he hadn't noticed.

I downed another shot and hiccoughed.

"Shae?"

"Hmm?" My head was comfortably foggy.

"Can I ask you a question?"

"Nope. Drinker not talker – that was the rule,

remember?"

"Right." Jared downed his shot and poured two more, but I knew there was a question coming anyway. "You don't like me very much do you?" And there it was. That was why I didn't want to talk. I sighed, rubbing my forehead.

"I neither like you, nor dislike you." I thought that would be the most diplomatic answer. "I'm ambivalent."

"I don't believe you."

I sighed again. "In that case, the answer is no, I don't like you."

"I see," he replied quietly, but when I looked at him he was frowning. "Can I ask why?"

"Because you have the arrogance of the young."

"I'm older than you are," he replied, laughing.

"Case in point." I shook my head and downed another shot. "You have the arrogance of those who haven't fallen on their arse – who haven't had the opportunity to learn from their mistakes. Who haven't learnt… humility." I spoke quietly so no one else could hear. Jared drank silently. "The arrogance to make judgement before getting the facts. People follow a captain because of his rank, but they'll follow the man because of his character. A true leader has honour, compassion, and modesty." I thought of Ash.

"You don't think I have those things?"

"I saw you display all of those today, and more, but you wear them under your uniform. They would serve you better if you wore them for people to see. I'm pretty good at reading people, Jared. You're a good man, and I believe you're an honourable man… but you're also a total arse."

I thought I'd gone too far, but Jared laughed and went to pour more drinks. I put my hand over my glass to stop him.

"I'm sorry," I apologised. "I shouldn't have said anything, it's not my place. Please forgive my arrogance. Ash's always telling me my mouth gets me into trouble."

Jared watched me carefully. "I like you," he said simply. "There's something about you I can't put my finger on, but I find you… intriguing." I'd been called much worse, and deep down I felt flattered. "On one hand, you're tough, beautiful, and an exceptional fighter, but on the other hand, you're unpredictable and emotional. Plus, you have this peculiar kinship with the Brotherhood." He paused. "You have to admit that's weird."

It was my turn to laugh. For someone who'd only just met me, he'd summed me up pretty well.

"So? What are you doing with the Brotherhood?" he continued.

Maybe it was the amount of alcohol in my blood, or maybe I was beginning to see a different side to Captain Jared Marcos, but I decided to answer.

"I can only tell you what Primus Finnian has told me about how I ended up with the Brotherhood – after all, he was there when it all happened. I assume the *Nakomo* was on a routine mission on the edge of Sector Three when they picked up a distress call from a small transporter. By the time they got there, the vessel was being ripped apart by explosions and the FTL engines were on the verge of going critical. They only just had time to rescue the two passengers before the ship exploded. My father was too badly injured and died almost the moment they got him onto the *Nakomo*. My mother," I paused to steady my breathing, "she was heavily pregnant with me, and very badly hurt. The monks had to do an emergency delivery, but just before she gave birth, she made them promise that the Brotherhood would look after me. They stayed true to their promise and now I work with them. They're family."

"I see." Jared put a freshly filled glass of Fire Whisky in front of me and I drank it without thinking.

"My mother gave me my name, but she died not long after I was born. All records of passengers, and what happened to the vessel, were destroyed when it exploded, so the Brotherhood have no idea who they were or what they were doing in that part of space. I lost both my parents that day and I don't even know their names." Jared looked sad for me. "It's all right," I said, rallying myself. "That was also the day I found my new family. The monks took me back to the monastery as they'd promised, and even though the Primus wasn't too happy about keeping a baby, they got used to me. I've lived, trained and worked with the Brotherhood my entire life. As I've said, our current Primus, Finnian, was one of the monks who answered my parents' distress signal. They were strangers to him, but he was there with them at the end and I take great comfort in that. I suppose you could call him the nearest thing I have to a father."

"I see," Jared said again. "Grainger and Roberts told me you fought like a monk, but I have to admit I didn't believe them. After what you've just said though…"

"To be honest, most people don't believe to begin with, but I've trained in Tok-ma since I was a kid," I explained.

"What level are you?"

"Delta."

"Really?" he said loudly. "You have to be, what, an Eighth or Ninth Degree Warrior Caste monk to be awarded Delta level? And you're no monk."

"Of course I'm not a monk, dumb-arse, but I can't believe you're still refusing to believe that I am Brotherhood." He raised an eyebrow. "Okay, Captain Know-it-all, how do you explain my Ident report?" I challenged.

"Data error?"

"Come on! Even the Royal Earth Force accepts my affiliation with the Brotherhood. And the Brotherhood itself? They treat me like one of their own – minus the oath and the robes, and being male, oh, and the whole abstinence thing."

The collar on my top was loose fitting and stretchy,

which allowed me to pull it over my right shoulder to reveal my tattoo.

"No way," Jared said, poking it. He cupped his hands to try and block out the light and moved in even closer. The tattoo sparkled slightly in the dark, a unique side effect of the sacred rock used from the original monastery. I felt his breath on my shoulder, and could smell the sandalwood and musk that still lingered on his skin. My chest fluttered and I pulled away. "Now that's something you don't see every day," he said.

"That's not all." I was showing off, fuelled by the Fire Whisky. I pulled the chain out from around my neck and on the end were two objects. One of them was a smaller version of the Ninth Degree medal that Ash wore on the belt of his robes. Jared took it in his hands and flipped it over.

"So now I'm officially impressed. I apologise for doubting you," he said graciously.

"It's okay. Most people don't believe at first."

"What's this? It looks unusual." Jared held the second object on the chain – a disc, approximately the same size as the Brotherhood medallion, but it was brushed bronze in colour, with a pale blue stone in the centre. "I don't recognise these," he added, referring to the delicate scrolling symbols covering both sides.

"It belonged to my mother," I replied. "She made the monks promise to give it to me when I was old enough. She said it was important… but she died before she could say why. There were three things I inherited from her: my name, this disc, and a tiny piece of ripped, blood-smeared paper with just three words written on it: Family, Honour, Courage. Perhaps it was a family motto or something. Whatever it means, they seem like pretty good words to live by."

"True." Jared let go of the disc and I tucked both items safely back under my top.

I was tired and feeling the effects of the Fire Whisky, so I put my head on the bar and let the cool surface sooth my hot forehead.

"Is everything all right here?" Malcolm asked. I lifted my head and focused on the older man.

"I would really appreciate a glass of water please, Malcolm."

"Sure, coming right up."

"Hey, Malcolm," I added, spotting a freezer behind the bar. "I don't suppose you've got any Carmichael's Chocamel ice-cream back there have you?"

"Let me have a look," he replied, rummaging through the chiller before pulling out the distinctive pink and cream tub. He placed the small pot on the bar along with two spoons. Jared looked at it and frowned.

"Don't tell me you've never had Chocamel ice-cream before?" I said. He shook his head, looking at me like I was halfway to crazy. "You haven't lived," I said pulling the top off the pot and picking up one of the spoons. "As a connoisseur of ice-cream, I can tell you that all of Carmichael's flavours are amazing, but Chocamel," I savoured a spoonful, "is the absolute best. All that chocolaty caramel loveliness..." I waved the second spoon teasingly in front of him.

He took it and dug in. After a moment, he shrugged his broad shoulders and merely said, "Hmm."

"Hmm?" I copied him, including the shoulder shrug. "Philistine! All the more for me then." I moved the tub away from him.

Jared put his spoon down on the bar. "Shae, there's one thing that's been puzzling me?"

"Just one?" I teased. He ignored me.

"Why were you at Finnegan's?" When I didn't answer, he asked, "Who was Nyan? He was obviously important to you." I winced at the mention of his name. "You blame yourself for his death?"

"I was responsible for his death," I hit back. "It was my job to protect him."

"Protect him from what?"

"That's Brotherhood business, Captain. I believe Ash made that quite clear back at Finnegan's," I replied, annoyed at him for asking the question. "You know, you should be more concerned with why your troopers died back there instead of worrying about us." It was a low blow, and I was ashamed when I saw the offended look on his face, but I couldn't take it back – it was already out there.

"Not that it's anything to do with you, but I've personally contacted the families of each trooper to explain they died bravely fighting for their Realm." When Jared spoke, he was all business.

"I'm sorry," I mumbled as my water arrived.

"And I wasn't born yesterday," he added.

"Huh?"

"I know when someone's trying to change the subject, and I know your man was killed by an Agent of Death." I choked on the sip I'd just taken. "I may be young, as you call me," he continued, patting me on the back, "but I can recognise the sound of an H'toka when I hear one. Who exactly was Nyan? Why were the Assassin Elite after him?"

There was no way I was going to discuss Brotherhood business with a Fleet Captain – no matter how under the influence of Fire Whisky I was. I knew I had to be careful, and decided another change of subject was required. "Tell me about Captain Jared Marcos," I said.

"I'm sorry?"

"We've talked about me, tell me something about you."

Perhaps he realised he wasn't going to get any further with his line of questioning about Nyan, or perhaps he thought it was only fair to tell me a little about him, either way he indulged me. "What do you want to know?" he asked.

"You must be, what, thirty-five?"

"Close. Thirty-four. Thirty-five in a few months."

"That's young for a Half-Wing Captain, let alone a Full-Wing Cruiser Captain." That fact still amazed me. "And let's not forget, the Full-Wing Captain of a brand spanking new Vanguard Class Cruiser, no less. Now I'm impressed. What gives?" When he seemed reluctant to talk, I added, "Come on, Jared."

"Fine. My father."

"Your father?"

"He's why I'm captain of the *Defender* at thirty-four. He never made it past a Lieutenant in Engineering, but he wanted more for me, so he pushed me to do better. All the time. Sometimes whatever I did wasn't good enough." He turned and looked at me and there was something in his eyes I couldn't read, but then he cleared his throat and said, "Why am I telling you this?"

"Because I'm a super-fantastic listener… and we've both had too much to drink?"

"You have," he said.

"You have, too," I countered.

"Ah, but I'm used to Fire Whisky." He slurred 'whisky' slightly.

"Yeah, I can tell." I was pleased we were back to a lighter, less stressful conversation. I didn't like the sneaky, arrogant Jared, but I liked relaxed, light-hearted Jared quite a bit. "Tell me more about your dad."

"Why?"

"Because I've never had one, not a biological one anyway."

"Is this a guilt trip?"

"Is it working?"

"Maybe," he said, but it must've been because he carried on. "He's a good man. He's always been hardworking, always put food on the table, and he looked after me and Mum."

"But he was hard on you?"

"I didn't get much of a childhood, but I did well at school. I went through the Academy in record time and was fast-tracked through Officer Training. I got my first captaincy at twenty-seven and was given the chair of the *Defender* six months ago, straight out of dry-dock."

Finnian was as close to a father as I was ever going to get, and he was the best, but sometimes I wondered what it would've been like to have grown up with my biological father. "He must be very proud of you," I said.

"He is. Tells all his mates how well I'm doing. I bet they love that."

"And your mum? Tell me about her?"

"She's beautiful, and she's patient," said Jared. I don't think he realised, but he smiled as he spoke about her. "Well, she would have to be to put up with the pair of us. She's a history teacher." I groaned. "What?"

"My worst subject," I replied, making a face.

He seemed surprised. "You went to school?"

"Of course I did, genius. Just because I grew up in a monastery with a bunch of mouldy old monks, doesn't mean I got away without a proper education. We have monks from all disciplines so I got a pretty good cover of subjects, and," I poked him to make sure he was paying attention, "probably some subjects you didn't even cover." I leant towards him, which probably wasn't a good idea because I could smell him again – and he smelled good. I did an exaggerated look around us to make sure no one was too close. "Shh, don't tell anyone, but I'm not very good at the whole academic thing."

"Is that so," he whispered back and I felt his breath on my neck. My skin immediately broke into goose bumps.

"Hard to believe, isn't it?" I said, leaning away so his breath wasn't on my skin anymore. "I suppose you could say I'm more a girl of action."

"You know, I can tell that about you." A boyish grin spread across his face and he poured us both another Fire

Whisky – even though I objected.

"Last one," I said definitely. "When we were kids it was always me that got Ash into trouble. I'd make him miss classes to go do something stupid like jumping off the Marulian Cliffs or swimming with the Mantra sharks. That was how we found out…"

"Found out what?"

"Umm… that I was the bad influence." Jared didn't need to know that that is how we accidentally found out I could heal other people as well as myself.

"The two of you seem extremely close."

"We are. I've spent more time with Ash than anyone else, ever. He's like a big brother, friend, confident, and protector all rolled into one big package. I love him."

"What about Brother Francis?"

"I was seventeen when this shy, scrawny, bag-of-bones arrived at the monastery." Jared raised an eyebrow. "I know, right? You wouldn't believe it to look at him now. I don't know how he got there, he just seemed to appear one day, but he was the same age as me so Ash and I were asked to show him the ropes, so to speak. We kind of became a three instead of a two after that."

"What happened to him before he arrived?"

"No idea; bad, I guess. I used to ask at first, but he obviously didn't want to talk about it so I gave up after a while. Besides, he fitted in so well that after a while it just never became a thing. We just moved on as a family." I paused. "Being a captain must be a pretty lonely job, I guess."

"Why do you say that?" If Jared was taken aback by my sudden change of subject, he didn't show it.

"I don't know really. Perhaps because I know how lucky I am to have Ash and Francis. You have to be professional with your crew – keep them at arm's length. Must be lonely is all I'm thinking."

I don't think Jared wanted to discuss it further because it

was his turn to change topic. “I understand the monks agreed to look after you when you were a baby, and I get that you’re close to Brothers Asher and Francis, but why are you still with them? I would’ve thought that as soon as you came of age, you would’ve been dying to get away from the confines of the monastery.”

“I have my reasons.”

“And they are?”

“Personal… and complicated.”

“I see.” He looked intently at his glass a moment. “Okay, here’s another question for you.” I groaned. “No, no, stay with me on this because I’m really interested. Do you believe in these Sun Gods the Brotherhood revere so much?”

I snorted a laugh. “That’s also complicated! Especially after this much Fire Whisky.”

“Try me.”

“Well, as you asked so nicely… so, for starters, you do know that we don’t actually believe there are Gods who live in the Sun.” He frowned and pursed his lips. “Just checking – it seems to be a popular misconception. Look, humans have always found something or someone to believe in, and Sun Gods are not a new thing. People on Earth have been worshiping them throughout time, and the sun symbol has popped up all the way through history. The Aztecs had Tonatiuh, the Egyptians had Ra, the Greeks had Helios, and even the Partizans had Volna. You want me to go on?”

“So it was a big thing on Earth. That doesn’t explain the Brotherhood.”

“It wasn’t just on Earth, that’s the point I’m trying to make. The exact same symbols can be found across the Four Sectors – different worlds, different times, but all with a similar lore, and they all seem to stem from the same derivation.”

“You’re saying you do believe?”

“Yes… no… hell, to tell the truth, I don’t know. The

Brotherhood believes that at one time a bunch of all-powerful, glowing, golden Gods ruled over the entire galaxy with divine righteousness. Do I share that unreserved faith? Maybe not. But you can't argue with hard evidence, and hard evidence says that something ties all these symbols together – there are too many for it to be coincidence. What I choose to believe is that there is something bigger than you and me – bigger than Humans, Santian, D'Antaran… I believe there is something that bridges the gap between races and worlds – and that's good enough for me… for now." Suddenly I was tired, and I'd about reached the limit of what I was prepared to share with a relative stranger. "Jared, I'm sorry, I'm exhausted and I've had too much to drink. I think I need to return to my quarters now."

"Of course," he replied, standing. "Maybe we can continue the conversation at another time?"

"Maybe," I replied. I stood and turned towards him, wobbling before I could get my balance. Jared reached out, grabbing my arm to steady me, but he let go immediately, like he'd touched a hot poker.

"I'm so sorry, are you okay?" he said, his blue eyes clouding over with worry.

I didn't understand. Was he apologising because he'd grabbed me? And why wouldn't I be okay? I couldn't read the look on his face, but he was staring at my arm. I thought perhaps I had something on my sleeve so I looked down, and that's when I understood – he'd grabbed my arm right where I'd been stabbed.

His eyes regarded me suspiciously, and he put his hand out to touch my arm again. I backed away, making excuses about needing my bed, but I knew my eyes betrayed the panic I tried to hide inside.

"I'll walk you back to your suite," he said calmly.

"I'm sure I can find my own way."

"Nonsense. What kind of a man would I be if I let you

walk back alone after the amount you've drunk?"

"Really, it's okay." I tried to protest, but Jared wasn't backing down.

"You can argue all you like, Shae, but at the end of the day, you can't stop me from coming with you."

"You know that's called stalking."

"Possibly. But I'm the Captain, so I can pretty much do what the hell I want." A boyish grin spread across his face, and I couldn't help laughing. Damn that whisky.

"Whatever," I finally agreed. "But no more questions, my head's starting to pound."

"Just one?"

"Do you ever give up?"

"No."

"Fine. Just one question," I said, but I regretted it as soon as the words were out of my mouth.

"When I grabbed your arm back there, you didn't blink."

"That's not a question, that's a statement."

"I'm getting there."

"I'll be an old lady by the time you do." I tried to stall, trying to think of an appropriate answer to the question I knew was coming.

"Why didn't you feel any pain?"

"Finally, a question," I said dramatically, but continued to walk in silence.

"Well?"

"Well what?"

"You can't keep avoiding the question. I'll just keep asking."

I believed he would, so eventually I said the only thing I could think of. "Drugs."

"Drugs?"

"Yup. Amazingly good drugs… and Fire Whisky," I added. "Just about every part of me is numb right now."

"Really?"

"Really," I repeated, getting into the lift while trying to ignore his sarcasm. Grace asked for a destination, which Jared gave, albeit with a bit of a slur. When we got to my floor, I stepped out carefully.

"So where did you get these 'amazingly good drugs' from?" he asked.

"Sorry, but you've already had your question," I replied, wobbling.

"Here," he said putting his arm around my waist. "You're all over the place."

"It's not me, it's you. I'm walking perfectly straight," I moaned, at which point both of us careened off a wall, almost taking out a pot plant. I felt light-headed, but I couldn't tell whether it was because of the alcohol, or because Jared's warm body was pressed against mine.

"You still haven't answered my question," he pushed.

"I told you, one question only, and you've had it." Fortunately, we arrived at my suite with perfect timing.

"Indulge me," he added smoothly. I turned to face him and realised how much I did want to indulge him, but not in the way he was thinking. Focus! I struggled to clear the liquor infused haze from my brain.

"Thank you, Captain, for walking me back to my room, which as you can see, is right here." I pressed my thumb on the pad and the door opened.

I had my back against the wall to steady myself and Jared was very, very close. He put his left hand against the wall by my right ear so that he was propped up, leaning in towards me. Was he going to kiss me? My pulse quickened and my face flushed, but to be fair, that could've been the alcohol.

What would I do if he did kiss me? I was never in that position – there was always a monk around to protect my virtue, so to speak. How the hell was I supposed to know what to do next? Part of me panicked, but the other part wanted him to kiss me. It wasn't as if I was ever going to see him again after we left in the morning.

Then my inner conscience kicked in. Sure he was good looking, but it didn't change the fact that he was also a prize arse, and sharing a few family stories didn't automatically make us best buddies. But then, perhaps I was beginning to really like Jared. Perhaps he wasn't the arrogant waste-of-space I'd thought him to be.

"Shae?" He bent down so his lips were close to my ear, and when he spoke, I could feel his breath on my skin again.

"Yes?"

"Why were you on Angel Ridge?"

"What?" I gasped, totally blindsided.

"Who was Nyan? Why were the Agents of Death hired to kill him?"

"Are you kidding me?" Realisation flowed through my veins like iced water. How could I have been so stupid? I'd let my guard down for the first time in what seemed forever, and he'd taken advantage. "Damn you, Marcos, that's low, even for you. I was beginning to think that maybe I'd been wrong about you, but I wasn't. You are a shit." I was angry and embarrassed.

Hell was I embarrassed.

I just wanted to get out of there, to remove myself from the situation as quickly as possible. Either that or hit him hard, right on the side of his big, fat, arrogant head, but something told me Ash would object – especially since the last time I'd thumped a Fleet officer, it'd taken him a week to patch up diplomatic relations. No, the best thing was to get away from him.

"You haven't answered my question," he pushed.

"No, I haven't. But you know what? Life's full of disappointments – get used to it. Goodnight, Captain Marcos." I spat out each word.

"You understand I had to try?"

"Actually, no, I don't. Oh, and, Captain?"

"Yes?" he said expectantly.
"Go to hell."
The door slid shut between us.

# 6

My head pounded. Damn that Fire Whisky – and damn Jared Marcos.

I pulled one of my boots off with too much force and it flew across the room, taking out a table lamp. I hopped towards the bathroom, taking off the other one as I went, all the while listing reasons why I hated Jared Marcos. I was already at number eleven and I hadn't even got around to brushing my teeth.

I was convinced I wouldn't be able to sleep. I was still angry with myself for failing to protect Nyan, but I'd also dredged up memories of my parents – which always left me melancholic – and then, then, I had to deal with the shit that was Jared. It was a triple whammy of gloom. I squirmed a few times to get the most comfortable position, finally putting my head back and closing my eyes.

It felt like I'd only just fallen asleep when I smelled the best aroma in the Four Sectors: freshly brewed Shatokian coffee. I thought I must've been dreaming, but the smell got stronger and I could hear Ash calling me.

"Shae, it's morning, wake up," he said gently. I didn't care. I didn't want to. "Wake up," he yelled. My eyes shot open and I sat bolt upright. "I brought you coffee," he added in a more appropriate volume.

There was a split second of calm… then my head exploded. I could heal myself from broken bones, internal injuries, knife wounds and bullet holes, but could I heal the hangover from Hades? Could I hell. I took the coffee gratefully, but still scowled at Ash.

My quarters where lit with artificial daylight, and Ash sat cross-legged on the end of my bed with his own coffee, as he'd done a thousand times before.

I thought about the thumb scanner on the door and a frown creased my forehead. "How did you get in?"

"Captain Marcos let me in with his override code," Ash replied. "He came to tell me that Harrison was going to be all right, as if we didn't already know that, and he thought you might need this." He threw a hypospray at me.

Jared!

The pain in my head had temporarily blocked out the memory. I wasn't embarrassed any more, I'd let that go, but I was angry and hurt, and like a volcano about to spew, those emotions rushed to the surface. Ash tensed, holding his coffee halfway up to his mouth. I knew he felt exactly what I was feeling, just as strongly as if he was experiencing it himself.

The Link was what we called the energy transfer that happened between me and an injured person – what observers would see as the silver-blue, shimmering arcs of light. The intensity of the Link depended on how bad the injuries were, so standard stuff like a broken bone, knife, or bullet wound was relatively easy to heal. I did my thing, the other person got better, and the Link broke. That was it. Nothing more between us.

Sometimes though, if the person was badly injured like Harrison, the Link needed to be stronger, and it took more effort to heal them. In those cases, there could be a residual energy trace for up to two or three days after.

During that time, I could feel the intense emotions of the person I'd healed – and they could feel mine – but only if we were in close proximity, and not everyday feelings, but strong, deep emotions like love, fear, anger and excitement.

The other person was usually none the wiser, just a little confused about why they had a random emotion that seemed out of place, but I was used to it. I've learnt to distinguish the differences, becoming practiced at building mental roadblocks to shut out feelings that weren't mine.

Ash is different though. Whether it's because I've healed him so many times, once bringing him back from certain death, or because we have such a close emotional connection, but the Link between us had never faded.

"Shae?" Ash said slowly. "Why do I feel like I want to punch someone in the head?" I groaned and rubbed my temples gingerly. "What happened?"

My head throbbed. "It's nothing," I lied. "I went for a drink last night because I couldn't sleep and Jared turned up."

"You should've got me. I would've come with you."

"I know, but I needed some space. Anyway, let's just say Jared is the shit I thought he was and leave it at that." I used the hypospray on my arm and it stung for a moment.

"What happened?" Ash repeated, but that time I felt his own anger rising.

"It's really nothing. I don't want to talk about it. I'm okay, and no harm was done – except for this killer headache. Remind me never to accept Fire Whisky from strangers again." I forced a smile.

"Umm…" He pulled his guilty face.

"Ash? What have you done?"

"Well, perhaps, given how you're feeling, I better go get rid of the Captain."

"He's here?" I gasped, pulling the covers up to my chin.

"He told me you'd had a few drinks last night and he wanted to check you were okay. Seemed pretty innocent, but now I'm guessing there's more to it." I felt his anger simmer though the Link.

"Tell him to go the hell away. And that's the polite version."

"No problem."

The end of the bed lifted as he got off and he headed towards the lounge, but I suddenly panicked. What was he going to say to Jared? He could be ultra-protective and I didn't want him to cause a diplomatic incident. That was usually my job. I threw myself out of bed, almost tripping over a chair in my haste to get to the door. I hid behind the frame and eavesdropped on the conversation.

"Captain Marcos." Ash used his formal Brotherhood voice. "I don't know what happened between you and Shae last night, she won't tell me, but—"

"Wait, I—"

"But something obviously did." Ash's voice was steely.

"Brother Asher—"

"Captain Marcos," Ash interrupted again. "We all appreciate your generous hospitality," I blurted out a sarcastic 'pah' then covered my mouth with both hands, "but I think it better if you leave immediately."

I heard movement and then the light swish of the door sliding open and closed. I guess Jared hadn't argued any further, taking retreat as the better option.

Ash appeared in the bedroom as I climbed back on to the bed. "He's gone," he said, propping up the doorframe.

"Thanks."

"Still don't want to talk about it?"

"Nope."

"Well I guess you'll tell me when you're ready. In the meantime, breakfast is in my quarters." At the word 'breakfast' my stomach heaved. "Oh, and the *Nakomo* will be ready to leave in an hour, the engineers are just finishing their final checks."

"Great – the sooner the better as far as I'm concerned. I

don't think I can manage food though."

"That's non-negotiable. You haven't eaten since yesterday morning." He paused. "And you need something to mop up that whisky." Just at the mention of it my stomach turned again.

"Okay, whatever," I conceded.

I reluctantly got out of bed and began searching for my clothes because I wasn't sure where I'd left them. Without a word, Ash wrapped his arms tightly around me, pulling me to his chest. That was what I knew. That was comfortable.

I relaxed, letting my head rest on his shoulder, and I breathed in his shower-fresh scent. The fist around my heart loosened, as if he physically sapped the anger from me. I felt calmer.

"Breakfast. Twenty. Or else."

By the time I'd showered my headache had completely disappeared, and I made a mental note to try and get some more of the hyposprays Jared had brought me for our med-kit. When I got to Ash's room, I was ravenous, which was just as well because there was enough food there for ten, including more fresh Shatokian coffee. We drank and ate well before an ensign arrived to escort us back to the hangar where the *Nakomo* was docked.

Francis and I were small-talking when the final double-doors opened on to the hangar. "Holy crap!" I gasped.

An engineer in dirty overalls rushed over as soon as he saw us. "Perfect timing," he said breathlessly. "The Captain told us to pull out all the stops and we've just this minute finished." He wiped at a smudge on his cheek making it worse.

I walked over to the *Nakomo* and ran my hand along her smooth hull, which had been scrubbed to within an inch of its life – not a lunar arthropod in sight.

"She looks amazing," I said.

"That's not all," continued the engineer, herding us around the ship. "We've changed all her hydraulic fluids, completely replaced her suspension system, updated her navigation control, boosted the range of your communications array and… well, the rest I'm sure you can work out yourself."

I wanted to kiss him. The *Nakomo* had been given a new lease of life, and she deserved it because she was part of the family. I was born on that old tub and she'd kept me safe ever since.

"Oh," he continued, as if it were an afterthought, "we've also restocked your medical and food supplies, with strict instructions to include Carmichael's Chocamel ice-cream." I couldn't help but smile, and I hadn't realised how happy I was until I turned around and saw Jared leaning casually against one of the empty crates. My smile slipped, but I decided I wasn't going to let him ruin the moment so I pasted it back on.

As the engineer led us back to the rear ramp, Jared wandered over. My first instinct was to run into the ship and hide, but I forced myself to stay put, besides, I had Ash by my side and that always made me feel brave.

"Captain Marcos," said Ash coolly. "I didn't expect to see you here after our conversation."

"I came with an offer," he replied cryptically.

"Really?"

"In appreciation for you giving us passage on the *Nakomo* yesterday, I would like to offer you passage on the *Defender* today." I was confused. "The *Defender* can get you back to your monastery quicker than…," I'm sure he was going to say something rude about our shuttle, but I think he caught the 'don't mess with the *Nakomo*' face I was making, "…your quaint craft," he finished tactfully.

"That's kind of you," said Ash, failing to keep the scepticism out of his voice. "But as you know, the location of our monastery is a secret to outsiders. Our 'quaint craft' will get us there just fine – especially with all the upgrades your engineers have given her."

"I insist," Jared pushed.

"You can insist all you like, Captain, but we will take the *Nakomo.* Thank you for the hospitality you have already shown us." Ash didn't wait for the Captain to respond, instead he indicated to me that it was time to leave.

I was about to enter the cabin when Jared called my name and I reluctantly turned. He stood at the bottom of the ramp, his hands on his hips and an expression on his face I couldn't quite read. For a moment, I saw what could've been regret, but if it was, it was gone quickly. And if it had been regret, regret for what? For the way he had treated me, or for not getting what he wanted?

"What?" I said dispassionately.

"I just wanted to say…" He paused, shaking his head, and then he seemed to change what he was about to say. "Maybe our paths will meet again?"

Was he kidding me?

"I hope not," I replied, thumping the 'close' button at the top of the ramp.

It was amazing how relaxed I felt once we were on our way back to the monastery. We travelled in silence for a while, but as the quiet continued, I began to think about Jared and anger bubbled in my chest.

Why did I let him get to me? Why was I so annoyed with him? Of course, the possibilities were numerous: he'd brought his troubles to Finnegan's, and Nyan was dead as a result; he was cocky and arrogant, two very unflattering characteristics in my book; he'd got me drunk to take advantage, and not in a good way; I thought he was going to kiss me, but he hadn't…

I could've gone on, but I had my answer.

I was angry with Jared because, for a while, I thought we might've been friends. I don't know why I'd shared my parent's story with him, something I've only told a handful of people outside of the Brotherhood, but he'd shared something about his past, too, and I thought on some level we'd connected. I'd been wrong though. He hadn't wanted to be friends; he'd just wanted information.

I corrected myself. I wasn't angry at Jared; I was angry at myself.

Ash sat next to me and I told him everything that had happened the night before. Most of the time he listened without saying a word, but occasionally he nodded his head. When I'd finished, he simply said, "You going to be okay?"

"Yes," I replied, and I was. I neither liked Jared, nor disliked him. I was ambivalent. That was the truth.

"Before we start," I said, as Francis joined us, "you know the drill." I waved my hands at them and they didn't resist. I put one hand on Ash's shoulder and one on Francis's and felt the tickling, tingling sensation build. The medical team on the *Defender* had done such a good job there wasn't much left for me to do but mop up. A brief silver-blue flash lit the cabin.

"Okay," said Ash, opening the discussion. "Fleet, Captain Marcos, the fight at Angel Ridge – they've all been distractions. It's time to get back to business. We know what we're going to say to the Primus about yesterday's events, so there's no need to go over it again, but we do need to think about what our next move should be."

"We know the original meeting went down on the Planet of Souls," said Francis. "We should be able to find out exactly where from the name on the mausoleum."

"We also know Nyan heard GalaxyBase4 mentioned," I added. "And somewhere called Frampton Edge."

"So not much then," replied Ash. "Francis, I want you to locate the exact spot on the Planet of Souls where our mystery group met; they may have left something there to indicate who they are." He caught the scepticism on Francis's face. "It's a long shot, but you never know. Shae, see if you can find anything on the Data-Net about this Frampton Edge place."

"On it," I replied, moving to the chair in front of a plexi-screen.

"Welcome to the Data-Net. What is your search parameter?" the computer said the instant I tapped the access button.

"Is that Grace?" Ash said, coming over.

"Got to be. Sure sounds like her." I replied. "Another upgrade?"

"Looks like it, but…" Ash's hand rested on his belt buckle. "As much as I appreciate the other enhancements they've given us, I'm not so sure about this one. I don't think I'm entirely comfortable having REF software on the *Nakomo*, and I don't think the Primus would be either." He sighed. "Not much we can do about it at the moment – use it for now and I'll get Brother Michael to de-install it when we get back to Lilania."

He and Francis left for the Flight area, and I turned my attention back to the computer.

"Search all accessible data-channels for information about a place or location named Frampton Edge in Sector Three." I rested my head back and closed my eyes, letting the computer work.

"Task complete," Grace stated, much quicker than I'd anticipated. "There are 256,672 results for places or locations named Frampton Edge within Sector Three."

"Damn it."

"However," she continued, "there are zero direct matches." I looked at the screen in disbelief. On one hand I was glad I wasn't going to have to trawl through 256,672 possibilities, but on the other hand it meant Nyan must've been wrong.

"Are you sure?" I asked.

"I'm sorry, but your question is imprecise. Please rephrase your enquiry."

"Useless piece of computer crap," I moaned.

"Would you like me to expand your search parameters?"

she offered.

"Yes. Same search, but this time include all Four Sectors. Give me direct matches only." I closed my eyes again.

"There are zero direct results for places or locations named Frampton Edge within the Four Sectors."

"Crap."

"Would you like me to expand your search parameters?"

"Why the hell not? Do a free-search of all accessible data-channels for any reference match to Frampton Edge. Again, give me direct matches only."

While I waited for the search to complete, I grabbed a data-pad and started to read up about GalaxyBase4. It must've been thirty minutes later when Grace informed me she was done. I crossed my fingers.

"There are two direct matches within your search parameters," she said impassively.

"Now we're talking. Give me the first entry." I sat up straighter in my chair.

The screen flashed up a death certificate for a middle-aged man. "Frampton Edge, Buildings Inspector. Died, aged 54, after falling from a 72-floor multiplex building under construction on one of the outer planets," Grace summarised.

"Not relevant," I replied, but the record had given me hope – maybe Frampton Edge wasn't a place, but a person. "What's next?" The screen flicked to an REF arrest warrant and I sucked in a surprised breath. "Grace, how were you able to access a restricted REF document?"

"You asked for a free-search of all available data-channels. Hermes was included in that search parameter."

"You have access to Hermes?"

"Affirmative."

It had to be a mistake. The engineers must've inadvertently given us access to the secure network during their upgrades. Jared would be pissed.

“Summarise,” I said.

“The arrest warrant was issued six months ago for the alleged transportation of illegal cargo including weapons and narcotics, and for human trafficking. Edge is also listed on an REF terrorist watch list as a suspected ARRO sympathiser. It includes his suspected bases of operation as Angel Ridge, The Trinity Planets, and GalaxyBases 4 and 5.”

“Result! Does it include any aliases or associates?”

“Affirmative.”

It was like pulling teeth. “Who are they?”

“Known aliases are Frampton Shaw, Charlie Edge, Charlie Shaw, Kingston Edge, Kingston Shaw...” The list went on so I cut Grace off, asking for possible associates instead. “Known associates are Moon Greenstone, deceased; Jack-knife Nash, incarcerated; Kat Stermon, incarcerated; and Jason Cady, owner of the Hotel Somnus on GalaxyBase4.”

“Well isn’t that a coincidence? Cross-reference Frampton Edge against Cady and all GalaxyBase4 records.”

“Charlie Shaw, one of Edge’s aliases, was booked into the Hotel Somnus for a period of three days, two weeks ago.”

“Is there any other information on the hotel booking form?”

“Negative. The hotel has been cited on four separate occasions for code violations, in particular, the omission of personal information on their booking forms.”

“Is there anything else linking Frampton Edge to GalaxyBase4?”

“Negative. That is the only reference accessible.”

“Check the manifests of all ships departing GalaxyBase4 since Edge was there. I want to know if he’s left.”

“There are no records of Frampton Edge, or any of his aliases, leaving the Base.”

I picked up the data-pad I’d been reading from earlier,

transferring the information from the main screen with a swipe of my hand before heading to the flight area to brief Ash.

"Perfect timing," said Francis when I got there. "We're approaching DeadSpace – you might want to grab a hold of something." I reached for the back of Ash's chair, ready for the jolt, but I barely felt the deceleration as the FTL engines powered down and we reduced to sub-light speed.

"Now that upgrade I can live with," Ash joked.

As Francis brought us up to the edge of the asteroid field, the lights and displays on the consoles flickered from the magnetic interference.

Like most kids, I'd been told the legend of DeadSpace during bed-time stories. Some believed Horatio Greystoke, Captain of the pirate ship, The Grey Shadow, found a way through the field and hid his cache of stolen plunder on the other side. The myth tells that Greystoke failed to disclose the exact route before he and his crew met a gruesome and untimely death.

Fuelled by the rumours of untold wealth, people have tried to navigate the field ever since – action men wanting the adrenalin rush, boasters who wanted to prove themselves, but mostly, your standard arsehole who got drunk and did it for a bet. Generally, they died trying, having no idea what the real treasure was beyond the field.

Francis leant forward and disengaged the ineffective nav-con system. There was only one way through the field, and that was by line-of-sight on a singular route passed down through the Brotherhood; a guarded secret that no outsider was privy to.

Francis was a natural pilot, and he knew the route well, but navigating the field could get a bit hairy. Most of the time we made it through without incident, but then there was that one occasion: the *Nakomo's* port thruster had needed an overhaul for months, but the fix had been bumped twice for more important repairs. It finally decided to crap-out just as we were navigating the field. We just about got through by the skin of our teeth and the thruster was repaired the very next day – as was the hull where we'd bounced off an asteroid.

It took about forty minutes of painstaking concentration to get to the far side of the field, and when we got there… a wide open space of nothingness. Francis brought the *Nakomo* to a complete stop before opening a secure com-link. After following some stringent identification procedures, an opening in the cloaking field materialised and I got my first glimpse of the most beautiful sight in the Four Sectors.

Lilania, a tiny, picturesque, gem of a planet, was hidden beyond the deadly asteroid field. Jared had asked why I hadn't left the monastery, and the planet was one of the reasons. I loved the place. It was home.

Francis took us down, skimming low over the pinkish waters of the Rosado Sea, so low that plumes of sea mist followed in our wake. Most of the planet was ocean, but a few islands punctuated the expanse of water and we headed towards the largest landmass on the southern hemisphere.

The sky around us was a washed-out rouge, and the flight area filled with a light rose tint, but in the distance storm clouds rolled ominously across the horizon, turning the sky a deep crimson.

It was the Rosado Sea that crashed its waves on the beaches nearest to the monastery, which itself sat on a rock plateau a way up the Marulian cliffs. Built in locally sourced stone, the buildings were almost camouflaged against the creamy-brown rock of the cliff face.

Francis glided the *Nakomo* over the Diamond Reef and across the small bay before taking us up to land in our designated area just above the main complex. After he'd completely powered down the shuttle, I listened for the usual groans and hisses, but all I heard were a few minor whimpers and a quiet growl. Then, out of sheer bloody-mindedness, the *Nakomo* gave one last loud moan, just to remind us that she'd got us home safely.

I walked down the ramp, raising my face to feel the warmth against my skin. The wind was light but it still ruffled the gentle curls in my hair, and I could smell the roseberries that grew in the kitchen gardens. When I opened my eyes, Francis was standing next to me doing exactly the same thing.

Brother Andre arrived panting. "Brothers, Shae, I'm afraid there is no time to…" He was distracted and his mouth hung open. "Good Gods, what happened to the *Nakomo*? Never mind, no time. The Primus wants to see the three of you immediately."

"Of course," said Ash. "I've a feeling we won't be staying long. Could you arrange for the *Nakomo* to be refuelled?" Andre agreed, practically pushing us towards the stone steps that took us down to the main complex.

We headed through the main entrance into the foyer, its walls adorned with drapes in shades of blue, and each one displaying the sun and rune symbols of the Brotherhood with honour. We hurried passed lower Degree monks practising Tok-ma, the smell of baking bread from the kitchen making me feel hungry again.

Leaving the foyer, we passed rooms used for prayer and meditation before walking out into the spacious central Courtyard where higher Degree monks practiced advanced Tok-ma. The Primus's Outer Chambers where on the far side, and Brother David stood at their threshold beckoning us. He ushered us straight into the Office of the Primus without delay.

Finnian sat behind a large, ornately carved wooden desk, but he got up and came around to greet us as soon as we entered. He guided us to a smaller round table to the side, and listened silently while we explained everything that had happened.

"So we have no corroborating evidence that the

information from Nyan is legitimate?" The Primus looked troubled.

"Correct," replied Ash.

"To be clear, you're saying we have no proof that an assassination is, in fact, going to take place."

"No." Ash sighed. "However, the fact that someone sent an Agent of Death to kill him, does give credibility to his information. We also believe that the event has not yet occurred or we would've heard about it. While there's still time, we would like your permission to start a formal investigation."

Finnian remained silent, his fingertips pressed together and raised to his lips.

"We've investigated less important matters, with a lot less information to go on than this," I pushed, winning a warning glare from Ash.

"I understand your frustrations, child, but there are implications I have to consider." Finnian rubbed his eyes, and for the first time he looked old. "I'll have my decision in one hour."

"But—" I stammered.

"One hour. Dismissed."

As soon as we stepped in to the Courtyard, Ash pulled me to one side. "Really, Shae? You think that was the most appropriate thing to say?"

"Don't tell me you weren't thinking the exact same thing," I replied. "Besides, I'm the only one who can get away with saying it."

"You know she's right," said Francis wading in on my side. I gave him a grateful smile.

"Maybe," Ash replied. "Freshen up, change, eat, whatever you want, but I want both of you back here in no more than one hour."

I didn't need telling twice. I bolted back through the inner Courtyard, almost taking out a couple of training monks along the way. There were several 'hellos' and 'heys' along the way, but I wasn't sticking around to chat. I burst through the outer doors, swung a sharp left, and followed the rock pathway to the patio overlooking the bay. I leant on the stone ledge overhanging the rocks and breathed in the warm sea air.

The wind had dropped and the shallow bay was almost still, except for the gentle waves that lapped the shore. I saw a group of monks swimming out by the Diamond Reef, careful not to go beyond into the drop-off where dangerous predators, like the Mantra sharks, hunted for easy prey. The water over the reef glinted hypnotically, but it was nothing compared to late afternoon. When the water level was just right, the coral would catch the sun, sparkling like a million dazzling gems.

I took the winding stone stairway to the beach below two steps at a time. By the water's edge, the wind took on a slightly salty taste, but it was still sweet and fragrant. I sat down to take off my boots, digging my toes into the warm, creamy sand.

In front of me, right in the middle of the bay, sat a small island – just a few tree's and some shrubs, but it was a good place to go when I needed to be alone. When I was a kid, I used to swim out there and spend hours just thinking and watching the reef-cabbles scuttle backwards and forwards.

Shielding my eyes from the bright light, I looked up at my home. The Marulian Cliffs, a dramatic geological formation of small outcrops and steep drops, dominated the far side of the monastery. Ash and I used to go cliff-jumping there when we were kids, until Finnian put a stop to it for being too dangerous. Behind the monastery was the Gateway, a precipice of rock which monks climbed and abseiled as part of their training. Ash and I were far too young when I used to make him bunk off classes and go there to climb it with me.

The monks realised I could heal myself when I was very young. They didn't know why, or how, just that I could.

The way Finnian tells it, I was about three when I tripped over a wooden staff and smacked my head on the corner of a table. Moments later the blood stemmed and a silver-blue glow formed around the wound. Since then, every time I've got damaged or broken, I've healed. It wasn't until I was much older that we realised my skills went beyond healing myself. It was that horrifying memory that I'd been so close to telling Jared the night before.

A bird flew overhead and squawked, bringing me back to the beach. I looked at my com-pad and noticed that half an hour had passed, so I pulled on my boots and made my way back up the beach to the stone steps.

By the time I got to my room, my ready-bag had been deposited on top of the hand-woven throw that was draped over my comfortable but basic bed. My old boots had been cleaned and placed neatly by the small writing table, pushed against the opposite bare stone wall, and no doubt my clothes had been sent to the laundry – one of the lower Degree monks had been busy.

My room was a million miles from my suite on the *Defender*, but I did have one thing that Jared's ship could never have. Almost one entire wall of my room was glass, with a set of double-doors leading out to a small enclosed patio overlooking the bay and Diamond Reef. There was nothing more beautiful than waking up to that.

I had a quick wash and threw on a fresh set of clothes. In hopeful anticipation that Finnian would authorise the mission, I packed my uniform, utility belt, Sentinel, hunting knife, Cal'ret, and credentials into my ready-bag.

I met up with Ash and Francis with four minutes to spare.

Finnian came out to get us himself and I couldn't decide whether that was a good or bad thing, or whether it meant anything at all. We sat at the round table again, but just as we got settled, Finnian stood up and started pacing. That was definitely not a good sign.

"This situation is weighing heavily on me," he said. "There are things occurring that I cannot share with you, but that may have great bearing on this investigation. It is with this in mind that I…" he paused and I held my breath. "I will authorise an official Brotherhood investigation."

"Yes!" I said, too enthusiastically.

"However," he continued, "there are two conditions. One I think you will appreciate, the other you most certainly will not." Unease bristled across my skin. "The first is that you have the full and complete backing of the Brotherhood. This means that we appreciate the timeframe involved and we are authorising you to use whatever methods you deem necessary to prevent this atrocity."

"Understood," said Ash. "What's the second condition?"

"The second condition…" Finnian paused again, as if he was preparing himself for our reaction, "is that only Ash and Shae make up the investigation team." He held up his hand to silence our chorus of objections. "I know you're not happy about this, but I have another task for Brother Francis – one which is of equal importance."

"But Finnian—" I began.

"Shae, you can stop there. I'm sorry, this is non-negotiable. I need Brother Francis for something else, and as I've already said, it is for something equally important. I would not have made this condition if it was not so. Ash, I believe the *Nakomo* is departure-ready so I suggest you don't waste valuable time. Francis, I'll give you a few minutes to say your goodbyes and then I need you to report back here to me." We got up to leave, but before we reached the door, Finnian added, "Ash, a minute if you please."

"I wonder what that's all about," Francis said as we walked to the *Nakomo*.

"No Idea. Perhaps he's telling Ash why you can't come." He winced. "Sorry," I continued, putting my arm around him. "I guess he has his reasons."

When we got to the shuttle, Francis and I stood for a moment in silence, then I held out my arms and he pulled me into a bear-hug. When I was running out of air and couldn't breathe, he let me go and we smiled at each other. He took hold of my hand.

"Be safe," he ordered. "And take care of Ash. You know how he gets himself into trouble."

I laughed, but underneath I was gutted he wasn't coming.

# 7

I sat in the navigation seat with my feet up on the console, something I would never have got away with if Francis had been flying. Ash hadn't said much since we'd left Lilania – if Finnian had shared his reasons for not allowing Francis to come, he was keeping them to himself. In the absence of fact, my thoughts filled with speculation. Occasionally I vocalised one of my more obscure and wilder conjectures, but Ash simply raised an eyebrow, or creased his forehead, and that said enough.

Eventually I got bored of asking and made my way back to the main cabin to rummage through the larder, finding the ice cream that Jared had specially requested be included in the re-stock. Part of me wanted to shove it out the airlock out of principle, but it was the best ice cream of all time, and I didn't really care how it'd got there, it was there. For all I cared, it could've been a peace offering, an apology, or a bribe. I picked up a spoon and decided not to think about Captain Annoying.

"You did the research on Frampton Edge, where do you suggest we start?" Ash asked, appearing in the cabin. He located a second spoon.

"The only definitive lead we have is that Charlie Shaw, an Edge alias, was booked into the Hotel Somnus two weeks ago, and that the owner of the hotel, Jason Cady, is listed on the REF arrest warrant as a known associate. I reckon we start with Cady – put the squeeze on him until he gives up Edge, and hope he's not already in another Sector by now."

"Okay. What Habitat Dome is—"

"Five."

"I hate it—"

"When I do that?"

"Hmm," he grumbled.

I decided to take a nap on one of the hammocks in the small sleeping compartment at the front of the shuttle. It'd been late when I'd left Jared, and healing Harrison had taken quite a bit out of me. Probably more than I'd realised.

The intercom buzzer woke me several hours later. "We arrive in thirty," Ash said through the speaker. "Gear up."

I pulled my uniform from my bag and dressed quickly in dark blue fatigues, smoothing down the left chest pocket where the Brotherhood Sun and Rune logo was embroidered. The utility belt was snug around my hips, and I holstered my Sentinel and Cal'ret before slotting a sheathed hunting knife down the side of my right boot. A mini data-pad, my credentials, and various other items, were zipped into trouser pockets.

I joined Ash in the flight area and peered through the front screen at the colossal metal construction looming out of black space. Ships arrived and departed in orderly fashion, from small shuttles like ours to larger cruise liners full of holiday makers. Each of the six metal habitat-domes was a sprawling metropolis simulating a different world's culture, so there was something to suit pretty much everyone.

I shivered and looked away – GalaxyBases always made me uneasy. I had an irrational fear that one of the domes would fail and everyone would be sucked into space, instantly freezing into human popsicles. Of course, that's never actually happened.

Ash contacted the Base, requesting a docking port in Dome Five, and was given priority clearance. As per protocol, he also requested to speak to the Senior Security Officer to inform them we were there to conduct a formal investigation. After a lengthy debate, the SSO finally accepted it was a classified operation and assured us her people wouldn't interfere.

We landed in Docking Bay C as ordered, the area closest to the Hotel Somnus, and I walked down the ramp breathing in the usual mix of exhaust fumes and oil. The *Nakomo* was dwarfed by the sheer size of the structure, and I began to get that uneasy Human Popsicle feeling again.

Like the outside of the structure, Bay C was mostly dull, grey metal; they saved the nice, fancy entrances for the cruise liners and wealthy holiday makers.

As the ramp creaked back up, securing the inside of the *Nakomo*, a girl and boy in dirty clothes, and equally dirty faces, rushed up with looks of expectant enthusiasm. The girl must've been in her mid-teens, if that, and the boy was no more than ten. Neither of them looked like they'd had a decent meal in days.

"Need your shuttle washed?" the girl asked.

"Cleaned inside?" added the boy. "Screens polished?"

"Best in Dome 5," said the girl quickly as she spotted a couple of older boys approaching. "Anything you want, we can do it." Her smile couldn't hide the desperation in her voice.

"That's kind," I said, thinking about the overhaul the *Nakomo* had just been given. "I'll tell you what, why don't you give the front screens and windows a good clean and polish. They haven't been done for ages." Both kids smiled widely. "I'm not sure when we'll be getting back though, so here..." I pulled out some credits and handed them to the girl. She looked stunned.

"Miss, this is too much for what you want done," she said in such an honest voice it almost broke my heart. She tried to give some of it back.

"All right," I said, thinking. "This ship is very special to me, and I would hate anything to happen to her, so here's the deal… you keep the money, all of it, and you do the best cleaning job you can. Then, when you're done, you pop back every so often to make sure everything's okay with her. How's that?"

"Deal," said the young boy, and the girl nodded enthusiastically.

"Just promise us one thing," added Ash.

"Anything," they chorused.

"Use some of those credits to get yourselves a hot meal."

"Can do," replied the boy as he dashed off.

"Thank you," said the girl, taking off after him.

The docking bays were in the rectangular base of the structure, so we had to get a lift up to what was essentially the ground level of the dome. Like everything else we'd encountered that far, the lift was vast, but it showed the first signs of the environment we were about to encounter. Grey metal had disappeared, and in its place muted colours with fixtures and fittings that sparkled in the warm glow of the chem-lights.

When I stepped out of the lift, I automatically put my hands up to shield my eyes. A simulated sun shone bright in a cloudless, blue, artificial sky, and a soft, warm breeze blew over the skin on my arms. In front of us snaked pathways and tram tracks. Luxurious, real-grass parks with lakes and play areas weaved between the wide bases of enormously tall, skyscraper buildings, some well over two hundred stories high. Criss-crossing between them at various levels were walkways and monorails. If you didn't know you were floating in a metal box somewhere in space, you could definitely be mistaken for thinking you were on Earth.

The buildings, made of stone, metal and glass, were diverse and magnificent, each one mirroring itself in the windows of the next so it looked like they went on and on into infinity. My neck ached as I craned my head skywards.

"The Hotel Somnus takes up floors twenty-nine to sixty-five in the Halcyon Building," I said, studying the mini data-pad I'd pulled from a trouser pocket. "Which is... two blocks down on the left. Reception is on the twenty-ninth, administration offices are on the thirtieth."

I didn't know what I was expecting of the Hotel Somnus, but given the owner's affiliation with wanted criminals, I was surprised when I got to reception. The décor was light, clean, and modern, and the furniture was obviously expensive. When I approached reception, the Other behind the desk stopped what he was doing and gave me that eerily false customer-service-smile they all seemed to perfect.

"Are you booking in?" he asked breezily.

"Not today." I showed him my credentials. "I'd like to speak to Jason Cady."

"I'm not sure if he's in," he replied, studying my details closely.

"Perhaps you could check?"

"Of course. I'll call his assistant immediately." The receptionist dialled a number, turning away slightly. "This is Rolt on reception. I have..." he paused, looking back at me.

"Shae."

"Right, yes. This is Rolt on reception and I have Miss Shae from the Brotherhood of the Virtuous Sun with me. She would like to speak to Mr Cady. Is he available?" It was obvious Rolt was buying time. "They're just going to check," he said amiably, but through my earpiece Ash informed me he'd apprehended Jason Cady trying to flee from his office on the thirtieth floor.

By the time I got to the thirtieth floor there was quite a

commotion. Ash's arrival had obviously caused intrigue, and groups of people held whispered conversations in corners and around desks. I stopped a young woman as she scuttled past and got directions to Cady's office. When I arrived, the door was locked until I informed Ash it was me and he let me in.

The room was old-school grandeur, and so over the top it was laughable: real-wood panelling, ornately carved desks, leather reproduction chairs, ancient paintings and – yuck – stuffed animal heads.

Ash had sat Cady in one of the less ornate chairs, using tiebacks from one of the heavy drapes to bind his arms and legs.

He wasn't what I'd expected either. He wore a stylish and expensive suit, his hair was neatly cut, his nails were manicured, and his shoes were polished. It was clear he wasn't the type to get his hands dirty and we would use that to our advantage. He stared at me in obstinate silence.

Ash pulled a chair forward and sat in front of him. "Mr Cady," he said. "We don't have time mess around, so I'll come straight to the point: we want Frampton Edge."

"Never heard of him," Cady said a fraction too quickly.

"Mr Cady," Ash leant forward, "we know you're acquainted with Frampton Edge, so there's really no point lying to us. All we need from you is where he is right now."

"Seriously, I've never heard of him. You've made a mistake." Cady kept his cool, but his cheeks pinked slightly.

Ash sighed dramatically. "We know that Charlie Shaw, one of Edge's aliases, was booked in to your hotel two weeks ago, and—"

"Hey," Cady cut in, feigning anger and offence. "This is a big hotel. How am I supposed to know everyone who stays here? You can't tie me up – I'll report you to your superiors. There are rules… you're finished." He played the wounded victim well. Under normal circumstances, he would've been right, but the authority the Primus had given us allowed for 'any means necessary'. Tying him to a chair was well within those boundaries.

Ash asked me for my mini data-pad and accessed our investigation authority before holding it up. Cady read the document, his wide eyes and dropped chin betraying the dent in his confidence. His face blanched.

"Tell us where Frampton Edge is. This is the easy way – I suggest you take it. No? Okay, so it's the hard way then." He got up and moved his chair out of the way.

"What?" Beads of sweat sprung up on his forehead and he pulled at his restraints. "What are you going to do?"

"Look, Cady," I said, stepping forward. "You can protest all you like, but we know you know Frampton Edge because you're listed as a known associate on his REF arrest warrant." Cady sucked in a surprised breath. "All we want is his location. It's not difficult."

"I can't help you."

"Think about it, Cady," I continued, ignoring him. "Brother Asher and I are Warrior Caste. That means we're trained in advanced interrogation skills. You may hold out for a while, maybe even a few hours, but trust me when I say you will crack eventually." I paced in front of him, his eyes following my every step. "But the thing is… we don't have time. So to speed things up, I'm going to give you two options. Option One…" I pulled my Sentinel out of its holster and showed it to him before placing it on the small drum table Ash had put in front of him.

"Wait. Whoa," Cady objected, his eyes wild.

"Hold on," I interrupted. "You haven't heard Option Two yet." I took a small rectangular box from my utility belt and placed it on the table next to the Sentinel.

"What's that?"

"Cruillian Truth Serum," I lied. In truth, it held a shot of painkiller for medical emergencies, but I wasn't going to tell him that. Cady went berserk, spluttering and choking on his own words. His face turned puce, and he pulled so hard on his restraints that welts formed around his wrists.

Between gasps he managed to get out various words. "You can't… it's illegal… need medical supervision… people die… side effects…"

"Calm down, Cady," I soothed. After a while he got himself in some order of control. "I'm guessing from that reaction you don't want the serum." I picked up the small box and fitted it back into my utility belt. "So we'll go with Option One." I picked up the gun. "Leg or arm?" I asked Ash.

"Leg I reckon… no arm… no, go with the leg. The leg's better."

"Stop! You can't do this. You're monks for God's sake."

"Do I look like a monk?" I yelled, trying to build the tension. "Last chance, Cady: where's Edge?" I raised the Sentinel to fire, aiming at Cady's kneecap. For one second I thought he was going to hold out… then he broke.

"Don't shoot. Don't shoot! Okay, okay," Cady blubbered, snot stringing from his nose. "I'll tell you where he is, just don't hurt me."

I put the Sentinel back in its holster, took the knife from my right boot, and cut through his binds. "Where is he?"

"Trinity Strip Club. Said he had a meeting there or something."

"Where's that?"

"Neva Building. Floor one-o-five."

"There you go," I said slapping him on the shoulder. He winced. "Isn't it just easier when you're helpful from the beginning?"

Before he had a chance to reply, Ash jabbed him in the arm with a sedative. Nothing dangerous, just enough to knock him out for a fair few hours so he couldn't warn Edge we were coming. We left him slumped in the chair.

The administration staff were still flapping around when we walked out. "You should all know that Mr Cady has confessed to all his illegal activities," said Ash, both loudly and convincingly. "The Authorities will be here any moment to take him into custody, so I suggest you leave now if you don't want to be involved."

As people dashed for the exits, I accessed the plexi-screen on the nearest desk. "If we take the lift to the hundredth floor, we can get the monorail to the Neva Building, then their lift to floor one-o-five. This place is like a bloody maze."

When the lift doors opened, it was full, so Ash held up his ID. "Official Brotherhood business, please exit the lift. Thank you," he added politely as people huffed and moaned in protest while they shuffled out. The lift doors shut and silence descended, except for the hideous, generic lift music you seemed to get regardless of what world you were on.

"Holy crap," I said. "At one point I didn't think he was going to give us the information."

"You were very convincing."

"Thank you."

"You're welcome."

I smiled.

The electronic voice of the lift informed us that we were on the hundredth floor and to mind the doors. There were clear signs to the monorail.

"Ash? How—"

"Haven't decided yet."

"Huh?"

"You were going to ask how we're going to get Edge back to the *Nakomo* if he's an unwilling captive."

"Yes, but—"

"It's irritating when someone finishes your sentences, isn't it?" He grinned. The monorail wasn't crowded and we found two seats away from everyone else. "If we can grab him easily, and he doesn't cause too much fuss, we'll cuff him and escort him back to the *Nakomo.* If he creates hell, we'll sedate him and get local security to help us. Agreed?"

"Agreed."

There were a few people milling around outside the Trinity Strip Club, and I got some leering glances from men who probably thought my uniform was a costume, or part of an act. I couldn't really blame them when I'm the only female to wear one legitimately.

As expected, we were stopped at the door, but we had our credentials ready and the bouncer waved us through with only the smallest amount of interest. The club was quite nice, for a strip joint – a central hexagonal platform surrounded by smaller stages against five of the outside walls, and a bar on the sixth.

"You go left, I'll go right," said Ash. "If you see Edge, contact me on coms and we'll go in together. Co-ordinated."

The house lights were down, but with the stage lights and strobes it was easy to make people out. A waitress asked me if I wanted anything to drink, which I did, but I declined. On the stage nearest me, a beautiful Other bent her body in ways that were physically impossible for Humans. Not surprisingly, she drew quite the crowd. Even I was impressed.

The smell of stale alcohol blended with the heady aroma of perfumes and lotions and it caught in my throat, reminding me of the tunnels at Angel Ridge.

I moved towards the next stage, the music changing instantly – I guess I'd crossed a sound-shield. Different cheering accompanied the new act and I scanned the crowd for Edge. I didn't see him, but there was someone else who caught my attention.

A thick-set Human male sat at one of the stages, his hair practically the same colour as his faded, black leather jacket. He was just different enough from the people around him to stand out – and even though the act in front of him was down to her skin, he hadn't looked at her once, his attention elsewhere. I noticed the bump in the back of his jacket from a weapon, but a group of leering customers prevented me from seeing what was drawing his focus.

I continued my sweep to the left, the new angle giving me a clear view of what the man was really interested in. Two men huddled together in a booth by the wall – one of them was Frampton Edge, the other was probably some scumbag villain he was doing business with. Occasional strobe lights fractured off a silver metal briefcase on the table between them.

The other guy tapped the case before glancing towards the bar. He was kind of sexy in a bad boy, hadn't-slept-in-a-week kind of way, and I wondered why it was that all hot men turned out to be arses… or criminals.

I pressed my earpiece to open a com-link and told Ash where Edge was, but before Ash had time to move, Edge looked up, startled. I followed his eye-line, unable to see what'd spooked him, but before I knew what was happening, he'd picked up the silver case and hammered the other man over the head with it.

Edge bolted towards an emergency exit and I followed, pushing people out of the way as I went. I probably would've got the first, too, if a group of drunks hadn't got in my way. I had to pull my Sentinel before they realised I wasn't an act and reluctantly let me through. The exit was closing shut when I got there.

I threw open the door before glancing over my shoulder to find out if Ash was behind me. I couldn't see him, but I did notice Leather Jacket heading my way, his gun pulled, and I decided not to hang around to find out what he wanted. I took off along the passage, which opened out onto a main thoroughfare before leading to the central column of the building. The open shaft, with roof to floor lifts, was surrounded by bistros and bars, their patrons milling around chatting and laughing.

I ignored the disapproving glances as I leapt on to one of the tables to see over the crowds. Just ahead and to the right, Edge picked his way through the mass of people, heading towards the lifts. I jumped down and tried to force my way to him, but it was like swimming against the tide.

"Brotherhood business… out of the way… move now… clear the way… make a hole," I yelled as loudly as I could, but it didn't seem to make any difference. I couldn't believe it when Edge made it to the doors just as a lift was arriving, and I skidded to a halt as they closed behind him. Even though I pressed the call-button repeatedly, they didn't budge, and Edge and I glared at each other through the glass. He smiled and waved as the lift descended. Smug bastard.

I was so furious I almost missed the ping of the lift doors opening in the next shaft, only just managing to get on board in time. A mother pulled her two children away from me and I did my best to calm them before pressing my forehead against the window to watch the lift below. It was only seconds until it came to a standstill.

There was no way to tell which floor it had stopped at, but I knew there was a monorail link on the seventieth, so I slammed my hand hard onto the button and prayed. Our lift came to a stop adjacent to the other one.

Edge had a head start and was nowhere to be seen – again – but I assumed he would do everything he could to leave the building as quickly as possible.

The monorail station was busy but I caught a break – Edge sat in the window seat of a carriage two platforms down. The flashing light above cabin told me it was due to leave imminently and I started towards him, but shouting made me turn around. Leather Jacket, now joined by a slim, blond man, raced through the crowds. For a second I wondered who the hell were they, but then I heard a train coming down the track between me and Edge and it didn't matter anymore.

I was out of time.

Without thinking, I jumped over the edge of the

platform, dived across the tracks, and hauled myself up the other side. It was so close that I felt the wake of the incoming train pulling me backwards, but somehow I managed to keep my feet.

The doors on Edge's train were shutting when I slid up to them. I shoved my hand between a set of double doors in one of the rear cars and prayed that the sensor would open them again. I stepped on, getting disgruntled glares from passengers who were seated and ready to depart. As the train left the station, I moved through the central isle, opening and closing the doors between the carriages until I could see Edge ahead. I decided to wait until we were at the next station before grabbing him, but it seemed he had other ideas. He must've seen me enter the car because he grabbed the young girl sitting near to him, her high-pitched scream startling the other passengers.

Edge pulled the Emergency cord and the train shuddered to a standstill, seventy floors up, halfway between two buildings. Great – just what I needed. The electronic voice told us to remain calm, help was on its way and in severe emergencies anti-grav chutes were available under each chair.

I held the Sentinel above my head, advising passengers to walk slowly past me to the next carriage, until only the three of us were left. I pressed my earpiece, opening a com-link to Ash, so that whatever happened from that point on, he would be able to hear it.

"My name's Shae, and I'm a representative of the Brotherhood of the Virtuous Sun," I said calmly.

"Sure you are," he replied.

"It's true." With my spare hand, I slowly reached for my credentials, holding them up for him to see. "I just want to talk to you."

"No, you don't. You're lying. The meeting at the club? It was a set-up, right?"

"I don't know anything about your meeting."

"Right," he said slowly.

"I'm telling the truth."

"Then why are you chasing me?" It was a fair question.

"Because you ran." It was a fair answer. "Let the girl go, you don't need her. All I want to do is talk." As a show of goodwill, I holstered the Sentinel and showed him empty hands, but Edge pushed the girl hard at me, catching me off guard.

We both toppled over and she fell on me. I'm not sure whether it was terror, or delight at being released, but she wrapped her arms around me and wouldn't let go. Behind her, Edge grabbed an anti-grav chute from under one of the chairs and fixed it around his chest. By the time I managed to untangle myself from the girl, he'd opened one of the doors using the emergency release. The wind beat through the carriage taking my breath away.

Edge stuck his middle finger up at me then jumped. Crap! That would mean I would have to as well. Not that I was frightened – I just subscribed to the view that jumping out of a perfectly good train was generally something to be avoided. I grabbed a chute, strapped it on, and held my breath. As soon as the harness detected I was far enough away from the rail, it automatically activated the anti-gravity system.

The wind buffeted my body and was actually quite invigorating, but that didn't mean I wanted to do it again in a hurry. I landed no more than thirty seconds behind Edge, but he was a small, wiry guy, and Gods-damn-it he was fast. He'd already put distance between us, but there was no way I was going to let him get away, and besides, I was pretty quick myself when properly motivated.

He'd set off across one of the parks, and I'd already caught up some of the distance between us as he cornered a building. When I skidded around the same corner, people were getting up off the floor and wiping themselves down, and the gap between us had halved.

We sprinted through a shopping district towards a crossway of paths between four of the shorter buildings. Edge had to take the corner wide because of an old-style horse and cart coming towards him, but I was able to take the inside line and went in for the tackle. I lunged forward, wrapping him up in my arms.

My momentum spun us around and we crashed through the front window of a restaurant, where, sandwiched between the glass and Edge, I took the brunt of the damage. Weirdly, the first thing I registered was the delicious smell of the food, but then a sharp, agonising pain reverberated through my chest as we landed on a wooden table, smashing it with our combined weight. I rolled onto my back, trying to ignore the sharp stings from where broken glass had ripped through my shirt and sliced into skin.

I felt someone shaking me, asking me if I was okay, but I ignored them, too busy looking around for Edge. "Where'd he go?" I asked, and several shocked customers pointed towards the back. I managed to get to my feet with the help of a waiter, and surveyed the damaged window. For a moment I thought I saw Jared in the distance, and wondered if I'd hit my head, but it was about the only part of me that didn't hurt. I pushed the thoughts aside as ridiculous, and took off through the rear.

I found a blood trail leading out the back and down a dark service ally, shadowed from the artificial light by the building. At the end, a high wall loomed, and I had to work hard to haul myself over it. On the other side, I shielded my eyes from the low sun simulating the first blushes of a sunset. Silhouetted against the orangey-red glow, Edge hobbled slowly towards a grass verge not too far ahead.

As I jogged over the verge towards Edge, he pulled a gun and started shooting. I wasn't really surprised, after all, he'd done everything possible to get away from me, but I was glad he didn't have the best aim. I un-holstered my

Sentinel, but didn't pull the trigger – he could barely even hold his weapon up anymore.

"Shoot him," Jared yelled, pulling one of his own Sentinels, but I was so surprised to see him running towards Edge I stopped dead. In any other situation, I'd have been glad Captain Courageous was there to take down someone who was trying to kill me, but I needed Edge alive. I hadn't gone through all that crap to end up with a corpse, besides, Edge wasn't a threat anymore. Jared was.

I ran full pelt at the Captain, who managed to get off a couple of shots at Edge before my body slammed into his and I bowled him over. We rolled down the verge a couple of times before coming to a stop.

I should've been worried about Edge getting away, but I wasn't. All I could think about was what in the name of hell was Jared doing there?

# 8

Once again, I was captivated by Jared's astonishingly blue eyes, so I noticed immediately when the shock cleared in them to be replaced with confusion – or was it annoyance? I, on the other hand, was furious.

I put my hands on his chest and pushed myself up so I was sat on his stomach. "What the hell do you think you were doing?" I asked.

He propped himself up on his elbows, a confused crease lingering between his eyebrows. "I thought I was saving your life," he replied.

"Well don't." I was petulant. "I need the guy alive. Don't you think I would've shot him myself otherwise?"

Jared looked unconcerned. "I just winged him." Edge groaned loudly. "See? Not dead."

"No thanks to you," I huffed, then realising I was still sat on him, and way too close for comfort, I got up, kneeing him intentionally in the ribs as I did. "Sorry," I added with little compunction. He stifled a grunt and got up after me, rubbing himself.

When I got to Edge, I was relieved to see that all wounds were superficial. As Jared had said, he would live, but his groaning made my head hurt, so I took the shot of painkiller from the small box on my belt and jabbed it in his arm. The moaning turned into a low whimper, but then another noise caught my attention and I spun around, pulling out my Sentinel.

"Easy. Easy," said Jared, putting a hand on the gun, adding enough weight to lower it. Normally, I wouldn't have allowed another person to do that, but I'd already seen the small group of troopers arriving.

There were six in total, but the only one I recognised was Roberts, who smiled and blushed when I caught his eye. One of them, a medic I presumed, went straight to Edge, but the others congregated around Captain Fantastic.

I was just about to go over and interrogate Jared as to why he was there, when more people arrived, putting me straight back on alert.

Leather Jacket and the slim blond guy had been joined by a dark-skinned man with a shaved head, and all of them had weapons drawn. I pulled my Sentinel out again, and taking their cue from me, Jared and the troopers followed suit.

The three men skidded to a halt, yelling at us to lower our guns, but we stood firm. Moving to shield Edge, I wondered how the hell I'd managed to get caught up in such a volatile situation.

"Ash? Can you hear me?" I said, knowing my com-link was still open. No response. Where was he? A shot of panic flowed like ice from my chest to the ends of my limbs. Had something happened to him? No, I rationalised. He was okay; I would've felt it through the Link otherwise.

The stand-off continued, and it was difficult to make out what anyone was yelling. Jared shouted that he was a Fleet Captain, though I thought that was obvious from his uniform, but I heard Leather Jacket say something back that changed everything.

"Wait, stop. Stop shouting," I yelled. "Everybody shut

up!" I added, positioning myself between the two groups, though in hindsight that probably wasn't one of my better ideas. "You," I said, pointing to Leather Jacket. "What did you say? Who are you?"

"Wolfpack," he replied, his voice deep and gravelly. "Marines. Special Operations."

If the situation wasn't so explosive it would've been laughable. Fleet and Marines – both on the same side, yet still with their weapons primed and aimed. I holstered my Sentinel because someone had to be the first to back down.

"Where's your ID?" Jared's tone was frosty, but he lowered his weapon slightly.

"We're undercover. No ID." The gun rose again. Leather Jacket mumbled something I couldn't hear to the blond, who glanced over at the troopers and laughed. "I got an authentication number," he told Jared. "Get me a data-pad and I'll verify the team."

Jared hesitated then motioned to Roberts to take his pad over, but as he did, the front doors of the nearest building crashed open and a team of local security officers piled out, guns waving haphazardly.

The small amount of faith that had built between Jared and Leather Jacket shattered in that single moment.

"Ash, if you're listening, I hope I'm doing the right thing," I said into my open coms before crouching down next to Edge. "Frampton Edge," my voice turned formal, official, "as I said on the train, my name is Shae and I'm a representative of the Brotherhood. I showed you my ID, do you remember?" Edge's eyes weren't quite focussed so I slapped his cheek. "Mr Edge? Do you understand what I'm saying to you?"

"Go to hell, bitch."

"Mr Edge?" My patience was wearing thin, and I was all too aware that things were not getting any better between the three groups behind me. "I have reason to believe that you may have information about a situation we're investigating, so I'm placing you in the custody of the Brotherhood of the Virtuous Sun. Do you understand?"

"Whatever," he said, repeating the hand sign he'd given me in the train. The medic shot me an interested glance before continuing his treatment.

"I don't care what these men want you for, but I can assure you, if you have been transporting stolen REF weapons, you'd be better off in my custody than theirs right now. Wouldn't you agree?" I asked. Edge thought about it for a while and then grunted. Clearly a man of few, if colourful, words. Eventually he nodded. "I need you to say it out loud. Do you understand why I've placed you in our custody?"

"Yes."

"Good." Where was Ash?

The shouting continued, and I feared things were going to end very badly. Enough was enough – I'd made a decision.

I took the Cal'ret out of the holster on my left thigh and gave it a hard shake, the baton seamlessly extending to a five-foot fighting staff. I stepped right into the centre of the arguing triangle, the volume decreasing slightly, but there was no point stopping once I'd committed. I lifted the staff above my head and spun it quickly before bringing it back down, hammering one end firmly into the ground by my left foot.

The moment the Cal'ret hit the earth, a high-energy pulse burst out in concentric circles. As it hit each person, the force created a sensory overload causing their bodies to simply shut down. In seconds, everyone – Jared and his troopers, Leather Jacket and his Wolfpack, and the local security forces – lay unconscious on the floor.

Admittedly it would only last a few minutes, but it was like pouring cold water over a raging inferno. I gave the Cal'ret another sharp shake, returning it to its resting baton length, before re-holstering it.

While I waited for Edge to come around, I collected weapons, starting with those belonging to the local security officers because they seemed the most volatile. When that was done, I sat listening to the silence, and it was bliss – even if it was only for a short time. I rubbed my eyeballs with the palms of my hands.

"Shae?"

I recognised the voice immediately. My eyes re-focused and I noticed Ash wasn't alone – the man who'd been doing business with Edge back at the strip club was with him. "What happened?"

"I was about to ask the same thing?" Ash cracked a grin because from the evidence he already knew, though he frowned when he saw Jared. The other man seemed more interested in the Marines.

I quickly filled Ash in on everything that'd happened, including the trigger-happy local security, and why I'd used the Cal'ret. As I finished, moans and coughs indicated people were starting to come around.

"Now you. What happened? Why weren't you on coms?" I asked. It wasn't an accusation, just concern.

"I was behind you all the way up to the monorail, but that's where you got away from us."

"Us?"

"Ah, yes," he said, sitting down next to me. "I see you've met the Wolfpack? Well that gentleman over there," he pointed to the man he'd arrived with, "is their Commanding Officer, Colonel Mitchell. We ended up getting into quite the jurisdictional tussle, especially as he didn't have any ID on him. I had to go off-coms, but we sorted it out in the end. I'm sorry it took so long for me to get to you."

"It's okay. I'm glad you're all right," I replied, watching Mitchell help the blond guy to his feet.

The security officers were just waking, but Jared was already on his knees, albeit pale and shaky. Gradually, as each group found their bearings, they started hunting for their weapons and discord flared.

"That's enough," I shouted, getting to my feet. "Captain Marcos, stand down your troopers." Jared mumbled something as he shook his head to clear it. "I said stand down your troopers. Now! Colonel Mitchell, stand down your team. I appreciate you don't know me, but trust me, you don't want to mess with me right now."

"I really wouldn't," Ash said under his breath, but I heard and nailed him with a glare.

"You lot," I pointed in the general direction of the security team. "Which one of you is in charge?" The group shuffled out of the way to leave one man standing out on his own. "What's your name?"

"Officer Winters," he replied, looking around him for the now absent support of his squad.

"Well, Officer Winters, over here we have Fleet, and over here we have Marines. There was a minor misunderstanding, but things are okay now. What do you say, boys?" There was a murmur of unenthusiastic agreement. "You can leave us now, we'll be fine."

Winters objected, but after Ash and Jared showed him their credentials, the squad reluctantly ambled back into the closest building. At least that was one group from three safely out of the equation.

While I checked on Edge, Ash stood between Jared and Mitchell, refereeing some kind of argument. Gradually, each of the two groups went to stand behind their respective leader and I rolled my eyes, wandering over to find out what it was all about. I was a minor distraction from the dispute.

"You can use a Cal'ret?" Mitchell asked. "I thought only Ninth Degree monks got one of those things."

"Ninth Degree monks… and Shae," Ash corrected.

"Well, I gotta say I'm impressed." Mitchell's eyes flicked between my face and the weapon, his expression perplexed.

"You must've got that thing to kick out quite a punch. Not too happy you used it on my men though." He returned his attention back to Jared. "Look, Marcos, Edge belongs to us. We've been working the little scroat for months and have proof he's been transporting stolen Fleet weapons. Your weapons, I might add." His lips twisted into a sneer. "Before you showed up, we were about to find out who else was involved – who the person in charge was – but that's hardly going to happen now, is it?" He squared up to Jared, his stockier frame compensating for a slight disadvantage in height.

"You know, it's interesting," Jared said ambiguously, crossing his arms.

"What is?"

"I was just wondering what a Lieutenant Colonel's doing leading a covert actions team?"

"That's full Colonel now, arsehole. And not that is any of your fucking business, but some of us actually work for a living. Let's just say I did a good job on a couple of highly sensitive missions and as a reward I got to pick my own gig."

"And you picked this?" Jared waved a dismissive arm towards the Wolfpack.

"Yeah, I did. It happens to be what I'm good at. I never did like all that paperwork-and-politics bullshit that seems to suit you so well. And while we're on the subject, I could ask you the same question. I mean, what's a Full-Wing Captain doing heading up a mission? Shouldn't you be drinking afternoon tea in your slippers or some shit? Isn't that what Fleet Captains do nowadays?"

"Don't push me Mitchell. I do what needs doing, and if that means getting hands-on, then so be it. Which reminds me: Edge is ours." Jared's tone was equally vicious. "We brought him down, so we get him. Simple as that. You can't have him."

"I wasn't asking for your permission."

"And I wasn't giving it."

"Like I give a fuck. Edge is coming with us, and if you try to stop us…" Mitchell looked ready to fight, and his men were poised, waiting for the word. I glanced at the troopers and idly wondered who'd win. I matched Mitchell and Jared as fairly equal, but I reckoned the Wolfpack would take the troopers, even though there were less of them.

But enough of the bullshit antagonism.

"When you're quite finished…" I said loudly. "In case you've both forgotten, I was the one who got Edge. He's mine. You can argue until the sun comes up – it's a done deal."

"I think you'll find it was my shot that actually brought him down," said Jared matter-of-factly, but the anger he'd displayed towards Mitchell had left his voice.

"You need to think very carefully about what you say next, Captain Marcos." I was furious. "So, tell me Jared." I knew using his first name in front of his troopers would annoy him. "What exactly do you want Edge for?"

"That's Fleet business," he replied without a moment's hesitation, but I saw a flicker in his eye.

"It's just that Colonel Mitchell here…" I turned to look at him, momentarily distracted by the incredible smile he returned. Where Jared was handsome in a clean cut, clean shaven, clean everything way, Mitchell was ruggedly gorgeous in a dishevelled, bad boy, twinkle in his eye, kind of way. I had to focus to remember what I was saying. "Umm… well… Colonel Mitchell's been quite clear about why he should stake a claim on Edge, but why you, Jared? What do you want with him? And don't give me that Fleet business crap."

"Feisty, isn't she?" Mitchell said to Ash. I turned to face him full on, giving him a 'don't mess with me' frown. His smile held. "My apologies, Babe. Carry on."

"Well?" I said, looking back to Jared.

"It's classified," he replied. He was so damn infuriating.

"I believe it was chance we crossed paths on Angel Ridge yesterday… but the same thing happening less that twenty-four hours later? I don't buy it. Why were you so insistent we stay onboard the *Defender* last night, Jared? Because I've got to say, I'm beginning to question your motives. And don't even get me started on the whole getting me drunk to take advantage—"

"What the…?" Mitchell roared, starting forward, fists clenched. "You need to get a girl drunk to get her into bed? That's fucking low, even for you, Marcos."

"No, wait, that's not what I meant," I said quickly, putting my hand on his chest to stop his advance. I was horrified I'd given the wrong impression, especially as Jared looked so wounded by the accusation, but I also quite liked that Mitchell had got angry. It meant he was a gentleman under that bad boy image – that he had honour.

"He got me drunk to get me to give up classified information about an investigation we're working," I clarified to Mitchell, but as I said it, it didn't really sound much better. Distaste remained on Mitchell's face, but he backed off and I thanked him before turning to Jared. "Anyway, what I'm trying to say is that last night you didn't know anything about our investigation, yet today… here you are, all tied up in it again. I don't believe in coincidences, Jared. Out of all the people in the entire Sector, why Edge?"

"Come here," he said, taking my elbow, leading me away from the rest of the group. "Why do I want Edge? Well, that depends on why you want him."

"That doesn't even make sense."

"Come on, Shae, think about it. I'm here because you're here. Well, not you personally, but your team. Where is Brother Francis by the way? Never mind, tell me later."

"I don't understand."

"Shae, we only met yesterday so you don't know me, but

I'm not the kind of person who would normally take advantage of someone the way I did with you last night. I'm not proud of what I did, I hope you believe that?" I thought for a moment then nodded. "I filed my After-Action report on Angel Ridge as per protocol, which included everything that happened: the Brotherhood, Nyan, and…" he flicked a glance towards the others, "the Agent of Death. I thought that would be the end of it, but then I got new orders. Command wanted to know why you were there, what you were up to, and I was ordered to find out. I knew I wouldn't get any information from Brother Asher… I assumed you would be the softer target."

"You were wrong."

"I know. I'm sorry." He studied his feet for a moment. "I reported back that I didn't get anything from you, but they were adamant I find out. So adamant they were willing to risk breaking the Constantine Agreement. I don't know," he shrugged, "it seemed like there was more to it, something they weren't telling me, but orders are orders. I had to take further action."

"What action?" As soon as the words were out, I knew I wasn't going to like the answer.

"When you didn't tell me what I needed to know… which I respect, by the way… you forced me to find another way. The computer upgrade—"

"The *Nakomo*!" I gasped, realisation dawning. "You gave us access to Grace so you could spy on us!" I was furious, biting the inside of my lip to stop myself from saying something I would regret. "How dare you?" I spat out each word, my voice ice-cold. It felt like the *Nakomo* had been violated, but worse, I felt naïve and stupid because I hadn't been more suspicious of the upgrade.

"I was acting on orders," he tried to justify. I didn't care.

My fingernails dug into the palms of my hands and I had to turn away because I couldn't look at him anymore. I was disappointed Jared had let me down again, and angry at myself. I'd only known him two days. What right did I have to expect anything from him?

"Shae?" he said, but I couldn't listen to any more. I wheeled around and punched him full on the side of the face, catching him off guard. He staggered backwards. The Marines cheered, but Jared wasn't so appreciative, and when he righted himself, I noticed I'd split his lip open. I shouldn't have done it, but I couldn't exactly take it back.

Jared was furious. "You've gone too far, Shae. You're under arrest," he said as he spun me around by the elbow so my back was to him. That's when Ash and Mitchell stepped in. They'd obviously heard the conversation because Mitchell told him he deserved it, though much less politely than that, and Ash reminded him he had no jurisdiction over the Brotherhood. Jared didn't seem to care – he cuffed me anyway. "Roberts," he said over the objections, "place Mr Edge in custody then find us a route back to the Warrior."

A moment later the trooper returned. "Captain?" he said cautiously. "There seems to be a problem."

"Just tell me Edge is in custody, Roberts," Jared grunted, holding me by the elbow, still fending off various verbal challenges from Ash.

"Yes, sir."

"Then what's the problem, Trooper?"

"That's the problem, sir." Jared nailed him with a deadly glare and Roberts physically recoiled. "Edge is in custody… just not ours."

"Then whose?"

"Hers, sir." Roberts pointed at me.

"I told you it was a done deal," I said smugly. "You should've listened to me. Edge has been in my custody all along – all sweet and above board."

"I don't believe it," said Mitchell, rubbing the stubble on his chin.

"Well, you better. I hate to say it, but it's true,"

confirmed the medic as he packed away his equipment. "It was just before we all got knocked unconscious. What happened by the way?"

I ignored his question. "Colonel Mitchell, please accept the Brotherhood's sincerest apologies for butting in on your op, but I can assure you it's totally necessary." I'm positive Jared knew I was purposely trying to wind him up. "Our investigation is time sensitive, so, Captain, if you could just get over your bruised ego for one second and take these cuffs off me, we'll get on with our work. If it helps any, I really am sorry for hitting you." Ash looked pleased I'd apologised. "But you know you deserved it, right?" His smile dropped, he sighed deeply, and he gave me his 'you just had to push it' frown.

"Forget it. You hit a Fleet Captain and you're under arrest. I'm taking you to the *Defender*, and... and," he said loudly as the protests started again, "as Edge is in your custody, he'll come too. Brother Asher, you're welcome aboard the *Defender* as my guest."

"Captain, may I have a moment with Shae?" asked Ash.

"I'm not—"

"It's not like I'm going to run off," I interrupted, turning my back on him to remind him I was still cuffed.

"Fine," he agreed. "But no more than a minute. Then we move out."

Ash and I walked a short distance away from the group. "I know, I know, I shouldn't have hit him, but you heard what he did to the *Nakomo*? Surely that breaches about a gazillion Constantine Agreement clauses? Don't look at me like that, Ash. Don't be cross with me. Please."

"I'm not cross with you," Ash assured. "But you do have a habit of making things more difficult for us than they need be. Good call on putting Edge into our custody though." A lopsided grin emerged from behind the frown.

"So what now?"

"Captain Marcos isn't going to let you go until he thinks

you've suffered enough, which means it looks like we're going back to the *Defender.* We can't fight everyone over this, we don't have time, but we can demand a closed interrogation of Edge – get the information we need then let Marcos and Mitchell scrap it out over who gets him when we're finished. Agreed?"

"Agreed. And Ash?"

"What?"

"I am sorry."

"Don't worry about it. It's not like you're going to change now, after thirty-odd years."

"Well?" Jared was still irritable, but he'd calmed slightly.

"We agree to your terms, however the cuffs aren't necessary. Shae will give you her word that she won't cause you any more trouble."

"Really?" There was a discouraging amount of cynicism in his voice.

"Captain Marcos," I said formally. "I give you my word, as a representative of the Brotherhood, that I will give you no further trouble regarding this incident."

"Okay then." He removed the cuffs and I stretched my arms out, feeling the blood pumping properly through them again.

"Shae and I will get the *Nakomo* and report to the *Defender* with Mr Edge forthwith." Ash was pushing it, and he knew it.

"Oh no," Jared said with a half laugh. "Shae and Edge are coming with me – there's no way I'm letting either of them out of my sight. If you want to pick up the *Nakomo*, be my guest. I give you my word you'll be allowed to dock on board the *Defender.*"

"As you wish," replied Ash.

"Captain," said Roberts, arriving at my shoulder. "The patient's stretchered and ready to go, and I've got us the fastest route back to the Warrior."

"Good, then let's move."

"Whoa, cool your jets a second." It was Mitchell with his team at his shoulder. "You're not going anywhere without us."

Jared squeezed the bridge of his nose. "I get one thing sorted, then more crap lands in my lap."

"Welcome to my world," I mumbled, rubbing my wrists where the cuffs had left indentations.

"Look, Captain," continued Mitchell. "Edge is part of our investigation, but if you insist on taking him under some bullshit pretext of arresting the person who actually put him in custody…" He turned and winked at me. "That was an awesome right hook though, Babe... anyway, what I'm saying is if Edge goes with you, so do we."

"You know what, Mitchell? Because I want to get us moving: fine. Skulk back to whichever ship you arrived in and I give you my word that you'll also be allowed access to the *Defender*."

"Oh no." Mitchell mimicked Jared so well I couldn't help laughing. "I'm not letting Edge out of my sight. I'll come with you. My team will get our ship. Besides, the view in yours will be so much better." I wondered what he meant until I realised he was looking at me. He smiled and I blushed. My stomach fluttered nervously and I looked down at my feet.

Mitchell gave his team their orders and they sprinted off. Ash said goodbye and promised me he wouldn't be gone long. "Don't worry, Brother Asher," Mitchell said with a wide grin. "I'll take great care of her for you. Won't I, Babe?" He put his arm around me and I felt how solid he was.

"That's what I'm afraid of," Ash replied before he left. I couldn't tell if he was being serious or not.

I felt uncomfortable being so close to someone I'd only just met, so I shrugged out from under Mitchell's arm and followed Roberts. Although there were more people on the streets, the sight of armed troopers moving with purpose was enough for them to shift out of the way.

It wasn't long before the Colonel fell into step beside me. "So?" he said, cryptically.

"So…? What?"

"Can I see it?" He pointed to my Cal'ret. "Only ever seen one from a distance before." I thought for a moment then handed it over. He studied the small runic carvings along the baton.

"From the ancient texts," I explained. "The monks believe they focus power and control."

"It's really light." He weighed it in his hand. "What's it made of? I always assumed it was allim, or something like that, but it's not nearly heavy enough."

"Stidium."

"No shit." He gave the baton a shake but nothing happened. "How does it work?"

"Well, for starters, that won't do anything," I said, watching him shake it again, an unexpected child-like awe sparkling in his eyes. "In fact, the only thing you can use it for is a truncheon." He raised an eyebrow. "There are two things that make it work – the first being the metal itself. They have to be made of Stidium because the alloy is fused on a molecular level with a bio-fission organism – that's what makes them so rare."

"And the second thing?"

"The person. When a Warrior Caste monk achieves ascension to Ninth Degree they're presented with a newly forged Cal'ret, previously untouched by anybody. From first contact, the Stidium becomes bonded to that particular monk at a cellular level, allowing only them to handle it – which is why it won't react to you." I held my hand out and he passed the baton back. As my fingers closed around it, the carvings glowed briefly. "The union also forms a higher-level connection between the baton and its wielder. A monk has to train both mentally and physically to use it – the stronger the mental connection, the more powerful the weapon."

"But you're not a monk, so how come you have one?" He eyed me suspiciously. "And how come you can use it so well?"

I couldn't tell him the monks attributed my skill with the Cal'ret to the energy I already have inside me – that I could command more power from the weapon than any other monk in history. "Because I'm special," I teased.

"You certainly are," he replied.

We were in the lift, heading to the Docking Bay, when I saw Jared dab his lip and wince. It would've been so easy to heal it for him, and I was annoyed with myself for wanting to.

I rested my back against the cool lift wall as Mitchell appeared next to me again. He stood side on, his right shoulder propped up to the wall, his body only a fraction from mine – even though there was plenty of room in the lift.

I turned my head towards him and suddenly had an urge to run my fingertips along his strong jaw line, prickly with at least two or three days' worth of stubble. His hazel eyes, which had been greener in the brightness of the Dome, were more hazelnut-brown in the muted light of the lift.

When he didn't say anything, I returned my gaze forwards.

I felt weird that he was so close, and I could tell out of my peripheral he was still staring at me. I tried really hard not to glance back so I concentrated on the wall opposite. Finally, I turned to him. "What?" I demanded quietly.

"Nothing." He seemed amused, his wide eyes crinkling at the edges.

"You were staring."

"I was?" A smile curled on his full lips.

"Yes."

"Oh." He raked his fingers through dark hair, and when he took his hand away, short, messy curls stuck out uncontrollably.

He was so close I could practically feel his body heat. The lift juddered and for a second his fingers touched the back of my hand. A shock jolted up my arm and through my body.

It was ridiculous, I felt… What did I feel? Nervous perhaps? But nervous in a good way? I took a deep breath and closed my eyes.

"You all right, Babe?" Mitchell's question surprised me and I opened my eyes to find him standing in front of me. My breath caught, and a shiver ran through me. "Babe?" He rested his hands on my shoulders and a jolt of electricity fired through my body again. Heat rose inside me.

For a moment, he looked directly into my eyes. Through the warm fog clouding my brain I thought about the previous night when I wasn't sure what I would do if Jared kissed me, or even if he was going to kiss me. But it was different with Mitchell. There was no confusion – I wanted him to. It was like my whole body ached for him to kiss me. It didn't even matter that I was in a lift with everyone else. They didn't exist.

It was insane – what the hell was I thinking? I closed my eyes again and rested my head back on the cold lift wall.

"Shae?" It was Jared that time. He sounded anxious, and it snapped me out of whatever spell I was under. He barged Mitchell out of the way with his shoulder and took his place in front of me. "What's the matter? Are you okay?" He seemed genuinely worried and put his hand on my forehead. "You're hot. Are you feeling all right?"

"I'm… I'm fine. I was…" I tried to think of something suitable to say. 'Amorous', 'lustful', 'aroused', didn't seem particularly appropriate. "Light-headed," I concluded. "I haven't eaten in a while. Low blood sugar probably." He studied my face and then turned to look at Mitchell with distaste and suspicion.

"You want to see the medic?" he asked, turning back to

me.

"Thanks, but I'll be fine," I assured him, though I was happy he seemed to care.

But then again, perhaps he just didn't want me keeling over while I was in his custody. How would he explain that to his superiors? 'Brotherhood Representative Dies in Fleet Custody'. It would certainly put a dent in his perfect golden-boy record.

# 9

The Warrior waited on the landing pad, its engines already impatient. Standing roughly five times the size of the *Nakomo*, it was as impressive as the *Defender*, and just as fortified – I counted at least four plasma cannons, and a scaled down Starflower railgun.

Inside was just as pristine – there was a place for everything, and everything was in its place. I felt I made the place look untidy just by being there. Mitchell looked around him with a mixture of amazement and disdain, and I wondered if he was thinking the same thing.

Roberts led us towards the upper lounge and I waited for the Colonel to sit before purposely taking the furthest seat from him. I wasn't expecting Jared to appear next to me.

"That seat's taken," I cautioned. He ignored me and sat anyway.

"Was he hassling you?" he asked, looking over at Mitchell, who stared back stubbornly. I was puzzled by the question. "Back in the lift?" he clarified.

"No. But you are."

He ignored my hostility. "Because if he was, I could

throw him in the brig… or blow him out an airlock."

"What?" I was shocked, but when I turned to face him, he had a twinkle in his eye and that boyish grin plastered across his face. That was the Jared I liked. "Honestly, he wasn't bothering me." I tried to keep my tone emotionless. He was in my bad books, and one mischievous smile wasn't going to wipe out everything he'd done.

"Shame. I could've used an excuse to get rid of him."

The Warrior took off so smoothly I wasn't even sure it had. "What do you want, Jared?" I asked.

"I…" He seemed surprised by my attitude, but what did he expect? I wasn't wearing the cuffs anymore, but I was still in his custody. "I wanted to talk to you about Mitchell." The smile disappeared and his eyes darkened.

"What about him?"

"He's Special Operations. Wolfpack."

"I got that. So?"

"Mitchell is… Mitchell's your typical Mud Monkey." I laughed at the name, but Jared gave me a look that told me he was serious.

"Mud Monkey?"

"It's the name Fleet has for Marines."

"Doesn't sound very friendly."

"You should hear what they call us," he replied with a half-smile.

"Jared, what exactly are you trying to say?"

"Spec Ops don't play by the rules. They think they're above the law and don't let anyone stand in their way – including other sections of the REF They're yahoos, and I don't agree with their methods."

I still wasn't following. So Jared didn't like their tactics? Well, boo-bloody-hoo. I didn't like his tactics much either. "I'm guessing you two have history?"

"Unfortunately. It was a while ago." He was reluctant to say more. "You picked up on that, huh?"

"Couldn't really miss it. You really don't like each other,

do you?"

"Look, do I have to spell it out for you, Shae? Mitchell's bad news. He's the kind of guy who'll use someone up and spit them out, just for his own pleasure – and he won't have any regrets. He takes what he wants, when he wants, and doesn't care about the carnage he leaves in his wake. He's probably got a girl in every spaceport."

"It's obvious you believe what you're saying, Jared. But I'm usually a pretty good judge of character and I'm just not getting that from Mitchell. But then I was wrong about you, so maybe my judgement isn't as good as I think it is."

"You know, Shae," he shook his head, "you're too naïve."

"Really?" I said, anger flaring. "Feel free to correct me, but to my knowledge Colonel Mitchell hasn't betrayed my trust, violated my privacy, or arrested me. Perhaps you're right, though. Perhaps I am naïve, after all, I trusted you. I even liked you. And you treated me like crap. So who should I really be looking out for, Jared?" Some of the troopers had turned to look at us, but Jared gave them a withering stare and they faced front immediately. "I may be naïve, as you say, but you're worse. It's like you have a split personality. One minute you can be pleasant and charming, even likeable, but then you have this other side to you which is arrogant and manipulative."

"I see," was all he said in response.

I sighed again because it all seemed too difficult. "Which is the real you, Jared? Because right now, I just don't know. And you know what? I don't care." He looked at me, stunned. "I don't have time to play games with you, and I can't keep letting you get to me. I'm sorry I hit you, but from what I know of Mitchell, he's an angel besides you." Jared opened his mouth but I held up my hand to cut him off. "I think it would be better if we stay away from each other as much as possible."

"If that's what you want," he said after a moment, but

he didn't sound happy. "Just… please remember what I've said about Mitchell." He got up without looking at me and headed for the flight deck.

Commander Tel'an waited for us in the *Defender's* hangar.

"Captain, Team Two located the *Hawkhurst*, Mr Edge's transport ship. They're towing it back now."

"Towing?"

"All onboard computers are on encrypted lock-down. Team Two couldn't get access to any of them, including the flight-com, so they decided to tow the ship and work on it here."

"Good call," said Jared.

"The *Nakomo* landed on board a few minutes ago." Tel'an continued her brief. "Brother Asher will meet you at Med-bay."

"What about my team?" asked Mitchell.

"The *Veritas* is about to land in one of our other hangars. I have an ensign standing by to take them to Med-bay also."

"Okay," said Jared. "Let's get Mr Edge to medical so Doctor Anderson can clear him for interrogation. The sooner the better."

Ash was already outside Med-bay when we got there, and I was so pleased to see him I gave him a massive hug.

"Everything all right?" he asked, studying my face when I finally let him go.

"It is now," I said, before hugging him again.

With perfect timing, the rest of the Wolfpack arrived, heading straight for their Colonel, and all of us stuffed into Med-bay behind Edge.

"Hold it," said Doc, putting up two hands to the approaching mass. "You four," he indicated to the Wolfpack, "unless any of you are injured… out. You, you and all of you," he motioned to Ash, Jared and the troopers, "the same. Out!" Anderson stood his ground as Jared objected. "Captain, this is a medical facility for people who need medical help. Mr Edge is restrained and going nowhere, and he's unarmed so he's no threat. I'll call you when he's well enough for interrogation."

"How long?"

Doc looked Edge up and down with an expert eye. "About an hour, I would guess." He began rounding up people, ushering them towards the door, so I followed. "Not you, little lady," he said. Several people stopped in their tracks. "You get to stay." I didn't understand why, but I wasn't going to argue. "The rest of you," he looked irritated, "do I need to tell you again?"

Reluctantly everyone else left and the doors closed behind them.

"Hop up." Anderson patted one of the med-beds. "According to Trooper Roberts's In-Field Report, you tackled Mr Edge through a shop window." He waved a data-pad at me as evidence of the fact. "Is that correct?"

"It was a restaurant window, but," I shrugged, "yeah, I guess so."

"I see." Doc's greying eyebrows knitted together. "You went through the window with Edge, you say?"

"Yes, but I'm totally fine, Doc. I really don't need any medical attention."

"I can see that." He studied my face carefully. "And yet while Mr Edge has abrasions, contusions, and an obviously dislocated knee, not to mention the hole Captain Marcos put in him, you have… nothing."

I panicked. "Just lucky I guess."

"Perhaps… Would you mind taking off your shirt?" His request threw me. "Indulge me, if you would?"

What harm could it do? I undid the buttons then pulled it from underneath my utility belt, but as I handed it over, I understood why Doc had made the request. Sometimes I wished everyone knew my secret – it would make my life so much easier. Anderson held my shirt up and light shone through the small cuts where the glass window had sliced through the material into my skin.

"Can you explain this?" he asked. "It's not immediately obvious because of all the dirt, but there's definite blood around the edges of these holes. Yet, you have no wounds."

"It must be Edge's blood." I shrugged, trying to look nonchalant. "Perhaps the glass cut my top, but didn't go deep enough to cut flesh. Either that or I've got the skin of a Rhinorian," I joked. Doc looked sceptical.

"I see," he said finally, having failed to come up with his own alternative explanation. "You're obviously a very lucky young lady. If you're sure you're fine, there's no reason for you to stay." He looked at the shirt again, and then at the holey vest-top I still wore. "There are clean t-shirts in the drawer over there. They're standard Fleet issue, but I don't suppose Captain Marcos will mind."

"Thanks, Doc," I said, removing the vest-top and replacing it with a new t-shirt. "You've been very kind."

"Don't mention it," he replied, still looking mystified. "I haven't done anything… again." He left my shirt on the med-bed and turned his attention to Edge who'd groaned loudly. I picked it up. "And, Shae?" I felt inexplicably guilty. "Please remind the Captain: one hour. I'll let him know when Mr Edge is ready. He really doesn't need to skulk around outside. I'm sure he's got far more important things to do."

As soon as the door opened I was surrounded by three men, all talking at once, all asking similar questions: what was going on? Why had I been allowed to stay? Was I all right? I answered Ash, because he was the only one I cared about.

"It's all right, Ash, I'm fine. Doc just wanted to check me over after my train jump."

Jared looked doubtful. I didn't care.

"You sure you're all right though?" That time it was Mitchell.

"Enough already," I said irritably. "Seriously, I'm fine. Captain, Doc asked me to remind you that he'll let you know when Edge is ready. I don't think he wants us all hanging around outside Med-bay."

I surreptitiously stuffed my ripped shirt and vest into the worn leather bag Ash carried over his shoulder.

"Roberts?" Jared called over his trooper. "Show our guests to the Mess Hall and get them some refreshments while they wait."

"Yes, sir," Roberts replied before Jared took him to one side and added something I couldn't hear.

I was about to trail after Roberts when Jared grabbed my arm to hold me back. "Shae, I—"

"Is this business?" I interrupted.

"Excuse me?"

"Do you want to talk to me about business? About my custody? About Edge?"

"No, but—"

"Then we have nothing to say to each another." I stalked away, and just because I knew it would piss him off, I went to walk beside Mitchell. When we got to the Mess Hall, Roberts ushered everyone inside, but I was still worked up about Jared and needed to let off some steam. "Roberts, are there any training rooms nearby?"

"Yes, except…"

"Except what?"

"The Captain told me to keep an eye on everyone, especially you as you're under arrest." His cheeks darkened.

"All I want to do is burn off some excess frustrations before Edge is ready for interrogation. I suspect Jared," Roberts winced, "sorry, Captain Marcos, told you to keep an eye on Mitchell as well?" The look on his face confirmed my suspicion. "So, stay here and do that. Just point me in the right direction and I promise to be a good girl."

"All right," Roberts conceded, just as Ash ambled up to find out what was going on.

"Do you want me to come with you?" he asked.

"Thanks, but I just want to clear my head."

"Okay, but if you need anything, anything at all, get on the coms and I'll be there."

I found the training room easily. It was typically uninteresting for Fleet – round, uncluttered and boring beige. The simulation control panel sat on a plinth to side of the door and I pressed the start button. Grace told me that as I hadn't used the room before, I needed to set myself up as a user, so I answered a heap of questions about my competency levels before I could begin.

After taking my Cal'ret out of its holster, I removed my belt and placed it on one of the benches pushed around the outside of the room. Standing on the slightly spongy fighting-circle covering the middle of the floor, I shook the Cal'ret, extending it to staff length.

"Grace, start Fighting Staff Simulation, Level Five."

"Fighting Staff Simulation, Level Five, starting on my mark. In three, two, one, mark."

As soon as she'd finished counting, a holographic opponent appeared on the mat in front of me. After circling the floor a few times, my simulated adversary stepped forward and we fought. I moved gracefully – ducking, dodging, and weaving as appropriate – my skill level far greater than that of my opponent. I took him out quickly, but as soon as he went down, another foe appeared.

"Grace, cancel current programme and advance to level seven."

"Fighting Staff Simulation, Level Seven, starting on my mark. In three, two, one, mark."

My new opponent was fitter and stronger, but it still felt like a warm-up. It took a little more skill and effort, but I felled the guy quickly, so I increased the difficulty level again to ten. On Grace's mark, two challengers appeared and I fought them simultaneously. My heart-rate increased, my breath quickened, and I started to sweat lightly. It was finally taking my mind off things… except I kept imagining that every opponent I hit was Jared.

I felled one opponent, then the second shortly after. Once the second was down, another two appeared and we started all over again. I was on my third pair when the programme unexpectedly stopped and they disappeared.

"How long have you been there?" I asked with more than a hint of irritation.

"Long enough to know you fight beautifully," Colonel Mitchell replied.

"What made you think it was okay to cancel my programme? Some would consider that rude, by the way."

"Holograms are all right, but they're no substitute for the real thing."

"Are you offering?"

"Are you asking?"

"Just pick up a damn staff, Colonel."

He grabbed a weapon from one of the racks punctuating the otherwise bare walls and joined me on the mat. We circled each other a couple of times.

"What's the matter, Mitchell? Having second thoughts?" I taunted.

"I was just working out how to kick your arse without hurting you too much." While he was talking, I stepped forward and did a standard manoeuvre, catching him across the thigh with the Cal'ret. "Nice move," he said. "What else you got?"

We fought and we bantered, we hurled friendly abuse, and we landed some good shots on each other.

"You're not too shabby, Mitchell," I said after a while.

"Jake."

"Huh?"

"It's Jake. Jake Mitchell. I noticed you call that prick Marcos, Jared, so—"

"So… you feel left out?" I teased. We fought some more, but he looked like he wanted to say something else.

"Spit it out, Jake."

"What?"

"Whatever it is you're stewing over."

"Okay, seeing as you asked… he's warned you off me, hasn't he? In the Warrior, on the way back from GB4?" I didn't say anything, but landed a pretty good blow to his side. "That was what you were talking about, wasn't it?"

"Yes," I said simply.

"Fucker!" He scowled. "Let me guess, he called me a Mud Monkey?" I laughed at the name again until he caught me on the arm with his staff. "He told you that I was a bad guy? Not to be trusted?"

"That's about it." I circled the mat. "He called you a yahoo as well."

Jake laughed, but the sound was hollow and humourless. "He's right, you know, in some respects." I must've looked confused. "I do have to do things that aren't strictly by-the-book, but that's my job. That's why they send in the Wolfpack. We get the things done that squeaky-clean captains like Marcos would never be able to do… and don't have the stomach for." The room filled with loud cracks as the two staffs met together in quick succession. "Doesn't mean I'm a bad person."

"He said you had a girl in every spaceport."

Jake laughed again, but that time he was amused. "I wish." He saw the look on my face. "I'm joking, Babe. Look…" He hesitated mid-manoeuvre, so I took the opportunity to land another good blow. "Hey! I'm not going to lie to you, my job requires me to play the bad guy sometimes, but I never forget I work for the good guys." I saw the conviction in his eyes. "And," he caught me across the shoulder with a surprising blow, "I don't have a girl in every spaceport. In fact, I don't have a girl at all. I'm not the love 'em and leave 'em type, whatever Marcos says."

"I believe you."

"You know, Marcos isn't exactly an angel," he said. "But

I think you already know that, being in custody and all."

"I don't want to talk about Captain Infuriating," I replied, hitting Jake much harder than I'd meant to.

"Fine by me," he replied cheerfully.

We stepped it up a notch after that, both working too hard to keep up the banter. Jake was good, but I was better, and after a particularly impressive manoeuvre on my part, he lost his staff. He grabbed my Cal'ret and we held it between us, our bodies almost touching. I grinned.

"What?" he asked, returning my smile, but his eyes narrowed. I sent a mental signal to the Cal'ret, which in turn sent an energy pulse down the length of the staff. It wasn't strong, but it was enough to shock him into letting go, disorientating him a little. A firm push landed him on his arse.

"Well, would you look at that? I win," I said, smiling happily. Jake shook his head and refocused.

"Interesting move, Babe."

"Why thank you, Colonel." I gave the Cal'ret a shake to return it to its baton length, and held out my hand to help him up. He took it, but instead of standing, he used his weight to pull me off balance and I tumbled to the mat beside him. With one quick move, he was on top of me, pinning my arms to the mat above my head with his hands. "Interesting move," I said.

He let go of my wrists but didn't roll away. We were so close and still breathing hard from the workout, our bodies moving together. I could feel his weight on top of me – it felt comfortable.

In a brave move for me, I put my hand up and touched his lips with my thumb. They were soft and warm, and I felt his breath on my skin. He dropped his head and kissed me, and it felt thrilling… exciting. I wrapped my legs around him, and he was the only thing on my mind. Everything else, every other thought I had, disappeared.

He pulled away slightly, looking deep into my eyes. He

stroked the side of my face, holding his hand on my cheek for just a fraction before he kissed me again. My hand curled around his neck and my fingers twisted in his hair. Our kiss was vigorous, full of desire, and I felt the heat rising in my body. I wanted him.

Jake pulled away again and started to say something, but I put my finger to his mouth before lifting my body to his, pushing myself against him. He moved and a bolt of lightning shot through me.

He nuzzled my neck – soft, gentle kisses that covered my body in goose bumps. I lifted my chin to expose more of my neck to his tongue.

His hand slipped under my t-shirt, and I trembled when he caressed the bare flesh of my stomach. His fingers were surprisingly soft, every touch like tiny electric shocks. He stroked my skin before moving his hand towards my breast and I gasped, wrapping my arms around his shoulders. That was what I wanted. Jake was what I wanted…

"Shae, can you hear me?" Ash's voice was clear over my coms.

"Wait, stop. Jake, stop." It was the hardest thing to say. I pointed to my earpiece when his forehead creased. "It's Ash."

"I know you're probably training hard, but Edge is ready for interrogation," Ash continued.

I giggled as Jake nibbled my ear. "Stop it," I said punching him gently on the arm. I felt light-headed and couldn't concentrate.

"Shae? Can you hear me?" Ash pushed.

I raised my hand and tapped my earpiece. "I read you," I said, but then I had to cut him off to hide the moan I couldn't stifle as Jake nuzzled my neck again.

I had to be serious; I had a job to do – no matter how much I wanted Jake to kiss me again, to touch me again. I tried to roll him off me but he was strong and resistant. I gave him my 'now's not the time' look, and he eventually let me push him away. We lay on our backs, side by side, while Ash chattered obliviously in my ear, telling me where they were taking Edge.

"Copy that, Ash. I'll be right there," I managed to say without further physical interruptions from Jake.

"I'm sorry, I've got to go," I said as Jake rolled on his side and put his hand on my stomach, stroking it lightly. "Seriously, I really have to go."

"I understand," he said, before leaning over and giving me a quick kiss on the forehead.

I retrieved the Cal'ret from the floor, where it had been discarded, and headed for the door. I was halfway down the first hallway when I stopped dead. "Where's my head? See what you've done to me? I can't even think straight. I don't even know where Interrogation Room Two is."

"It's all right, Babe." His face glowed. "I know where it is." He put his hand on the small of my back and led the way.

After navigating several floors and hallways, we turned a corner which led to a large square lounge area with doors off each wall and an operations desk in the centre surrounded by chairs. Ash, Jared, and the rest of the Wolfpack congregated on the far side of the room and I took a step towards them. Jake stopped me.

"I need to ask you something," he said quietly, a puzzled look in his green-flecked eyes. "Marcos gave you a pretty convincing warning about me, yet…" He studied his fingernails.

"Yet?" He looked up but didn't say anything. "Jake, I don't know what's going on between you two, and quite frankly it's none of my business, but I believe you should make up your own mind about people… and, well, I like you. I kind of hoped that was obvious."

"I've never met anyone like you."

"People say that to me a lot."

"Do those same people tell you you're the most

astonishingly beautiful, passionate, and exquisite person they've ever met?" I blushed outrageously and he smiled because he had his answer. "I'm not what Marcos has made me out to be."

"I know."

"It's important to me you believe that."

"I do."

"Because that, back there, I've never done that with someone I've only just met."

"Except me."

"Except you." He laughed quietly.

I looked over to the others. Jared and Ash were deep in conversation, the rest of the Wolfpack separated off slightly. Unexpectedly, Jared glanced over and caught my eye.

"We best go," I said reluctantly. "It looks like Jared's about to come over and save me from the big bad Mud Monkey." Jake laughed so hard the whole group looked over.

"Let's go, Babe," he said when he got his breath back.

As soon as we approached, the rest of the Wolfpack gathered around their Colonel. "What the hell happened to you two?" asked Leather Jacket.

"Staff training," Jake answered calmly. I tried not to blush.

"Who won?" asked Ash.

"I did, of course," I replied. He nodded proudly, but the Wolfpack weren't convinced that I could best their Colonel.

"It's true," Jake said, shaking his head. "She's truly incredible… with a Cal'ret." Jared and Jake exchanged a distinctly unfriendly glare.

"Right," said Ash, breaking the tension. "Shae and I require a closed interrogation of Edge—"

"No way," interrupted Jared. "It's Fleet policy—"

"Do I have to remind you that Mr Edge is in Brotherhood custody? That doesn't change just because he happens to be on a Fleet ship. And," he said loudly for emphasis, "having Shae in custody doesn't change that fact either. Fleet protocols don't apply."

Jared conferred with Tel'an. "Fine," he said reluctantly.

"That means no guards or senior staff in the interrogation room," Ash continued. Jared nodded. "And no holographic, visual, or audio recording." Jared remained silent. "Captain, I want your word on that."

"You have it," he said eventually.

And just because I knew it would annoy Jared even more, I added, "Jake, we'll pass custody of Edge over to you and the Wolfpack when we're done – as an apology for gate-crashing your investigation."

"Jake?" grunted Jared. I wasn't sure whether he was objecting to me handing over Edge to the Colonel, or my casual use of his first name. I didn't really care.

"Yes, Captain. Jake can have Edge when we've finished." Jared scowled, Ash raised an eyebrow, and Jake smirked. I ignored all of them. "Let's get on with it, shall we?"

# 8

Edge sat on a metal chair in the middle of the small, circular interrogation room, shackled to the table in front of him. The two well-armed troopers wore matching scowls.

"Please release Mr Edge's restraints," Ash said to one of them, who looked to Jared for agreement. "Captain? Do I have to remind you this is our interrogation?"

"On your heads." Jared nodded his permission to the trooper before ordering them both to leave the room. He followed reluctantly.

As soon as the door shut, Ash took a small red box from his bag and placed it on the table. He turned it on and it beeped twice before falling silent. Edge looked at it suspiciously while rubbing his wrists, red-raw from pulling on the cuffs.

"Mr Edge," Ash began politely. "As you're aware, my colleague placed you into the custody of the Brotherhood because we believe you have information about a situation we're investigating." Edge remained silent, staring at Ash with open loathing. "While we've been given the hospitality of the *Defender*," I involuntarily let out a dry laugh, "I need to make it clear that the REF has nothing to do with this interrogation. That's why we've asked the guards to leave, and for all recording equipment to be turned off."

"If you believe that, you're an even bigger moron than I thought," Edge scoffed.

"That's what this box is for. The fact it's silent confirms all recording devices, except for our own of course, are turned off. It will let me know immediately if any of them are reactivated." Edge shifted in his chair. "I'm going to cut to the chase because time is of the essence. We believe that very shortly an assassination attempt will be made on somebody important, and we believe you know something about it."

"You're talking out your arse. I don't know nothing."

"You're lying," I said.

"Screw you, bitch. Go die." Edge was venomous.

"Hey! Watch your mouth," Ash growled, leaning forwards, his eyes suddenly dark and intimidating. Edge recoiled and Ash sat back in his chair, his face smoothing over. "We have evidence that links you to a group of people who recently met on the Planet of Souls. We believe you transported them to there, and that you know everything there is to know about the assassination."

"You got me all wrong," Edge replied, a cocky sneer appearing. "I'm a paragon of virtue, me."

"And that would be why you're on a terrorist watch-list, would it?" Ash goaded as Edge's sneer faded. "Yes, we know about your sympathetic tendencies towards ARRO."

"You got no proof of that." The bravado was back after a momentary waver. "I'd be in REF custody otherwise."

Edge folded his arms and sat back in his chair, but Ash wasn't put off by the mocking grin he'd adopted. He kept talking, trying to catch him off guard – making statement after statement, interspersing them with questions. He even threatened that Edge would be an accessory to murder, throwing in all sorts of punishments and sentences, but still nothing.

As valuable time went on, Edge showed the first small signs of discomfort. He fidgeted and chewed at his nails, but remained silent except to offer some colourful insults.

About an hour later, Edge sat up straighter, his eyes clearing. "Bollocks to you," he said unexpectedly. "I'm not scared of the Brotherhood. There's been no assassination – no murder attempt. All you got is rumour, or you'd have charged me by now." He spat at Ash. "You got nothing, 'coz nothing's happened. You can't fit me up for some non-existent crime."

A thought floated through the back of my head and I had to concentrate through Edge's taunts and insults to bring it into focus. It was a long shot, but at that point we didn't have anything else. I signalled to Ash that I was stepping out.

Jared and Jake were by my side in an instant, and I had to raise my hand to silence them. As much as I hated to admit it, I needed Jared.

"Captain, have your techs cracked the *Hawkhurst's* lock-out codes yet?" I asked.

"No, they're struggling. Apparently, the encryption code is complex – they can do it, it's just going to take time."

"Time's something I don't have. Can you use your authority to find out whether the *Hawkhurst* was docked at Angel Ridge yesterday?"

"Shae, what's going on?"

"Please, Jared," I practically begged. "I can't tell you why, but I need to know if Edge was at Angel Ridge yesterday."

"After what went down," Jared looked sceptical, "I don't think they'd give us the time of day."

"Can you try? It's really important – I wouldn't ask otherwise."

"I think it's a waste of time, but I—"

"You're such a fucking dick, Marcos," Jake growled.

"Don't push me, Jake," Jared snarled back, squaring up

to the Marine, but Jake wasn't backing down.

"Why don't you just help her? Man up for a change."

"Watch it, Mitchell, or I'll throw you, and the rest of your Mud Monkeys, off my ship quicker than you can form your next half-wit thought."

The combined objection from the rest of the Wolfpack drowned out Jake's response.

"Enough!" I shouted, standing between the two men. Not one of my better ideas, but it seemed to break the tension.

Jake rubbed his stubble for a moment. "I might be able to help, Babe."

"How?"

"Kaiser?" He called to Leather Jacket – so that was his name. "That scroat on Angel Ridge, what was his name? You know, the low-life snitch who gave us information on the Forrester narcotics bust last year?"

"Bishop?"

"Yeah, that's the dude. He still there?"

"I think so."

"Good. Try and get hold of him. We need to know if Edge was on Angel Ridge yesterday. It's important, so free rein on the intimidation tactics."

"On it," Kaiser replied before disappearing.

Jared had stepped away to talk to Tel'an. As I approached, the Commander nodded her agreement of something then headed towards the ops desk, but he stayed put, arms folded tightly across his chest. He looked serious, his eyes flashing dangerously.

"Jared?" I said quietly. He unfolded his arms but his face was still hard. "Jared, please?"

"He just makes me want to punch…" He raised an arm in Jake's direction then took a deep breath and unclenched his fist. "I'm sorry. I wasn't trying to be obstructive, just realistic. Mitchell has no idea what went down at Angel Ridge yesterday. He's got no right to judge."

"I know," I replied, trying to appease him, although I found myself wondering why. I was supposed to be mad at him.

"I won't allow him to speak to me like that, especially not on my own ship."

"And that's your right," I said diplomatically. His face lightened.

"I've asked Commander Tel'an to contact Angel Ridge, see if we can get anything from them. She can be quite persuasive."

"I bet she can. If you get anything, can you let me know?"

"Of course." I turned away. "Shae?"

"Yes?"

"I haven't filed any reports. You're not under arrest."

"Thanks," I said, meaning it. It didn't get him out of my bad books though.

"Just… well… just don't hit me again. You've got some punch on you. It kind of hurt." The boyish grin returned.

"Try not to do anything to deserve it then."

"Deal."

When I returned to the interrogation room, Ash was still firing questions at Edge, and Edge was still sitting in smug silence. I gave Ash a barely noticeable glance which only he would understand meant no new information. He continued his questioning.

Half an hour later, Jake stuck his head through the door and motioned for me to step out. Ash decided to follow, prompting Edge to spit abuse and obscenities as we left.

"Jake, please tell me you have something," I implored.

"Babe, this is me you're talking to."

"What's going on?" Ash ignored Jake's arrogance.

"I'm hoping everything will make sense in a minute," I said. "What've you got, Jake?"

"Our snitch on Angel Ridge confirmed that the *Hawkhurst* was docked there yesterday, between roughly seventeen-thirty and nineteen-thirty."

"Yes!"

"That's when we were there," Jared interjected, frowning.

"I know," I replied, turning to Ash. "Edge is cocky because he knows we haven't got anything concrete on him. Plus, we don't have any actual proof that anything is going to happen. All we have is hearsay and supposition, and that's not enough leverage to get him to talk. But..." I paced as I spoke. "The Agent of Death had to get on and off Angel Ridge somehow."

"You think Edge took him there in the *Hawkhurst*?" said Ash.

"It's a long shot, but it adds up."

"Even if it was him, we don't have any proof."

"But Edge doesn't know that. The Agent of Death killed a Human citizen, which puts that very real murder under the jurisdiction of the REF Right?" Both Jared and Jake nodded. "So you could argue that Edge, who took the Agent to Angel Ridge for the sole purpose of murdering Nyan, was instrumental in his death. Jared, what's the minimum sentence for accessory to murder?"

"Seven years."

"I know how we get him," I concluded.

"How you get him," Ash clarified. "I'll stay out here."

"What? Why?"

"I've got nowhere with him so far. You haven't questioned him yet, and it may catch him off guard. You're totally capable, and this was your hunch. You should run with it."

"What if I go blank?"

"Shae, you've run hundreds of interrogations by yourself."

"I know, but..."

"If it makes you feel better, Captain Marcos can turn the recording equipment back on. We'll be able to see and hear everything, and I'll be in like a shot if you need me… but you won't. I have faith in you."

"But—"

"Edge is almost certainly guilty of an REF crime, so they have the right to evidence whatever he says. Besides, I think we're long past trying to keep this situation contained within the Brotherhood."

Commander Tel'an re-joined the group. "Sorry, Captain. No joy with Angel Ridge," she explained. "I tried my best, but I won't repeat in present company what they said. It seems they're still smarting over your 'contemptible behaviour' yesterday."

"Our contemptible behaviour," Jared snorted.

"Thanks for trying, Commander," I said.

"You're very welcome." She returned my smile, her amber eyes shining brightly.

"Right then," I said. "Let's do this. Jared, can you give me two minutes in the room with Edge before turning your equipment back on?" His forehead creased but he nodded. I took a few deep breaths to calm the swirling knot in the pit of my stomach, and when I entered the interrogation room, I was steely.

"Look who's back." Edge spat out each word. "You come to tell me I can go, bitch?" I didn't say a word, keeping my expression completely neutral. I looked straight at him the entire time. "Where's your boyfriend? Scared him off have I?" Still I said nothing. I moved one of the two chairs away from the table and placed it against the back wall, manoeuvring the other so that it was directly in front of Edge, the table between us.

I sat and casually crossed my legs, still watching Edge, and still not saying anything – my face emotionless. He kept eye contact for a bit then dropped his gaze and picked at his nails.

After two minutes, the box on the table began beeping loudly and Edge started, his eyes wide.

"What the hell?" he spluttered, appearing rattled for the first time. "Why's that thing beeping?"

"This?" I leant forward and tapped the box. "This is telling me the recording equipment has been reactivated." I silenced the alarm.

"Why? What the… Why?"

"I'm glad you asked." My voice was calm and confident. "Captain Marcos is recording the rest of this interrogation to use as evidence in your trial." Edge shifted position nervously.

"Oh, I get it." He forced a laugh. "You think you can trick me into saying something? Well you can't, bitch. I've done nothing, and you have nothing on me. I suggest you let me go before I bring my own charges of harassment and unlawful detention."

"Are you sure about that?"

"Am I sure…? Are you high, bitch?" He was belligerent and losing his cool – exactly what I wanted. "Of course I can bring my own charges." He tapped his fingers on the table between randomly waving his arms around.

"No, I was talking about the bit where you said you hadn't done anything wrong," I explained calmly.

"You're twisted… and desperate."

It was time to switch things up, to catch him off guard.

I stood up so quickly the chair flew backwards, hitting the wall with a loud, metallic clang. Edge was wide-eyed when I slammed my hands down on the table, leaning over so my face was closer to his.

"I'm not talking about possible assassinations, Edge. I'm talking about actual murder. Murder!" I shouted. He looked like he was about to say something, but I didn't give him the chance. "We know you were at Angel Ridge yesterday. We know you transported an Agent of Death there. And we know that the Agent went there for the sole purpose of killing someone. That makes you an accessory to murder."

Edge blanched, beads of sweat running down the side of

his face. I changed tactics again to keep him off balance. After retrieving the chair, I sat back down opposite him. "This time we have proof," I lied. "Actual, undisputable, first hand, eye-witness evidence that puts the Agent of Death with you at Angel Ridge. There's not a jury in the Sector that won't find you guilty."

"But—"

"Accessory to murder," I clarified. "That's seven years minimum."

"You're bluffing."

"Really?" He flinched as I got up. "Because that witness is on their way here. Captain Marcos sent a squad to go pick them up – shouldn't be long now." I paced in front of him, never breaking eye contact. "This started out as a Brotherhood investigation, but accessory to murder? That's big time, Edge. That's REF business. Why do you think we let them turn the recording equipment back on?" He looked startled. "Because this is bigger than Brotherhood now," I answered for him. "This is seven years in a Max-Four penal complex."

Edge tried to get some swagger back. "So what? Seven years? I'll be out in four."

I walked the circumference of the room so I stood behind him, out of his eye line. He tried to stand but I was prepared and used my weight to force him back into his seat.

"Maybe that's true," I reasoned. "But I'm betting you won't make four days when the Agents of Death find out you spilled your guts to Fleet about one of their own."

I was still finishing my sentence when Edge tried to stand and swing for me. Before he could turn, I grabbed his arm, twisting it behind his back, and smashed his head on the table. Not too hard, I didn't want him unconscious, just enough to put him back in his place. I let go of his arm and he sank back into his seat, rubbing his forehead and flexing out his shoulder. I gave him a moment to digest what I'd said as I returned to my chair.

"I never said nothing about the Agent of Death." He looked half petrified. "I'd never."

"I know that, you know that, and even the records will show that, but people talk. It's difficult when there are so many departments involved… things get exaggerated, information gets distorted… then before you know it, the Agents hear you told us everything. And don't think you'll be safe just because you're in lockup." I leant forward and whispered, "I heard they got to someone in solitary confinement in a Max-Five High Security Prison. Now that's not easy to do, I can tell you."

The cold sweats and shakes told me I had him, but I switched tactics again. Leaning forward I shouted, "Did you take the Agent of Death to Angel Ridge?"

"No!"

Still yelling, "You're lying, we have proof. Do yourself a favour and admit it. Did you take the Agent of Death to Angel Ridge?"

"No!" But he hesitated.

I fired questions in quick succession: "Did you take the Agent of Death to Angel Ridge? Did you know that he was there to kill someone? Do you know who the Agent was? Do you want to go to prison? Do you want to be the next target for the Agents of Death?" After each question, his face crumbled a little bit more. I paused for effect then shouted, "Did you take the Agent of Death to Angel Ridge?"

"Yes! But you gotta protect me. Please, I don't wanna die. Yes, I took him there, but I never saw his face and I don't know who he was. Don't let them think I told you anything."

I had him for his part in Nyan's death, but I still had to tie in everything else. "What about the Planet of Souls?" He looked confused through his tears. "What was your involvement? Who else was there? Were they ARRO? What do you know?" I was back to the rapid-fire questions. I wanted to draw him in while he was still unbalanced.

"I—"

"Talk to me, Edge," I demanded. "This is your last chance to tell me what I need to know, or I walk away and you're on your own."

"If I tell you, you have to protect me from the Agents."

"I'll do my best."

"Promise me."

"I promise I'll do whatever I can to protect you." There was no distinction between my two responses, but Edge must've been happier with the second.

"I was there," he said.

"Where?" I needed him to be specific.

"On the Planet of Souls. I took them there, the people you was talking about, but I don't know who they were. Swears. They had cloaks and hid their faces, and they made me stay on the *Hawkhurst* during the meeting. I took them there and then brought them back. They were well pissed on the way back though – thought something bad must've happened."

"What was the meeting about?"

"No idea." He saw the scepticism on my face. "I dunno, all right? It was none of my business."

"Were they ARRO?"

"Huh?"

"ARRO? Were they an ARRO cell? Come on, you don't get on a watch-list for nothing – we know you're a sympathiser."

"They… they could've been, but nothing was said to me. Swears."

"Where did you pick them up and drop them off?"

"Angel Ridge."

"How did they get in touch with you to make the booking?"

"Didn't."

"What do you mean?"

"It was arranged through a dude called Cady. He's—"

"I know who he is." I was thinking hard. "Can you tell me anything else? Anything at all?"

"That's all I know. Cady contacted me through the usual channels, told me he had a job. He gave me the pick-up and drop-off locations as normal, so I thought nothing of it. There's nothing else. You have to protect me now, right? Right?" He had panic behind his eyes but I had no sympathy for him.

"The Angel Ridge job – how was that booked?" I asked, but I had a pretty good idea what the answer would be.

"Cady," Edge replied.

"Where did you pick the Agent up?"

"Merron's third moon, Quenia."

"And drop him off?"

"Same place."

"So, for the record, Jason Cady booked you to do both the Planet of Souls and the Angel Ridge runs. You picked up a small group of people from the Ridge and took them to the Planet of Souls, then returned them back to Angel Ridge. But you have no idea who they were, or what the secret meeting was about. Then later, you transported an Agent of Death to Angel Ridge from Quenia, but you don't know who he was or who he was going to kill. Is this correct?"

"I think so."

"Think so, or know so? Our records need to be accurate."

"That is, was, umm, yes."

"And there's nothing else you want to tell me? This is your last chance."

"That's all I know. Swears."

"Thank you, Mr Edge," I said, standing. "That's all I need for the moment." I walked to the door and left the room without a backwards glance.

Ash, Jared and Jake stood at the ops desk where they'd obviously been watching the show on the monitors. All of them were grinning, but only Ash's smile was tinged with the same disappointment I felt. I slumped into a chair in front of the desk and put my head in my hands.

"Damn it, Ash." I felt him sit next to me.

"I've briefed Captain Marcos and Colonel Mitchell on everything." I looked sideways at him. "The whole situation. They know as much about the assassination plot as we do. I figured at this stage in the game, we could do with all the help we can get."

Jared crouched down in front of me. "It would've been easier if you'd confided in me from the start," he said. I had a sudden urge to reach out and push him over.

"So Edge is a bust – just a low-level runner with no real information to help us," added Jake, who'd stood behind Jared with his arms crossed. It irked me that he'd used the word 'us' and I wondered whether pushing Jared over would take out Jake as well. My hand twitched.

"We need to speak to Cady again," Ash looked at his com-pad, "but the sedative I gave him may have worn off. If he's bolted, he could be anywhere. He's certainly not going to stick around after Shae threatened to blow a hole in his kneecap."

"You what?" Jared almost toppled over.

"Relax, Jared, I was bluffing. I wouldn't have done it, not really. Anyway," I pulled the mini data-pad from my trouser pocket, "I chipped him before we left." I pressed a few buttons on the pad until a map appeared. "According to this, he's still in his office."

"Colonel Mitchell," Ash said, adopting an official tone, "the Brotherhood turns Mr Edge over to your custody, as previously agreed, but on the understanding we may need to interrogate him further."

"Agreed," Jake replied, equally business-like.

Jared, who'd stood as I had, smiled broadly, and I didn't

understand why until he said, "Perfect. You and your team can stay here and interrogate your prisoner, and I'll take a squad of troopers with Shae and Brother Asher to pick up Cady." I closed my eyes and prepared for the inevitable.

"No fucking way," steamed Jake. "My team are a far better protection detail than your pansy-arsed troopers."

The predictable verbal slanging match started, but we didn't have time for it, and they were so caught up in their own pissing contest, they didn't even see us leave.

"Wait," puffed Jared as they caught up, still giving each other looks of pure loathing.

"This has gone far enough, gentlemen." Ash was irritated; I felt it through the Link. "While I appreciate the support both of you have given, this," he waved his hand between the two of them, "whatever this is, is proving detrimental to our investigation." Jake started to say something but Ash hadn't finished. "I don't care what's going on. Enough is enough."

"Of course," Jared said. "I apologise for our lack of professionalism."

"Do I have to remind you that we are Brotherhood? We don't require protection," Ash continued.

"I meant no disrespect," Jake said. "I—"

"My apologies for interrupting." Commander Tel'an had appeared so silently she made me jump. "Captain, your vid-com with Admiral Pritchard is scheduled for fifteen minutes' time in your office."

"Damn it! Commander—"

"The Admiral says that after missing the last two, if you cancel this call, he'll be extremely displeased." She gave the news as diplomatically as she could.

"Jared, you shouldn't get into trouble because of us," I said. "This is a simple extraction mission – nothing Ash and I haven't done a million times before."

"However…" Ash added slowly, taking the time to think. "If Cady does run, some extra manpower may come in handy. Colonel, perhaps we could use the Wolfpack as back-up?"

"It would be our pleasure." Jake smiled smugly. "We can take the *Veritas*."

I checked my data-pad, which still placed Cady in his office. "Jared, could you arrange for someone to call ahead to the local security office and ask them to sit on Cady until we get there?" He nodded. "Don't worry; we'll be back before you know it."

As expected, the *Veritas* was more like the *Nakomo* than one of Jared's Warriors. Probably about twice the size of a Warrior, the *Veritas* was an interesting ship. At first glance, she didn't look anything special – old, worn, and in need of some attention, but like the Wolfpack, she was definitely not what she first appeared to be. State-of-the-art weaponry, and top of the range engines, were hidden behind a scruffy carapace.

The inside was rough and ready, built for action not comfort, so there were few mod-cons. I took a seat next to Ash in the main cabin and watched Jake give orders to the Pack before following Connor to the flight deck. With Jared he'd been argumentative and volatile, with me he'd been charming, even vulnerable, but on the *Veritas* he was in total control. I liked seeing that new side to him.

We were well on our way to Base4 when he eventually sauntered over, propping himself casually against a bulkhead.

"It's about time I introduced you to the rest of the Wolfpack. This is Kaiser, my second in command." Kaiser, who was cleaning his gun at the table opposite, looked up and nodded. "The blond guy on the flight deck is Connor – our weapons and explosives expert, in addition to being pilot. And the other one," Jake looked around for the last member of the team, "who seems to be missing, is Ty – our communications and technical specialist. Oh, and resident ladies' man."

"Glad to have you all on the mission, Colonel," said Ash. "As Shae said earlier, this should be simple. We go in, grab Cady, get out, and do the interrogation back on the *Defender.*" He glanced around. "Colonel, you have an interesting ship. With your permission, I'd love to take a look around."

"Of course. Please, be my guest."

As soon as Ash wandered off, Jake sat in the newly vacated seat and leant towards me. "I was wondering when I was going to get you all to myself again," he whispered. I felt his breath on my neck and memories I'd tried to suppress flooded back. My stomach flipped.

"We're hardly alone," I replied, looking to see if anyone was watching. He lifted his hand to my cheek and touched it gently sending shockwaves down my spine, but I brushed it away with another quick glance around the cabin. I was trying to decide how to respond when Jake ran his hand up the inside of my thigh and I practically leapt out of my seat. Kaiser glanced over.

As much as my body seemed to want Jake, it wasn't the time or place to be messing with my feelings, and I compensated with anger. Trying to keep my voice down, I practically ordered him to the weapons storage room.

"Jake, enough," I said as he propped up one of the bulkheads again, skimming his fingers through his shaggy hair. Damn he looked sexy. "You're driving me crazy," I continued, even more frustrated that he seemed pleased by the comment. "I'm serious. You can't keep doing this to me. We're both professionals, and we have a job to do. I need to focus, but every time you touch me my head gets fogged up. You confuse the hell out of me, Jake."

"I'm sorry, Babe, but I can't help myself when I'm around you." He smiled, his eyes crinkling at the edges.

"Pull it together, Colonel, please. Or…" I didn't finish because I didn't actually know what to say next. Jake's smile faltered.

"Or what?"

"Or…" I thought hard. "Or I'll tell Ash we can't work with the Wolfpack anymore. He'll listen to me, you know he will." It was a pathetic threat, but Jake stood upright.

"Okay, Babe. Okay." He held his hands up in surrender. "I get it, and I'm sorry. It's just you're too irresistible." I gave him another look. "I promise I'll do my best, but you…" he sighed, looking me up and down slowly, "you've got to try your best not to light my fire as well." I was stunned. I hadn't even imagined I was having the same effect on him that he was having on me.

"It's a deal," I mumbled.

Fortunately for both of us, Connor's voice came over the intercom telling us we were about to land. I walked past Jake, taking special care not to brush against him, and returned to my seat.

# 11

As soon as the *Veritas* was powered down, Ash and I were out and heading towards the lift. The sedative would've definitely worn off by that point, but the data-pad map told me he was still in his office so I guessed the local security officers had detained him.

I positioned myself on the opposite side of the lift from Jake and looked at my feet, but even with the distance between us, memories swam through my head and I felt my cheeks burning. I looked up and caught him grinning at me, which only made me blush harder.

The mid-evening sky was black and rain pelted down. Artificial light seeped from the buildings, and the streetlights were so bright it almost felt like daylight.

We hit the Halcyon building only minutes later, taking the elevator to the thirtieth floor. Kaiser cracked his knuckles before pulling a huge pulse-cannon from the holster on his back. "What?" he asked innocently after catching my eye. "Nothing wrong with being prepared."

I could appreciate that.

The lift doors opened, and the first thing I saw was a security officer throwing up into a pot plant; that wasn't a good sign. Everyone shifted to alert, and weapons were readied. Kaiser glanced at me and tapped the side of his cannon as if to say, 'told you so'.

The open-plan office had been trashed, and there were no staff in sight – just the security guy, still heaving over a hikas plant.

"Ty, take the officer. Find out what he knows," Jake ordered.

As Ty peeled off wordlessly to the side, the rest of us headed towards Cady's office, an uncomfortable knot tightening in my stomach. Two officers flanked the wooden doors, but they let us through after we identified ourselves.

I recognised the three men pacing the room from our encounter earlier – included Winters, who still looked as pale and out of his depth as he'd done before. Then I noticed Cady.

"Shit," I cursed, kicking out at the nearest cabinet. "Shit, shit, shit!"

Cady was exactly where we'd left him, just not exactly how we'd left him. His head was bent back, blank eyes staring at the ceiling, and a small, dark hole punctuated the middle of his forehead.

"I'm assuming you didn't leave him like this?" Kaiser joked humourlessly.

"What do you think?" I replied, stepping carefully around the skull fragments and grey-matter peppering the carpet.

Plexi-screens were smashed, and paper littered the floor; desk drawers had been pulled, their contents tipped out haphazardly.

"We didn't do it. He was like this when we got here," Winters babbled. "Thought it best to leave him until you arrived. I've never—"

"Kaiser," Jake said, cutting him off. "Debrief Winters and his team outside, then get rid of them – they're contaminating our crime scene." Winters blanched, but he allowed Kaiser to usher him and the other two out of the office. "Con, do a sweep. I don't want any surprises," Jake continued.

I approached Cady's body, bending over to get a closer look at the small wound on his forehead, careful not to touch the body or stand on anything. I twisted so I could see the back of his head, most of which was on the carpet. Congealing blood seeped from the ragged bone edge of skull, adding to the dark puddle below.

"Look familiar?" Ash said. The hit of anxiety I got from him through the Link unnerved me far more than the dead body.

"Something you want to share?" Jake muttered as he circled the body.

"Looks like the Agent of Death is tying up loose ends," I replied.

"Well, whatever's going on, Cady ain't talking anymore. What do you want to do now?"

"Cady's death is certainly a setback," Ash replied, "but we do this by the book. We check everything to see if the Agent missed anything." He surveyed the office then caught my doubtful expression and shook his head. "I know – you don't need to say it."

I picked up a cracked data-pad from the floor, wiping off blood splatters before putting it on the desk. "Jake, this equipment is trashed. Can you get Ty to take a look, see if he can't work some magic?"

"No problem, Babe," Jake replied, tapping his earpiece. "Ty, I need you—"

He was cut off by a two-tone emergency siren.

"Warning. Incendiary device detected. Evacuate the floor immediately." The electronic computer voice was clear over the alarm.

For a split second we looked at each other – then we ran for the door. All thoughts of preserving evidence were lost as my boots squelched through bloody carpet, but a sudden thought stopped me in my tracks. Ducking around Jake, I ran back into the room, snatching the shattered data-pad from the desk.

Ash had waited for me at the door, and together we headed to the open-plan office. Jake was just in front of us, ordering his team to head for the stairs before the automatic lock-down sealed off the floor to protect the outside walls and bulkheads from damage. The energy shield ensured the integrity of the rest of the building – anyone left inside when the shield activated was considered collateral damage.

"Floor lockdown in thirty seconds," the building's computer continued dispassionately.

Ty held the main stairway door open on the far side of the vast office and we headed towards him. I ran as fast as I could, weaving around upended furniture, slipping on strewn paper.

"Floor lockdown in fifteen seconds."

Connor was on the other side of the room, practically pushing Winters and his team towards the exit. Jake was right in front of me, but he stopped and turned, holding out his hand.

"Floor lockdown in ten..."

I don't remember exactly what I yelled at him, but I'm sure it was something to do with not waiting for me – only I know it wouldn't have been that polite.

"Nine..."

One of the security officers fell, but Connor was in front of him and didn't realise. Without thinking, I detoured towards him.

"Eight..."

Ash, unprepared for my sudden course deviation, ran straight past me, slipping as he tried to stop.

"Seven..."

An agonising pain shot through my shoulder, and it felt like my arm was being ripped from its socket. I just managed to secure the data-pad before dropping it.

"Six..."

I tried to twist out of Jake's grasp, desperate to help the officer, but his grip on my wrist tightened as he corrected my course back towards the exit.

"Five..."

I made another attempt to pull away from him, but in response he wrapped an arm around my waist and half dragged, half carried me towards Ty.

"Four..."

I looked behind me, watching the officer trying to pick himself off the floor, but Jake's hold was vice-tight.

"Three..."

We slid through the exit door, practically bowling over Ash and Kaiser. Conner was directly behind us with Winters and one of the other officers.

"Two..."

Ty held the door wide open, careful to remain on the stairs side of the opening. He yelled at the last officer to hurry, waving his free arm in encouragement.

"One... Shield activating." The computer's voice was final.

The man was a metre from the door when the translucent, green-tinged energy barrier blocked his escape. He skidded into it, disorientated with panic, and I looked into his wide, scared eyes as the bomb went off. The floor on our side of the shield vibrated softly, but a swirling, maelstrom of fire engulfed everything in the office.

I ducked away from the flames, even though my brain knew they wouldn't breach the shield, and when Jake put his arm around me, I tucked myself into his chest.

Through the shield, I watched the office filling up with fire suppressant foam. If the Agent of Death had missed anything, it was destroyed by the explosion, or the fire... or the foam. He was nothing if not thorough, I would give him that.

Emergency crews arrived moments later, and we were ordered to move to a rally-point at the base of the building. Ash rounded us up, ushering the group towards the stairs, but I noticed Jake hang back. He opened a com-link and began talking quickly, but I couldn't catch what he was saying above the chaos.

Outside was equally frenzied. A middle-aged officer with a severe, bony face guided us to a hastily erected marquee where we were told to remain until someone came to get us. Jake nodded his understanding, but as soon as she was out of sight, he turned to the group and said, "Okay people, we're outta here."

"Thank God," replied Ty. "This place blows."

"That's enough!" Jake nailed him with a glare.

"Sorry, boss," he mumbled.

As we rounded the side of the tent, our path was blocked by a woman flanked by two guards. "Hold it right there," she said, putting up her hand. "Where do you think you're going?"

"Who are you?" Jake asked.

"Watchfield," she replied, her eyes narrowing as she looked him over. "Senior Security Officer for Dome Five. And none of you are going anywhere until I've found out what happened up there." She pointed up at the building – the windows of the thirtieth floor still tinged green.

"Actually," Jake was at his politest, "we've been cleared to leave."

Watchfield snorted her disbelief. "Seeing as how I'm in charge, just who exactly—" She stopped talking, listening to someone on coms. "But—" she replied, her face darkening. She turned away. "No, but I… I realise that, sir, but… Of course, sir… Yes, sir… Watchfield out."

"Everything okay?" Jake asked overly politely.

"I don't know who you people are," her cold eyes studied us carefully, "but you're free to go." The words came reluctantly, each one sticking in her throat.

"Appreciate it, Senior Security Officer Watchfield." I heard the faintest ring of sarcasm in Jake's voice, and I'm sure she did, too, because her fingers tightened around the handle of the weapon on her hip. After a moment, she huffed and stomped away without further word.

As we continued towards the *Veritas*, an unexpected wave of irritation washed over me. We were on a Brotherhood mission, yet Jake had taken it upon himself to start giving the orders. I wondered if I was being unfair and over emotional, given the circumstances, but the frown on Ash's face suggested he felt the same way.

In the lift to the hangar, Ash asked, "Colonel Mitchell, as much as I appreciate the fact we're not stuck with Dome Security right now, would you care to fill the rest of us in on why that is?"

"After the explosion, I briefed Commander Tel'an on what happened. Knowing how time-critical the mission is, I asked her to contact the Base Security Captain and persuade him that holding us would have severe and detrimental repercussions on a current REF investigation." For a moment, he sounded just like Jared. "Guess she did a good job."

I felt guilty for being irritated with him.

Jared waited for us in the *Defender's* hangar. He was a pain in my arse, and definitely still top of my 'people I'd most like to thump' list, but something inside me calmed when I saw him.

"Hey, Jared, I—"

He grabbed my shoulders, twisting me backwards and forwards, checking me over. "Are you all right?" he asked. "Shae? Are you injured? Are you okay?"

"I'm okay," I replied, stumbling as he let me go. Jake appeared beside me out of nowhere, putting his arm around my waist to steady me.

"What the hell's the matter with you, Marcos? She's fine.

Brother Asher's fine. We're all fine. Thanks for asking."

I freed myself from his hold.

"You were supposed to protect them," Jared shouted, a storm raging in his sharp, blue eyes. "Not get them half blown up."

"Fuck you, Marcos. Who the hell do you think you are?" Jake yelled back, hands clenched in to rock-hard fists. I'd had enough.

"Do it!" I yelled, stepping out the way. "Go on – do it. The tension between you two has been nine kinds of crazy since the Dome. If the only way to fix that is to knock the crap out of each other, then go ahead. This is as good a place as any to do it." I indicated the wide open hangar floor. "Just get on with it and let us know when you're done. We've got a job to do."

I slipped my arm through Ash's, and he didn't resist as I led him towards the exit. I hoped Jared and Jake would see sense and follow, but they didn't.

The lift doors at the end of the hallway slid open as we approached and we stepped in silently, but when Grace asked our destination, I didn't know what to say. I looked to Ash, but he merely shrugged his shoulders. Neither of us knew where we were heading, and for some reason, on top of everything, I found that ironic. It fitted with the situation and I laughed – proper, genuine laughter. Ash joined in, the tension lifted, and things felt better. I laughed so hard my sides began to ache.

When Jared and Jake appeared, I was wiping away tears with the back of my hand. Neither of them was bruised or bloodied, so it was safe to assume they hadn't fought, but I thought it diplomatic not to comment.

"Level Two conference rooms," Jared said as they stepped in.

"Where are the others?" I asked.

"They're staying on the *Veritas* until we decide what to do next," Jake replied.

The table in the conference room was covered in food and my stomach rumbled at the smell. "Thought you might be hungry," Jared said, as if he'd read my mind. "You can eat while you debrief me on what happened."

I was surprised when Jake took a backseat and let Ash give the primary brief – chipping in only with additional thoughts and views. Between them they covered everything from the moment we landed on GalaxyBase4 to the moment we left.

"So, to summarise… we're screwed," Jared said at the end of the brief.

He got up, stretched, and then went to what looked like a storage cupboard at the far end of the room. When he came back to the table, he slid a carton of Carmichael's Chocamel ice-cream and a spoon towards me.

"You remembered! You're a legend," I said, digging in.

"It's nothing," he replied as Jake choked on his coffee.

After talking at length about the events at Base4, Ash suggested we spend some time going back over the whole affair – starting with the meeting we'd had with Nyan on Angel Ridge. He thought Jake might pick up on something we'd missed.

"Is that everything?" Jake asked when we'd got to the end.

"That's it," Ash said.

"Well…" He looked deep in thought for a moment. "We're screwed," he said, echoing Jared.

"Not quite," replied Ash. "We still have two leads we haven't followed up on yet."

"If you say the Agent of Death, I might have to maim you," I grumbled.

"That is one of them, but I agree, unless Edge suddenly remembers something, it would be like shooting in the dark. Agents cover their tracks too well… as we've just witnessed for ourselves."

"We've been interrogating Edge since you left. He

hasn't given us anything – nothing he didn't give Shae, anyway. I don't think he knows anything else," Jared added.

"Did you get the lockdown codes to his ship's computer systems?" Jake asked.

"No, that's the one thing he's absolutely not budging on, but we've got the manifest of what he had on-board. Nothing spectacular: some contraband weapons, level three narcotics, and some medical supplies I've never heard of. Bits and pieces really."

"So our final lead is the Planet of Souls," Ash concluded. "It's the only other piece of information Nyan gave." He looked around the room at our sceptical faces. "I know the chances of finding answers there are slim at best, but what other choice do we have?"

For a moment, the room was pin-drop silent, then Jake stood.

"Okay then, we go to the Planet of Souls," he said, as if he'd finalised the decision. "I'll get Con to ready the *Veritas*."

"Belay that," said Jared, also standing. "The *Defender's* faster. Even with her new FTL engines, it'll take a good seven or eight hours to get there."

"Fine," Jake agreed grudgingly.

"Brother Asher, Shae, the quarters you used last night are still available to you. There's a bag in the bathroom, if you put your clothes in it and put it outside your door, I'll make sure they're cleaned and returned to you by morning. Colonel, I'll arrange quarters for you and your team."

"No need," replied Jake. "We'll stay on the *Veritas*."

"As you wish."

"Jake, when was the last time you slept in a decent bed?" I asked. "Please accept Jared's offer. I wouldn't be comfortable knowing you and the guys are all cramped up on the *Veritas*."

"Well, when you put it like that… besides, I would hate for you to be uncomfortable, Babe." He winked. "Thank you, Captain, we accept your hospitality."

"Great," Jared grumbled. "I suggest we all meet in the Mess Hall at zero-eight-hundred for a breakfast briefing."

Ash walked me to my room, and as he said goodnight he suggested I avoid any late-night visits to the bar. I kissed him on the cheek and assured him that all I wanted was a shower and a bed.

"Grace, play music. I don't mind what, just as long as it's mellow and chilled. Not too loud," I added. The room filled with a tune I didn't recognise, but liked.

I unbuckled my utility belt and placed it gently on a glass-topped coffee table, adding a mini data-pad, a couple of stun-grenades, a torch, and all of the other paraphernalia from my trouser pockets.

I found the linen bag on the counter in the bathroom – between the warm, fresh bath-towels, and the luxury body lotions. After turning on the shower, I took off my clothes and stuffed them in the bag, ready to put out later.

I stepped into the shower and let the hot water wash away the day's grime. I closed my eyes and listened to the music, lost in the softly undulating tempo of the melody.

I decided to try the roseberry body scrub from the vast selection of luxury toiletries, because it reminded me of the gardens on Lilania. I scooped some up in my hand and began rubbing it into my arms and shoulders, the scent bringing back images of home. As I massaged the scrub into my stomach, a jolt pierced though me, releasing a different memory – one I'd tried to bury.

The warmth radiating through my body was no longer from the hot water, it was from the memory – it was from Jake. I felt his touch, his body, his breath. I was back on the floor of the training room, the comfortable weight of his body on top of me. I felt his tongue exploring my neck, his hand caressing my skin. I remembered his kiss, passionate and desperate, and I could almost taste him…

"Captain Marcos is requesting access," Grace said over

the music. The memory shattered and I tried to ignore her, desperate to get it back. I closed my eyes and forced my mind back to the training room, but the memory was gone. "How would you like me to respond?" she continued.

I puffed out a long sigh then lifted my chin to let the water splash off my face. "Tell him it's late and to go away."

"The Captain says it's important," she said a moment later.

"Then tell Captain Marcos… no wait, I'll tell him myself. Put me through. Jared?"

"Shae, I know it's late—"

"It is late, Jared. Whatever it is, can it wait until morning?" The sound of running water washed through the background.

"I'm sorry, I didn't realise you're in the shower, but please, it won't take long." When I didn't answer, he added, "I come bearing gifts."

"Give me a minute," I said, turning off the water. I dried myself quickly before pulling on one of the warm, scented robes.

When the door opened, Jared was propped against the frame, that trademark boyish grin spread wide across his face. Damn him! No matter how irritated I was, he managed to clear it all away with one soppy look and that bloody smile.

"Can I come in? I've brought a peace offering." The two beer bottles chinked softly as he held them out. I paused, thinking about the previous night's drinking session, and then wordlessly waved him in.

"Don't make me regret this, Jared."

"I won't, I promise." He looked sincere. "Nice robe by the way," he added. "Sorry I got you out the shower."

"Are you?" I sat at one end of the long couch, pulling the robe tightly around me. "What do you want, Jared? And please don't tell me you've come to warn me again about Jake."

Jared didn't say anything, instead he unscrewed the cap off one of the beers and handed it to me. I hesitated before accepting it.

"It's just the one," he promised, sitting at the opposite end of the couch. "Cheers." He lent forward and we chinked bottles. He drank, but for someone who just had to speak to me, he wasn't doing much talking.

"What is it, Jared?" I asked again, preparing myself for Jake's character assassination.

"I… I wanted to say… I'm sorry," he replied, but his unexpected apology caused me to choke on the swig of beer I'd just taken. He immediately moved towards me, but I held up my hand to stop him.

"I'm okay," I said through a small cough.

"I didn't realise my apology would have that kind of effect."

"Funny," I wheezed. "So?"

"So?"

"Jared! You're incredibly infuriating." He looked slighted. "So? So what? What are you sorry for? I mean, there are so many things, it could be any one of them."

"Funny," he mimicked.

There were many reasons for me to hate Jared, but being there with him seemed quite normal, even comfortable. I'd only known him twenty-four hours, yet somehow it felt like I'd known him forever – a fact that still confused me.

"Where do I start?" he said, the grin reappearing.

"Try the beginning," I suggested helpfully.

"Okay… I'm sorry for getting you drunk."

"Honestly, I think I was well on my way there before you arrived. And I could've said no to the Fire Whisky, but… it wasn't getting me drunk that was the problem."

"I know." He looked down at his beer bottle and picked at the label. "What I told you about my mother and father, I want you to know that I don't just talk about them with anyone. I can't remember the last time…" He trailed off. "Being with you last night, it wasn't just because I wanted information. I felt…"

"Felt what?"

He seemed conflicted, but then he shook his head and sat up straighter. "I'm sorry for using your drunken state to try and get information from you. I'm sorry for bugging the *Nakomo*, and I'm sorry for putting you in custody." He said it quickly, as if he needed to get it out all in one go. I looked into his eyes and I could tell he meant it.

"I'm sorry too," I said.

"For what?"

"For hitting you." I really was sorry, but couldn't help the smile that came with it. Fortunately, Jared saw the funny side as well.

"I deserved it. Anyway, I wanted to tell you that it's okay if you hate me. I wouldn't blame you. I just want you to know that, for some reason I still don't understand, I feel…" he seemed to dredge his brain for the right word, "connected to you. I can't explain it. Am I making any sense at all?" Weirdly he was, but he didn't give me time to respond. "Shae, I need to talk to you about Mitchell."

"Jared, please—"

"Wait, before you say anything, let me speak."

"I don't—"

"Please? I need to say this one thing, and then I'll go and never say another thing on the subject."

"You promise?"

"You have my word." He was so sincere, I nodded my agreement. "It was wrong of me to warn you off Mitchell the way I did. I know you like to think the best of people, but sometimes you don't always have all the information. I can see you're taken by Mitchell, that you have feelings for him." He looked directly into my eyes, and I betrayed those feelings by turning away. "I thought so," he said quietly, but there was a change to his tone I didn't understand.

"Jared, I…" It was my turn not to know what to say.

"I know it's none of my business what you feel for Mitchell, but be careful. I don't want you to get hurt."

"What happened between the two of you, Jared? What caused this amount of hostility?"

"It's not my place to say," he replied. "It's up to Mitchell if he wants to tell you, but you should know we've drawn a truce for the time being." Jared finished his beer. "Just try not to get hurt. That's all I wanted to say."

Even though he had no right to warn me off Jake, I was happy he cared enough to try, so I shuffled along the couch and gave him a hug. For a second he froze, then his arm wrapped around me. I rested my head on his shoulder and a new memory surfaced – the one where I'd hugged him on Angel Ridge to stop him pulling his gun. I felt comfortable and relaxed, so when the pad by the front door buzzed, I was annoyed at the interruption. Jared moved his arm so I could get up.

"Who is it?" I said, pressing the intercom button.

"Babe, it's me."

I had just enough time to register that Jake was freshly showered and shaved before he swept me off my feet.

"I missed you, Babe," he whispered into my ear, breathing in my scent. "I'm glad you're still—" He stopped abruptly, scowling over my shoulder. "Babe?" he said carefully, not taking his eyes off Jared. "What's he doing here?" He set my feet back on the carpet.

"Jared stopped by for a beer and a quick chat," I replied, gently wriggling out of his hold.

"Did he now? You're some piece of work, you know that, Marcos? There's no way in hell I'd have agreed to a truce if I'd known you were going to come bad-mouthing me to Shae the first opportunity you had. I should have gone with my first instinct and beaten the crap out of you back in the hangar. I bet you enjoyed telling her your one-sided version of what happened before?"

"It wasn't like that," I said, shocked by the venom in his voice.

"No?"

"Not at all. I asked, but he wouldn't tell me." I saw the doubt in his eyes so I placed my hand gently on his cheek and turned his face towards me. "He said it was up to you to tell me – if you wanted to."

The frown-lines smoothed out and the light crinkles returned to Jake's eyes. He lifted his hand and stroked my cheek gently with the back of his fingers, but I felt uncomfortable knowing Jared was watching.

"So, what are you doing here so late, Mitchell?" Jared said, earning another glare.

"Not that it's any of your business, but I came to see if Shae was all right after our excitement at Base4." Jake looked down into my eyes. "So he really did just come for a beer?"

"Yes."

"Well then... that beer looks pretty empty to me," Jake said pointedly to Jared. "Guess you'll be leaving then?"

"Actually, I won't," Jared replied, but truce or not, I was too tired for their crap.

"Actually, you will," I corrected.

"What?" He was stunned. Jake smirked.

"You, too, Jake."

"But, Babe..." His grin slipped.

"Don't 'but, Babe' me. It's late, and I'm tired."

When I woke the following morning, I was disorientated, and it took me a moment to remember where I was. I instructed Grace to turn off the alarm then pulled the covers over my head. Five minutes later the alarm went off again, and I sat bolt upright, rubbing my eyes.

"You have one appointment reminder for today," Grace prompted. "Breakfast Meeting with Captain Marcos at zero-eight-hundred in the Mess Hall."

"I know. That's why I'm up, damn it." I was tired and

irritable, and couldn't shake the feeling that the day would be much less challenging if I could get an extra couple of hours in bed.

I washed in silence, declining Grace's offer to play music. Instead, I chose to run through the events of the previous two days, working at the problem from different angles, trying to come up with new insight. I hoped that I'd have a eureka-moment, and suddenly everything would make sense, but it didn't happen.

I dressed quickly, carefully replacing all the gizmos and gadgets into my pockets before buckling on my belt and strapping the holsters around my thighs. I put my coms earpiece into my ear and it bleeped to tell me I had a message – Ash was going for an early morning run and would meet me in the Mess Hall. I did one last check of my quarters to make sure I hadn't forgotten anything then headed out.

Ty and Connor were eating alone at one of the long refectory-style tables when I arrived at the Mess Hall. Even though it was busy, none of the *Defender* crew had sat anywhere near them so it looked like there was an invisible exclusion zone around the two members of the Wolfpack. I grabbed some hot food from the counter and went to sit with them.

"Careful," Connor whispered conspiratorially, "the natives are restless. Are you sure you want to be associated with us bottom feeders?" He grinned, stabbing at a sausage.

"I think I'll cope," I whispered back. "Hey, Ty, I don't suppose you've had a chance to look at Cady's data-pad, have you?"

"I had a quick look. It's pretty trashed – the control crystal's fried and the memory disc's corrupted."

"Damn it!"

"Hey, hold on now. I didn't say I couldn't work a little Ty magic on it." Connor groaned, but Ty ignored him. "I'm going to run a restoration algorithm on it later when I got more time – see if I can't recover anything."

"Could you keep me informed?"

"Sure, no problem," he replied, massaging his shaved head.

I felt the atmosphere change in the Mess Hall and looked up to see Jared sauntering over to the food counter.

It would've been logical for him to sit next to Ty, so there were two people on each side of the table, but he didn't. He sat next to me. I didn't mind, but Connor and Ty stiffened in their seats – uncomfortable in the company of a Fleet Captain without their own commanding officer. They fell into silence and concentrated on eating.

"Please tell me that's what I think it is," I said, drawn to the two mugs on Jared's tray.

"Depends what you think it is," he teased.

"Don't play games with me, Jared. It's way too early," I warned, only half joking.

"Wouldn't dream of it." He smiled mischievously. "Here," he said, handing over one of the mugs. "Fresh Shatokian coffee. Ash said it's your favourite."

I slowly inhaled the deep, rich aroma, took a sip, and sighed contentedly.

# 12

It wasn't long before Jake and Kaiser appeared. I looked up and Jake caught my eye, holding my gaze while giving me a smile that made me feel I was the only person in the room. I was captivated, and even though he was the other side of the room, he had stolen my complete attention. Jared coughed loudly and I had to apologise because I couldn't remember what we'd been talking about. He shook his head and I brushed away a twinge of guilt.

Ash got there moments later, and by the time they'd all got something to eat they arrived at the table at the same time. Jake sat opposite me and I made a point of tucking my feet under the bench to avoid any accidental touches under the table.

Ty put his cutlery down noisily and pushed his plate away. "Are you leaving that?" I asked.

"Man, you can sure eat," he said, looking down at the sausage he'd left. I wasn't sure whether he was amazed or appalled.

"I've got a fast metabolism," I explained. "And I'm also not a morning person – which means I need a good breakfast and at least two cups of coffee before the urge to punch someone goes away."

"I can vouch for that," added Ash. Everyone laughed.

"So… are you going to eat that, or what?" I pushed.

"It's all yours." Ty handed his plate over. "And Captain, I recommend you rustle up another one of those coffees – double-time."

"Copy that," Jared replied, laughing.

When everyone had almost finished eating, Ash asked, "When do we reach the Planet of Souls, Captain?"

"We're already here," Jared replied.

"In orbit?" Jake exclaimed, standing. "Then what the hell are we still doing sat here?"

"Relax, Jake, the search area's still in darkness. Sunrise isn't for another…" he looked at his com-pad, "forty-two minutes. I thought we had plenty of time for a decent breakfast."

"You thought?" Jake began to flare.

"Captain Marcos is right," Ash said, defusing some of the tension. "Colonel, why don't you sit down and finish your coffee? We've plenty of time, and you have to admit, it will be a lot easier to search the area in daylight."

Everyone settled back down onto the benches, but unease crept over the group.

"Do you think they have Chocamel ice-cream back there?" I asked to break the silence.

"For breakfast? What is it with you and the ice-cream, Babe?" Jake said.

"It's an addiction."

"Maybe you need an intervention," Ty suggested.

"Maybe you're right. Still, there are worse things to be addicted to."

"True," decided Connor. "Hey, Ty? Do you remember that Other you got with on—"

"Leave it!" Ty waved his fork in warning.

"You know, the one who could bend herself in—"

The rest of Connor's sentence was muffled as Ty

launched himself across the table and held him in a headlock. I heard something about 'addiction' and 'positions', but that was about it.

They wrestled energetically, and I moved sideways along the bench to avoid getting caught up in it. Jared closed a protective arm around me, pushing them away when they got to close.

That's when Jake decided enough was enough. "Stop," was all he had to say to break the two men apart. I thought they'd be mad at each other, but they were laughing. "You can let her go now," he added.

I hadn't realised Jared still had his arm around me. "My hero," I joked, pulling myself up straight.

"Always," he replied as Jake gagged. They glared at each other across the table and I noticed the Wolfpack watching keenly, almost hoping for some kind of action.

"Time to go, I think," Ash said, picking up on the tension.

"I agree," replied Jake, standing. "Con, ready the *Veritas*."

"Already prepped and good to go," Connor replied.

"Outstanding. Well, Captain, guess we'll see you when we get back."

"Not this time." Jared also stood. "I'm coming too."

"We don't need you," Jake replied bluntly. "Between Brother Asher, Shae, and my team, we have enough manpower for a search."

"Actually, it's not such a bad idea," said Ash. "Another set of eyes wouldn't hurt."

"It's settled then." I smiled happily. "We all go."

Connor barely waited for Kaiser to close the hatch before he took off and burned out of the hangar.

"There's a speed limit inside the ship for a reason," Jared said, making no effort to hide his irritation.

Ty and Kaiser disappeared to the lower cargo hold while

Jared and Ash sat in the corner of the cabin talking about serious stuff, judging by the look on their faces. I took apart my Sentinel, placing each part neatly on the table before starting to clean it. I was so engrossed I didn't notice Jake until he sat down beside me. My stomach flipped, just as it always did when he was near.

He shifted position so his leg touched mine, and he rested his elbow on the back of the seat, his forearm pressing gently against my shoulder.

"It drives me crazy that I can't kiss you right now," he whispered, gently rubbing my shoulder with his forearm. I tried to keep my wits about me, but his touch was all my body needed to remember what had come before. I found myself unconsciously leaning towards him, my chin raised slightly towards his lips, before I realised what I was doing. I pulled away, nervously looking around. He sighed and removed his arm from the back of my chair.

"So what's the deal with you and Captain Charisma?" he asked unexpectedly.

"What do you mean?"

"I mean one minute you're so mad at him you don't even want to hear his name mentioned, the next you're having cosy late night beers with him – wearing nothing more than a bathrobe."

I thought about it for a moment. "Honestly, I don't know – I'm not really sure I understand it either. After all the shit he's done…" I trailed off because I didn't have an answer, and because I felt bad that some of the sparkle had left Jake's green-flecked eyes. "I do try to stay mad at him, but even after everything he's done... I like him."

"Better than you like me?"

"Are you jealous?" I teased.

"Damn right I'm jealous. You've no idea how much I want to lean over and kiss you, to touch you, to hold you in my arms. I'm using all my willpower to stop myself from dragging you into the weapons locker so we can pick up where we left off yesterday... but I won't, because I know you need to concentrate on this investigation. And I respect you for that, by way. Yet he gets to put his arm around you whenever he wants. He gets to be your hero. When Marcos touches you, I want to punch him in the face – really, really hard. But you… you don't seem to think anything of it."

"Jake, look at me," I said as he started to turn away. "I don't know how I feel about Jared... but it wasn't him I was with on the training room floor yesterday. It wasn't Jared I was thinking about in the shower last night – it wasn't his kiss I remembered, or his touch, it was yours."

"Really?"

"I wouldn't have said it otherwise."

"No, I mean were you really thinking about me in the shower last night?" His eyes sparkled playfully as I nodded. "Because I was thinking about you taking a shower last night." I blushed fiercely.

"Colonel?" Ash said and I looked up, wondering how much he'd heard. "Connor wishes to speak to you."

Jake cleared his throat and stood. "We'll finish this discussion later," he said before loping off towards the flight deck.

It was my first visit to the Planet of Souls, but I wasn't in a hurry to get there. The thought of an entire planet just for dead people weirded me out a little, maybe more than a little, and the hard, bumpy landing jangled my already on-edge nerves. I cursed Connor under my breath.

"Sorry about that, guys," he said over the intercom. "The ship's instruments are a little temperamental at the moment."

I descended the *Veritas'* ramp but hesitated at the bottom, reluctant to take that last step onto land, but then Kaiser gave me a shove and I didn't have a choice. I scowled at him but he just smiled and shrugged.

I took a quick look around while I waited for the others

to sort themselves out. I guess the burial plots had started out in some kind of order, but years of adding new graves, and the gentle shifting of the earth, meant they looked disorganised and untidy. Huge ornate mausoleums sat next to smaller tombs, and some graves had nothing more than simple, stone markers.

You could tell that at one time the graves had been maintained, probably by families grieving for their loved ones, but we were in an older part of the cemetery, and those relatives were probably long gone themselves. I tried to read some of the stones, but names and messages were mostly unreadable. Headstones had fallen, or were covered in weeds, and mausoleums were cracked and crumbling.

The monuments left to the dead were dying themselves, and I shuddered in the cool of the early morning.

Some of the tombstones and mausoleums were bathed in a pale orange glow, while others remained in cold shadow. A grey mist clung to the ground and it swirled ominously around my ankles, waiting to be burned off by the heat of the day.

To say the place smelled of death would've been contrived, but it did smell. The vegetation, doing its best to reclaim the planet, gave off a damp, rotting stench, and I tried to remember to breathe through my mouth.

We'd assembled around a tomb at the base of the *Veritas'* ramp, when Connor appeared at the top, his blond hair shining in the morning sun. "Just to let you know, the ion particles in the atmosphere are playing shit with the ship's sensors and communications," he explained.

"Perhaps that's why Nyan managed to get so close to our mystery party without the *Hawkhurst's* sensors picking him up," suggested Ash.

"Makes sense," said Jake. "Okay everyone, coms-check." Sound quality wasn't great, but at least they worked. "Con, stay with the *Veritas* – see if you can do anything about those sensors."

"On it," Connor said, disappearing back into the belly of the ship.

Ty placed a holo-pad on the tomb, a map of the area floating above it. It flickered sporadically with interference.

"This is where we are now," he pointed to a small cluster of dots, "and this is where the mausoleum is." He pointed about four miles away on the map. "Where we're standing is the only logical place the *Hawkhurst* could've landed, but there are countless routes they could've taken to get to the meeting site... I believe these are the most likely, though." He tapped the holo-display and three directions lit up.

"If it's agreeable with you, Colonel," Ash said, taking the lead, "I suggest we split into pairs and follow the three paths to the mausoleum. We'll rendezvous there and agree our next steps." Jake nodded. "Good. Shae, you and Kaiser take the green path." I took the mini data-pad out of my trouser pocket and uploaded the map. "Colonel, you and I'll take the red, leaving Captain Marcos and Ty with the blue."

"Con," Jake said, tapping his earpiece. "We're heading out in pairs. If you get a hit on anything out of the ordinary from the sensors, direct the nearest pair to investigate." He listened for a bit. "Okay, keep me informed. Jake out." He turned back to us. "Connor says he's doing his best to boost the sensor signal, but be prepared for communication blackouts. Let's go; stay safe."

Kaiser and I headed out on our designated route, but the path was more perilous than I expected. A thin layer of mist still covered the ground, hiding fallen tombstones and plant roots, and Kaiser mocked my inability to stay upright. I got my own back, though, when he slid on a patch of slimy weeds and ended up on his arse.

"You okay?" I asked, trying not to laugh. He ignored me. "You sure you don't need a hand?"

"No," he grunted. "What? You think this is funny?"

"A little."

He wiped the slime from his trousers. "What about now?" he said, flicking it in my direction, a playful grin lightening his craggy face.

"Hey! Watch it! Okay, truce, yeah?"

"Truce," he agreed, holding out a hand to help me over a gravestone.

"So, how long have you been with the Wolfpack?" I asked, changing the subject.

He studied me silently, as if deciding whether to answer or not. "Four years, give or take," he said eventually. "Jake recruited me – then together we recruited Ty, and later, Connor."

"Why did he pick you? Oh, I'm sorry, that sounded rude. I didn't mean to imply that… I was genuinely interested. I hope I didn't cause offence?"

"None taken. Honestly, I don't know. At the time, I was on a spiralling road to hell, or the stockade. One or the other. I never fitted my old unit – always considered the rebel or troublemaker for not just accepting shit orders. My CO was a useless fucking retard, umm, pardon my language." He shrugged apologetically. "His incompetence got good people killed, and I felt it was my duty to tell him just how inept he was – with my fist." He smiled, a brief look of satisfaction crossing his weathered face. "Anyway, the bastard wrote me up and I was heading for a court-martial when Jake offered me a place in the Wolfpack. A second chance. I was sceptical at first but Jake's a do-right leader, even Ty and Connor aren't that bad when you get to know them. Best decision I ever made."

I was about to ask another question when I heard Connor through the static in my earpiece. "Sensors are picking up a metal object about seven metres from your current location. Follow my directions." We did, but it turned out to be a tarnished silver flower bowl left by one of the graves. "Sorry guys, I'll keep looking," he said.

"You call Jake, 'Jake'," I said to Kaiser as we continued

on our original route.

"So do you."

"He's not my CO."

"True. None of us in the Wolfpack use our ranks. Less likely they'll slip out when we're undercover and get one of us killed – particularly Jake. He's not hung up on titles anyway. He's a good guy. You should know… wait, I'm picking something up." He studied a hand-held sensor.

"What is it?"

"Traces of plasma fire and bullets." We walked on a bit further. "Look at this." He pointed to a headstone with a chunk out of the corner. "Fits with what your man said about them chasing him. Problem is the plasma residue and bullet fragments are showing as general issue, sold on tens of worlds. There's nothing specific enough to tie down where the weapons came from." I was disappointed, but not surprised.

Ash and Jake were already at Barrington-Huntley's mausoleum when we got there. Jared and Ty arrived just after we did.

"Anything other than the generic evidence of a gunfight?" asked Ash.

"Nope, just an old flower bowl," replied Kaiser. "You?"

"A beer bottle and a walking stick."

"Only thing we got was an ancient trombone," added Ty.

My earpiece crackled and I heard Connor's voice, but interference was significantly worse and I could only pick up the odd word.

Ash gathered us around. "This is where Nyan first said he heard voices, and that they came from the south. That's supported by the fact that the weapon's fire is all directed from south to north." He indicated directionality with his arm. "I'm amazed Nyan got out alive given all the firepower they threw at him."

"Agreed," said Jared. "Looks like a small war's been

fought here."

"Hey," said Ty suddenly, looking up at the inscription on the mausoleum. "This guy's name reminds me of Bartington Huntley."

"Who?" Kaiser asked.

"The Sky Orb player for the Tamon Tigers," I replied.

"I'm impressed," said Ty.

"Don't be. I didn't have a clue who he was until Nyan told me." It didn't seem to matter; I'd gone up a notch in Ty's estimation.

"Are you three done?" asked Jake. "Can we get back to business?" We nodded. "Thank you. I suggest we form a search line, moving southwards, and pray we come across something. I know coms are hinky, but keep an open channel."

Kaiser took the left flank, I took position about five metres from him, Ash was five metres from me, then Jake, Jared, and finally Ty out on the right. We walked slowly, painstakingly checking our areas before moving on. The ground-fog had finally lost its vice-like grip, burned away by the heat of the sun, so I could see the soil and vegetation beneath my feet. I think I preferred it when I couldn't.

"Something definitely happened here," said Ty when we reached an open area. Although he was at the opposite end of the line, I could just about hear him through the open com-link.

"I agree," said Ash. "The vegetation's been disturbed relatively recently, and by the size of the area, I'd say there were quite a few people here. Look sharp everyone; let's see if they left us anything useful."

We followed a grid pattern and I redoubled my concentration.

"Got something," yelled Kaiser, clearly forgetting the open com-link and nearly blowing my eardrum in the process.

"Everyone stay in your grid," said Jake. "Kaiser, what

you got? And Kaiser? No need to shout it."

"Sorry, Boss. Looks like a brooch or badge or something." He knelt down, looking closely at whatever it was on the ground. He flipped it over with the point of his knife. "It's a pin – like those bloody politicians and royal officials wear. Looks new."

"Bag it up, but don't touch it. We might be able to get some useful biologicals from it," Jake said.

"Will do."

We continued forward until all evidence that something had happened was clearly to our rear. We'd turned to do one last sweep when I thought I heard Connor over coms again, but I wasn't sure – it could've just been static.

"Did anyone—" I started.

"Quiet! Did you hear that?" said Ty.

"I think I heard Conner," I said.

"No, not on coms. Something... closer."

"I didn't hear anything," said Kaiser. "You need your ears checked again, Ty."

"No wait, I heard something, too… Look out!" Jared yelled.

In the split second it took me to look sideways, he'd tackled Jake to the ground, and a bullet shattered the stone wall just behind where he'd been standing. The open com-link between the team cut out completely.

I threw myself behind a tomb, pulling my Sentinel out of its holster as bullets ricocheted off stone around me. I heard Ash, Jake, and Jared all yelling jumbled orders, and decided we really needed to sort out the whole leadership issue before it got one of us killed.

Kaiser was tucked precariously behind a gravestone, quickly breaking up under a hail of bullets. It wouldn't protect him much longer.

"I count eight, maybe nine," I shouted over the gunfire, before leaning around the side of the tomb to take out an Other with a shot to the head. "Make that seven, maybe eight," I corrected, ducking to avoid flying stone chips. "Kaiser, you can't stay there. I'll cover you. Get somewhere safer." He nodded his understanding.

I popped the caps off a couple of stun grenades, pressed the buttons, and counted five seconds before lobbing them. Kaiser bolted from behind the headstone and disappeared off to the side, silently flanking the hostiles. When he made his move, so did I. We worked well together, managing to take out the few remaining targets in our sector with little trouble, but gunfire to the left told me the others were still engaged.

Ash was pinned down, taking heavy fire, and I headed towards him. I hadn't got half way when someone shouted, "Grenade!"

Before I could react, the blast wave flung me backwards through the air until I hit the side of a mausoleum. My head whipped back, cracking against the brick, and a white-hot pain shot through every nerve in my body. I only knew I'd fallen to the ground because I felt damp vegetation on my face – then I couldn't feel anything at all except the lightening pain in my head. I thought I was going to vomit, and when I couldn't bear the pain anymore, blackness descended.

I tried to open my eyes but they refused, as if my eyelids belonged to someone else. I heard voices, urgent, fearful, but it was like listening to a conversation under water.

I concentrated hard through the torturous throbbing in my head, eventually feeling my eyelids flutter. My eyes half opened but it took a while to focus, and even longer to realise I was on the *Veritas*. Jake and Jared were at my side, both covered in so much blood, and I tried to reach out but my body was unresponsive. I wanted to say something, to ask if they were okay, but my head hurt so much I lost my battle against the darkness.

The next time I managed to claw my way back to consciousness, I felt sick from being in motion. I forced my eyes open, recognising one of the homogeneous, pristine corridors of the *Defender*. The bright lights burned, and my head hurt so bad it felt like my brain was trying to claw its way out of my skull.

Jared and Jake were still by my side, but I didn't know who the other men were, Med-techs probably, and it didn't take a genius to work out we were heading for Med-bay. When they realised I was conscious, everyone spoke at the same time, and I was relieved that my hearing was a little better.

"Don't move, Babe."

"We're nearly there."

"Hold on, Shae."

"Everything will be okay."

"You'll be all right."

"Does she look bluish to you?" asked one of the men I didn't know. Thankfully, the others ignored him.

Through the killer pain in my head, I remembered blood-soaked clothes, and was filled with panic. I tried to speak, but before I could, the swirling blackness snuck up on me.

I was conscious again. I wasn't on the move anymore, but I felt movement around me, and I heard voices and medical equipment bleeping. My head wasn't as bad as before, but I was exhausted, and couldn't even summon up the effort to open my eyes.

I knew Jake and Jared were close because I could hear them whispering, though I couldn't tell what they were saying. Then a woman's voice joined the conversation.

"Nurse Julo, please give our patient a shot of Frotine," she said with a broad Earth accent.

"Yes, Doctor," replied another woman I presumed was Nurse Julo.

"What? Why? You can't!" said Jared, clearly anxious.

"Captain," the doctor said carefully, "there's no reason to keep the patient's body medically immobilised any longer."

"No reason? Did you look at the same scans we did?" Jake said, his voice drained but angry.

The doctor overlooked his tone, and in contrast kept hers even and calm, soothing almost. "About that, Captain… look at this," she said, a note of confusion creeping in. "This is the scan you took of the patient—"

"Shae," interrupted Jared.

"Yes, Captain, of course. This is the scan you took of Shae on the *Veritas*. The one you sent to us before you got here. Is that correct?"

There was a moment's silence. "Yes," Jared concurred.

"These lines here, here, and here, show where the patient's… sorry, Shae's neck was shattered during the explosion."

I shouldn't have been, but I was quite impressed – I'd never had a broken neck before.

"We've seen these already, Doctor. What's your point?" Jared's voice was harsh.

"Please, bear with me. In addition to the neck injuries, these spider-lines show multiple skull fractures, and this dark patch indicates an extensive brain haemorrhage." That would certainly explain the pain in my head. "Can I ask… who bandaged her head?"

"I did," Jake replied. "But what the hell's that got to do with anything?"

"It was an impressive field-dressing… but it's not who bandaged her head so much as why?"

"This is bloody ridiculous," Jake snorted. "You're making no sense, and you're wasting time asking us stupid questions when you should be treating her."

"Please, you'll understand in a minute. Why did you bandage Shae's head?"

"Fine," he huffed. "But isn't it obvious? I bandaged her head because she was bleeding, a lot, and I had to stem the blood."

"I see." The confusion in the doctor's voice increased. "I hope you don't mind, Colonel, but I sent one of our engineers to check the medical scanners on your ship – to make sure they're accurate – and they are; one hundred percent."

"Doctor, even I'm beginning to lose patience." Jared sighed wearily. "Where's this going?"

"I'm getting to the point."

"I suggest you get there quicker."

"Yes, sir." Her voice wavered slightly. "Take a look at this next scan. What do you see?"

"I'm not a doctor, but… a small brain haemorrhage maybe," said Jared. "Whose is this?"

"It's Shae's latest scan," the doctor said. Busted! There was no way I was keeping my gift a secret after that.

"Is this some kind of joke? What's going on?"

"That's just it, Captain. I've no idea what's going on. And I can assure you it's no joke. We've run the scan three times, and every single one has come back the same. No broken neck, no skull fractures, and no head laceration that would explain where the blood you're all covered in came from – even though tests conclusively prove it's hers. Take a look at her if you don't believe me."

A moment later, I heard a curtain being pulled back, then felt someone gently touch the side of my head.

"When we removed the bloody field dressing you put on, Colonel, we expected the worst, but there was nothing there," the doctor explained. "The new scans show a small amount of bleeding on the brain, but nothing like your original scan. I'm at a loss to explain it."

I felt a hand brush over my upper left arm where I'd been stabbed at Angel Ridge, and knew it was Jared. He lifted my arm to look at the back and I found it difficult to keep my eyes shut. Perhaps I should've just opened them and dealt with the consequences, but I was wiped out, and my head still felt like it'd been drilled into.

"What are you looking for?" asked the doctor.

"She was stabbed."

"No, she wasn't – are you sure you're not the one with brain damage?" Jake said rudely.

"She was stabbed two days ago on Angel Ridge. Right here." He stroked my arm gently. "Now there's nothing. No scar, no mark; nothing."

"You must've imagined it."

"Jake, I was as close to her as you and I are now, and I'm telling you, she had a knife straight through her arm. It went in here, and came out here."

The cat was well and truly out of the bag. Part of me was relieved, but I knew that Ash would be…

"Ash!" My voice was harsh and my throat stung. I sat up quickly, swaying as my head objected to the sudden movement. The bright lights of Med-bay burned and I blinked furiously.

"Keep her still," yelled the doctor urgently. Jared, who was closest, pressed me back down onto the bed by my shoulders.

"Where's Ash?" I cried. Why wasn't he with me? And why wasn't anyone answering my question? I tried to fight against Jared, but Jake pinned my other side to the mattress. "Where's Ash, Jared?"

"Shae, he's…"

"Jared, tell me." I fought to sit up, but they were too strong. "Is he alive?" They shared a glance. "Is he alive?" I repeated.

"For now," Jared said reluctantly. "But it's not good, Shae. They don't think he's—"

"No!" I cried. "I can help him. Let… me… go."

"Nurse, hand me a sedative stat," the doctor said. "Keep her still. She needs to stay calm."

I couldn't let them sedate me. I had to help Ash.

I brought my leg up to knee Jared in the ribs in the hopes that he would release me, but he removed his hand from my wrist and pinned my leg back to the bed. Once my arm was free, I was able to grab the Sentinel from the holster on his thigh and press it to his chest.

"Back off," I demanded. "You, too, Jake."

"Shae, you're not thinking straight. Put the gun down, Babe," Jake urged.

"I'm sorry, really I am, but I need to see Ash. And I'll do whatever it takes. Whatever it takes. Please, Jared, I can save him." The weapon was heavy in my hands, and I didn't want to, but I forced myself to point it at him. "Please…"

He backed away and directed Jake to do the same. A couple of security officers burst into Med-bay, weapons raised, but he told them to stand down.

Pain shot through my head when I slid off the side of the bed, and I staggered, on the verge of vomiting. Jake took a step towards me, but I swung the gun towards him. He retreated, holding his arms up.

"Where is he?" I asked through bouts of nausea. "Where's Ash?"

"There." The doctor pointed to a large rectangular window in the wall towards the far end of the room. It was weird, I hadn't noticed it before. The window was brightly illuminated and I shuffled my way along the ward, holding on to things to steady myself. When I got nearer, I saw it was a viewing area for an operating theatre.

I looked through the glass, frozen to the core by the amount of blood on their scrubs and on the floor, but instead of fixing Ash, the medical staff just stood there, looking at him. My heart stopped.

"You can't be in here," gasped Doc, momentarily thrown by my appearance, but he stepped back when I pointed the Sentinel at him.

"Is he alive?" I demanded, tears hot on my cheeks.

"I'm sorry, we've done everything we can."

"Does he have a pulse? Right now? Does he have a pulse?"

Doc looked confused. "Yes… but it's being artificially maintained. Shae, his injuries were—"

"You don't understand. It might be enough… it has to be enough," I mumbled. "Get out." I waved the gun indiscriminately at the staff. "Get out now." Doc ushered them towards the exit. "Quicker. Out!"

I shut the door behind them and stood by Ash's side. He was a mess, I was a mess, but I had to pull it together. For him.

I looked up and saw a sea of faces watching through the glass, and realised there was no putting the genie back in the bottle after what I'd done. I put the Sentinel down on one of the side tables and tried to focus, but my head pounded. I tried to clear my thoughts, but all I could think about was the thud, thud, thud of my brain against my skull.

I glanced back to the window and saw Jared watching me, one hand pressed against the glass. My breathing calmed and I took a deep breath, trying to banish the pain long enough to clear my mind.

I placed one hand over Ash's open chest, the other just above his stomach, and was relieved when I felt the tickly, tingling sensation in the pit of my tummy. It was faint, but it relaxed me enough to concentrate, and the feeling began to spread. As soon as I'd connected with him, I knew he was bad, but the fact I had connected with him told me it wasn't too late – I could still save him.

My skin shimmered with a silver-blue glow, just as it had when I'd healed Harrison. A pale sparkle pulsed down my arms, collecting at my hands briefly before whisper-thin strands of energy arced to Ash. He began to glisten under my fingers, and then the glow radiated out until it covered his entire body. I didn't dare look up – I didn't want to see the faces of those who were watching.

The room bathed in the silver-blue shimmer radiating from the pair of us, and the more I concentrated, the brighter the glow became. Strands of crackling energy reflected off metal instruments, creating dancing patterns of light on the walls.

I focused everything I had on Ash, but I was already weak from healing myself. His body vibrated, and I could feel life being drawn back into him, but I was so tired. I kept telling myself over and over again that I only had to hang on a little bit longer, but the light in the room waned.

I hung on to the connection by my fingertips, using every last ounce of strength to heal him. Eventually I had absolutely nothing left to give and pulled my hands away. The last of the fading light vanished.

That's when I died.

# 13

At least, that's when I died according to Doc Anderson.

I woke up in Med-bay. It smelled clean and antiseptic, but the normal harsh, white light had been replaced by the warm glow of a single lamp angled off the wall behind my head. I closed my eyes and evaluated my condition: my head was no worse than after a night on the beers, and I could feel everything else was how and where it was supposed to be – but I was exhausted.

Ash sat by the side of my bed with his eyes closed, holding one of my hands gently in his own, our fingers intertwined. Our hands were raised to his face and he was saying a silent prayer – I felt his lips moving against my skin.

"You know that tickles?" I said and he opened his eyes. A lopsided grin spread across his face but he looked drained. "Ash, are you all right? Did I not heal you enough?"

"Hush," he said gently, looking nervously at the heavy white curtain pulled around the bed. "Everyone thinks you're still unconscious; let's leave it that way for the moment. The last thing you need is them all rushing in asking questions."

I looked at him carefully, the dark circles under his eyes prominent against pale skin. He stroked my hand softly. "You haven't answered my question," I said, trying to sit, but then gave up and settled my head back on the pillow.

"Shae, I'm fine. You did well. Don't even think about me – concentrate on yourself. You… you scared me."

"I scared you?" I cried, then tried to take it back by covering my mouth with my free hand. We both froze for a second, listening, watching the curtain, but after a moment of nothing happening, we relaxed. "I was so frightened I wouldn't be able to save you this time. They tried to stop me. I had to… Oh no! I had to—"

"I know what you did, Shae. Captain Marcos told me everything."

"Is he angry? I bet he's mad, isn't he? I wouldn't blame him. I—"

"Don't worry about the Captain." Ash smiled, picking up my hand again. "You need to relax. I mean it." He had his serious face on. "Healing yourself, then me… I was worried you'd pushed it too far, that you weren't going to come back to me." He looked sad as he kissed the back of my hand. "Doc says you clinically died. Twice. Don't ever do that to me again, do you understand? I don't know what I'd do without you."

"I know how you feel," I said quietly, tugging at the high neck of the pale green medical gown. Crisp, white sheets were pulled tight across my chest and I felt pinned down, trapped. The sound of distant conversations drifted in from the other side of the curtains. "Was it really that close?" I asked.

"Yes." His eyes glistened as he spoke and I got a heart-breaking hit of anguish through the Link.

"How long was I out?"

"Too long."

"I'm sorry. If it makes you feel better, my head doesn't

hurt anymore... well, not much. I'm just exhausted. You know how I get after a tough heal."

"I do. Tired and hungry... and irritable." He forced a grin and I appreciated the effort.

I yawned and stretched, but then a thought turned my skin ice-cold. "What happened to the Wolfpack? To Kaiser and Ty? I haven't seen either of them. What happened on the planet? What—"

"Hush," Ash soothed again. "Everyone's safe. That's all you need to think about right now. You need to rest, why don't you go back to sleep?"

"I would if there wasn't all that noise. What is going on out there?"

"The Colonel and Captain wanted to sit with you, but I persuaded Doc that it would be less stressful on you if only I was present. I don't think he expects you to make it – he said keeping a monk close would probably be prudent."

"Some people have so little faith," I quipped.

"I know. Crazy isn't it?" he joked back, and I saw some light return to his pale, grey eyes. "Anyway, I'm fairly sure they're still arguing over whether they can come in."

"What have you told them about… about what I can do?"

"Nothing."

"Really?"

"I thought it would be better if we told everyone together, the both of us. Get it over and done with in one hit."

"Do you think they might just forget it happened?" I knew it was wishful thinking.

"No." He gave me one of his 'are you kidding me?' frowns he was so practiced at.

"You didn't answer when I asked if Jared was angry with me. I'd be pretty mad if someone took my gun and then threatened me with it."

"I think he's more annoyed he allowed you to get his

weapon, but under the circumstances, he understands. I don't think he'd be very happy if you did it again though."

I stifled a yawn but my eyelids felt heavy. "Ash?"

"Hmm?"

"I'd sleep better in my quarters."

"I'm not sure you're strong enough—"

"Please." I said it like I did when we were kids – when I tried to get him to do something he knew he shouldn't. I also gave the corresponding look – for good measure.

He thought for a second. "All right. Nobody really sleeps well in Med-bay anyway. Can you stand?"

"Yes, but how am I going to get past everyone?"

"I'll distract them. They think you're at death's door so they're not exactly expecting you to get up and walk out." I removed the covers with difficulty and stood. I felt tired and light headed, but on the whole, better than expected. Ash looked unconvinced. "Are you sure you're okay?"

"I'm fine. Trust me. I can make it if it means getting out of here. I'll drag myself along the floor if that's what it takes." Fortunately, Ash was used to my flare for the dramatic.

"Here, put this on," he said, passing me his jacket. It was warm and smelled of him.

"Okay, it's now or never. Go. Be a diversion. I'll see you back at my quarters."

Ash kissed my cheek, his lips brushing my skin as if to kiss me any harder would break me.

I peeked around the side of the curtain and watched him draw everyone into a conversation on the far side of the room. Jake and Jared were there, still arguing with Doc, and a wave of relief washed over me. They were both well and unbroken.

I slipped around the curtain and headed for the main door, my bare feet silent on the cold, sterile floor. I made it the short distance to the lift without meeting anyone, but when it arrived it was occupied by two crewmembers, deep in conversation until they saw me. They studied me with narrowed eyes but I simply smiled and said, "Hello," as if it was perfectly natural for a strange girl in a medical gown to be wandering the ship. After a moment, they returned my smile and carried on their conversation.

I rested against the wall because the simple task of standing had become a challenge.

The last hallway to my quarters was an endurance test. I recalled what I'd said to Ash about dragging myself along the floor if I had to, and thought it ironic that it might come to that. The only thing stopping me from curling up on the hallway carpet, was the thought of that ridiculously large, comfortable bed only a few metres away.

I walked in the door, passed through the lounge without stopping, and literally fell on the bed, only waking when Ash picked me up to put me under the covers. He pulled up the sheets and kissed me on my forehead.

"Go back to sleep," he whispered.

"I made it without being seen," I replied sleepily.

"Actually, you were spotted leaving Med-bay. It took all my powers of persuasion to stop them coming after you. I would've been here sooner otherwise." He started to walk away.

"Wait—"

"Sleep," he ordered, looking back over his shoulder.

"Will you stay?"

"I'll be right out there on the couch."

"Don't be an idiot," I said, pulling back the covers on the other side of the bed.

"Someone won't be pleased with us sharing."

"Jake will have to get over it. It's not like we haven't done it a hundred times before."

"I wasn't thinking of Colonel Mitchell." Ash slid in, fully dressed. "Now will you sleep?"

"Yes," I said dreamily. I snuggled up against him, my head on his chest, and my arm across his tummy. I listened to his soft, rhythmic breathing, and the gentle beating of his heart – his chest rose and fell in symmetry with mine, and I felt his arm close around my shoulders.

I don't know what time I fell asleep, early evening perhaps, but I woke at just gone zero-eight-hundred. I was lying in exactly the same position, and Ash was still fast asleep – his breathing slow and steady, his face peaceful and beautiful. I wanted to stay there in his arms, but I had an urgent need to pee. I unfolded myself, careful not to wake him, and headed for the bathroom. I took a shower while I was there, turning up the water temperature to as hot as I could stand it. I stood under the massaging jets for ages, my body heating to the core.

I felt good – no, I felt really good... and starving. My head was clear, my joints were free and loose, and through the rumbling, a comforting warmth pooled in the pit of my stomach. I finished washing and stepped out of the shower, wrapping a large towel around me. After wiping the condensation from the mirror above the sink, I looked at myself closely. My skin was pale, as it always was, but it had a radiance I hadn't seen for a while. My hazel eyes were clear, and the colour was true. I couldn't believe how healthy I felt.

I put on my robe and went back into the bedroom where Ash was starting to stir. I jumped on the bed right next to him, bouncing him awake like I used to when we were kids, only the beds weren't quite so soft back then. He groaned and half opened his eyes.

"Morning," he mumbled, pulling back the covers and swinging his legs over the side of the bed. He rubbed his head and then his eyes.

"Are you sure you're okay?" I asked, still bouncing gently on the bed.

"I'm really all right... but clearly not as good as you." He frowned. "How do you feel?"

"I feel great." I got off the bed.

"You look great. Death suits you… just don't do it again," he added hastily, as if he'd given me some kind of idea. "What time is it?"

"Nearly zero-eight-thirty."

He groaned again, shaking the last bit of sleep from his head. "To stop the others taking off after you last night, I had to promise we would meet them this morning to tell them everything. You okay with that?"

"Guess I have to be." I shrugged. "As long as there's breakfast."

"There is. I made it a condition."

"You know me so well."

"After the interrogation's finished, the Captain wants to bring in the Wolfpack and debrief everything else that happened yesterday. Oh, and the quartermaster was kind enough to provide us with new clothes." He pointed to a pile of black, Fleet-issue fatigues. "Man, I need a shower. Mind if I use yours?" he said before striding into the bathroom. After a moment, I heard the water running.

A bit later Ash returned to the bedroom, dripping water on the carpet.

"Have you seen my boots?" I asked.

"Over there," he replied, pointing towards the bureaux. I was too scared to look. "They're fine." He sighed. "You've got to get over your weird boot superstition at some point – they're going to wear out eventually whether you like it or not."

"I know, but not right now. These boots have seen me through some shit. They're my lucky charms… as well as you, that is. You and my boots."

"I don't get it." He shook his head, grabbing his own fatigues.

We left my quarters and I headed in the direction of the Mess Hall, but Ash corrected my course, telling me we were meeting the others in the conference room where our conversation would be more private. I might've imagined it, but as we walked, people seemed to pay more attention to us than they had previously. Small groups stopped what they were doing and broke into hushed conversation.

The door to the conference room slid open and I took a couple of steps in. Jared, Jake and Doc turned to look at me at exactly the same time, and there was silence for a second before all of them, without exception, started towards me, their questions merging into a confusing blur.

I did an abrupt about-face and walked straight out of the room.

I couldn't breathe or focus properly, but I heard Ash shouting – then he was beside me in the hallway, talking to me, calming me. My heart pounded and I was sweating; my hands shook, and I had a lump in my throat I couldn't swallow. I was dizzy and light headed, but through all of that I tried to concentrate on his voice. My one constant. Gradually I managed to get my breathing under control and the shaking calmed.

"I know you're scared – the Link, remember? But why?" he asked as we sat on the floor of the hallway, his arm around me, my head on his shoulder. He stroked my forehead lightly.

"What if they think I'm a freak?" I said, my voice trembling.

"What?" He laughed. "You're not a freak. You're not," he reiterated after he caught the look I gave him. I was mad he'd laughed and I pulled away from him. "I'm sorry, Shae, really I am, but you know you're not a freak. Please tell me you know that." Worry burned in his eyes.

"I know you and the Brotherhood don't think I am, but what if they do? What if the Brothers have just been too polite to tell me the truth all this time?"

"Now you listen to me." Ash measured his words. "You are not a freak – no matter what anyone else says. Do you hear me?" I looked away. "Do you hear me?" he repeated firmly. I nodded slowly.

"Can you brief them, Ash? I'll stay here... unless the bar's open. I could wait in the bar," I suggested hopefully.

"I don't think we'd get away with that. I think they'd actually hunt you down. Especially Doc, he thinks you're a medical miracle." He gave me his lopsided grin, which I usually couldn't resist.

"You do know that 'medical miracle' is code for freak, don't you?" I replied, but I couldn't help smiling back. Once again, he'd brought me back to reality. "Okay, let's get this over with, but please can you do most of the talking?" He agreed.

Whatever Ash had said – shouted – before he'd come out to me, must've worked. There was no sudden dash towards me, no cacophony of questions, just lots of smiles. I could cope with that.

Jared, who was closest, approached cautiously. Without saying a word, he drew me into a soft hug, and I relaxed against his chest. "It's good to see you looking better," he said quietly into my ear, and I noticed he smelled of sandalwood and musk – like he had in the bar the night we'd got drunk on the Fire Whisky. He lent back and kissed my forehead, his lips warm against my cool skin, but then he let me go, stepping out of the way.

Doc was next, but he didn't hug me. Maybe he thought he didn't know me well enough for that, but he did take one of my hands in both of his, and he beamed brightly as he squeezed it. He started to ask something, but Ash coughed loudly and he cut himself off, saying his questions could wait.

Then it was Jake's turn. He looked deeply into my eyes before brushing his fingers lightly across my cheek, as if he was checking I was really there – really alive. Then he hugged me. Not the careful hug Jared had given me, but an intense, emotional hug, and I couldn't help holding him just the same. He pulled back, but instead of releasing me, he raised his hand to my face again and traced my lips with his thumb before kissing me on the mouth. It wasn't a long kiss, but my heart fluttered and those embers started to heat up inside. As he released me, Jared and I made eye contact for the briefest of moments. I blushed and looked away.

There was a moment of awkwardness, then my stomach did the hugest rumble and the moment passed.

"Are you sure you're okay, Babe?" Jake asked.

"I'm fine. In fact, I'm better than fine." That particular fact still amazed me, but I wasn't going to complain. "Please, everyone, stop staring at me. You're creeping me out."

We sat around the table – us on one side, Jared, Jake and Doc on the other – and Ash took control, as promised, while I tucked into breakfast.

"We'll tell you everything we can, and then we'll try to answer your questions at the end," he said.

He told the story of a three-year-old girl who'd cracked her head open before miraculously healing in seconds, and who'd continued to spontaneously heal injuries and broken bones ever since. He told the story of two adventurous teens that'd got into difficulties rock climbing, and how the girl had mended someone else for the first time. He didn't go into details.

The assembled group were deadly silent, perhaps afraid to halt the flow of the story.

Ash explained about the energy transfer and the silver-blue shimmer as best he could, but as we didn't really understand it, that part of the story was particularly vague. He was able to tell them more about the Link, though, drawing on first-hand experience. He confirmed to Jared that he hadn't been imagining the knife in my arm, and that I had healed Harrison on Angel Ridge. Finally, Ash confessed that, even though the Brotherhood had been studying me since I was three, we were no closer to knowing why or how I could do the things I do. I frowned at him because that last bit made me sound like I was some kind of lab rat.

"And that's it. Over to you," he said with trepidation.

Silence.

I glanced at Jared, Jake, and finally Doc, unable to believe we'd stunned them in to silence. Finally, Jake spoke. "Well, I always knew you were special, Babe." He winked at me and I blushed.

"Who else outside the Brotherhood knows?" asked Doc.

"I could probably count the number on one hand," I replied. "Jared, I'm so sorry we kept you in the dark about Harrison. I hope you're not too mad." He looked stunned.

"Shae, Harrison would've died if you hadn't helped him. Why on Earth would you think I'd be mad at you? I'd give you a medal if I could."

"It feels liberating that you know. Do you realise how difficult it is to keep a secret like this? Well, I can tell you – it's hugely difficult. It's exhausting." The conversation was light, but a wave of panic washed over me again.

"Really?" Ash said, watching me keenly. The others looked baffled. "Surely you can't still think that?"

There was definitely a downside to being emotionally connected to someone. "Bloody stupid Link," I huffed.

"What's going on?" asked Doc. "Am I missing something?"

"I just got a hit from Shae – through the Link," Ash explained. Doc sat up straighter in his seat, eyes narrowing with concentration.

"Because you're physically close?" he asked.

"Yes. And because Shae healed me yesterday, the Link is…" he searched for the right word, "super-charged."

"It's also a super-pain-in-the-arse," I grumbled.

"So, what did you feel?" Doc pressed Ash.

"Stop! Is nothing private? If you must know, Ash can feel I'm scared – scared you all think I'm a freak," I said heatedly, annoyed I'd been put in that position, but the outcry of denial was so strong, I couldn't help but believe them. After that, it was like a dam had opened and a wave of questions followed.

"So what happened yesterday was quite normal?" Doc asked.

"Absolutely not!" Ash practically choked on the muffin he was eating. I'm not sure whether it was the choking, or the revelation that events had been uncharacteristic, but the atmosphere changed abruptly.

"Please explain," Jared said carefully, his attention drawn to me. All the concern and worry that'd been etched on his face at the beginning of breakfast was back.

Ash started to answer, but I put my hand on his arm to indicate that I would take the question.

"There are side effects to healing myself or someone else from serious wounds or life-threatening injuries. Usually those side effects are fatigue and hunger – like I need to recharge the energy in my batteries, or something like that." They seemed to follow my explanation so I pressed on. "Over the last few days, even before yesterday, I've done quite a bit of healing. The knife wound and Harrison on Angel Ridge, and then—"

"The cuts from the glass window at GalaxyBase4," Doc interrupted, comprehension finally dawning.

"Yes. A few broken ribs and probably some internal bleeding as well," I clarified. Doc was astonished.

"After the explosion, Shae had to heal herself from some horrific injuries," Ash said. "That would've been draining enough, but then she healed me as well. And that… that pushed her further than she's ever gone before." His voice was quiet by the time he finished, and I think everyone realised the gravity of the situation.

"So dying, twice… that's not normal?"

I don't know why Doc had to keep making a thing of the fact that I died at all, let alone twice. And what made him think dying even once was normal – even for me?

"No, it's not. It's the first time," Ash confirmed.

The silence in the room was deafening. Jared stood up and stretched his back out, and I could see his muscles working under his top. He started to pace.

"Still, on the upside… I'm okay, and Ash's okay, and neither of us got dead," I said cheerfully, trying to lighten the mood. "But there is one last thing I need to apologise for." Jared turned, raising an interested eyebrow. "I'm really sorry for taking your gun, Jared – and for pointing it at all of you, and your staff, Doc. Please accept my apologies, but I couldn't let you stop me from getting to Ash. I had to heal him while he still had a pulse. I hope you understand." It came out in a hurried jumble.

Jared didn't say anything for a moment, but then his lips parted into that boyish grin and he simply said, "Don't do it again."

I felt guilty because he still had the raw, cracked lip where I'd punched him back at the Dome, so I got up and took the few steps between us. I looked up into his dazzling blue eyes, momentarily disoriented before pulling myself together.

"Hold still," I said, touching his lip with the tips of my fingers. It was such a small injury there was no glistening or silver-blue light – just a tiny amount of tingling. Jared's lips parted, curling into a smile, and a second or two later, the split was gone. I ran my fingers over his cheek, and so were the wounds left over from the fight at Angel Ridge.

I noticed Jake watching carefully from the other side of the table. "Should you be doing that after everything you just said?" His voice was stilted, as if he was trying to stop himself from saying more. I gave him a reassuring smile.

"Easy peasy. Besides, you're next," I replied.

"Huh?"

"Come on, Jake. I saw Edge lamp you over the head with that metal case at the strip bar. I bet you haven't had anyone look at it." I prodded his skull a couple of times and he drew away.

"Hey! Easy, Babe, that hurts."

"As expected. Men!" I healed him in seconds. "I know you probably think I'm saying it to make everyone else feel better, but I really do feel good. It's bizarre really, but I actually feel better – healthier – today than I've done in a long time. Tell them, Ash."

A mischievous glint sparkled in Ash's eyes; one I'd seen many times before. "It's true. She was the one jumping on the bed to wake me up this morning. Then she moaned at me for dripping water on the floor when I got out of the shower. So I'd say she must be feeling okay." He got the reaction he was looking for from Jake and Jared. I don't think Doc understood what he was implying.

Before things got out of hand, I thought it best to get us back on point. "Anyway, that's it; there's no more we can tell you. You know pretty much what we do now."

Doc was convinced that, given enough time and tests, he would be able to get to the bottom of 'my condition' as he called it. I declined politely, but he didn't get the message until Jared dismissed him.

"I suggest we get back to business," Ash said, pouring himself a mug of coffee. I nodded as he waved the jug at me. "We missed quite a lot of yesterday given the, umm, circumstances."

Jared was staring through the window, looking out at the blackness, when I joined him. He shifted slightly at my arrival, but his gaze remained fixed somewhere in the distance. I wondered whether we were still orbiting the Planet of Souls, but somehow the star configuration didn't look right.

"I promise this is the last time I'll ask, but…" His voice was quiet and calm, but his knuckles were white where he gripped the polished wood railing. "Are you sure you're okay?" I placed a reassuring hand on his back, feeling tense, knotted muscles under his shirt. He turned his head slightly and he looked older.

"I'm fine, honestly."

"When I saw you lying there, I…" For a moment he looked stricken, but he cleared it away as we both turned to see the Wolfpack arrive.

Kaiser came in first, but he stopped abruptly when he saw Ash casually chatting to Jake. Ty and Connor, who were not far behind, walked straight into the back of him so that all three practically fell into the room. Connor called him all the names under the sun, until Kaiser pointed their attention to Ash.

"Morning, guys," I said cheerfully. Three faces turned abruptly towards me, then back to Ash, then to me again. It was almost farcical. "Coffee anyone?" I asked, holding up the pot. Not a single word.

Eventually Kaiser stepped forward. "I know Jake briefed us while you were recovering… but I didn't believe… not really." That broke the ice and Jake allowed them a few moments to pull themselves together before starting the brief.

When they finally accepted what'd happened, Connor said, "Do you know how much blood you two left in the *Veritas*? It took me ages to mop that shit up. If I'd known you were going to be all fixed up like this today, I'd have left it for you to clean." Kaiser kicked him in the shin. "Ow! What the…?"

"Brotherhood, Dude. Show some respect."

"Oh, yeah, umm, sorry – no offence meant."

"None taken," replied Ash. "But I suggest we get started."

"Hang on." I held up a hand. "You know the rule, Ash – no work until everyone's fixed. You first, Kaiser," I said, pointing at his broken nose and the massive bruise covering half his face. For a grown man, let alone a member of an elite Special Ops team, he was a complete baby, and when I raised my hand, he backed off a step. "It won't hurt, I promise – maybe it'll just tickle a little."

"Yeah, but—"

"Don't be such a girl," I teased. I think that did the trick because he stood still then. A pale, silver-blue light danced between my fingertips and his face, and when I moved my hand away, he was perfect. Well, back to normal, anyway. "How does that feel now?" I asked.

"Fuck me, that feels great," he replied, then grinned sheepishly. "Pardon my language." He was stunned. "Doesn't hurt a bit. What does it look like?" he asked Connor.

"Damn ugly – same as it always does." Connor poked at Kaiser's face until he swatted him off and went to look at his reflection in the window.

"Now you." I looked at Ty. "What happened?"

"He got shot in the arse," Kaiser called over from the window, laughing raucously.

Ty's face darkened and it looked like he was about to rage. "I did not get shot in the arse," he bellowed, starting towards Kaiser, but Connor put out a hand to restrain him. "I didn't," he clarified as I stifled a laugh.

"So what did happen?"

"A bullet ricocheted off one of those damn tombstones and caught me in the back of the leg."

"Arse," Kaiser corrected.

"Leg! Doc got it out. It's fine."

"Drop your trousers," I said, not thinking twice about it, but he was hesitant. "Come on Ty, it's not like I haven't seen men's legs before, and the healing works better over skin, not trousers." I caught him throw Jake a questioning look, so I pinned Jake with my own stare, folding my arms tightly across my chest, irritation clear on my pursed lips. I raised an eyebrow and sighed deeply, refusing to take my eyes of him. Eventually he nodded briefly at Ty, who slowly unbuttoned his trousers, drawing it out as if he was being forced to do it at gunpoint.

"Suck it up, Ty, we haven't got all day," I said. "Besides, from what I've heard, you're not exactly shy about getting naked."

# 14

With everyone mended and recovered from the shock of seeing Ash and me fully fit, we were able to get down to business. The first part of the debrief consisted of going over the events that led up to the ambush on the Planet of Souls. Connor started by half explaining, half apologising, for the sensors not picking up anyone else on the surface with us – but as we already knew, the ions in the atmosphere had played havoc with the equipment.

Each member of the team walked the group through their account of what'd happened during the fire fight. From what I could make out, our attackers were guns-for-hire from Angel Ridge. Most of them were killed in the fight, but the few that survived and been captured, had named a man called Polanski as their leader. They knew nothing other than it was he who'd recruited them back on the Ridge.

"Who hired Polanski?" Ash asked.

"Polanski was the idiot who threw the grenade that got you guys," said Kaiser. "The retard got caught by some stone and shrapnel from the blast – died before we could get anything from him. You ask me, anyone dumb enough to get killed by their own grenade must've been pretty simple to start with."

"So let me get this straight: all we know is a band of half-useless, guns-for-hire were recruited on Angel Ridge by a local man called Polanski... who's now dead and can't tell us who hired him?" I said.

"Sounds right," Jake confirmed. "You're really not very popular are you, Babe? I mean, what's this now… the fourth time in as many days someone's tried to kill you?" Jared scowled at him.

"To be fair," I said, "the first time really wasn't our fault – it was Jared's."

"Whoa, hang on a minute," Jared replied, his coffee poised halfway to his lips. "No, you're right, that was our fault," he clarified.

I mulled over whether it was worth trying to persuade Jake that Edge wasn't really trying to kill me either, he was simply trying to escape. After all, he'd shot at Jared, too. But Cady's office? That was different. The Agent of Death definitely wasn't trying to kill anyone – he was just destroying evidence. I put my case forward, and Jake was on the verge of agreeing with me, when Jared interrupted.

"Normally, I'd concur," he picked at a cold bacon sandwich, "but don't you think it's strange the building's computer detected the explosive device after you got to Cady?"

"Perhaps we tripped something when we got there?" suggested Connor.

"Not possible," Jake said. "Local security got there before us. If it was tripped on entry, they would've done it. That bomb wasn't armed until after we got there. It was meant for us."

"After yesterday's ambush, I'm inclined to agree, Colonel." Ash blew out a slow breath.

"Brother Asher, please call me Jake. It seems everyone else is." He glanced purposely at Jared.

"You can lose the Captain with me, too," Jared added,

raising his hand as if to identify himself.

"As you wish – as long as you call me Ash."

"Deal," agreed Jake. "So we all agree then: we've rattled a few cages over the last few days."

Ash looked deep in thought. "But how did they know we were going to be there?" he asked eventually.

"Where?" I replied.

"Take your pick: GalaxyBase4… Cady's office… the Planet of Souls…"

"Now you're asking the right questions," said Jake.

"We had the same conversation yesterday when you were…" Jared looked reluctant to finish his sentence, choosing to clear his throat instead. "Only the Wolfpack and the crew of this ship knew where we were going. I asked Ty, as an impartial communications expert, to check both our incoming and outgoing coms logs for the last few days. He discovered that Lieutenant Grainger had received several calls from her partner, Peter Sharman."

"I don't get it. What's that got to do with anything?" I asked.

"Sharman works as a mid-level Court Official in the House of Palavaria," Ty explained, but I was still blank.

"On its own, the information doesn't mean anything," Kaiser added. "But remember the pin I found yesterday? Biological tests confirmed it belonged to a man named George Black – who just happens to be a member of King Sebastian's personal staff. He also lives in the same domicile block as Sharman."

"So, you're suggesting the target of the assassination is King Sebastian?" Ash rubbed his hand over his mouth as Jared nodded.

"Sebastian rules over every Human colony, planet, and space habitation in Sector Three. By the very nature of his position, he's got his fair share of enemies," said Jared. "I know he's supported by hundreds of staff and officers, but two people linked to his administration can't be a coincidence."

"Sounds like a stretch to me," said Ash.

"Maybe," Jake agreed. "If we didn't have the evidence Shae collected for us."

"Me?" I said, surprised. Jake smiled and indicated towards Ty.

"Remember the pad you snagged from Cady's office?" Ty asked. "Well, it took some genius-level work on my part, but I managed to recover most of the information on the data-disc. Buried real deep, beneath a layer of wicked black-shadow encryption, was a set of financials. It's only because I'm so awesome that I managed to crack the code."

"Nobody likes a cocky bastard, Ty. Get to the point," said Jake.

"Yeah, well… as I was saying… fortunately Cady was thorough. He kept track of all payments he made to Edge, as well as some other equally shady characters, but more importantly, he logged where the incoming money came from. It was tough going, but I managed to follow the payments back through numerous shell-companies and ghost organisations, and, well, the upshot is the money came from a known ARRO source."

"Put palace staff together with money from the Anti-Royalist Rebel Opposition, and it's not so much of a stretch anymore," Jared said with a seriousness I'd not seen in him before – not even when we were being shot at on Angel Ridge.

"Someone of great importance," I said, and all eyes were on me. "Something massive. Something no one was ever going to forget. That's what Nyan said he heard." Cold goose bumps ran over my skin. "I know ARRO have shown they're not afraid to take lives, but there's a difference between blowing up a couple of consulates or ambushing REF patrols, and assassinating a ruling monarch."

"It's clear from increased activity and violence that

ARRO are mobilising across the Four Sectors," said Jared. "And as you said, they've already proved they can coordinate multiple cells to take out well-guarded, high-profile targets. With the right people on their side, I believe ARRO would target the King – or at least a member of the Royal Family. No doubt in my mind."

I sat back in my seat trying to take in the enormity. Maybe Jared was right about ARRO, but Grainger? That didn't fit at all. "What about the Lieutenant? I know I've only met her a couple of times, but she didn't seem like the terrorist type to me."

"We've interrogated her, and I don't believe she is either," Jared replied. "Naïve maybe, but not a terrorist. I think she was simply being used for information. I've put her in custody until we get to the bottom of things."

"I guess we need to speak to Black and Sharman then," I said, my brain still processing the information. "I'm sorry, of course you know that. I'm still catching up." I tried to smile but it was a lame attempt.

"You're right, we do need to speak to them, but as they're both members of the House of Palavaria, we can't interview either of them without express permission from a Senior House Official or member of the Royal Family," Jared explained.

"You've got to be joking," I said.

"Unfortunately, he's not," said Ash. "It's all to do with protecting the confidentiality of the House."

"We're in orbit around Decerra now, but even with our pull," Jared indicated between himself and Jake, "we can't get in to see anyone until eighteen-hundred this afternoon. They won't even give us authorisation to land a transporter before then. Apparently, they're all preparing for some big Royal event – they said we were lucky to get an appointment at all."

"Didn't you tell them about the threat to the King? About ARRO?" I asked, stunned that we had to wait seven hours to warn them.

"Hang on now, Babe," Jake said. "We can't just walk in to the Royal Court and start yelling assassination without proof. We'd be thrown out on our arses and our credibility would be shot."

"But you said we had proof."

"We have circumstantial evidence that ARRO may have sponsored an assassination plot. Nothing concrete – and certainly no proof that the target is anyone from the Royal Family. We need to tread carefully."

"This is absurd," I moaned pushing the plate in front of me away with a clatter. "Jared, you said we could get permission from any member of the Royal Family, right?" He nodded. "So it could be Princess Josephina?"

"Yes, but apparently she and Prince Frederick are busy preparing for this mystery event. We couldn't even get access to their aides." Jared got up and paced.

"I might, might, be able to get us in sooner," I said. "I'm not promising anything, but I could give it a try."

"Right now, a try is better than nothing, Babe," Jake replied. "What've you got in mind?"

I pointed at the com-panel in the middle of the table, and asked Jared to get his Coms Officer to connect us to the Palace switchboard.

"Good morning," I said politely when the call was placed. "My name's Shae, and I'm a representative of the Brotherhood of the Virtuous Sun." The operator didn't seem impressed, or she didn't believe me – which was probably more likely. "I'd like to be connected to the offices of Princess Josephina." Silence. "As soon as possible," I pushed.

"The offices you request are busy, please try again in a week or so." The operator was blunt and full of self-importance. "Is there anything else I can help you with?"

"Actually, there is. You can put me through to the offices of Princess Josephina, as I have requested." I tried hard to keep the irritation out of my voice. "And before you tell me again that the offices are busy, I suggest you consider the fact that the Princess and I are close personal friends. Should she find out that you prevented us from speaking… well, I'm sure she would be most displeased."

"Hold the line."

I hated bureaucratic bullshit.

"Close personal friend?" Jake questioned. I don't know whether he was impressed or confused.

The operator came back, and she'd added a snippy, sarcastic tone to her voice. "If you and the Princess are personal friends, as you say," I wanted to punch her, "then you'll have a PIC… that's Personal Identification Code if you don't know." She failed to keep the disdain out of her voice, probably convinced she'd won our com-link duel.

"You mean Phoenix-Delta-Seven-Two-Seven?"

The operator nearly choked on the other end of the line. "Umm… my apologies, Miss… umm… I'll put you straight though."

"Nice one," said Ty. "What a bitch." Kaiser punched him hard on the arm and made a shushing noise.

"Shae?" The voice was hesitant.

"Princess Josephina!" I replied, surprised she'd answered personally.

"My goodness, it is you. What a surprise. We haven't seen each other in what?" She paused. "Four years? When are you coming to see me?"

"Actually, that's just it, Princess. Some friends and I are in orbit now, and I've been telling them how beautiful and amazing you are. I would love for them to meet you." I crossed my fingers on both hands and held them to my temples.

"Oh, Shae." She sounded apologetic. "I'm so sorry, but now is a really bad time. We're right in the middle of something."

"Of course, I understand. It's such a shame we won't

get to see you, but Ash says maybe we can catch up on our next visit."

"Ash is with you?" she asked before a moment's silence. "Maybe I can fit you in for a short visit. I'm sorry, Shae, that's sounds dreadful, but we're terribly busy."

"Seriously, we understand, I'm just glad you can fit us in at all. I promise we won't take up too much of your time. We'll be there in an hour," I said before she had a chance to change her mind.

"Oh my! An hour?" For a horrible moment I thought she was going to cancel, but then she said, "No, no, that's fine. It's okay. I'll see you shortly." The connection terminated.

"Looks like you've got an admirer," Jake said to Ash, openly smirking.

Less than fifteen minutes later we were back on the *Veritas* heading towards Decerra, home to the House of Palavaria, and the political and administrative centre for the whole of Sector Three.

"Here," Connor said, handing me a box that contained my belt and weapons. "I cleaned the blood off them as best I could, but I can't guarantee they're spotless. I'll give them another go for you when I've got more time." I wondered if that was his way of apologising again for not detecting the bad guys back on the planet.

"Thanks. I'm glad I've got them back, I felt naked without them," I said, doing up the last fastening around my thigh. I'm sure Connor was about to make a rude comment, but he thought better of it as Jake sauntered past.

The short trip was uneventful, but it gave me the opportunity to spend a few minutes on my own. I sat on the floor in a far corner of the main cabin and closed my eyes, tucking my knees up under my chin. Under the circumstances, I thought everyone had reacted quite well to my gift – but they knew me, even if it'd only been a few days.

My secret was out, and I couldn't help but worry how senior military staff would react when they discovered it. Visions of labs and test tubes, scalpels and operating theatres, passed through my head like bad nightmares. The only thing keeping me calm was the thought of Ash; Ash and the entire contingent of the Brotherhood of the Virtuous Sun. They'd protect me, just like they'd always done.

The nightmarish visions started to dissipate the more I thought of the Brotherhood, and instead I began to pick up a faint conversation. I opened my eyes and watched Jake and Jared talking quite amiably over the far side of the cabin. If those two got over themselves, they might realise they could actually like each other. I was stretching my luck, but there was no harm in wishing. Maybe if we all lived through the mission, I would subtly work on the pair of them – with a sledgehammer.

Ash joined them and I focussed on the conversation. It wasn't like I was eavesdropping; it was just that I could hear their discussion more clearly once my brain wasn't concentrating on other things – like being chopped into tiny bits in the name of medical research.

The conversation was about how we knew Princess Josephina. Ash explained that when we were younger, part of our education involved going on placements to various worlds – so we could experience all aspect of life and cultures. We'd spent time teaching a version of Tok-ma to the Prince and Princess when we were in our late teens, and as the Princess was of a similar age to me, we'd hit it off. Other placements had involved far less salubrious places, designed to give us a rounded education.

"I think the Primus worried that Shae's education was a little too rounded at times," Ash said. "Francis and I had to dig her out of trouble on more than one occasion. You didn't think she got that attitude from living at the monastery twenty-four-seven, did you?"

"I heard that," I said.

"I know you did," replied Ash, unfazed. "And you know I'm right."

I thought for a moment then shrugged my shoulders. "True. But if I remember correctly, it wasn't just me who got us into trouble. What about that time on Annerro when you and Francis ended up in that whore-house?" Jake and Jared both swung their gaze from me to Ash – who was keen to clarify.

"They were having problems with some of their customers. We were purely there to help." He was telling the truth, but it still got us into one hell of a fight.

I stood up and looked out of one of the small portholes. Decerra was a pretty place, although not nearly as beautiful as Lilania, and it was chosen as Sector Three's central planet because of its remarkable similarity to Earth. There were more oceans and fewer continents than Earth, but the Palace was built on a landmass with long sunny days, adequate rainfall, and good soil. The lush vegetation and abundant wildlife were so similar to Earth's that visitors often believed they were brought there on transporters.

What was brought there from Earth, was the pale, almost white marble used to build the Palace of Palavaria. Through the window, I saw the building standing proud against the green landscape, magnificent by anyone's standards. I'd been blown away the first time I'd seen the beautiful stained-glass windows in tall towers, with boldly coloured flags flying at full mast. It was such a contrast to the monastery.

Connor followed Palace orders and brought us down on the South Landing Pad. As soon as we descended the ramp, we were accosted by a middle-aged woman, bossy and overbearing, and not at all happy to see us.

"My name is Martha O'Donnell, Princess Josephina's personal aide. I'm assuming you're Shae," she said haughtily. I did an exaggerated look around me then nodded my head. "I had no idea there were going to be so many of you, and that you'd be quite so… underdressed. Who are you all? What is your business with the Princess?" she questioned, oblivious to the waves of dislike flowing rapidly in her direction from our entire team. She tapped the data-pad she was holding with exceptionally long, false nails.

Ash introduced each of us quickly and politely, but I could feel from the Link how he really felt. The aide tapped our information into her pad with an irritating click-click-click from her nails, and when she had all our names, she raised an eyebrow that was plucked to within a millimetre of its life.

"And our business with the Princess," Ash said, his voice super-calm and super polite, "is none of yours." Martha looked like he'd just hit her in the face with her own data-pad. She turned an interesting shade of puce and looked like she was about to bust something.

As much as I disliked the aide, we were in a hurry, so I took her by the arm and guided her towards the security check-point. "Martha, um, may I call you Martha?" I continued without waiting for her to answer. "We appreciate your assistance, and understand the Princess is extremely busy. If you could take us to her, we'll be out of your hair in no time at all."

She seemed to like that idea because she huffed loudly and began to stride purposely towards the check-point, waving her arm furiously at the others to follow.

"Sign in and leave your weapons here," she ordered, devoid of any manners, but I was more disturbed that I'd forgotten that particular rule: only the King's Guards were allowed to carry weapons within the walls of the palace. After a short and pointless discussion within our group, we had no choice but to relinquish our combined arsenal, but being unarmed made me feel uneasy – even in the Royal

Palace of Palavaria.

We walked, or rather matched, through the palace, trying to keep up with Martha's pace. As we strode through the inner courtyard, surrounded by high stone walls, bay windows and arched doorways, the air seemed to still and a quiet hush descended – except for the loud, echoing, clack-clack-clack of Martha's killer heels on the flagstone. Our military boots made little sound in comparison.

We passed through the Great Hall at speed, and I noticed it hadn't changed since the last time I'd been there. King's Guards were stationed throughout the room, conspicuous in their bold, purple tunics with the Palavarian coat of arms on the chest.

The Great Hall was marvellously vast, with gigantic, gilded brass chandeliers hanging from the high ceiling. On the left wall, about half way down, a massive fireplace burned, and above, the Palavarian coat of arms hung proud. The walls were covered in paintings and tapestries, and the stained-glass windows depicted events from the Royal Family's history. Bold colours and luxury materials were used liberally, offsetting the severity of the marble.

There was no time to stop and reminisce as Martha marched us on. I marvelled at how quickly she could walk in those heels – I would've broken both my ankles within the first ten metres. By the time we got to Princess Josephina's personal quarters, I couldn't have disliked Martha and her fake nails, clacky heels, prissy outfit, and three inches of make-up, any more. I was also pretty sure the feeling was mutual.

We entered an ornate antechamber, where two King's Guards flanked an ancient, wood and wrought iron door.

"You three," Martha pointed at the Wolfpack, "you'll have to stay here." Then, as if purposely trying to make the atmosphere worse, she added to the guards, "Make sure they don't go anywhere." I watched Kaiser struggle against an inner demon, desperate to come out. "The rest of you, wait here until I've introduced you."

She strode forward so quickly the guards had to scramble to open the heavy doors. The minute delay caused exaggerated irritation in the aide, who tapped her foot, tutting loudly.

A few minutes later the doors swung open again and Martha reappeared. And if it was possible, she looked at us with more distaste than ever.

"The Princess will see you now. Remember, she's very busy, so keep your business brief and to the point," she ordered over her shoulder as we followed her into a lounge area. It was just as ornate and luxurious as the rest of the palace, and it reminded me of the quarters Jared had given me on the *Defender*. "The Princess will be out momentarily."

All children grew up hearing about beautiful princesses, dashing princes, and dastardly villains. Josephina was your quintessential fairy princess, which, or course, made her the complete antithesis of me. Her long, golden-blond hair framed a petite heart-shaped face, which glowed when she saw us, and her full, red lips broke into a genuine smile.

I was reminded of Martha's acerbic 'underdressed' comment when I noticed the Princess's beautiful figure-hugging, deep-red velvet gown. The v-shaped bodice accentuated her long neck, and the thin straps showed off her shoulders – which were almost as smooth, pale, and flawless as the marble surrounding us. Where I normally wore a gun belt around my hips, Josephina wore an ornate gold belt of linked royal medallions, inset with a variety of twinkling gems.

"Please, everyone," she purred in a polished, educated voice. "These are my personal quarters. There's no need for such formalities here." Ash and I relaxed immediately, after all, for us it was like stopping in for tea with an old friend – albeit a hugely important one. The aide, who was still lurking, looked disapproving. "Martha, that will be all, thank you. I'll call you when I need you again."

"But—"

"I'll let you know when I am ready to continue our work."

"Yes, Princess." She spun on her high heels and stalked from the room.

The moment she was gone, Josephina's face broke into a wide grin, and she kissed me on each cheek before pulling me into a hug. Then she did the same thing to Ash, and I could've sworn he blushed before introducing her to Jared and Jake.

Up close, the Princess looked tired, with unusual dark circles under her wide, green eyes – which keenly surveyed our group.

"Please, sit." She pointed to a cluster of chairs and couches in deep, opulent fabrics and gold brocade. "I've had tea prepared. Shae, would you help me pour? Then you can tell me why you're really here."

I don't think Jared and Jake quite knew how to take being served tea by a member of the Royal Family. They perched on the edge of their seats and looked uncomfortable.

When we all had drinks, I started to explain. "Firstly, Princess—"

"Good grief, Shae," she interrupted. "Personal chambers, remember?" She waved her arm around to make her point. I really liked Josephina. She was almost certainly the nearest thing I had to a best female friend. Come to think about it, she was probably my only female friend.

"Of course. Phina, I'm really sorry I had to use our friendship to get in to see you, but something has happened. I'll let Ash explain."

"My, this does sound intriguing," she said, turning her attention towards Ash. As her gaze passed Jared, she caught his eye and gave him the briefest of enigmatic smiles. I'd seen her do that before to men she liked; a brief smile, a gentle glance up from under those long eyelashes, the slightest of touches… She was flirting with him, and it irritated me beyond belief, though I had no idea why. It wasn't like he belonged to me. I realised I was frowning and swiftly cleared it off my face, hoping no one else had noticed.

Ash spoke quickly, briefly explaining the events that had led us to her quarters. Throughout, Phina sat quietly, her tea left untouched and cooling, and by the time Ash had finished, an ominous mood had settled on the group. Phina took a long deep breath then blew it out slowly while she digested the information.

"Your Highness," Jared started, but the Princess cocked her head to one side and raised a delicate eyebrow. "Josephina," he corrected himself, "I appreciate we've no hard evidence to prove that there's an imminent ARRO threat to your family, but—"

"But when two high level representatives of the Brotherhood, a Fleet Captain, and a Marine Colonel, believe it's an extremely high possibility, I would be a fool to ignore it," she finished for him.

"Precisely," he agreed. "Not that I'm implying you're a fool," he added hastily.

"Relax, Captain." Phina smiled sweetly at him, but that time she leant forward and added a gentle touch to his knee. She stood suddenly, and we scrambled to follow suit. "We need to speak to my father immediately," she said.

"Phina, there's something else we need. We'd like your authorisation to interrogate Peter Sharman and George Black, the two men Ash mentioned. We're hoping they'll be able to shed further light on the situation," I said.

The Princess walked over to the com-panel on her desk. "Sergeant Mollere, I need you in my private chambers immediately. There are some gentlemen in the antechamber, please bring them in with you." When she turned back towards us, I had a really strong feeling there was something else she wanted to say, but was holding back.

"Josephina, I have to ask," said Ash. "What's the event everyone's preparing for? There's nothing in the official engagements calendar, yet we were told all staff are busy preparing for something important. ARRO may use the cover of a special occasion to make their move."

"My dear Ash, I wish I could tell you, but unfortunately I can't; it's not my place." She opened her mouth to say something further, but the doors swung out and Sergeant Mollere walked in, followed by two King's Guards and the Wolfpack.

Sergeant Mollere was an older gentleman, possibly in his early fifties, with greying hair and a moustache, but he looked fit enough to give any of us a run for our money. He had a concerned look plastered across a lined face.

"Sergeant, thank you for coming so promptly," Phina said. She looked to me and added, "Shae, my father trusts you. Would you come with me to tell him?"

"Of course," I replied.

She turned to Ash. "The King's Guards are at your disposal. How do you wish to proceed?"

"I suggest we split into two teams. Jared, Kaiser and I will go after Sharman. Jake, Ty and Connor will go after Black," he replied.

"So be it. Sergeant, I've authorised these men to find and detain two members of House staff. Please extend your full resources to them. I'll leave it to you gentlemen to sort out the details. Where's my father?"

"The King's training in the dojo," the Sergeant replied, still looking troubled.

# 15

Dressed in long, wide trousers and jacket, and protected by a breastplate and helmet of metal and leather, King Sebastian looked a formidable fighter.

He'd once told me that Kendo helped centre mind and spirit, as well as building character and honour, and in that respect, it was very similar to Tok-ma. He looked just as imposing as our own Warrior Caste, although fortunately for his opponent, he fought with a flexible training weapon rather that the lethal katana sword that would've been wielded in true battle.

He was mid-challenge, and for a man of his age, he was fit and lithe, moving purposely around the mat. The stale smell of sweat hung in the air, and the crack of the swords clashing echoed around the room.

The King couldn't abide people kowtowing to him on the training mat, even if that meant he lost, so the challenge was fierce – both men battling for physical and mental superiority. The crowd cheered and roared their encouragement, but I heard Jake's voice in my earpiece and moved away so I could hear him better.

"Shae, do you read me?"

"Go ahead."

"Black's not in his office. He left about the same time we arrived, so I reckon the scroat's definitely got something to hide. Jared's having the same problem finding Sharman, but we've got the King's Guards helping to track them down."

"Copy that. Jake… stay safe okay?"

"You know me, Babe." The com-link terminated.

The King landed a heavy blow to his opponent's arm and I winced at the sound of snapping bone. As soon as the fight was officially pronounced over, a medic ran on to the mat to help the man, who held his arm gingerly. Both fighters bowed and removed their helmets.

"Good challenge, Bruik," the King said. "I thought you had me a couple of times."

"I thought so too, sire," said Bruik, trying to smile through the pain.

Phina took my elbow and indicated to me that it was time. "Pardon my interruption, Father," she said to get the King's attention.

"Ah, there she is; my beautiful daughter." His narrowing eyes told me he'd picked up the tone in her voice. "Shae! Good grief! I'd no idea you were here. How lovely to see you again, you haven't changed one bit." He smiled, stepping forward before thinking better of it. "I would hug you both, but…" He indicated to his sweaty clothes.

"Father, we need to talk." Phina tried to keep the urgency out of her voice, but his eyes narrowed further.

"One moment," he said, before turning his attention back to Bruik. "Report to Doctor Ford. Tell him I sent you and he'll get you fixed up in no time." He thought for a moment then looked questioningly at the medic. "We do have our Royal Physician, don't we?"

"Yes, sire. I believe Doctor Ford is on duty," the medic replied.

"Good. That man never seems to be here. There's a

different bloody doctor in his place every time I go to the infirmary."

"Doctor Ford has been on a… I guess you'd call it a Royal Physicians exchange programme," the medic explained. "The doctors from all Four Sectors have done placements with each of the Royal Families to improve their skills and knowledge. He's back now, sire."

"Did I know about this?" The King didn't seem angry, just perplexed.

"Yes, Father. You agreed to it several months ago," Phina replied. It looked like there might've been some recognition in his eyes. "Please, Father." She was more insistent. "We need to talk."

"Of course, my child," he said, holding her chin and looking down in to her deep-green eyes. "Give me some time to shower and I'll—"

"No," she said bluntly, and the atmosphere instantly shifted as everyone collectively held their breath.

The King didn't say anything, but his eyes blazed. "Everybody out," he ordered, and I wasn't going to argue. The sound of quiet shuffling filled the room, but as I turned to comply with the King's command, I felt Phina wrap her delicate fingers around my wrist.

"Phina, you'd better explain your behaviour." The King's voice was cool, but the inflection was ominous, and I recoiled when he turned his attention to me. "Shae, I believe I asked everyone to leave." I tried to move away, but Phina tightened her grip.

"Father, please excuse my insubordination, but I would not have done it if what we have to discuss was not of vital importance. Shae, please stop trying to pull away," she added in frustration. "Father, believe me when I say Shae needs to stay." The King paused then nodded his agreement. "Thank you," she said.

"This better be good," he grunted, starting to undo the numerous straps holding his breastplate in place.

"Let's sit, and we'll tell you everything," she replied pointing to one of the benches.

I was impressed. I chipped in now and again to give more detail, or clarify bits, but on the whole she did a remarkable job at telling it straight. During the account the King said nothing, but occasionally he stood and paced.

"And you think two of my staff are involved?" Sebastian asked.

"Yes, we believe so, Your Majesty. We're working with your Guards to locate them now, but so far they've avoided capture," I replied.

"I see. Shae, please excuse my bluntness, but I must leave to convene my senior staff. There's more going on than you are aware of – things that may have serious implications," he explained, and I was reminded of the Primus saying exactly the same thing before we'd left Lilania. What the hell was going on? "I'm afraid I cannot include you in these discussions just yet."

"I understand. With your permission then, sire, I would like to re-join my team in the hunt for Black and Sharman."

"Of course. I'll be in touch shortly." With that, King Sebastian and Princess Josephina left the dojo through a side door.

I linked to Jake via coms. "How's it going?" I asked. He was out of breath, the sound of pounding feet in the background.

"One of the King's Guards spotted Black heading towards the north landing pad. We're heading that way now."

"I know where it is, I'll meet you there," I replied, setting off at a sprint.

After crossing the walled garden, I broke out onto the patio above the north lawn, so immense it was more like a park than a lawn. I stopped and shielded my eyes from the bright sun, scanning for Jake and the team. Faint shouting drew my attention to the distant right, and I saw a small figure emerge through a shrubbery patch and pelt across the grass.

I ran down the steps to the lawn two at a time, working out an angle that would put me on an intercept course with Black before he made it to the landing pad. I was already half-way to him when I heard Jake shout and I turned my head to see him, Ty, and Connor appear through the exact bushes Black had.

I was only ten metres from Black when the distinctive H'toka 'pop' echoed across the gardens. I instinctively dropped to the ground, struggling to process the fact that there was an Agent of Death on Decerra – but not only on Decerra, within the Palace of Palavaria itself.

The Wolfpack had dropped as I'd done, but without our weapons we were easy targets. He should've stayed down, but instead Jake launched himself off the grass and ran towards a small wooded copse.

"He went this way," he yelled over his shoulder, and in seconds, Ty and Connor were behind him. I turned to follow, but then his voice was on coms telling me to check on Black – telling me to see if there was anything I could do, emphasis on the word 'anything'. I knew what he meant.

Every bone in my body wanted to follow the Wolfpack, but I did as Jake asked and headed towards Black, noticing two King's Guards standing and brushing themselves off – they must've followed me from the patio.

Black lay motionless on the grass, a dark red puddle extending from under his head. I knew he was toast, you could tell that just by looking at him, but the King's Guards were watching so I bent down and felt for a pulse.

"He's dead," I confirmed, frustrated and tired of being one step behind. Two loud pops rang out, and a flock of birds took flight from the copse. "Stay with the body," I demanded, taking a few steps towards the trees, but then I stopped and turned back. "Give me your weapon," I ordered the nearest guard.

"What?" He looked indignant. Another loud 'pop' echoed and my flesh turned cold.

"You hear that sound?" I shouted. "That's an Agent of Death. You know what that is, right? My team's up against a trained assassin with nothing to defend themselves. I'm Brotherhood, working in conjunction with the REF" I showed them my identification. "Princess Josephine gave Sergeant Mollere strict instructions to put the Guard at our disposal… now give me your damn gun before I put you on your arse and take it anyway." I held out my hand and glared at him. The guard checked my ID again then relinquished his weapon.

I set off towards the copse, aiming for the break in trees where the Wolfpack had disappeared. "Jake, where are you?"

"We've got the Agent pinned down at the Water Terraces," Jake whispered. "Trouble is we're a little pinned down ourselves." Another 'pop' rang out and I wasted no time in sprinting towards the sound.

When I was near, I slowed, keeping low and quiet. I made my way around the elegantly shaped ponds, built to fit together on descending terraces. I saw Ty and Connor hunkered down behind one of the short walls, Jake about five metres to their right.

"Jake, I'm at your ten," I whispered.

"I see you. The Agent is behind the base of the horse statue."

"Got him. Jake, I've got one of the guard's guns."

"I'm impressed, Babe," he whispered. "Ty, Connor," he brought them in on the com-link, "Shae's got a gun, and I don't think the Agent knows she's here. I'm going to move right – you two move left and draw his fire. He'll think he's safe to move around the base of the statue to engage you, while keeping shielded from me, but it'll put him in direct line of fire with Shae."

The Agent of Death took the bait and moved around the statue, but it wasn't far enough for me to get line of sight. I moved to my left until there was no more wall for me to hide behind.

He opened fire on Ty and Connor, who had little cover to keep them safe, but I still couldn't get a good enough shot to take him down. I had no choice. I stood up, vaulted the low wall, and ran left, yelling to get his attention. The Agent spun towards me, his wet cloak clinging to his body, and from my new position I had a clear target.

Two guns fired simultaneously. The bullet from the H'toka sailed past my head, so close to my temple I heard the rush of air, but the blast from my gun hit the Agent centre-chest. He stumbled back, falling in to one of the ornate ponds.

Jake threw himself into the water after the Agent, and by the time I got to them, Ty and Connor were already helping to pull him out. I knew we had to take him alive, and I guessed that was why they were trying to save him, but I was surprised that Jake had his fingers in the Agent's mouth. He and the Agent were both soaking wet and covered in tiny, bright-green lily pads.

The man was alive, barely, but barely was good enough for me. I could heal him, and then we'd be able to interrogate him. Maybe that was the break I'd hoped for. Although he was weak, he bit down on Jake's hand, and blood ran between his teeth and through Jake's wet fingers. He gagged as Jake pushed his hand further into his mouth.

After a moment, Jake pulled his hand away, allowing Ty and Connor to lay the bleeding Agent on the pristinely maintained grass walkway. Jake sat down heavily beside him, holding a tooth in his hand, looking triumphant. I didn't understand why until Ty told me that all Agents had a suicide pill in one of their teeth.

"It's old-school, low-tech, but it works. Damn hard to detect," he explained.

Jake's hand bled from the deep, jagged bite-mark, but he had all his fingers and the injury wasn't life threatening, so I figured I could deal with him later. I knelt next to Connor.

The Agent struggled to breathe. His lips were blue, and his skin was greying from loss of blood. I knew I needed to heal him, quickly, and fortunately there was no one else around to witness it.

"Shift out the way," I said, giving Connor a nudge, but he and Jake exchanged a glance I didn't like the look of.

"Give me a minute to think," Jake said, holding his hand away from his body so the blood dripped on the grass. He shook his head, spraying pond water out of his hair. "He'll never talk," he concluded.

"He will. I'll heal him, and you can interrogate him," I said. "Jake, you can get what we need, I know you can." I sounded desperate because I was sure the Agent didn't have much time left.

"Jake's right, Shae. We'd be wasting valuable time," explained Ty. "Agents of Death are trained to resist even the strongest of interrogation methods. Sure, our experts would be able to break him eventually, but there's no way we would get the answers we need from him in the time we have."

"Then we find his weakness. He must have one – everyone does, right? But I have to heal him now or it'll be too late, and we'll have lost the best lead we've had so far. Why are we waiting?"

"Jake, a moment?" said Ty, holding out his arm to help Jake off the floor. The two men stepped away. I couldn't hear what they were saying, but Jake listened intently as he dripped water and blood, staining the grass red. He evaluated the wounds on his hand, eventually nodding before slapping Ty on the shoulder in agreement.

The Agent of Death fell unconscious and I decided I couldn't wait any longer. I started to move his robes out of the way to begin the healing.

"Connor, stop her!" Jake shouted, making me jump. I was so shocked I didn't even put up a fight when Connor pulled me away from the Agent. "I'm sorry, Babe, I didn't mean to scare you, but we have a plan. I don't think you're going to like it, but actually it was your idea." The bristles stood up on the back of my neck. "Ty, wake him up."

Ty took a small vial from one of his trouser pockets, snapping it under the Agent's nose. He came to instantly, spluttering bubbles of blood from the sides of his mouth.

"This is ridiculous, Jake. Let me heal him before it's too late," I said, moving back towards the Agent. Connor tried to stop me again, but that time I was prepared and managed to wriggle out from his grasp. I hadn't counted on Ty, though, who pulled my arms behind my back before I had a chance to fight him.

"Stop wriggling, I don't want to hurt you," said Ty, but I was too angry to register the pain.

"What the hell, Jake?" I shouted.

"I'm sorry, Babe, but it's for the best," Jake replied. He looked genuinely remorseful, but as he'd given the order to restrain me in the first place, I still wanted to kick him in the jewels.

The Agent, once de-masked, didn't look anything special, but much younger than I'd expected. He watched our interaction with a pained, perplexed expression, but then his chest heaved and more blood oozed from the wound.

Jake knelt next to him, leaning in so he was sure the man could focus on him. He held up the tooth and watched the reaction spread across the Agent's face. To begin with, it was somewhere between panic and horror, but then his expression cleared and he became almost serene. He started to make a choked, gargling noise, which I realised was laughter.

"Take a look," he said weakly, trying to raise his head to nod towards his gaping chest wound. "Even without the tooth, I'm a dead man. Game over." His voice was quiet, but harsh, and more blood trickled from the side of his mouth. When he coughed, bubbles of spittle and blood sprayed on to his cheeks.

"That's just it, my friend; you're not going to die. Shae here is going to heal you. You're going to live, and you're going to be taken into custody – where you'll be beaten down by the best interrogators the REF has to offer. And one day, one day," he reiterated, "you will crack, and you'll tell us everything about the Agents of Death. How you're recruited. How you're trained. Who else is an Agent. Everything." Jake was so calm it was almost eerie, but at least he was seeing sense about letting me heal the man. "Now that's got to be an Agent's worst nightmare."

"Nice speech, but I'm not an idiot. Death's coming." He laughed again and my skin crawled. "You can't stop it."

"Is that so? Shae?" Jake indicated for Ty to release me. "Would you mind showing our friend here what you're capable of?"

"Oh, now I can?" I said sarcastically, moving towards the Agent, but Jake held his bitten hand above the man's chest.

"Maybe a small demonstration to start with?" I studied his face, hoping I'd see something in it that would explain what he was up to. "Please?"

For a moment, I hesitated, still mad at him for having Connor and Ty restrain me, but who was I kidding? There was no doubt I would heal him; he knew that. He'd counted on it.

The Agent's eyes started to close and his head lolled to one side, so Ty broke a second vial under his nose and he came around, spluttering. Once he'd refocused on Jake's hand, I held it between mine and healed the bite-marks. The silvery-blue shimmer reflected in the wide, scared eyes of the Agent, and once I was done, Jake wiped the blood off on the grass. He showed the completely healed skin to the man, rotating and turning it slowly to prove there was no damage left.

The Agent looked at me aghast, starting several sentences. "I… You… How…? Who…? What are you?" he finally settled on.

"That's not important." Jake was happy his point had been made. "The fact is, you're going to go down in history as the first Agent of Death to ever let himself be captured alive. The first person to give up the closely guarded secrets of the Assassin Elite. Man, I would not like to be in your boots right now." The Agent spluttered and coughed, and more blood oozed from his chest wound. "But… I'm going to offer you a deal." The Agent raised an eyebrow. "Option One is that Shae heals you, like she did my hand, and you spend the rest of your life in REF custody – subjected to hard core interrogation, day after day, eventually giving up everything you have sworn to protect. Or… there's Option Two: I let you die right here, right now."

"What the…? Jake, are you mad?" I spluttered because I'd gasped so hard I'd choked. Ty even banged me on the back to get me breathing again. "This is ridiculous." I moved towards the Agent, but my head was still swimming from Jake's offer and I'd forgotten about Ty. A second later I was locked-down again.

"What's the catch?" the Agent barely whispered.

"I want information about the job you're working now. Give me that and I'll let you die. All your other secrets go with you to the grave. It's a good offer, but it runs out in, oh, about thirty seconds." He looked at his com-pad.

"How do I know you're not bluffing? Get the information and then heal me anyway?"

"I give you my word. You should know what that is, being an Agent and all."

The man closed his eyes. "Fine," he grunted through gritted teeth.

Jake didn't hesitate. "Who hired you? Was it ARRO?"

"Above my pay grade."

"Okay, who gave you your orders?"

"I get my instructions via secure coms. I couldn't tell you who sends them even if I wanted to."

"Who's your target? Is it Sebastian? The Prince? Princess Josephina?"

The Agent looked surprised. "We're assassins – we kill people for money – but there are lines even we don't cross. None of them are on my Kill List."

"Really?" For a split-second Jake's look matched the Agent's. "Then who is on your target?"

"Five names on the current list: Black, Sharman, Peterson, Kraven, and Doctor Ford," he said, his speech stilted as he struggled to talk. During a coughing fit a large blood clot dislodged from the chest wound, and he deteriorated further.

"No one else?" Jake pushed.

"No." It was barely a whisper.

"Who have you crossed off the list?"

"Black… Sharman…"

He had very little time left. I needed to heal him, but Jake continued the questioning.

"Were you the Agent who killed Nyan on Angel Ridge?"

"Yes."

"And Cady on GalaxyBase4?"

"Yes."

"Did you intentionally try to take us out with the bomb in Cady's office?" The Agent's eyes closed so Jake slapped him hard on the cheek to rouse him. "Did you intentionally try to kill us?"

"Yes." There was a combined intake of breath from the group.

"So we were on a Kill List?"

"No. You… getting too close… had to… stop you…" He slipped into unconsciousness again.

"Jake," I said desperately. "You got what you needed.

Let me heal him before it's too late."

"I gave him my word, Shae," he replied quietly, unable to look at me.

"Jake, come on? It's got to be now," I pleaded, pulling against Ty even though it hurt.

"No," he said flatly, and even as he did, the Agent's body convulsed and his chest stopped moving. Jake bent over and placed two fingers on his neck. "He's dead. Let her go, Ty."

I put my hands over the Agent's chest, but Jake was right, he didn't have a pulse – it was too late. Jake leant towards me, but I pushed him away, so angry with him that I didn't know what to say or do.

"Shae—"

"You son of a bitch, Jake! You used me. You used what I can do."

"I'm sorry, I—"

"Go to hell," I hissed, turning to walk away.

"Wait, where are you going?"

"What do you care? Oh, I'm sorry, was there something else you needed to exploit me for?" It was sarcastic and childish, but I didn't care. What I did care about was getting as far away from all of them as I could. Ty tried to put his hand out to me as an apology, but I shoved him away before stalking off.

I didn't know where to go, I just knew I couldn't be there – with them – with the body of a man I could've saved. I needed to get my head straight.

I stomped through the small wood muttering to myself, but the more I thought about what'd happened, the angrier I got with Jake. And the angrier I got, the more I wanted to punch him in the head.

I returned to the Water Terrace to confront him, but when I got there I couldn't see him anywhere – and that irritated me even further. The King's Guards had finally arrived, and I heard Connor and Ty briefing them. When

Ty saw me, he made his excuses and came over.

"Are you okay? Did I hurt you much?" he asked.

"Where's Jake?" I asked, ignoring his questions.

"He went back to the *Veritas* to get some dry clothes. Shae, I—"

"Don't worry about it, Ty. It's your meathead boss I have the issue with, not you. He and I need to have words. I'll be back shortly."

I jogged towards the South Landing Pad, replaying events in my head, and the more I did, the more furious I got. By the time I arrived at the ship, Colonel Jake Mitchell had definitely replaced Jared at the top of my 'People I most wanted to punch' list.

I sprinted up the *Veritas'* loading ramp and took the stairs to the main cabin two at a time, spoiling for a fight.

"Jake?" I yelled. Nothing. I began to worry I'd missed him, but I couldn't have been that far behind the bastard, so I stomped towards the weapons storage area at the back of the ship. "Jake? Jake, where are you?" I bellowed, followed by, "you son of a bitch," in a quieter voice.

"Babe, is that you?" His voice was clear through the ship's internal coms.

I pressed a button on the wall unit. "We need to talk," I replied, no niceties.

"Sure. I'm in my quarters – floor below. Take the stairs off the main cabin and my crib's the one right at the end." His voice was natural, and he seemed pleased I was there – he had no idea what was about to hit him. Adrenaline pumped, and I felt heat rising in my cheeks.

The hatch to his room was open and I walked towards it preparing my first killer sentence, but when I got there I couldn't get my words out.

I couldn't even breathe.

# 16

Jake stood in the middle of the room towel-drying his shaggy hair, wearing nothing more than a pair of combat trousers. They weren't done up and hung low on his hips, the waistband of his underpants contrasting white against tanned skin. Before I could stop myself, I imagined my fingertips running along the furrows of defined muscles, down towards his…

"Hey, Babe," he said casually, with a cheeky smile that promptly brought me back to reality.

"Don't you, 'Hey Babe', me," I shouted, angry I'd let myself get distracted. I was so mad I could barely think straight, and Jake's semi-nakedness was not helping matters. "What the hell was that?"

He stopped drying his hair, lowering the towel slowly. "What the hell was what?"

"That. Back there. Don't play ignorant, Jake, it doesn't suit you. You know damn well what I'm talking about."

Colour crept into his cheeks, but he was totally still. "I did what I had to."

"You what?" I exploded.

"Damn it, Shae. I told you who I was, and I thought

you'd accepted that. I did what I had to do to get the information we needed… or is my job only okay with you unless you happen to be caught up in the middle of it?"

I tried to ignore that last bit because I realised he might have a valid point. "You let a man die, Jake," I accused, pointing at him, trying to move the conversation away from me.

"You shot him!" he retorted with a hollow laugh, pointing back at me. "What did you think was going to happen? He would've died anyway."

"Not if I'd healed him." I took a step forward because right then I wanted to lamp him right in the face. "Who gave you the right to play God?"

"Me?" He seemed genuinely taken aback. "Who gave you the right, Shae?" He was in front of me, his eyes flashing dangerously. I backed away into the bulkhead, but he took another step forward, pinning me. "How do you decide who lives and who dies, who you heal and who you leave broken?"

Guilt ripped through me. He was right – I did have the power to make that decision – but I didn't want to think about it because it wasn't supposed to be about me, it was supposed to be about him.

"You had me restrained." I was embarrassed, and that made me angry, but Jake was less than a metre away from me with hardly any clothes on and I found it difficult to focus. I told myself I wasn't going to get distracted again and focussed on my rage instead. "You used me. You knew I would've healed him. I should've healed him," I yelled, my voice hoarse.

"Grow up," Jake barked, moving forward so his face was only a fraction from mine. He took a deep breath to calm himself, but he didn't take his eyes from mine. "Not everything is about you," he continued in a quieter voice.

He looked like he was about to add something but changed his mind, instead he lowered his eyes and punched the wall beside me. He turned away, both hands behind his head, fingers knitted together. Muscles knotted tightly across his shoulders.

The argument was not going how I planned, and I realised I was fighting back tears.

"I'm sorry I had to use your gift… use you," Jake said, still facing away from me, his voice low but nowhere near calm.

"That was the one thing, Jake," I sobbed, failing to stop the tears. "The one thing that was guaranteed to hurt me more than anything."

I was done, there was nothing more to say.

I peeled myself away from the bulkhead and made for the door, but before I got there Jake grabbed my arm and spun me around to face him. His eyes studied my face for the briefest moment, and then he bent his head and kissed me. After the argument we'd just had, I was furious.

How dare he?

He moved one hand behind my back and the other behind my neck, pulling me to him. I tried to push him away, but my strength was nothing compared to his and he didn't move.

I struggled to release myself, but somehow a line got erased and I found myself kissing him back. I parted my lips and his tongue found mine, hungry and desperate.

My hands, which had tried to fend him off moments earlier, wrapped behind his head, my fingers grasping at his damp hair, pulling him closer.

It wasn't like before, back in the training room, it was more urgent, more desperate. I didn't love Jake, hell, I'd only just met him, but he was dangerous and exciting, and I wanted him. Even if my brain had said, 'walk away', I don't think my body would've listened. Every part of me remembered our last encounter, and I wanted to carry on where we'd left off.

With effort, I pulled away from him, and he looked at

me with eyes that blazed with passion. He wiped away the tear tracks from my cheeks with his thumbs, and I could barely think straight.

"Jake," I whispered. "You know I'm still really mad at you, right?"

"Yes," he replied, before leaning forward to kiss me again.

Even though Jake was taller than me, our bodies fitted perfectly. I pressed myself against him and could feel from his hardness that he wanted me just as much as I wanted him. For a split second my head made one last attempt to remind me that I wasn't in love with him, but so what? We were both consenting adults, weren't we? Who was going to care?

A bolt of lightning shot through my body as Jake's hand wandered under my T-shirt, finding bare flesh. His other hand tilted my head slightly to one side as his tongue softly caressed my neck, and his teeth gently nipped my skin. Goose bumps covered my entire body, and I ached for him to take me. His thumb stroked my lips and I took it in my mouth, gently sucking on it. He stopped kissing my neck to let out a low groan.

He pulled away from me and I moved forward, not wanting our bodies to separate. I put my hands up and started to stroke his smooth, bare chest. He was strong and warm, and his muscles flexed as I drew my fingertips lightly over them. I gently stroked one of his nipples with the tip of my index finger, smiling as goose bumps immediately appeared on his tanned skin and his breathing changed. The very tip of my tongue flicked around his nipple, and that time Jake's moan was deeper and louder.

His hands found their way under my t-shirt again, caressing the skin on my back, working their way up to my bra, which he flicked undone. He lifted my face gently and we kissed again, his warm, soft tongue caressing mine. Deep inside, I burned for him.

He pulled me away again and I tried to resist, but he whispered, "Trust me."

He turned me around and slipped his hands under my t-shirt, lifting it up over my head. Then he slid the straps of my bra off my shoulders, dropping it on the floor next to my top. His fingers gently traced the vertical line of graceful, ancient script tattooed down my spine. "What does it say?" he asked, his breath hot on my neck.

"It's a long story," I replied, not wanting to be distracted from the shivers his fingertips were triggering. "I'll tell you about it later."

His hands were on my skin, searching and desperate, and at the same time he nuzzled my neck. Another round of goose bumps covered my body. His hands cupped my breasts, caressing them gently before his fingertips found my nipples, which were already hard. My back was up against his chest and he was firm and warm.

The combination of Jake's moist lips and searching tongue drove me crazy. He blew gently on my glowing neck and I shivered with pleasure, my breathing fast and shallow. My brain fogged over.

He lowered both of his hands, tracing the line of my stomach, then quickly undid my trousers. He moved his left hand back up to my breasts while he slipped his right hand into my trousers and underneath my panties. I opened my legs slightly and gasped.

His fingers flicked and massaged, quickening in speed and rhythm, and my back arched against his body. My gasps got stronger and louder as his touch became more vital. Bolts of lightning shot out from my centre, and just when I felt it couldn't get any better, he gently nipped at my neck with his teeth and everything exploded.

"Oh, Jake!" I cried as my entire body convulsed on a surge of pleasure that flowed to the very ends of my fingers and toes. My knees completely gave way, and if Jake hadn't moved his free hand around my waist, I would've been on the floor – and I wouldn't have cared.

After the original explosion subsided, gentle aftershocks pulsed out from my core. Jake turned me back towards him and we kissed again, over and over, his stubble tickling my skin.

Eventually, his hands lowered, caressing my bottom, and then in one quick move, he grabbed me and lifted me off the ground – my legs instinctively wrapping around his hips. He was so strong he was able to support me with one hand while the other brushed everything off the top of the table in a sweeping movement. I'm sure something broke, but neither of us cared. He placed me down carefully and I didn't even mind that the smooth metal was ice cold.

"Let's get these off you, shall we?" Jake said as he bent to undo my bootlaces. After they'd unceremoniously thudded to the floor, he pulled my trousers off in one tug before his hands made for my panties. I stopped him and his eyes immediately clouded with worry. "Babe, I thought this is what you wanted."

"Oh, I do," I said through the continuing aftershocks of the orgasm he'd already given me. I leant forward and kissed him quickly before pointing to his own trousers. He smiled in recognition and took a couple of steps back so I had a better view. Then, while holding his waistband, he looked up through his eyelashes and gave me a boyish grin that reminded me so much of Jared. A brief shot of guilt ran through me but I pushed it quickly to the back of my mind.

I jumped down from the table and took his hands in mine. I guided them to my panties and helped his fingers slide under the sides. He took over and removed them the rest of the way, kissing my breasts and tummy as he bent. Then he took my hands and guided them to his underwear, not that I needed much encouragement. I kissed his nipples and ran my tongue down his stomach as I bent, and when I was low enough, I took him in my mouth and heard him gasp.

I started slowly, steadily, rhythmically, and then gradually increased speed while he made little noises that got louder and deeper. "Wait," he suddenly said through ragged breaths.

He picked me up and carried me to the firm, simple bed against the wall, setting me down gently before lowering himself on top. I felt his hardness against my stomach as he propped himself up so that he could see my face.

"Are you sure, Babe?" he asked, and I nodded because I didn't think I could speak if I wanted to. He shifted slightly to getter a better position and I lowered my hand to guide him to exactly the right place.

I thought I'd prepared myself, but as he pushed inside me I gasped. Our bodies were perfect together, and I responded to his every movement, flexing and adapting. As Jake's urgency increased, I felt the little bolts of lightning intensify, and then the rush of my second orgasm pulsed through me. Seconds later, I felt his body tense and shudder, and then he sighed. He relaxed against me, our bodies hot and sweaty.

We lay in each other's arms as the aftershocks subsided, occasionally kissing, occasionally caressing. Gradually my breathing returned to normal and reality crept back in. Jake propped himself up on one elbow, facing me, his fingertips tracing patterns on my tummy. It was comfortable lying together.

"You're so beautiful, Babe," he said casually. "Unique, amazing, special."

"Stop it." I blushed.

"Annoying, emotional, argumentative," he joked. "I've wanted to do that since the very first time we met. I'd have taken you right there and then if I'd thought for one moment you'd have agreed to it." Jake's lips curled up at the sides and his eyes shone deep green.

"Get a grip! Not the first time we met – we were in the

middle of Dome Five surrounded by a bunch of people, remember?"

He thought for a moment. "Even with all those people there." I pinched him playfully on the arm, feeling completely and utterly satiated. He idly touched my lips with his thumb.

"Oh, Jake!" I said trying to sit up, but I was pinned by his arm.

"Really? A third?" He looked impressed, and smug, and he lay on his back, folding his hands behind his head.

"No, you idiot! I told Ty I was coming here to have it out with you."

"And you did. Twice, if I recall correctly." He smirked and I hit him on the stomach with my fist.

"Jake, please be serious. We've been gone ages. What if they come looking for us? At the very least, we've got to get back to work."

"Let Jared deal with it. He likes being in control." I didn't understand the stab of guilt that pierced my chest at the sound of Jared's name. "He's such a dick," Jake concluded.

"He saved your life," I said, feeling that I needed to defend him – no, I wanted to defend him. "If you two would just put all this macho bullshit behind you, you might find you have more in common than you think. Come on." I tugged at his hand and he reluctantly let me pull him up off the bed, but as soon as we were up, he pressed his solid body against mine, his arousal pushing on my tummy. "Jake!" I exclaimed.

"What?" He smiled mischievously.

"Pack it in." I wriggled free and picked up a black pair of combat trousers, but they were way too big for me so I threw them at Jake. I had to hunt around the room to find my various items of clothing, and when I had them all, I turned to find Jake propped against a locker, a hungry look in his eyes. He was still completely naked, and I had to tell myself to focus because part of me wanted him inside me again. "What are you doing?" I demanded.

"Watching you."

"Well don't. Get dressed."

Even though he tried to convince me that we wouldn't be missed, I finally managed to persuade Jake that we had to go back to work. A few minutes later we were both fully clothed and I checked myself in the mirror, trying to see whether it was obvious we'd just had sex. My skin glowed, and the curls in my hair were slightly less curly, but I convinced myself that could've been down to the encounter with the Agent of Death.

When we got to the stairs up to the cabin, Jake said, "Ladies first." I was halfway up when I realised it wasn't because he was being a gentleman.

"Stop staring at my arse," I ordered.

"Babe, I'm hurt that you would think me so shallow… but you do have a great arse."

We were crossing the cabin, heading towards the second set of stairs leading to the cargo hold, when Jared suddenly appeared at the top of them, making me jump. Jake didn't seem fazed in the slightest.

"There you are," Jared said. "Are you okay?" He sounded tense.

"Yes thanks, I'm fine. Nice of you to ask," Jake replied.

"I wasn't talking to you."

"I know."

"I'm okay, Jared," I said, pleased that he cared, although cared about what? "Why do you ask?"

"Ty told me what happened. I was concerned about you." He kept turning his head to scowl at Jake. "He told me you were furious with Jake and came here after him. I came…" He didn't finish.

Guilt crept through my chest, but again I couldn't understand why. It wasn't because Jake and I had just had sex – I'd wanted that as much as he had. Perhaps it was because we were almost caught, by Jared of all people. I'm sure I looked guilty, but Jake… Jake looked smug, and that annoyed me.

"So, you've come to tell me what a lame trick I pulled on Shae," Jake taunted. "To tell me what a despicable person I am for the way I interrogated the Agent of Death." He squared up to Jared, arms folded tightly across his puffed-out chest.

"Actually, no," Jared replied. "I agree with the way you handled the situation. You and your team were right – it was the only way to get the information in the timeframe we had. It was a good call." Jake deflated. His arms unfolded and he took a half step backwards. He didn't seem to know how to react to the compliment. "As I said, I came here…" he turned to face me, "because Ty said you were upset, and mad at Jake, and I wanted to make sure you were all right."

"It's true, I was mad at Jake," I said.

"She's still mad at me," Jake corrected, winking, and I flushed. So he had listened after all.

I couldn't look him in the eye in case I gave something away, but I couldn't look at Jared either because of the inexplicable guilt swimming around in my chest. I looked at my feet instead. It was safer.

"Shae?" Jared said slowly and I looked up. He didn't say anything else, he simply studied my face, and then he looked at Jake, who was back to being relaxed and calm. He looked at me, then Jake, and then at me again. With each look, his expression altered a little, like he was trying to work through a puzzle, but then his whole body stiffened. "Oh no," he growled. He stared at the ground for a few heartbeats and when he glanced up he looked me directly in the eyes. "Please tell me you didn't?" he said, so quietly I wasn't sure I'd heard him right. He placed the palm of his hand on my cheek. "I warned you about him. Why didn't you listen?" A darkness fell over his face and his lips tightened into thin lines.

I may not have understood what was going on, but Jake obviously did because his posture changed as dramatically as Jared's. He just had time to ready himself before Jared lunged, and they stumbled backwards until Jake crashed into one of the crates.

"Son-of-a-bitch," cried Jared as he clasped his hands around Jake's neck. "I didn't think even you'd sink low enough to seduce her during a mission."

Jake got in a blow to Jared's ribs and he released his grip slightly, allowing him to land another punch to the side of Jared's head.

"This… has… nothing… to do… with you," Jake wheezed.

"Stop it," I yelled, but it was like I wasn't even there.

I couldn't believe they were fighting, although in hindsight, perhaps their relationship had been building towards that particular conclusion from the start. Still, they were not going to use me as an excuse to beat out their unresolved issues. I was angry at the pair of them – angry and terrified.

I tried to wade in to break them up, but after ducking an elbow from Jared, meant for Jake's chin, and a fist from Jake, meant for Jared's ribs, I backed off again. What was I thinking? Did I really believe I would've made the slightest difference like that?

Neither held anything back, and at the rate they were going, one of them was going to get seriously hurt, or worse. Even if I could patch them up after, I didn't want to see that happen – I cared about them too much.

My head swam as Jake and Jared continued to fight, punching and kicking. They were strong and fit, and excellent fighters – clearly equally matched. They chucked each other around and I had to leap out of the way a couple of times to avoid getting caught up in it.

Every time one of them landed a punch on the other, I

felt a tug inside me, and the longer they fought, the stronger the tug got until a swirling ball of energy eventually knotted together under my ribcage. It felt almost like the force that built up in me before I healed someone, but it was different somehow – more powerful, more potent – and I was terrified. I had no idea what was happening to me.

I felt light-headed as the energy built, getting stronger by the second. My hands started to shimmer silver-blue, and my heart thumped hard in my chest, the rush of blood deafening in my ears. I needed Jake and Jared to stop fighting because I needed them, but they continued, oblivious. When Jake picked up a piece of broken crate, I couldn't stand it any longer.

"That's enough," I cried, unconsciously holding my arms out in front of me. A powerful wave of energy pulsed from my hands, knocking them both off their feet and throwing them clear across the cabin.

I fell to my knees in shock, eyes wide with fright as I stared at the motionless men on the other side of the room. Were they dead? Had I killed them?

They were slow and groggy, but in time they picked themselves up off the floor. They scrutinised each other, trying to piece together what'd happened, and then they both turned to look at me. The energy build-up had gone – there was no more tingling, no more twisted knot in my chest, and certainly no more glowing hands. All that was left was shock, and the relief that they weren't fighting anymore.

Nothing made sense. I was confused and scared, and I didn't know what to do. So I cried.

When Jared sat on the floor next to me, I reached out for him, pulling myself closely into his chest, tucking my head under his chin. He put his arms around me, and that was exactly what I needed. He couldn't give me the answers I desperately wanted, but I knew he would do everything he could to protect me. He would keep me safe.

My body heaved against his chest as I cried. My tears fell onto his shirt as he held me, and he said nothing. And to give Jake his due, he didn't say anything either, but he sat right next to me with his hand on my knee – his way of saying he was there for me as well.

Jared's heartbeat began to calm me, and when I was ready, I released him and he unfolded his arms, wincing. I wiped my eyes and nose and apologised to him for the tear stains on his t-shirt. He looked down at them and politely told me that you could hardly see them against the blood. I laughed weakly. More red trickled down his chin from a split lip, and he wiped it away gingerly, being careful not to press too heavily on the lump already forming around his mouth and cheek.

"That was you, wasn't it, Babe?" Jake asked, dabbing at the cut above his eye – which was swollen shut.

"I wanted you to stop hurting each other," I replied, sniffing.

"Hey, I was just defending myself," Jake said, pressing a finger to his eye again and grimacing.

"I know, Jake." I placed my hand on his cheek because I didn't want him to think that hugging Jared was a snub towards him. He lent forward with some effort and kissed me carefully on the lips, and then he wiped a rogue tear away from my cheek with his thumb. He must've thought I was a total freak. I wouldn't have blamed him if he wished he'd never got involved with me in the first place.

"And you," I turned to face Jared, "I'm a grown woman, in case you hadn't noticed."

"Oh, I think he's noticed," said Jake, but I ignored him.

"I like that you look out for me, but really, it's not necessary. I wasn't seduced," Jake made a small coughing noise and I blushed again, "well, okay, maybe just a little… but Jake didn't make me do anything I didn't want to."

Jared looked miserable but resigned as we sat in silence.

"You two drive me crazy," I said, when I couldn't stand

it anymore. "You know my life is with the Brotherhood. The monks are my family, and my friends – they're my whole life. I don't know that many people outside the Brotherhood, and I don't trust easily… but you two?" I frowned. "I've known you a matter of days, yet both of you have managed to get under my skin. Believe it or not, you're probably the closest friends I have outside the Brotherhood – even if I do want to kill you half the time." I wondered if they understood what I meant. Even I thought I sounded a little crazy.

"Babe—"

"I'm not finished," I continued. "What I'm trying to say is that you mean a lot to me… and I have no idea why. I can't stand it when you argue, let alone fight. I'm not saying you have to be the best of friends, but…" I stopped talking because I noticed the raised eyebrows they'd given each other when I mentioned the word 'friends'. "This is exactly what I'm talking about!" I wanted to bang their heads together but I didn't have the strength, so I did the next best thing – I slapped them both upside their heads.

"Hey," huffed Jake.

"What the?" said Jared.

"Pack it in, the pair of you. If you just got over your own egos, you'd realise what everyone else already knows."

"And what would that be?" Jake said, though I don't think he wanted the answer.

"Well, I'm glad you asked," I replied sarcastically. "It happens to be that the two of you… no, the four of us, make a good team. And it would be better still if you would stop trying to tear each other apart. You don't really hate each other," I said confidently, but Jake snorted and Jared choked. "Okay, whatever. I'm sick of trying to stop you from beating on each other. Just go for it." I stood up, wobbled, and two pairs of hands shot out to steady me.

"Shae's right," Jared said. "Jake, we can be professional about this. What happened before… I'm prepared to put it aside while we work this thing together. Deal?"

"I can do that," Jake replied after mulling it over for a moment. "Deal." He held out his hand and the two men shook firmly – very firmly.

"Jake, I think two new T-shirts are in order," I said. He hesitated, but I made shooing motions with my hands and he reluctantly wandered off. "Jared, you know the drill: shirt off."

"Do you think you should, after what happened?"

"Just do it," I ordered. He had trouble getting his top off over his head because of the blows Jake had delivered to his ribs, so I helped. It was the first time I'd seen him shirtless, and even though I knew he was fit, I was still pleasantly surprised. "You okay?" I asked when the pain subsided.

"Yeah." He didn't sound convinced. Before he had time to protest, I wrapped my arms around his torso and squeezed until he eventually groaned and buckled. I let go.

"Hurts, doesn't it?" I said. "Next time I won't fix you and you'll have to live with the pain. Got it?"

He managed a half smile. "Yes. You made your point."

"Good. Hold still."

"Do I need to lie down or something?"

"No, we can do it standing up." I realised how that sounded and giggled. I was nervous. What if things had changed in me? What if I couldn't heal anymore? I put my hands to his chest, and was just about to start when I had a sudden thought and lowered them again. "How attached are you to that scar on your forehead?" I traced the line with my finger and he shifted slightly.

"Why?"

"I can fix it when I'm healing you… if you want. I only ask because some people like to keep scars that mean something to them. I don't have any myself, but I can understand how people feel they define their past."

He thought for a moment and then said he wanted to

keep it. I was intrigued and made a mental note to ask him about it later. I raised my hands again, instantly relieved when the usual tickle started deep inside me. It was all over as Jake reappeared.

"Good timing," I said. He'd already removed his torn shirt and was naked from the waist up. Something inside me remembered what it was like to be pressed against his warm skin, and tiny embers smouldered inside of me. "Come here," I said as I squeezed him, giving him the same warning I'd given Jared. "And before you say anything… yes, I'm okay to heal you; no, you don't have to lie down; yes, we can do it standing up… and yes, I do know that sounds smutty, so no rude remarks."

With Jared and Jake healed and clean, we were ready to get back to work. I headed for the stairs before the inevitable questions began.

"Hold it right there," Jared said and I stopped abruptly, turning slowly. Crap. So close.

"So?" Jake said. Where they a tag team now? Perhaps it was better when they weren't talking to each other.

"So, what?" I decided to play dumb, heading for the stairs again, but they were blocked by both men.

"So… you didn't tell us you could do that." It was Jared's turn again. "Whatever that was."

What should I do? Lie? Say, 'That old trick? Oh yeah, that happens every time I want to break up a fight. I just put up my hands and blast them apart with a freaky energy pulse'? Or tell them the truth and admit it'd never happened before, and that I was more terrified than they could possibly imagine?

Fortunately, or unfortunately, depending on how you looked at it, the question was answered for me. Jared had seen the panic in my eyes. "Wait a minute," he said. "That's never happened before, has it?"

I tried not to have another meltdown. "No." Fear rose inside me again and I began to tremble.

"Babe," Jake soothed. "It's okay. It'll be all right."

I squashed the fear back into the pit of my stomach and straightened myself up. I wasn't going to let what'd happened get the better of me. I was okay. I could still heal, and I felt just the same as I always did. No, that wasn't true. I felt like I had since I'd clinically died. Better. Stronger.

I put on a brave face. "It's true that's never happened before, but I'll deal with it. In the meantime, we've got a job to do, and we've been gone too long already. Ash is going to be pissed with us for disappearing."

"Yes, but what about—" Jake started.

"We have work to do," I interrupted, shaking out my joints to psych myself up. "If you really want to help me, you can get your heads back in the game. Time's running out, and we can deal with…" I couldn't even say it, "we can deal with the other thing later."

"If you're sure?" Jared made one last attempt.

"I am. One more thing though, you have to agree not to say anything to Ash." They looked surprised. "He's the only one of us that's truly focussed at the moment. I don't want him distracted by this as well. I hate keeping secrets from him, but he'll be worse than you two for worrying. If you promise not to mention anything to him, or anyone else, I'll promise to talk about it later when we have more time."

They agreed, reluctantly, but at least they were actually agreeing on something – it was a step in the right direction.

# 17

I crossed the landing pad, keen to get back in the investigation, but stray thoughts flashed through my head – Jake's warm body on top of mine; Jake and Jared fighting; and what I was only going to refer to as 'that thing that happened'. I tried to ignore all of them. The sooner I filled my brain with proper work stuff the better.

As we neared the Security Checkpoint, I noticed it was unusually busy. I didn't have time for the delay and picked up the pace, ready to push my way through if necessary, but Jared pulled me to one side.

I studied the group – which seemed to be one man surrounded by an entourage of personal guards and staff. "Why are we stopping?" I asked.

"To let him pass," replied Jared, looking puzzled. He threw Jake a questioning look, but got a shrug in response. "We can afford to wait a minute."

"But—"

"Trust me, we have time. Besides, his guards won't let you anywhere near Security while he's there."

"While who's there?" I felt frustration flutter in my chest. "Who is he?"

"That's Maximilian Colderon, Babe," Jake said. "Earth's Lord High Chancellor, and the second-highest ranking civilian in the Four Sectors. He's about as VIP as you get."

"What's he doing here?"

"That's a bloody good question," he replied. "Things just keep getting more interesting, don't they?"

"Well, whatever he's doing here, he doesn't look happy."

"Neither would you be in his position," said Jared.

"What do you mean?"

"Well, like Jake said, Colderon's the second highest ranking civilian. The only person above him was William Kensington as Lord High Steward."

"So when Kensington died six months ago," Jake said, "Colderon probably thought his promotion was in the bag."

"I'm guessing things didn't go the way he expected?" I said.

"No. In a surprise move, the Tetrarchy gave the honour to Samuel Bellamy."

"Colderon's own deputy," clarified Jared.

"Ouch! That had to hurt. The Tetrarchy must've had their reasons though," I suggested.

"Guess so," replied Jake, lowering his voice as the group cleared Security. We moved out the way. "But I bet that left one extremely pissed-off Lord High Chancellor," he whispered.

As soon as we were back on Palace grounds, I contacted Ash on coms.

"Is everything okay?" He sounded concerned.

"Everything's fine," I replied as cheerfully as I could under the circumstances.

"Have you seen Jake or Jared? They seem to have disappeared."

"They're with me. We've been…" I searched for the right words, "working out a few issues."

"I see."

"We're heading to you now. Where are you?"

"We're all at the Water Terrace. There's quite a commotion, I'll explain when you get here. Quick as you can, please."

Ash hadn't been kidding – the Water Terrace was a circus.

Kaiser stood over the body of the Agent of Death, scowling at a couple of medics who looked like they wanted to take it away. Ty and Connor held back a group of King's Guards, and Ash was in heated discussion with Sergeant Mollere, just off to the side. Additional guards lurked in small groups, whispering incessantly.

We headed to Ash and I caught the tail end of the Sergeant's sentence. "…since he was a teenager. I just can't believe it." Mollere's worn face was pale and damp with sweat, and he looked like he was about to vomit. Ash took his arm and guided him to a stone seat next to one of the ornate ponds, signalling for a medic.

When Ash returned, he moved us further away from the Guard. "The Agent was a King's Guard. Sergeant Mollere knew him personally," explained Ash quietly.

"Really?" I said, leaning around him to look at the man on the bench.

"His name is, was, Castilian Santiago. Apparently, the Santiago family are highly thought of within the Court. Castilian joined the Guard at eighteen and has worked his way through the ranks. Sergeant Mollere's having trouble believing that the Agents have infiltrated the Palace without them knowing."

"Maybe he was a sleeper agent? Dormant until recently activated," Jake suggested.

"It's not an approach that's been previously attributed to the group," Jared said, rubbing his chin. "But if Jake's right, there could be sleeper agents anywhere."

"Let's not start speculating and concentrate on one problem at a time," said Ash, looking at the mêlée still going on around the Agent. "Jake, is there any value in holding on to the body?"

"No, I think we got everything we're going to."

"Then why not turn it over to the Guard? That'll get them off our backs and free up the Wolfpack. What do you think?"

"Agreed," Jake replied before heading off to deal with the situation. I watched as he spoke briefly to Kaiser, to the medics, and then whistled to get Ty and Connor's attention before motioning for them to join our group. By the time the full Wolfpack had returned, Mollere had re-joined us.

"Let's recap," said Jake. "The Agent—"

"Santiago," Mollere interrupted. "His name was Castilian Santiago." I noticed Jake bristle.

"Okay then… Castilian Santiago, who let's not forget was a highly paid, highly trained, and deadly assassin," I knew Jake was rubbing it in on purpose, "had five men on his Kill List."

"What?" Mollere practically exploded. "Why wasn't I told of this earlier?"

"Need to know, Sergeant. You're lucky I'm telling you now – let's not forget, Santiago was one of your men." Jake's voice was firm to the point of rude.

"We've kept the list quiet until now because not everyone on it is dead, and we didn't want word getting to them that they're targets," Ash said, more diplomatically. "We believe each of them has been involved in planning an assassination, and if they catch wind that we know about them, they might go to ground. Plus, someone's cleaning house, and we need to get to them first."

"Well, clearly Black's dead." Jake pointed his thumb over his shoulder towards the woods.

"And Sharman, too. We found him in the Orangery – single shot to the forehead. The usual," added Jared.

"That leaves Peterson, Kraven and Doctor Ford," I clarified. Mollere coughed and turned white. "What is it?"

"Are you sure it was Kraven on the list? You couldn't have been mistaken?" He looked like he was about to vomit again so I took a step backwards.

"Who's Kraven?" Jake asked.

Mollere ignored the question, but I thought that was probably because he didn't like Jake much. He took a deep breath and seemed to compose himself, recovering quickly from the obvious shock the name had caused.

"Kowalski," he called to a guard standing by the horse statue. "I want you and your men to detain Doctor Ford and Peterson from Logistics. Make sure you do it quickly and quietly. Take them both to holding cells, and let me know when you have them. I want your team to guard them personally until we get there. Do you understand?"

"Yes, sir," Kowalski replied before disappearing.

The Sergeant turned back to us. "Peterson is a low-level logistics coordinator, but Doctor Ford is Personal Physician to the King. They couldn't be two more different people. I don't understand how they can both be involved."

"That's for us to work out," Jake said stiffly. "What about Kraven?"

"You must be mistaken. It's not possible."

"Who… is… Kraven?" Jake spelt it out slowly and carefully, having already lost his patience.

"He's…" Mollere shook his head, "Captain of the King's Guards."

"I don't understand," said Jared. "I thought Sanghara was Captain of the Guard?"

"He was… is. It's complicated. Sanghara's sick, has been for a while, but with medication he's able to function quite normally… up until a few weeks ago when he had a complete relapse."

"Convenient timing," Jake muttered.

"With all the planning for the…" Mollere stopped himself dead and changed what he was about to say. "Look, Kraven is Sanghara's protégé, so he was the logical choice to step in to the role." He sounded bitter. "The promotion's only temporary until Sanghara's better."

"But even if it's only short-term, Kraven currently has full responsibility for the protection of the Royal Family and Palace Security. He has unrestricted access to the King, Prince and Princess," Jared said.

"That's true, but it's ridiculous to think he's involved," Mollere tried to rationalise. "As Sanghara's protégé, Kraven's worked with the King for over a year. He's had plenty of opportunities to do something before now."

"I agree, it is puzzling," said Ash, "but we need to speak to him, none the less."

"It's not possible."

"Stop stalling, Mollere." Jake grabbed him by the collar and he looked startled for a second, then angry.

"Take your hands off me," he ordered.

"Jake, look," I said, pointing towards several, unhappy guards heading towards us. Jake let go of Mollere's collar and straightened his uniform.

"I'm not stalling, Colonel," he said stiffly, waving off the advancing men. "You can't talk to Kraven because he's not here. He's off-world. Did you not wonder why I was coordinating the search with you, and not the Captain of the Guard?"

"Where off-world is he?" Jake demanded.

"That, I can't tell you. And before you threaten me further, Kraven's current location is confidential. I'm not at liberty to offer that information… even if I knew it." The uncompromising look on his face told me he was sincere, and even Jake backed off. "May I also remind you, Colonel, that an assault on one of the King's Guards is an assault on the Crown – regardless of who you are, or what rank you might hold."

"Whatever," Jake mumbled, looking unconcerned by the threat.

"Excuse me," Jared said, pointing to his earpiece to

indicate he was receiving a coms. He stepped away from the group.

"This news is very troubling," said Ash. "Sharman, Black and Peterson all hold relatively low-level positions within the House. I'm guessing they were probably patsies, easily manipulated into doing what ARRO wanted, but Kraven and Doctor Ford? How did ARRO get to them? If indeed ARRO is behind all this – we still don't have concrete proof. And as Sergeant Mollere said, they're both in positions that put them close to the Royal Family on an almost daily basis."

"Maybe that's it," I said.

"What's it?" asked Jared, returning to the group.

"The timing. Nyan said he heard the assassination would be big. Something people wouldn't forget. Take out a member of the Royal Family in their Palace and it would be big news, granted, but take them out during a large event, like the one that's obviously being organised, and it would be phenomenally huge. A real statement for ARRO."

"That sounds credible," agreed Ash.

"There's something else," I continued. "If Sharman, Black, Peterson, Kraven, and the Doctor are all part of an ARRO cell, who's leading it?"

"I don't understand," said Mollere.

"Well, if I was planning an assassination—"

"Are you trying to tell us something, Babe?" Jake joked, but I scowled at him and he mouthed 'sorry'.

"If I was planning an assassination, and if I had other people doing the grunt work, I might consider them loose-ends. So—"

"You might hire an Agent of Death to kill off anyone who could cause you, or ARRO, trouble at a later point," Jared finished for me.

"Exactly. But I wouldn't have them killed until—"

"Just before the assassination was due to take place. In case you still needed them," Jake said.

"Precisely. But will everyone please stop finishing my sentences? Do you have any idea—"

"How annoying it is?" That time it was Ash, but even he wasn't above receiving a punch on the arm.

"You get my point," I concluded. "There has to be someone higher in the food chain than Royal Physician and Captain of the King's Guard."

"I guess we need to talk to Peterson and the Doc then," Jake suggested. "If they're the weak link, let's see if we can't break them."

"Agreed," Mollere said. "If you follow me, I'll take you to our Detention Suite."

We headed across the lawn after Mollere had given his men their orders. The Sergeant and Ash led the group, behind them Jake and Jared took up flanking positions beside me, and behind us was the rest of the Wolfpack.

"Hey, Jared, who was your com-link from?" Jake asked.

"Commander Tel'an," he replied. "The techs have finally cracked the encryptions on the *Hawkhurst's* computer."

"That's excellent news," I said. "Isn't it?"

"Hmm," Jared grumbled. "Depends on how you look at it. We've enough evidence of weapons and drug smuggling, not to mention human trafficking, to put Edge away for good, but the rest of his flight-log was pretty standard. He had a few jobs transporting some hooker to the other Sectors over the last couple of months, but there's nothing else. Certainly nothing that would shed any light on our current investigation."

"Perhaps he really is just your average piece-of-shit scroat in the wrong place at the wrong time," Jake said.

When we arrived at the Palace holding cells, Mollere called over Kowalski. "Did you have any trouble, Corporal?"

"No, sir. We found Peterson in his quarters, packing. Looked like he was getting ready to leave in a hurry, but he didn't put up a fight. I think he was more petrified than anything – kept saying we had to protect him. I've put him in holding cell one with one of my guys keeping an eye on him."

"What about Doctor Ford?" Ash asked.

"Ford was in the infirmary, but he seemed more curious than anything. He kept asking questions like what the charges were, and where we were taking him. I've put him in cell four."

"Thank you, Kowalski, we'll take over from here," Mollere said. "But stay close, I might need you again." The Corporal nodded and faded into the background.

Almost simultaneously, Jake and Jared said that they would interview the Doctor, but after Ash questioned the sanity of them interrogating together, we agreed that Ash and Jake would take Ford, and Jared and I would take Peterson.

Before we went in, I had a thought. "Sergeant Mollere, could you find out if anything unusual has happened within the Palace over the last couple of months? Maybe something odd or out of place. Anything at all really, even if it doesn't look much."

"Of course. I'll get my people on it immediately."

When Jared and I entered the interrogation room, Peterson didn't say anything, but he tapped the table nervously and fidgeted in his seat. He was an average sort of guy: average size, average weight, average looks – not someone who'd stick out in a crowd. Maybe that's why he'd been recruited by ARRO in the first place.

There was already fear in his eyes when Jared started. "Jeremy Peterson," he said. "Let's start with an easy question… what do you know about an assassination attempt on a member of the Royal Family?"

Silence.

"Okay. Do you know that Peter Sharman and George Black are dead?" Peterson picked at a loose thread on his trousers, unable to hold eye contact with either of us for more than a second. "You do know that Sharman and Black are dead, don't you, Mr Peterson? That's why the Guards found you packing? Because you know you're next?" Peterson's right leg jiggled incessantly under the table.

"Mr Peterson? Jeremy?" I said gently, deliberately contrasting against Jared's harsher tone. "It was an Agent of Death who killed Sharman and Black." He gulped loudly. "The Agent's dead, but do you know who he was?"

I'm not sure whether he was genuinely interested, or he simply couldn't stay quiet any longer, but he finally spoke. "No. Who was it?" Dark sweat patches soaked through his beige shirt, and he wiped his forehead with the back of a shaking hand.

"Castilian Santiago," Jared said, but Peterson showed no signs of recognition. "He was a member of the King's Guards, and your name was on his Kill List."

Peterson's bloodshot eyes widened. "But he's dead? You said…" He looked desperate.

"Yes, he's dead," I confirmed.

"But that doesn't mean another Agent won't be activated to complete Santiago's mission," Jared added. I thought we made quite a good tag-team.

"You… you have to protect me," Peterson stuttered. "It's your job."

"Strictly speaking, it's not our job," Jared said. "It's up to the King's Guards to protect you, and as Santiago was one of their own, I…" he paused for effect, adopting a sceptical expression, "I can't guarantee someone else in the Guards isn't an Agent. I'm not sure you would be entirely safe."

That's when the dam burst.

Peterson shook and sobbed. He rocked backwards and forwards in his chair, repeating, "I'm a dead man," over and over. I got up and walked around the table to put my arm around him. He was hot and sweaty, and didn't smell pleasant.

"It's a pity," I said. "Had you known something about the assassination, you would've fallen under our purview and protection."

By the time I'd returned to my seat, he was spilling everything he knew – which unfortunately wasn't very much, and not much more than we already knew. But amongst all the crap was one crucial piece of information.

When we finally got up to leave, Peterson lunged across the table, grabbing my wrist. It wasn't an attack, just the actions of a desperate man, but Jared bought his elbow down hard on the side of his head and he let go, slumping to the floor. Jared hadn't hit him that hard, but probably harder than he needed, so as we walked out of the room I gave him my, 'that wasn't really necessary,' look.

"What?" he said innocently. "The guy assaulted you. He could've hurt you."

"He was no more capable of hurting me than a cantooa kitten."

"Perhaps." He shrugged his broad shoulders apologetically, and then turning back towards the room, he yelled, "Sorry for hitting you in the head, Peterson." I laughed, hard, and it felt good. I knew I shouldn't have, but I just couldn't help it. It's like when someone trips up the stairs in front of you, and you know you shouldn't, but you laugh anyway. "Is that better?" he asked, his blue eyes sparkling.

"Much. Now all I need is coffee."

Jared asked the nearest guard for directions to a drinks machine, and I was about to take my first sip when Mollere approached.

"We've gone over the security logs for the last couple of months," he said. "There were a couple of drunken misdemeanours, the theft of some Pendoldine, the harassment of one of the Scholars – but that turned out to be a bunch of dissatisfied students – and some vandalism to one of the old outbuildings, which isn't even used any more. That's it. Nothing very exciting I'm afraid."

"What's Pendoldine?" asked Jared, cautiously sniffing his coffee.

"According to the report, it's a drug for some kind of genetic disorder."

"Never heard of it."

"It's relatively new, and quite expensive by all accounts. Probably stolen to sell on the black market."

"So that's a bust then," I said, choking on the coffee – which should've come with a biohazard warning.

Jared made an odd gargling sound and spat the mouthful he'd taken back into the cup. "Wow, that's bad," he said as Ash and Jake rounded the corner.

"Great, coffee," Ash said.

"Wouldn't bother," replied Jared. "Seriously," he added, pouring the contents of his cup into a plant pot.

"How did you go with the Doctor?" I asked. Jake opened his mouth but closed it again when Kowalski appeared.

"My apologies for interrupting, Sergeant," he said, "but our visitors have been summoned to the King's Office."

The King's office was exactly the same as I remembered – large, ornate and beautiful. Apart from the King, only Princess Josephina and Prince Frederick were present, and I thought it strange there were no Senior Staff. An aide guided us towards a suite of ornate couches and asked if we needed anything, but Sebastian dismissed him before anyone could reply.

"Brother Asher," the King said, holding out his hand. "I didn't imagine that when we met again, it would be under these circumstances."

"Neither did I, Your Majesty," he replied before introducing Jared and Jake.

Sebastian motioned for us to sit, and Phina purposely slid in next to Jared on one of the sofas, her knee touching his leg. He looked uncomfortable, and I was glad.

"Shae, where are we with the investigation?" the King asked, straight to business. "I want to know everything. How far does this go?"

"You already know some, but I'll recap quickly. We believe a middle-man called Cady took money from ARRO to transport a group of men, included a number of your staff, to a rendezvous on the Planet of Souls. He passed the booking to a pilot called Edge, who completed the mission as agreed. Nyan, our original informant, heard some of the meeting on the planet, but he was killed before he could tell us everything."

"By an Agent of Death?" Sebastian clarified.

"Yes." I took a sip of water from the glass Jake passed me. "The Agent, who we now know was Castilian Santiago – one of your Guards, sire – was hired to clean house. He killed Nyan on Angel Ridge, and Cady on GalaxyBase4, but fortunately we were able to get to Edge before him. Further investigation led us to Sharman and Black… which is what brought us here today."

"I see." Sebastian rubbed his eyes. "Continue."

"Sharman and Black were both killed by Santiago before we could bring him down. He was shot and killed at the Water Terraces."

"By you, I hear."

"Yes, sire. I didn't have a choice; my team was under heavy fire."

"That wasn't a criticism, Shae." He smiled briefly. "What happened after that?"

"Before he died, Santiago gave up three more names: Peterson, Doctor Ford and Kraven." I stopped because the King's eyes had clouded over and his lips had drawn into a tight line. I wasn't sure whether to continue.

"Go on," he said, answering my question.

"We have Peterson and Ford in detention. Peterson's not much use, but he did give us a key piece of information. Up until now, we were only speculating about who the target was, but Peterson confirmed it. It's you, sire." I waited for the group to process the information. "He has no real affiliation to ARRO that I can tell – for him it was all about the money. Black recruited him, and it wouldn't surprise me if they kept him out of the loop."

"What about Doctor Ford?" Prince Frederick asked.

"We didn't get anything from the Doctor," said Ash. "He insists he has no idea why he would be on a Kill List. He's also adamant he has no affiliation with ARRO, and knows nothing of an assassination attempt. He speculated that someone might want him dead so he wouldn't be around to heal you if the attempt on your life wasn't immediately fatal."

"Do you believe him?" asked the king.

"Not in the slightest," replied Ash without hesitation. "But we've no proof one way or another, and we don't have any leverage at this point to persuade him to talk. He's certainly a smart one, I'll give him that, and he knows we can't hold him indefinitely."

"So what now?"

"Kraven's the only lead we haven't been able to follow up on. Because his name's on the Kill List, we know there's at least one person above him, possibly calling the shots. If we can get to Kraven before anyone else does, we might be able to persuade him to tell us who that person is. I have to ask, Your Majesty, where is he?"

Sebastian took a moment to think. "This is a very grave situation indeed, but I'm most relieved it's I who is the target, and not my children." He held up a hand to silence the joint protests from the Prince and Princess, but I noticed he hadn't answered Ash's question.

"Sire," Ash pushed. "We believe that the attempt on your life will be made during an important event, and we know something big is being planned. With respect, our team is working blind. We need to know what's going on."

"I appreciate your candour, Ash." The King paused, thinking again. "Shae, gentlemen, there's something you need to know." I sat forward in my seat, placing my glass carefully on the coffee table. "What I'm about to tell you is classified Alpha Secure. I've already had your security levels increased accordingly." Jake's eyes widened, and Jared crossed and uncrossed his legs. I felt intrigue flow through the Link from Ash. "I'm assuming you know about the Tetrad Summit?"

Of course we did. It was one of the best, and worst, kept secrets in the Universe. The four presiding monarchs made up the Tetrarchy of Souls – a group which was responsible for every Human, every soul, in the Four Sectors. The Tetrarchy had absolute power over everything, including the military, politics, business, and commerce. What they tried, and failed, to keep secret, was that every four years the Tetrarchy, their immediate families, and Senior Officials, got together for a four-day, joint Summit.

"As you probably know," the King continued, "during the Tetrad Summit, various topics are discussed, agreed or rejected. Disputes are resolved, and Laws are reviewed and updated. What you may not know is that each House is allowed to take a maximum contingent of one hundred people, not a person more. Our representatives include high level House officials and administrators, council members from the ruling planets, high ranking military personnel, and prominent members of the Brotherhood."

I finally understood why Finnian had been so cagey when we'd been back on Lilania. He would've known about the Summit all along.

"Each Sector takes its turn to host the Summit at some point during the fourth year. As I've said, the fact that we have a meeting isn't exactly a secret, but the actual details surrounding the Summit are kept Alpha-Secure. The exact location and time is revealed a matter of days before the event, and to key personnel only. This year it should've been Sector Two's turn to host the event, but increased ARRO activity in their Sector raised serious security concerns, so it was agreed to move it to ours, as next in line."

"That's why Colderon was here," Jared said, realisation dawning. "Makes sense now."

"Yes," confirmed the King. "One of his official duties is Master of Ceremonies at the Summit. He was here to finalise details before heading there."

"Which planet is hosting?" asked Jake.

"That's just it," Prince Frederick said. "It's not held on a planet. It's held on a ship." I'm sure my shock was apparent because Phina laughed.

"The *Athena*, after the Goddess of Wisdom, never stays in one place," Phina explained. "She moves around, both before and during the Summit. She has the transponder signal, and all the relevant credentials, of an environmental research vessel, and is very unassuming to look at. Most people would pass her by without a second glance."

"I'm stunned," I said.

Phina smiled fondly and continued. "Each delegate is given an exact time and location to arrive at the *Athena*, and when they get there, they have to hold at an agreed distance. Once the *Athena* completes their security checks, they send a shuttle to collect them. The delegates are searched thoroughly for any kind of threat, including weapons, explosives, and bio-hazards, before being brought to the *Athena*. Their ship is told to leave the area immediately and given a time and place to return for their representatives. The *Athena* has to get four hundred people on board, so it's like a military operation. I'm sure you can appreciate the difficulty of it, Captain?" she said, touching his knee gently.

"When does the Tetrad Summit begin?" Ash asked.

"Tomorrow."

"Tomorrow?" I practically choked.

"We rendezvous with the *Athena* at fifteen-forty-five precisely," Frederick said.

"And that's where Kraven is now? On board the *Athena*?" Ash asked.

"Yes," the King replied. "The Captains of all four Royal Guard meet on the *Athena* before the event to work with the on-board security team, making sure everything is set to our expectations." He paused then turned to Prince Frederick. "We must contact the *Athena* on the emergency channel to warn them about Kraven."

"Wait," Ash said, causing Frederick to stop in his tracks. "My apologies, sire," he added hastily. "I didn't mean to be disrespectful." He lowered his head, but the King asked him to explain. "If you contact the *Athena*, it's highly probable Kraven will realise we're on to him – and ARRO. It may cause him to panic, alter his plans – improvise. That could be dangerous."

"Brother Asher's right, sire," said Jake. "The last thing we want is for Kraven to get spooked and do something unpredictable."

"What are you suggesting?"

"I recommend we don't tip our hand about Kraven at this stage," said Ash. "However, it's vital that the four of us, and the rest of the Wolfpack, get access to the *Athena*."

The King drew in a deep breath, and the Prince shook his head vigorously.

"The delegate list is agreed well in advance," Phina explained. "There's no way we could change it now, not without explaining our reasons in full. Even if you came with us tomorrow, you'd never get from our ship to the *Athena*. And if we gave you our rendezvous coordinates for you to turn up in your ship, the *Athena* would simply leave. They won't hesitate to go without us – even if that means leaving the King, the formal host of the Summit. And even if it were possible to get you on board, you're making a huge assumption that Kraven won't hear about what's happened here."

"Okay, you're probably right, but here's a thought," I said. "I bet it's already common knowledge that an Agent of Death was taken down on palace grounds by an external team – us."

"I'd say that's a safe bet," agreed Sebastian.

"And I'm guessing that gossip is rife as to why we were here in the first place. Most of your guards have probably put two and two together and worked out that we were here to stop an assassination on a member of the Royal Family."

"But you haven't stopped it," said Frederick.

"They don't know that."

"Okay, I see where you're going with this," he said.

"All we need to do is confirm the gossip. We tell everyone that just before the Agent of Death died, he told us that he was here to kill the King. Agent dead… assassination foiled… everyone safe and happy."

"I don't see how this gets us even near the *Athena*." Jared looked doubtful.

"One step at a time, stay with me on this. As far as everyone's concerned, the danger has been averted and the King's life is no longer in imminent threat. This alone means that if Kraven gets wind of what has happened—"

"Which, as the Princess said, is probably a given," interrupted Jake, but I ignored him and continued.

"—he won't get spooked, believing he's still free and safe to continue with his original plan. In the meantime, as the Agent was one of his own staff, it wouldn't be unreasonable for the King to order a comprehensive security review of the Guard to ensure there aren't any more sleeper agents. Given the timing of the threat, surely it would be acceptable – prudent even – for the King to use an independent security team, and to procure alternative transport to the *Athena*. To be on the safe-side. It would be logical for him to utilise the prestigious Vanguard Class Cruiser, which just happens to be in orbit, and whose captain was part of the team responsible for neutralising the assassination threat. Would the *Athena* security not believe that?"

"It sounds convincing," Phina said, shifting slightly so her knee rubbed against Jared's leg. She gave him one of her finest enigmatic smiles.

"So that gets all of us to the ship," I continued, trying to ignore them. "We get on the *Athena* as the new Royal Family security detail."

Sebastian shook his head again. "You had a valid plan right up until the end. The *Athena* has its own protection detail; no House security is allowed on the ship – except for the Captains of each Guard."

I was out of ideas. "It's not like we need to attend the actual Summit – we just need to get on board. Can't we go as observers?" I added in frustration.

"Of course!" Frederick almost fell off the arm of the chair he was perched on. "Shae, you're a genius!"

# 18

Frederick radiated excitement.

"Father, I was reading through the ceremonial regulations of the Summit a few weeks back, and there's something in there I think we could use to get everyone on the *Athena.* What Shae said just jogged my memory." As he talked, he routed through the bookshelf that covered the entire end wall of the King's office. He pulled out an old, worn book, leafing through it quickly.

"Frederick?" questioned Sebastian.

"Nearly there," he said, stalling. "Here we are; this is the bit." He brought the tome back to the chairs and laid it open on the coffee table. "This book is effectively the ultimate set of laws regarding the Tetrad Summit. The codicil I'm referring to is hidden away at the back, and may have been overlooked. It's also kind of wordy. Listen: In addition to the maximum one-hundred emissaries endorsed by any Sector, the presiding monarch of the Hosting Sector may invite a small number of his or her more remote relatives to attend the extracurricular activities of the Tetrad Summit, though not the actual legal proceedings of said Summit."

"I haven't heard that before," Sebastian said. "And I certainly haven't heard of any hosting monarch using it to bring additional family to the Summit."

"Like I said, they're probably not even aware of it. This book is ancient," said Frederick, blowing dust off the cover as proof.

"I'm sorry, Frederick, but I don't see how this helps," I said. "We're not exactly family, distant or otherwise."

"I have an idea about that, too. We would have to go with a wide interpretation of the rule, but," he turned to his father, "we might be able to make them family using the Order of Royal Battle."

"What are you talking about, Freddie?" The Princess had lost patience.

"Careful, Phina," the King chastised. "Your brother has an interesting idea."

"He does?" Her small nose wrinkled.

"Interesting, yes, but I'm not sure… An Order of Royal Battle hasn't been awarded in over five centuries."

"What is it?" Phina asked, just as in the dark as the rest of us.

"It's a particular tribute given to individuals who've excelled themselves in a war fought with, or on behalf of, a ruling monarch. It went out of fashion because as well as receiving one of the most prestigious titles in the known worlds, the individual was also welcomed into the monarch's extended family. With all the benefits associated," Frederick explained.

"That's some award," Jared said.

"Yes, well, don't get your hopes up yet," said the King, standing. "Strictly speaking, they should only be awarded during times of war. I'll need to confer with my Chief of Staff."

It must've been almost an hour before the King returned with a harried looking gentleman wearing ceremonial robes almost as ancient as he was.

"I've spread our concocted story, and no doubt the gossip is making its way around the Palace as we speak." The King smiled. "I've also spoken to the *Athena* on the emergency channel to explain we'll be arriving on the *Defender* tomorrow. They weren't happy, but given the circumstances they've agreed to make an exception. In addition, I've invoked the codicil quoted by Frederick. I would've been back sooner, but it took their administrators some time to agree it's still an active clause. I've given them your names, and they're expecting you. Of course, you'll not be able to enter the actual Summit, but one step at a time, I say. That leaves us with one last bit of business."

Sebastian ushered the old man forward then asked the four of us to step into the middle of the room.

"Mr von Appler is going to formally officiate in these proceedings. I apologise they don't come with more pomp and circumstance, but I'm sure you understand."

When von Appler spoke, his voice was weak and phlegmy, and I wanted to cough for him. "King Sebastian the Third, Head of the House of Palavaria, Esteemed Ruler of Sector Three, and Protector of the Third Seal, has nominated the four of you to receive the Order of Royal Battle."

"Wait, what about the rest of the Wolfpack?" Jake asked.

"I'm sorry, Colonel, but it was difficult enough getting the four of you on the guest list," explained Sebastian. "I'm afraid the Pack will have to remain behind this time."

The old man continued. "The King has informed me that you were all instrumental in saving his life, thwarting an imminent and heinous threat to the Crown. While we're not at war in the strictest of terms, one could argue that, as Castilian Santiago was a member of the House of Palavaria, you were fighting a war on domestic terrorism. I can therefore confirm that your activities exceed the criteria for 'battle fought on behalf of the ruling monarch'. I'm pleased to confirm that the King is able to award you the Order of Royal Battle, and all that it bestows on you." He looked so frail I didn't think he was going to get to the end of his sentence, and I wished he would just cough already – that phlegmy wheezing made me queasy.

The King retrieved a ceremonial sword from one of the cabinets and ordered us to kneel in a line, which we did as best as we could, given the space. After some formal words, a tap on the shoulder with the sword, and a signature on von Appler's scroll, we were members of the Royal Family. Simple as that.

"Welcome to the House of Palavaria," Sebastian said quite cheerfully. "We'll have a party if I live through this."

"Father," Phina cried. "That's not funny. You shouldn't even joke about it."

"You'll need to take this scroll with you to the *Athena*," said von Appler. "It will confirm your official Palavarian family status." He handed it to Ash before retiring from the room, shuffling and wheezing.

"All right," said Jared loudly to get everyone's attention. "While King Sebastian has spread the story that he's no longer in danger, reality is very different. I apologise for my bluntness, Your Majesty, but there's no telling how deep your Guards have been infiltrated."

"No need to apologise," said the King. "What do you propose?"

"I think we should get you to the *Defender* as soon as possible."

"Father, I agree. I never thought I would ever say this, but it's not safe here." Phina turned to us. "We're already packed and prepared to leave, so most of our luggage can go on the shuttle tomorrow. We just need to get some essentials for tonight."

"Here's the plan then," said Jared. "Ash, you go with the King; help him pull together a few bits and then escort him to the *Veritas*. Shae, you do the same with Princess

Josephina, and I'll go with the Prince. Jake, you explain everything to the Wolfpack then get Peterson and the Doctor to the ship. Get Connor ready to fly as soon as we're all on board." Jake nodded. "Stay quiet and off the radar. No one's to know you're leaving; not even your personal staff. Agreed? Okay, let's go."

Not half an hour later, the Royals sat together in the main cabin of the *Veritas* as we headed towards the *Defender*. As I walked passed, I heard the tail-end of Jake's apology for the condition of his ship, though I thought, given the circumstances, the King and his family wouldn't care about the used coffee mugs, discarded rations packets, and dirty gun cleaning cloths. I did, however, think it prudent to pick up and hide Jake's blood-splattered t-shirt from earlier.

I joined Jared and Ash at the rear of the main cabin, where they were talking to Commander Tel'an on Jared's com-pad.

"That's right," Jared confirmed. "I want you to lock down the ship. No shuttles or communications are to leave the *Defender* until further notice. Is that clear, Commander?"

"Of course, Captain." Her voice had a note of intrigue in it.

"I also need VIP quarters one, three and five ready for our arrival, and I want you and three of our best security personnel to meet the *Veritas* when we land."

"Yes, Captain."

"Thank you. That will be all, Commander. No wait, one more thing. As soon as we're on board, I want the *Defender* moved away from Decerra. A short trip should do it, destination your choice, but keep us away from any mainstream planets."

"Aye, sir." The connection terminated.

Ash decided to check on the prisoners, leaving me alone with Jared for the first time since his fight with Jake, and more importantly, since 'the thing that happened'.

"I don't want to talk about it," I said, pre-empting any questions.

"You promised you would," he reminded me, trying to make eye contact, but I looked in every direction but his.

"Later," I suggested, fixating on a faded warning plaque on the wall. "Ash needs to know too, right? Might as well do it all together." I still hadn't given him the eye contact he was looking for, so he took my chin in his hand and raised my head up until I had no option but to look at him.

"You promise?"

"I—"

"Shae, Captain," Jake called and we both turned to see him gesturing for us to join him. "King Sebastian and his family would like to be shown to their quarters as soon as we land, and if it's acceptable with you, Captain, I've agreed that the Wolfpack will continue to provide security."

"Of course," Jared said, nodding towards the King.

"You've all done so much for us today, I cannot thank you enough," Sebastian said. "My children and I will be going through last minute plans for the Summit, and will be ably protected by the Colonel's Wolfpack. Please don't concern yourselves with us this evening. I'm sure you've other things you need to be doing."

"As you wish, Your Majesty," Jared said.

As soon as we'd disembarked on the *Defender*, Jared introduced Tel'an to the Royals before she, the security detail, and the Wolfpack, escorted them to their rooms. The rest of us took our prisoners to the brig. We'd just finished booking them in when Jake stepped away to take a call.

"That was Kaiser," he said, moments later. "The Royals are safe in the King's quarters, and he's set up a rota to cover the door at all times. Looks like we're done for the evening. So what now?" he asked, stretching.

"Now we need to talk," replied Jared, looking deliberately between Ash and me. "Why don't we go to the conference room and I'll have dinner delivered? We can plan for tomorrow… and Shae can tell us about that thing that happened."

"What thing?" Ash asked, unease suddenly flooding the Link.

"It's nothing, Ash. You know what? I'm not really that hungry. I might just head back to my quarters," I said.

"Nice try, but you're not getting away that easy. What thing?" he repeated, and I knew he wasn't going to let it go.

"Fine. I'll explain everything over dinner," I said, glowering at Jared.

So there we were, back in the conference room – again. I couldn't settle and paced the room until Ash said if I didn't sit down and tell him what was going on, he would tie me to the chair like he had when I was nine. We both ignored the questioning looks from the others, but the threat worked and I eventually sat. And like pulling off a band-aid, I decided to explain everything as quickly as I could.

"Something happened, Ash. Jake and Jared were fighting; I wanted them to stop; I held up my hands and… poof! Next thing I know, energy pulse-thingy; they were on the floor; all over." I took a breath. It hadn't been so bad after all. Three faces stared at me in frustration. "What?"

Ash was open-mouthed, his eyes wide. "What are you saying?" he asked slowly, his voice serious. "Are you telling me that… what exactly are you telling me? And for goodness sake, speak slowly this time. I need to know everything that happened."

A wave of fear flowed through the Link from him, catching me off guard. I turned to the others for support, but they looked at me the same way Ash was. Like I wasn't just a freak, I was a super-freak.

My stomach churned and I felt sick. I tasted bile in the back of my throat as I explained everything in as much detail as I could recall. Ash look dumbfounded, and by the time I'd finished, an unnatural stillness had settled over the room. I couldn't stand it. "Somebody please say something. Even if it's to tell me what a super-freak I am."

"Shae, you've always been a super-freak to me," Ash said. It broke the tension and I laughed, but I noticed he still had his serious face on. "So you were emotional when it happened?" he clarified.

"Yes," I said, although I wasn't comfortable admitting it in front of the others.

"And nothing like that has ever happened before?" Jared asked. Obviously he thought it was safe for him to talk, but he was wrong. I nailed him a brief, 'this is entirely your fault,' glare.

"No. I've told you that already."

"Have you tried to do it again?" Jake asked from the corner of the room, where he perched on the edge of a cabinet, his arms folded lightly across his broad chest.

"Of course not! Why, in the name of all things sane, would I want to do that again?" I noticed Ash's grey eyes narrow. "What?"

"It's just…"

"Just what? Ash, please tell me what you're thinking."

"It's pure speculation..."

"I don't care; tell me. You're scaring me."

"Okay, but I'm simply thinking out loud here. The monks found out you could heal yourself after you hit your head when you were three, right?" I nodded. "It wasn't until years later that your gift advanced to being able to heal someone else – me. Do you remember how you felt at the time?"

"I was scared you were going to die."

"Just like you were scared Jake or Jared was going to get hurt."

"Yes… are you suggesting this is another evolution of my gift?"

"I think it's clear we don't know anything for sure. You have an energy in you we don't understand. Over time, you've learnt to use that energy to heal, but maybe what you experienced today is another application of that power."

"Am I hearing this right? You're saying Shae can use her gift as a weapon?" Jake said, moving back to the table.

"Whoa!" I sat bolt upright. "Nobody said anything about being a weapon!"

"All I'm saying, Babe, is if you've got a bunch of gun-thugs coming at you, being able to blast them away with an energy pulse wouldn't be such a bad thing, right?"

"I think we're getting off point," interrupted Ash. "Like I said, we don't know for sure what happened, or whether it will even happen again, so I suggest we don't get carried away. Jared, Jake, let me make this clear, this is Brotherhood business – I trust I can count on your discretion?"

"Of course," Jared replied.

"Yeah, sure. My lips are sealed," added Jake.

"Good. And you," he turned to me, "promise me you'll tell me if you feel anything remotely similar again."

"I promise. And Ash? I'm sorry for not telling you earlier, but you were the only one still concentrating on the case."

"I understand," he replied. "Has anyone got anything else they need to add on this matter?" The question was there, but his tone implied the conversation was over. "Right then, I suggest we move on to other concerns."

With perfect timing, dinner arrived, and as we ate we agreed our plan for the following day, finishing around mid-evening. Jared excused himself to see to Fleet business, and Jake left to check in with the Wolfpack, so Ash and I headed back to his room.

It turned out the King's quarters were opposite mine, and as we strolled past, we said, "Hi," to Kaiser, who was on guard duty.

I settled myself on the couch in Ash's lounge, tucking my feet up under me.

"Okay, I've left it long enough. What's going on?" Ash

said, handing me a cup of coffee.

"I've told you everything I can remember."

"I'm not talking about that." I couldn't quite place the look on his face. "You're unsettled, Shae, and it's not like you. I want to help, but I can't if you don't tell me what's going on."

"I slept with Jake."

"I see," he replied, not a hint of judgment in his voice.

"It's not the fact that I slept with him that's the problem, it's the fact we slept together during a mission. It was unprofessional, and I'm disappointed in myself."

"Sometimes these things happen," he said philosophically. "You can't change what happened, so there's no point beating yourself up about it. No harm done."

"That's just it, there was."

"Captain Marcos?"

"Yes." My voice was quiet. "That's why they fought."

"I thought it might've been."

"It was all my fault, Ash. Perhaps Jared thought he was defending my honour or something."

"Or something," Ash said cryptically.

"Huh?"

"Don't blame yourself, Shae. Those two have been spoiling for a fight since the moment Jake came on the scene, but that's another story. Tell me what happened with Jake."

"I don't know; it's weird. From the first time we met, there was something… something between us. Every time he got near it was like I knew he was there – even if I couldn't see him – and a small touch from him would make my insides flutter. Am I making sense? It wasn't that I set out to sleep with him today, I actually went to kick his arse, but it was like I couldn't help myself."

"Did he…" Ash cleared his throat, "did he take advantage of you?"

"No! Oh no, Ash, not at all. Please don't think that."

"So how do you feel about him now?"

"Well, the physical attraction's definitely still there, but things are complicated… and confusing," I said, my cheeks warming. "I feel like we have this strange connection. And I do care deeply for him, more than I really should for someone I've only just met, but… oh, I don't know. I'm sorry; I'm probably not making any sense."

"I can't say I understand completely, but then I gave up trying to understand you a long time ago," Ash said, smiling. "I know it's difficult, but you do need to try and recognise your feelings for Jake. It's only fair on him."

"I know," I replied. "But that's easier said than done."

"What about the Captain?"

"What about him?"

"How do you feel about him?"

"There's no way I'm opening that can of worms tonight, Ash," I replied, forcing a laugh. "I can only deal with one emotional nightmare at a time."

"As you wish."

"I'll leave you in peace," I said, taking my cue from his yawn.

"Shae, don't beat yourself up about this. I hate to tell you, but sometimes things just don't make sense." He smiled and hugged me, giving me a gentle kiss on the forehead. "Everything happens for a purpose. It will all become clear at the right time. Have faith."

I headed back to my room, stopping for a brief chat with Kaiser along the way. I poured myself another coffee and wandered restlessly around the room until the com-panel by the door pinged and I went to answer it, thankful for the distraction.

"Hey, Ty," I said, surprised to see him. He stood in the doorway, hands in pockets, rocking from foot to foot. He'd showered and shaved, and looked remarkably presentable. He smelled much better, too.

"I… umm… I came to say I'm sorry again for… umm… restraining you earlier," he mumbled.

"It's okay, Ty, I know you were just following orders."

"Yeah, well, I'm sorry anyway."

I suspected Jake had sent him, but I didn't say anything because Ty already looked uncomfortable. When I'd said we were okay for the fourth time, it finally sunk in and he slunk off down the hallway. I caught Kaiser smirking, so I threw him a withering look before going back into my room.

I cleaned my Sentinel for something to do, wondering whether I'd secretly hoped it'd been Jake at the door – or even Jared. Still, it'd been neither of them. Perhaps they were both avoiding the super-freak.

I was thinking of Jared when I remembered something. Earlier, before the fight, he'd seemed so upset, so disappointed, I hadn't listened to him about Jake. Whatever his reasons, he genuinely seemed to want to protect me, and I'd ignored him. I felt bad.

I asked Grace for his location – he was in his quarters – and decided to take the risk he was still up.

"Can't sleep?" Kaiser asked as I left my room.

"No. Too much caffeine probably," I lied.

I'd never been to Jared's quarters, but I'd worked out the logic behind the *Defender's* design, and it was easy to find. I was about to knock when I stopped myself. What if he was already asleep? What if he didn't want to see the Super-Freak? Or worse still, what if he thought I was an awful person for sleeping with Jake? I turned to leave, but then the door opened.

"Shae?" Commander Tel'an seemed pleasantly surprised to see me. "You're here to see the Captain?"

"Umm… I… well," I stuttered ridiculously. "I'm sure he's busy. I'll catch him tomorrow."

"We've just been going over duty rosters. I'm sure…" She turned to call back into the room, but Jared was already in the doorway. "I'll leave you to it," she said, excusing herself.

Not that I've seen many captain's quarters, but Jared's looked relatively standard, though nothing compared to my quarters for luxury and size. I looked around, catching a glimpse of his bedroom, and perfectly made bed, through an archway to the rear.

I felt ridiculous. What was I doing there?

"Give me a second," Jared said, walking over to a huge desk, where he added a data-pad to the stacks already there – just catching a mug as an avalanche of pads almost knocked it off the edge.

Most of the furniture was standard Fleet issue, but he motioned towards an overstuffed couch in faded brown leather. It had been patched and re-patched, clearly seeing better days, and even though I thought it looked a little dubious, I had no option but to sit. I sunk into the soft leather and squashy cushions, and it was the most comfortable thing I'd ever sat on. Jared's smile widened.

"It was in one of the lounges at Fleet Academy," he explained. "I spent many nights studying on it to get me through exams, and in the end, I started to see it as a bit of a good luck charm. When I graduated, I persuaded a friend to help me liberate it. It's come with me on every ship since."

"I understand lucky charms," I said, looking at my boots. "But I can't imagine you stealing anything," I teased.

"Liberating," he clarified, his eyes sparkling.

"Of course: liberating. That makes all the difference." Talking to 'nice' Jared was uncomplicated, and as comfortable as the cushions.

"Now I know you didn't come here to try out my couch, or talk semantics with me, so what gives?" Jared asked, seating himself at the other end from me.

"Would it be ridiculous if I said I don't really know why I'm here?" I replied vaguely. He rubbed his chin and I expected him to say, 'yes, you're crazy', so I was surprised when he launched into an apology for the way he'd reacted in the *Veritas*.

"It was unprofessional, and it's none of my business what you get up to... but I guess it did give me the opportunity to beat the crap out of Jake," he concluded. For a moment I didn't know what to say, but then he gave me that boyish grin and I knew he was joking. We agreed to leave the topic and move on to something less contentious.

I don't know whether it was conscious on the part of either of us, but we avoided talking about the House of Palavaria, Jake, the Wolfpack, and even the mission. We chatted about his family, and what it was like for him growing up, and we talked more about my weird childhood with the Brotherhood. I'd already told him pretty much all there was to know about my biological family, but I explained why Finnian was the closest thing I had to a father, and why Ash was so important to me.

"Earlier, in the conference room," Jared said, "Ash mentioned he was the first person you healed – other than yourself that is. You can tell me it's none of my business, but I'd really like to hear what happened."

"It's not an easy story to tell," I replied, my skin already cold.

"It's okay, I understand. It was too much to ask."

"No, you know what? I'd like to tell you."

"You sure?"

"Yeah. I've only talked about what happened with a handful of monks, and they were more interested in analysing why my gift advanced. This is going to sound strange, but it'll be nice to talk about it with someone who's just interested in what happened."

"Well, I can promise I won't analyse you once," Jared replied, pummelling the back of the couch to make himself more comfortable.

"You better not," I said, swatting him with a cushion.

"Okay, here goes. It was a hot day in summer not long before my fifteenth birthday, so Ash would've been seventeen. I can't remember whose idea it was to go to the Gateway after classes, but we got there late afternoon."

"The Gateway?"

"Sorry, I forget you don't know. It's a cliff-face the monks use for training – rock-climbing and abseiling, that sort of thing. Ash and I were always competitive, and I clearly remember Ash challenging me to a race to the first staging point. We set off, climbing as fast as we could, joking and laughing until we were out of breath. Ash was beating me, which, to be fair, was pretty normal. He was way stronger and faster than me, and when I did actually beat him, I was sure it was because he let me."

"You're smiling," Jared commented.

"Those were good times… mostly," I replied, surprised that he was right. "Good memories, except this one."

"You don't need to continue if it's too hard."

"It's fine. I'm okay. So, Ash was quite a long way in front of me, and almost to the first staging-point, when I heard him cry out. At first I thought it was a tactic to let me catch up, but my heart froze when he said he'd been bitten by a rock snake. Ash would never joke about something like that, so I knew it was serious. I couldn't think straight, but I managed to open a com-link to the monastery. Brother Benjamin tried to keep his voice calm, but I knew it was bad."

"So you saved him from the snake bite?"

"No. Well, yes, I suppose I did in the end, but what happened was much worse." Jared sat up straighter. "Benjamin told me to climb back down to safety, but I couldn't, I had to get to Ash. I could see he was having trouble keeping his grip, and I was almost to him when the venom finally took hold. It was like one of those surreal, slow-motion moments as he dropped past me. I lunged out to grab him, but he was out of my reach."

Jared passed me a glass of water and I realised my pulse was racing.

"I'll never forget that dull, sickening thump as Ash hit the rock platform below." I shuddered.

"Shae—"

"No, let me finish. I need to finish."

"Okay." His eyes darkened with concern.

"By the time I reached him, I was convinced he was dead. His body was broken and bent, blood trickled out of his nose and mouth, and his head was split open." I pointed out where the split was on my own head, my hand shaking. Jared shuffled along the couch and took it in his own. "There was so much blood, Jared. It pooled underneath his head and there was nothing I could do. It was like I'd broken inside as well."

"But he couldn't have been dead," Jared said.

"No, thank the Gods. I heard him moan. It was barely audible, and at first I thought it was just wishful thinking, but then I forced myself to really listen. His breath was faint and uneven, but it was there, and I remember pleading with him not to die. Actually, I guess it was more like an order." I laughed sadly. "It was like I was angry he'd got himself broken. Finnian was the first monk to arrive, and he tried to pull me away, but I wouldn't leave. Apparently, I was hunched over Ash's body, crying and shouting, 'You are not going to die,' and then it happened."

"You were healing him?"

"Yes. I didn't even know I was doing it at first. Finnian said my whole body shimmered then something like fine strands of light crossed between my hands and Ash's chest. Then Ash shimmered too, and all I could think was, 'You're not going to die. You're not going to leave me'. I heard people talking and shuffling around me, but nothing mattered to me except Ash. I passed out moments later."

Jared puffed out a long breath. "What happened after that?"

"When I came around, I was in the hospital wing of the monastery and Ash was sitting on the side of the bed next to me, smiling that big lopsided grin of his. It was like nothing had happened to him. He didn't even have the scar on his chin from when we'd been Staff training and he'd ducked when he should've dived. I couldn't remember what I'd done, but the monks filled me in on the details. At first I didn't believe them, but then how else could Ash have been there… perfect? I tried to heal people for a long time after that with no success, but eventually I got the hang of it, and now, as with Harrison, it's relatively easy."

"I don't know what to say," he said, finally letting go of my hand to rub his chin.

"Oh my gods! Put out the bunting and call a national holiday – Jared's speechless," I joked.

"Funny," he replied. "Seriously though, now I understand the connection you have with Ash. It means a lot that you trust me enough to share something so personal."

"Well, I appreciate you kept you word and didn't try to analyse me."

"There's still time," he said, grinning. I swatted him again with the cushion.

I sat back, breathing in the faint aroma of sandalwood and musk, and it reminded me of the way Jared smelled after a shower. It seemed homely, and even though I'd just relived one of the most painful memories I had, I felt comfortable with him.

I didn't want to leave.

# 19

When I woke the following morning, I had no idea where I was. I wasn't in my own bed on Lilania, and I wasn't in my quarters on the *Defender*. I sat up, trying to get my bearings, and it took me a while to realise I was in Jared's bed. I put my hand over to the other side of the mattress, disappointed he wasn't there.

I slid out from beneath the covers, fully dressed, and as my eyes adjusted to the dark, I noticed Jared asleep on the couch. I crouched beside him, watching his chest rise and fall with each breath, and idly traced the scar above his eye with the tip of my finger, wondering what history it told. He woke with a start, which made me jump, and I spent the next five minutes apologising to him.

"How did I…?" I asked, pointing towards the bedroom, my cheeks warming.

"You fell asleep on the couch," he replied. "You looked so peaceful I didn't have the heart to wake you, and it was easier to carry you there than back to your quarters. I hope you don't mind?"

"Of course not." I couldn't argue with his logic.

"I need a shower," he said, stretching. "You're welcome

to stick around, but I have a staff meeting at zero-eight-hundred."

"I need to get cleaned up myself," I replied, thinking I hadn't showered since before Jake and I had… I felt quite disgusting all of a sudden.

"Why don't you meet me in the Mess Hall for breakfast at zero-nine-hundred? It'll give me an excuse to keep the meeting short and sweet."

"Sure. Sounds like a plan," I replied, returning his smile.

I stopped outside my quarters to retrieve the fresh set of clothes left by the quartermaster and said, "Good morning," to Connor, who was on guard duty.

A note was pinned to the package: 'My Dearest Shae. I've made an appointment for us to see the ship's seamstress at ten-hundred in the Kit Room, Level 12, Room 14B. We need to agree your wardrobe for the Summit. Please let me know if this time is inconvenient, otherwise I'll meet you there. Deepest Regards, Commander Tel'an.'

It hadn't occurred to me that I wouldn't be able to wear my usual combats on the *Athena*. I was supposed to be the privileged recipient of the Order of Royal Battle and a member of the Royal Family – of course fatigues weren't going to cut it.

A little before zero-nine-hundred, I left my quarters for the Mess Hall. Jared and Ash sat at the same refectory table as before, and they both rose as I approached. I climbed over the bench next to Jared, put my tray on the table, and leant forward to kiss Ash good morning, but then, without thinking, I turned and kissed Jared on the cheek. My stomach flipped when I realised what I'd done, and I desperately hoped he hadn't thought it inappropriate. It's not like I could take it back, but I tried to look out of the corner of my eye to catch his reaction. He'd returned to his breakfast as if nothing had happened.

"How was your meeting?" I asked, trying to sound

natural.

"Urgh. I hate staff meetings," he said quietly. "Bane of my life."

He filled us in on what was happening on the *Defender*, at least what he could tell us, and it was actually quite interesting. I hadn't realised being the captain of a Vanguard Class Cruiser was so demanding, and I was sure his life hadn't been made easier by our current situation. Of course, he could choose to sit out the investigation, but I knew there was no way in hell he would do that.

We were so engrossed in conversation I didn't notice Jake until he sat down heavily next to Ash. I contemplated whether I should give him a kiss to offset the one I'd given Jared, but decided it might give him the wrong impression. Things were far too complicated. In the end, I decided a friendly, "Good morning, Jake. How did you sleep?" would suffice.

"Fine thanks." His voice had an edge to it; not much, just enough to make me think something was up. "You?" he asked me directly, ignoring the others.

"Very well, thank you."

"Good," he replied. He lowered his eyes and began to eat, but I noticed he seemed unusually interested in me. Every time I glanced at him, he was already looking at me, and it began to make me feel uncomfortable. In the end, it got too much, and when I caught him staring at me for about the hundredth time, I snapped.

"What is it, Jake? What's with you this morning?"

"It's nothing," he said, trying to convince me with an award-winning smile. "We'll talk about it later, okay?"

"Oh, okay. Sure," I replied, confused.

"She was in my bed," said Jared, casually.

"What?" Jake and I chorused.

"That is what you wanted to ask Shae, wasn't it, Jake? I'm guessing one of the Wolfpack told you she was out all night, and you want to know where she was. Well... she was in my bed," he repeated.

Jake's eyes flashed, his lips thinned, and his knuckles turned white from gripping his cutlery so tightly. It looked like he was using every ounce of self-control he had to stop himself from sticking the fork in Jared's neck. Ash didn't look surprised, so I guessed Jared had already told him what'd happened, but he shifted position and readied himself to intervene if necessary.

"Relax, Jake." Jared grinned. "I'm just playing with you. Shae fell asleep on my couch and I moved her to the bed – fully clothed. I slept on the couch." Jake continued to glare at him dangerously, but he loosened his grip on the cutlery.

"I don't believe it," I hissed. "Just when I thought you could be trusted to play nice together, you prove you're nothing more than oversized kids. Jake?" I waited until he gave me eye contact. "If you wanted to know where I was – not that it's any of your business – you should've just asked." I caught Jared smirking again as I turned to face him. "And you? You're lucky you have your crew around you, otherwise I would smack you upside your head for being an arse." Anger rose in my chest and I hated myself for letting them have that effect on me. "Grow up. Both of you." I stood so suddenly I knocked the tray and a mug tumbled over, clattering on the plate. "Sort it out by the next time I see you. I'm not kidding."

"Wait, where are you going?" Jake asked.

"I have an appointment with Commander Tel'an," I replied before turning to Ash. "Perhaps you can knock some sense into them?"

"I'm not sure that's possible," he replied, shrugging.

"Please try."

By the time I found the Kit Room, I had a killer headache. It was as if I had Jake bitching away in one ear, Jared slinging childish insults in the other, and my brain was caught in the middle. I rubbed my temples with my fingertips, hoping to squash them away, and prayed that

Ash would deal with the pair of them.

"Hello, Shae," Tel'an said brightly. "I hope you don't mind my being here to help pick out your wardrobe, but the Captain felt you might like another woman's opinion."

"Are you kidding? I live in these." I picked at my loose-fitting trousers. "The more help the better as far as I'm concerned." Tel'an was so beautiful I imagined she'd have perfect taste; she even made her Fleet uniform look good.

"Well, Henrietta's the best Senior Seamstress in Fleet," she explained. "She's a little… eccentric, but a genius when it comes to clothes."

As she finished talking, a slightly crazed-looking woman with wild hair popped up from behind a counter. She spoke too fast, I had to really concentrate to understand what she was saying, and she was so animated, she had to keep pushing her glasses back up her nose to stop them falling off.

Eventually I made out that she wanted us to go with her and we followed her through several rooms, each filled with different items of standard issue uniforms, until we reached a locked hatch. She ushered us through, and when the lights came on, I stood open-mouthed and unable to speak.

The seamstress dashed off, weaving in and out of glittering racks, and a little more than ten minutes later, she came back with a rail bursting with the finest dresses.

It took me the best part of two hours to try them all on, and I was grateful Tel'an was there to help. I hadn't realised putting on fancy dresses was such an ordeal, but by the end of it the seamstress said I had a wardrobe fit for a princess. She told me the outfits would be packed and ready for collection by the *Athena* shuttle, except for one, which she'd have delivered to my quarters for me to wear that afternoon.

"What about the trousers?" I asked.

The seamstress threw her hands up in exasperation. "You explain it," she said to Tel'an as she pushed us out the door. "I've got a lot of work to do."

"No trousers," Tel'an said as we left the Kit Room. "Unless carrying out an activity where a dress would be impractical, female members of the Royal Family must wear dresses at all times."

"Is this the Dark Ages?" I grumbled. "How am I supposed to protect King Sebastian and his family if I have to hitch up three layers of skirt before I can fight anyone?" I saw the look on Tel'an's face and knew there was no point discussing the matter further. I said goodbye and returned to my quarters.

I spent so long in the shower that by the time I got out, I only had twenty minutes until I had to meet the others for our final briefing. As the seamstress had promised, a dress bag hung in my bedroom with a note attached: 'Found this and knew it would be perfect'. I unzipped it with an increasing sense of dread and pulled out a full-length, silk gown in dark purple. I stepped in it, knowing before I'd even pulled it up the bodice would be tight fitting. It had narrow straps and a low-cut neckline – too low-cut. The last thing I wanted was to take off after a bad guy and have my boobs spill out of the damn thing.

I struggled to do the zip up in the back, wondering whether you had to dislocate a shoulder to be able to do it on your own. In a fit of frustration, I considered doing just that, after all, I would heal, but I figured a more sensible option would be to ask whichever member of the Wolfpack was standing guard outside the King's room.

I shuffled to the door, one hand on my chest to hold the bodice in place, and one gripping the flowing skirt so I didn't fall flat on my face. I must be the only person in existence who could look so unladylike in something so beautiful. I was agitated and beginning to fluster, so the last person I expected, or wanted, to see was Jake. But there he was, right outside my door talking to Ty.

"Jake!" I gasped, letting go of the skirt so that it fell

gracefully to the floor. He looked incredible. It was the first time I'd seen him in his uniform, and damn he looked sexy.

"Holy crap," he exclaimed, openly staring at me, a hungry smile on his lips. "You look… awesome."

"No I don't," I replied irritably as one of the straps fell off my shoulder. I put it back in place but it fell down again, and I noticed Jake and Ty both watching. "Stop staring," I demanded, adding, "Jake, I need you."

"That's what every man wants to hear, Babe."

"Shut up, and get in here," I said, pulling him into my quarters by his arm – he didn't resist. As the door closed behind us, I turned to him and tripped over the hem of the skirt, practically falling into his arms. I put my hands out to stop myself falling, only just managing to grab the bodice before exposing myself.

"You look stunning, Babe," he said as I righted myself.

"Can you help? I think you need to be some kind of contortionist to do the bloody thing up. I look ridiculous."

"You look perfect." He stepped closer. "That is a great dress... how easy does it come off?" he added with a mischievous sparkle in his green-flecked eyes. "I'm guessing if you let go of that bodice, it comes off quick enough."

I struggled to focus as he lifted his hand and touched my lips with his thumb, and I knew I should've stepped away from him, but I couldn't make my legs work. He moved his fingertips down my throat and over my neck, and I lifted my head in response, sighing. His fingers continued along my collarbone, moving the strap of the dress off my shoulder before he bent forward and kissed my neck.

"Jake, no," I choked as the embers stirred, and the inevitable goose bumps sprang up on my skin. I couldn't stop myself from leaning closer to him, and as my hand reached around the back of his head, my fingers tangled in his hair before I even knew what I was doing. Fire burned inside me as he continued to kiss my shoulder. "Jake, I—" His lips were on mine, his tongue searching and hungry, and I kissed him back. Flashes of previous intimacy blazed through my head and my body reacted, just as it had done before.

He ran his fingers down the bare skin on my spine, and excitement rippled through me. How could a simple touch make me want him so badly?

I was completely captivated again, but a single thought kept trying to punch its way through the fog in my head: I had a job to do. I pulled away. "Behave," I said, straightening my skirt.

"Now where would be the fun in that?" he replied, holding his hands out to me. Flushed skin and hungry eyes betrayed his lust.

"Seriously, Jake... you'll crease the dress." It was weak, but it was the only thing I could manage.

"Then let me take it off you, and we won't have that problem." It was clichéd, but it was actually a rational solution. I even thought about it – just for a moment.

"Jake, please can you just do me up." I turned my back to him, but instead of pulling the zip, he pulled me into his body, and I could tell from his hardness pressing into the small of my back how much he wanted me. He moved my hair to the side to kiss the nape of my neck, and I was way too close to giving in to him. "Don't," I said, pulling away.

"You're angry with me."

"Of course not." I touched his cheek with my hand. "I'm angry at myself for being so damn weak when you touch me, but I'm not angry with you. There's nothing I want more than to give myself to you, but we have a job to do. And I think you know that, or you'd have had me out of this thing already." I flapped the skirt for emphasis. He looked away, and I took it that I was right.

"I was worried you regretted yesterday. That you thought you'd made a mistake," he said in a moment of seriousness.

"You're such an idiot," I replied, but when his eyes

flicked to mine, I could tell he didn't know whether I was being serious or not. "No, I don't regret it. I regret the timing of it. Just like now."

He was silent for a moment. "I know it shouldn't bother me you spent the night with him, but it does. I admit it: I'm jealous when you're with him."

"I spent the night in Jared's quarters, not with him." I clarified the distinction again.

"I know you like him."

"I do, most of the time. I like nice Jared. I'm not so keen on Jared the Arse though. I've never known a man who makes me so mad."

"And yet you always forgive him."

"No, I…" I let the sentence hang because I realised he was right. I turned my back and asked him to do me up again, which he did without any further attempt at intimacy – just as well because the door pinged moments later.

When Jared walked in, I had my elbows out at shoulder height with Jake's arms around my waist, trying to do up a delicate belt buckle from behind. He moved his body closer to mine, and I was sure he was making a deal of doing up the belt so he could keep his arms around me for longer.

"You might find that easier to do from the front," Jared offered. "Just a suggestion."

"I'm good, thanks," replied Jake, his breath warm on my neck. When he'd finally done it up, he kissed my bare shoulder before stepping away.

I straightened myself out then turned to face them. "How do I look?"

Silence.

Eventually Jake said I looked exotic and stunning, and Jared said I looked like a true Princess, but I wasn't convinced. I glanced down at the dress and frowned. "How am I supposed to catch bad guys in this?" I despaired. "I can hardly even breathe in it."

Ash arrived, wearing the spare set of ceremonial robes

he kept on the *Nakomo* for emergencies, and the four of us went to the King's quarters for our final briefing. After a short discussion, we set off en masse to the landing bay to meet the shuttle from the *Athena*.

If I thought the dress was bad, the heels were worse, and after tripping several times, Jake put his arm around my waist to support me. While I appreciated his attempt to save my dignity, I was surprised by the effect that small action had on almost every other person in our party.

By the time we got to the hangar, the unassuming shuttle from the *Athena* had docked, and the Officiator informed us our cases had already been cleared and loaded on board. While we waited to be checked for weapons and biological hazards, I pulled and tugged at my dress until Phina pointedly told me to stop fidgeting.

"Your Majesty," Ash said before we entered the shuttle. "Are you sure you want to do this? Your life is still at risk and you're putting yourself in great danger. No one would think less of you if you withdrew from the Summit."

"Your concern for my wellbeing is appreciated, Brother Asher, but my place is at the Summit. Besides, I'm sure you would agree it will be easier to draw out Kraven and his collaborator if I'm there as a target. This is something I have to do – I will not let ARRO dictate my actions."

From the outside, the shuttle looked reserved and modest, but inside it was all luxury and comfort. Our Officiator, Rew Albright, was a gently spoken man, and when we were all seated he started his briefing by handing us all leather-bound folders containing Summit information and itineraries.

"Welcome to the Tetrad Summit, Your Majesty, Your Highnesses. I'm sure you don't want me to bore you with too much information at this stage, so I'll keep this short. Everything you need to know is in your folders, however I will be your House Aide for the duration of your stay on the *Athena*. If you want to know anything, anything at all, please ask. As Royals, you'll have access to dedicated facilities, dining rooms and lounges; details of which are in your packs. Alternatively, you can have anything you wish delivered to your rooms. There is one small change to the itinerary for tonight: the Royal Welcome Dinner will start with cocktails at six-forty-five instead of six. The Summit will start at nine tomorrow morning, as planned. Please, enjoy your stay on the *Athena*." He smiled genuinely, and I decided I quite liked Rew.

After the initial brief he came to our group, where he crouched down and lowered his voice. "Sirs, Lady Shae, due to the late nature of your inclusion in the Summit, we've had to rearrange some rooms. We've only two suites in the Royal Zone available, but the Captain and Commander have offered up their quarters. They're very adequate, but obviously in a different part of the ship. I can only offer our humble apologies for this inconvenience."

"Do the Royal suites have a couch?" asked Ash.

Rew's forehead creased. "Yes, of course. All the suites have full lounge and bedroom accommodation."

"Then please thank your Captain and Commander for their very generous offer, but we won't inconvenience them. The four of us will share the two suites."

Rew's eyebrows knitted together in bafflement. "But, sir, Royalty should never have to share a suite. It's unheard of."

I'd forgotten that as far as the *Athena* was concerned, we were members of the Palavarian Royal Family and it made me smile. "Rew, it's okay. Honestly. Captain Marcos and Colonel Mitchell will take one suite," I caught the shared look of irritation on their faces and smiled again, "Brother Asher and I will share the other."

"My Lady, I cannot put you in such a compromising situation." Rew looked horrified. "My superiors will be dreadfully unhappy if they find out I've allowed this to happen."

"Brother Asher isn't just a Brother, he's my brother –

family. We'll be quite all right sharing. In fact, I insist. And if your superiors give you grief over it, tell them to come talk to me and I'll put them straight. Okay?"

Rew reluctantly agreed, but he didn't look happy as he disappeared to make the new arrangements.

When we landed on the *Athena*, there were several stewards waiting to show us all to our individual rooms. Instead, much to their bewilderment, we all escorted the three true Royals to the safety of the King's suite. After Sebastian promised they would remain there until we came back for them, we left.

It was time to find Kraven.

# 20

I hoped Kraven would be easy to find, but I knew we weren't that lucky. As we headed towards the Central Security Hub to begin our search, I recognised the bald head and stocky frame of the man walking towards us.

"Francis," I cried, flinging myself into his arms.

"I couldn't believe it when I heard four additional members of the Palavarian Royal Family were attending the Summit," he said after putting me down. "And Finnian nearly had heart failure when we found out it included you two. How did you pull that one off?"

"It's a long story, and one for another time, Francis. It's good to see you, old friend," said Ash.

"You, too, my brother."

"Hey, where is Finnian?" I asked, just as the Primus appeared.

I was happy I had my family back together, and even though I'd only known them a matter of days, I included Jake and Jared in that as well – a fact that still surprised and confused me.

After the greetings and introductions had concluded, we found a quiet corner so Ash could brief Francis and Finnian on everything that'd happened.

"So, is everyone happy with the plan?" he asked when he'd finished. "Jake, Jared, pull whatever military strings you can with *Athena* Security. Find out what they know about Kraven – what he's been up to, where he's been on ship, and where he might be now. Primus, with respect, can you and Francis use our Brotherhood network to do the same? Shae and I will head to his quarters. I doubt it'll be that easy, but we might find something. Please try to be inconspicuous, and remember, we need him quickly... and we need him alive." Everyone nodded their understanding, but as we were about to split up, he added, "And gentlemen? Try not to kill each other."

I was pretty sure that wasn't aimed at Finnian and Francis.

When Ash and I reached Kraven's room, my hand automatically fell to my thigh and I cursed the no-weapons rule again. I knocked on the door and Ash gave me his 'are you kidding me' face. "No harm in trying," I said. "Jared, we're at Kraven's. Can you get us access?"

"Working on it."

"Can you work faster?"

"We're still negotiating with Walden, the Chief of Security." I picked up the irritation in his voice and decided not to push further, instead Ash and I loitered silently in the hallway. "You should have access now," Jared said after a couple of minutes. I heard the quiet click of the lock, and when Ash pushed the door lightly, it swung open.

Kraven's room was a maid's worst nightmare; clothes left where they fell, and ready-food dishes littering most surfaces. "I don't know what you're expecting us to find – except a new strain of mould, that is," I said, rooting through some papers on the desk.

"Maybe nothing," replied Ash. "But maybe he's not as careful as he thinks."

We searched the room meticulously, trying not to

disturb anything, but the mess made our task difficult. The only interesting thing we found was hardcopies of the ship's blueprints, but as Ash pointed out, he had legitimate access to them in his position.

"Security hasn't seen Kraven since yesterday," Jake said through my earpiece. "And that's unusual, given the imminent start of the Summit. They also said he seemed vague and preoccupied."

"Did anyone question him about it?" The voice belonged to Finnian.

"No. Apparently they were too busy with their own tasks – useless bastards. They're going to check surveillance cameras to see if they can locate Kraven, but there are hundreds on board and large areas aren't covered at all for guest privacy. Waste of time if you ask me."

"Jake, Kraven's got a data-screen in his room. Can you get someone to check the coms-log?" I asked.

"Already on it, Babe. He's received a number of messages over the last couple of days, but they're all encrypted."

"Of course they are."

"The tech guys are working to decrypt them, but in the meantime, we've identified some of the places Kraven liked to hang out. Jared and I are going to check out a couple of bars, but there's a training room near you he used regularly. I'm sending you the coordinates."

"We'll take a look," said Ash.

We left Kraven's quarters and headed straight to the location, but it was another waste of time. "This is a nightmare," I grumbled. "Kraven has access to the entire ship – he could be anywhere. What now?"

Without any better suggestions from the team, we decided to head back to the Security Hub, but as soon as we walked in the door, we were collared by the Senior Duty Officer.

"What's going on?" Ash asked.

"We were able to decode Kraven's last message," he replied.

"Hold on." Ash opened a com-link to the team. "Go ahead," he prompted.

"We've decoded the last message Kraven received. There's no originator identification so we don't who sent it, but it reads: 'Meet eighteen-hundred today, usual location'."

"Is that it?" I asked.

"I'm afraid so."

"When was the message sent?" Ash asked.

"Just before ten-hundred this morning."

"Great!" Jake's disembodied voice was sarcastic. "So we know Kraven's meeting someone in a little under half an hour, but it could be anywhere on board. That's helpful."

I was about to thank him for making such a fantastically useful comment, when a woman hurried over.

"Sir, I apologise for interrupting, but I've just come on shift and found out what's happening. I don't know if it's much help, but last night, while I was doing my usual security sweep, I saw Kraven exiting a maintenance hatch. I challenged him but he said a repair crew had reported a suspicious item and he'd gone to check it out. Said it turned out be a kit-bag left behind by a worker on a previous shift. It sounded like something those guys would do so I didn't think anything of it – until now."

"Where exactly is this maintenance hatch?" Ash asked.

"And what size boots do you wear?" I added.

Ash and I met up with Jake, Jared, Finnian, and Francis at maintenance hatch 12-4F. Thanks to the security team, we'd been issued torches, and data-pads loaded with schematics for the maintenance shafts that crisscrossed the belly of the ship.

"We've less than twenty minutes until the meeting and miles of tunnel. You know your directions – if you find them, call in your location and the rest of us will converge.

We'll take them down together. Together," Ash emphasised. "Be safe everyone."

The tunnels were dark and dirty, and I felt ridiculous tramping through them in my dress – but at least I wore the sensible boots I'd managed to liberate, as Jared would say, from the security officer. Ash held the torch, leading the way, and I marked off junctions and tunnels on the data-pad as we passed through them. The com-link was ominously quiet, and our search became more urgent as time moved closer to eighteen-hundred – then it started to move past.

"Found them. Sending location now," whispered Francis over coms. "Can't see who Kraven's talking to, but he's giving Kraven a package."

"We're on our way," I said, plotting the quickest intercept path on the data-pad before sprinting off down the tunnel.

It was Finnian's quiet, calm voice on coms next. "The meeting's finishing and they're about to leave… we're going in."

"No, wait," Ash said.

"We'll lose them both if we don't," whispered Francis.

"Hold fast. Wait for backup," Jared said urgently. "We're nearly with—"

Two gun shots echoed through the tunnels.

I knew we were close because I heard them without the aid of the com-link. My blood turned cold, and I ran as fast as I could through the gloom, desperate to get to them.

The first thing I saw was Francis restraining a man on the floor. I could see it wasn't Kraven, but Francis had him well under control, so I turned my attention to the rest of the scene. Through the dim light, I made out Jared kneeling over someone on the floor. I guessed that was Kraven, but where were Finnian and Jake?

When he heard me, Jared rose quickly, closing the short distance between us in a couple of steps. He grabbed my shoulders, blocking my way, and I looked up into his face. There was something in his eyes, something that frightened me.

"I'm sorry," he said. "Shae, I'm so, so sorry."

I leaned around him to look at the figure on the floor. "No," I gasped, struggling against his grip. "No! It can't be."

I watched helplessly as Ash dropped to his knees next to Finnian's body, his whole body sagging. Jared pulled me closer, wrapping his arms tightly around me, but what was he thinking? I could heal Finnian. He would be okay. I tried to back away, but he wouldn't release me.

"Let me go," I cried, finally pulling free. "I can fix him, you know I can."

I sank down next to Ash, my breath faltering at the sight of the two bullet holes in Finnian's chest, but it was okay he would be all right. I closed my eyes and put my hands over Finnian's chest, trying to clear my thoughts so the healing could begin.

"He's gone," Ash said, his voice trembling.

"No, he's not. I can do this." But as I looked between my father's motionless body and my brother's face, realisation crashed through me.

"He's gone," he repeated, gathering me up in his arms, but I didn't want to be held. Not by Ash, and not by Jared.

It was like a switch flipped in my head. I pulled clear of Ash and stood, facing Jared. "What happened?" I asked calmly – the kind of weird-calm people get when they're scarily angry. Jared looked to Ash. "Don't look at him, he was with me. What happened here?"

"Shae, I'm worried about you," Jared said, rubbing my arm, but I shrugged him off. My father was dead, and the only thing keeping me going was the thought of finding the bastard that did it... and taking him down. I was running on revenge – pure and simple.

"Don't make me ask again, Jared," I said, my tone

cautionary.

"Okay, Shae, but I don't know exactly. Jake and I arrived just after the gunshots. Francis was getting him under control." He pointed to the man trussed up on the floor. "I went to Finnian, and Jake took off after Kraven. There was nothing I could do – nothing you could've done. He was already dead."

My resolve wavered, but I held on to my anger.

"It was Kraven," Francis said quietly. "We had no idea the package was a gun, and when Finnian went to take him down they struggled. Kraven shot him – I couldn't do anything." He looked distraught, even in the dim light. "I'm sorry," he added as Jake reappeared.

Jake was breathing hard and he bent over, putting his hands on his knees to get his breath back.

"Tell me you got him," I said, but he shook his head silently.

A data-pad pinged and Francis picked it off the floor. "Seems this is Quentin Gabriel – Lord Master for the House of Palavaria."

"Seriously?" Jared was stunned. "Gabriel?" He rubbed his chin and went to take a closer look. "I didn't recognise him in the darkness, but it explains a lot."

"Why?" Ash asked.

"Because Lord Master is the highest civilian rank within the House. Gabriel would've known everything about the Summit from the moment it was changed from Sector Two to Sector Three. He was in the perfect position to organise something like this."

"I heard rumours that the head of Sector Three's Rebel Opposition was someone in the administration," said Jake. "But I never thought—"

"You knew, and you did nothing?" A flash of anger burst through my steely-calm. Gabriel laughed, but Jake stood between us.

"Look at me, Shae. They were rumours. Nothing more

than drunk-talk and urban legend. Over the years, the REF has put various squads on the case, but they've all came up empty. There wasn't a shred of proof to act on."

"Well, there is now," I replied, stepping around him.

Quentin Gabriel leant against the tunnel wall, his hands tied behind his back, his ankles bound. I didn't care that he was restrained when I put my full weight into the punch that I landed on the side of his head.

"What's the plan?" I demanded.

A cruel smile crept across his face. "There'll be a white moon over Larrutra before I tell you anything," he mocked.

"Really?" I said, before landing another punch. Blood tricked from his nose and he licked it off before spitting it at me. The red was barely visible against the dark purple of my dress.

"You can't stop ARRO." He smiled again, smug with self-righteousness. "We're too big, too strong, and we're getting more powerful by the day."

"Save the speech, I'm not interested."

"Look at you," he continued unabated. "The oh-so-principled Brotherhood's Warrior Caste – nothing more than the REF's lapdogs. And what about you two?" He turned to Jared and Jake. "You think you're any better? You follow your orders blindly, too stupid to realise that the people who give them to you are fools themselves."

"That's enough," Jake grunted.

"What? Can't take the truth? Well, here's some more for you: the time of the Monarchy is over. The Leadership of Humans will be reclaimed by the people – by force if necessary. No longer will power be taken by pathetic, weak individuals just because of an accident of birth. Royal families are a fabrication of power – a lie fed to the masses to keep them compliant. They smother the democratic rights of—"

"Someone shut him up," said Jake, and I obliged by punching him hard in the face again.

"So all this is because you think you should lead Sector Three instead of King Sebastian?" asked Jared.

"Me?" Gabriel laughed loudly. "You don't have a clue, do you? This isn't about me, it's much bigger – it's always been about giving power back to the people... all the people. A new era will begin, I give you my word on that. Everything I've done has led to this point, and I'm proud to have played my part."

"You're really going with that old cliché? Couldn't think of anything more original?" I said.

"It doesn't matter, there's nothing you can do to stop us. ARRO is more powerful than you know. Sure, you can take me out of the game, but one of my generals will step up into my place, and one of their lieutenants will step into theirs. You might even get to one or more of them, but the movement can never be stopped."

"We'll see if you're still singing the same song after the REF interrogators get through with you," Jake said.

"Ah, yes," Gabriel replied. "The inimitable Royal Earth Force; what a joke. You know, the advantage of working with true professionals – like the Assassin Elite – is that you pick up a few useful tricks along the way."

Gabriel made an odd movement with his jaw, and before I could do anything but open my mouth to object, he'd swallowed the suicide pill from his tooth.

"He's dead," Jared said after checking his pulse. "The only reason I can see for Gabriel to risk meeting Kraven now, is because they're about to make their move. You think Kraven's going to try and assassinate the King at the Royal Welcome Dinner?"

"Killing Sebastian in front of a room full of Royals would certainly make the statement Nyan mentioned," agreed Ash.

I paced, digesting Kraven's words, hardly listening to the conversation as it continued, but then Jake appeared at my side.

"Babe, I'm worried about you," he said.

"I'm fine."

"But—"

"Kraven knows we're after him, but we're going to get the bastard, yes?"

"Of course, but… wait, where are you going?"

"Isn't it obvious?" I said rationally. "I have to get ready for the Royal Dinner. If we don't get to him first, Kraven's going to come to us eventually."

"No way," Jake exclaimed. "We don't even know for sure there aren't more cell operatives out there. Besides, Kraven's armed – you're not."

"Neither are you, so your point is?"

"That's—"

"I'll go with Shae," Ash interrupted as Jake and I squared off against each other. "They'll think it's odd if I'm not there anyway."

"Fine," I agreed, because he was right – and because I couldn't argue any longer and still keep it together. Facing up to Jake had already weakened my determination. Before we left, I took one last look at the men surrounding me. "No one else except Kraven is going to die here tonight. Understand?"

I stood in front of the bathroom mirror and wiped the grime of the tunnel off my face and neck, the ruined dress discarded on the floor. My skin was pale, with an unhealthy tinge of grey, and my eyes were cold and rimmed red. Tears started to well, but I told myself it wasn't the time. Eventually they subsided.

The dress labelled 'Royal Dinner' was stunning – an off-the-shoulder design in vibrant red velvet – but I felt suffocated by the luxurious gold lace and velvet ribbons that ran over the bust and down the sleeves. At any other time I'd have felt beautiful, but right then, it was just a means to an end.

"I know you're hurting," I said to Ash while we walked the short distance to the King's suite. "I don't need the Link to tell me that. The others don't understand why I have to do this… but I know you do."

"I'm with you all the way, Shae. There'll be time to grieve after we get Kraven – we owe it to Finnian to finish the mission," he replied.

We entered the King's suite moments later and the Royal Family were ready to go, looking magnificent in their ceremonial finest.

"Oh my goodness, you look awful!" Phina gasped.

"I thought the dress looked quite good on me," I replied, trying to keep my voice light and cheerful.

"She's not kidding, Shae," added Prince Frederick. "You both look terrible. What's happened?"

"We found out Kraven was due to meet someone," Ash replied. "But by the time we were able to intervene, he… unfortunately he evaded us, Your Majesty."

"I see," said Sebastian.

"We detained the person he was meeting – the person we believe orchestrated the attempt on your life. The same person we believe is head of Sector Three's ARRO chapter."

"Well? Who is it?"

"Your Lord Master. Quentin Gabriel."

"I don't believe it," roared the King.

"I can assure you, sire, that—"

"Oh, I'm not questioning your information, Brother Asher. I just don't believe… Quentin? ARRO? I've been betrayed by one of my dearest friends? Wait until I get my hands on him."

"I'm sorry, sire," I said carefully – I'd seen that side of Sebastian before. "Gabriel's dead. We had him in custody, but he took his own life with a suicide pill."

"That cowardly…" The King paced the room, muttering angrily, but then he looked suspiciously at Ash.

"There's something else?"

I thought Ash was going to tell them about Finnian, but instead he avoided the topic. "We believe the attempt on your life will be made tonight, at the dinner. The rest of the team are trying to track Kraven, but if they can't, we think he'll come for you there."

"That's a suicide mission!" said Frederick. "Surely he must know he won't get out of the room alive."

"I don't think he plans to. Gabriel's already shown that ARRO members are willing to be martyrs to the cause," replied Ash.

"Father, you mustn't go," pleaded Josephina.

"This is exactly why I should go," he replied. "We cannot let terrorists believe they can get away with things like this."

"But father—"

"Don't 'but father' me, Phina. We need to make a strong stand against ARRO. I've made my decision."

When we arrived at the Royal Dinner, we were introduced to the room by the Officiator, and I couldn't help a sad smile as I was presented as Lady Shae of Palavaria. It didn't suit me, but Finnian would've found it funny and we'd have laughed about it after.

The large room had been decked out in all things luxurious, although it seemed over the top to me. The crests of the four Royal Families were proudly displayed on the walls, with the Palavarian colours prominent at the far end as the hosting House. Women wore the finest dresses, made from the most expensive materials, and men looked extraordinary in suits adorned with ribbons, medals, and feathers.

The smell of exotic spices and aromatic elixirs overpowered my senses until I acclimatised.

I knew I shouldn't drink, but as the waiter offered, I accepted a cocktail and downed it in one. A vision of Finnian lying on the floor of the maintenance tunnel filled my head, and I felt my face begin to crumple.

"Are you okay?" Phina asked.

"I'm fine," I replied, pulling myself together.

"Do you really think Kraven will dare come here tonight?"

"Yes, I do. Excuse me please, Princess." I turned to Ash. "Stay with the King, I'm going to do a sweep."

"Okay… be safe," he replied.

I walked the room, avoiding eye contact with the other guests. The last thing I wanted was to be dragged into any introductions or discussions. I was almost to the opposite side of the room when I heard Jake through my earpiece, his voice urgent. "I see Kraven. Francis, he's heading towards you. Corridor four."

"On my way," Francis replied.

"Ash, Shae, he's coming your way." Jake was out of breath. "Francis, do you have him? You must be right on top of him."

"I was, but he… he just disappeared."

Through a break in the guests I noticed Ash gathering up the King and his family. "What the hell's going on?" he asked.

"Bit busy at the moment," Jake snapped. "Does anyone have eyes on him?"

"No," said Jared.

"Nothing," confirmed Francis.

"Fuck!" shouted Jake. "Okay, everyone converge on the Royal Dinner. Shae, Ash, watch yourselves. We'll be there shortly."

I'd made it about a third of the way back to Ash when something caught my eye. A waiter held his silver drinks platter slightly differently to the others, and he looked down at the floor instead of the guests. He glanced up briefly when he almost walked into Princess Hannah from the House of Mercia, but it was long enough for me to see his face.

"Kraven's here," I said quietly. "He's dressed as a waiter."

"Don't do anything stupid, Shae," Ash ordered, but all I could think about was Finnian… and revenge.

Kraven hadn't seen me in the tunnels, and the dress made me inconspicuous amongst the other guests, so I was able to get close without raising his suspicion. I was only a metre or so from him when he caught sight of Ash protecting the Royals, and I guess he got spooked because he made his move early. He pulled the napkin away from the silver platter, and picked up the weapon it concealed.

"Gun!" I yelled, throwing myself directly in the line of fire between Kraven and Sebastian. I made a grab for the weapon, but my fingertips gripped his shirt cuff instead. I got my other hand on his wrist, forcing his arm up, so when the shot rang out the gun was pointing at the ceiling. I cursed the damn dress as I struggled with Kraven, restricted by velvet ties and tight lace.

The gun waved precariously in the air as we struggled and a second shot fired, hitting one of the walls. I got in a good punch and Kraven's legs buckled, but thanks to my high-heels and stupid dress, I lost my balance and toppled over with him. When we landed, the force knocked the gun from our hands, and it skittered across the floor, out of reach. At least that was one problem solved, but I was winded from the fall and Kraven got in a couple of good hits of his own.

Ash headed towards us, and I tried to motion for him to go back to the King, but I took another punch to the head, disorientating me. Kraven grabbed a waiter's knife from some scattered cutlery on the floor before clasping a clammy hand around my neck, pulling me to my feet. Using me as a shield, he pointed the blade at Ash to back off.

The rest of the team fought their way through the mass of people trying to exit the room, and Kraven waved the knife dangerously between them and Ash before finally deciding to press it into the soft skin of my throat.

"Give me your weapon," Jared ordered the Security Chief, who'd appeared panting behind him. Walden hesitated, then seeing the look on the King's face, he handed it over. Jake and Francis stood motionless, their eyes flicking between gun and knife.

"Put the knife down, Kraven," Jared demanded. "It's over, you failed. ARRO's failed and Gabriel's dead; killing her will serve no purpose now."

"Shoot him, Jared," I demanded, but he ignored me.

"Put the knife down," he repeated slowly. I felt Kraven shift his position behind me and the weapon tightened against my throat.

"Shoot him," I implored.

The King made a sudden lunge, startling Kraven, and he reacted quickly, twisting me towards Sebastian to protect himself from the attack. Whether he meant to do it or not, the knife sliced into my throat. The blade was sharp and I barely felt more than a tickle as it bit into my skin, but warm blood dribbled down my neck. I'd no idea how bad the cut was, but I saw the startled looks on the faces of the assembled men.

I couldn't wait any longer. I'd been injured, and could already feel the tingling in my throat as I started to heal – the last thing any of us needed was the added complication of me starting to shimmer. I slammed the heel of my shoe into Kraven's foot, catching him off guard long enough to allow me to grab the hand holding the knife. I sunk my teeth into it as hard as I could and he dropped the knife, screaming.

I wriggled my body to the side, giving Jared the target he needed. I don't know where the bullet hit, but as Kraven was thrown backwards, he managed to get his fingers around my throat and I collapsed with him.

His grip weakened as I looked directly in his eyes. "We got you, you son of a bitch," I said coldly.

It was difficult to understand his reply because it was faint and he was gurgling blood, but I thought he said, "I've done my bit."

I could've healed him, there was still time, but I wasn't going to. Not him. Not after what he'd done.

Jake pried Kraven's fingers from around my throat as his last breath left him. "Here, Babe," he said, gently putting a cloth napkin over the cut on my neck. He stroked the side of my face with a warm hand and my lips quivered – not because of his touch, but because the steely anger that'd kept me going had dissolved the moment Kraven died.

Sebastian leant over Kraven's body before kicking him, as if to make sure he was really dead. "Get this piece of crap out of here," he ordered. "And Shae? You need to get that seen to." I followed his troubled gaze down to my dress, surprised at how much blood had seeped into the material.

"It's nothing. Looks worse than it is," I replied.

"Well, it still needs seeing to." He surveyed the stateroom and cleared his throat. "I guess I've got some explaining to do. Gentleman, Shae, thank you again for everything you've done. When the Summit's over you'll all be my guests at the Palace, and we'll discuss just how grateful I am."

"You're welcome, Your Majesty," Ash said. "With your permission though, we'd like to take our leave. We have a few things to sort out."

"Of course. Whatever you need to do." The King headed off to talk to Walden.

As I watched him walk away, it sank in that we'd won.

We'd saved the King, but in the process I'd lost my father.

That was the moment my resolve shattered into a million pieces. I started to shake, nausea roiling through me, and if it hadn't been for Jake, who gathered me into him, I would've crumbled into a heap right there.

# 21

We left the Welcome Dinner in chaos. Royals had scattered to the four corners, and security officers tried their best to calm them and herd them back together.

I'm not sure if we were escorting Kraven's body to the infirmary, or just heading that way to see Finnian – either way, we trailed behind the officers transporting him on a stretcher. We passed groups of huddled guests and angry mummers rippled as they began to digest what'd happened.

I walked like a ghost between Ash and Francis, not really paying attention to them, only capable of concentrating on putting one foot in front of the other.

When we got to the infirmary, we were met by a tall, formidable-looking woman who introduced herself as Miriam Offenbach – the *Athena's* Chief Medical Officer.

"Brothers, I'm sorry for your loss," she said. "Your Primus is laying in rest over here." I didn't have the energy to be offended that she hadn't addressed me, but when she tugged back the curtain and there were only two chairs pulled up next to the bed, I was upset. "Are you injured?" she asked me.

"I'm sorry?" She pointed to my bloodied dress. "Oh...

no, it's Kraven's blood," I lied.

Finnian's body had already been cleaned and covered by a crisp, white sheet pulled up to his shoulders. His arms rested on top of the covers, and apart from being pale, he looked like he was in a peaceful sleep. I half expected him to open his eyes and tell us it was all a bad joke.

I felt Ash leave my side and turned to see him talking quietly to Jake and Jared. I caught Jared's eyes and saw pain in them, but unusually for him, he didn't turn away or force the hurt from them. He held eye contact and a lump caught in my throat, but then Ash said something directly to him and he broke his gaze before he and Jake left the infirmary.

Ash picked up a third chair before he re-joined us at Finnian's bedside, pulling the curtain closed behind him.

"What did you say?" I asked, not taking my eyes from Finnian.

"That this was Brotherhood business."

"They didn't look too happy," Francis said, wiping his cheek with the back of his hand. His eyes were red and puffy.

"Well, I don't think they wanted to leave, but they accepted this was family time. They're good men."

"Thank you," I said, placing my hand on his arm. I wasn't sure whether I was thanking him for arranging time for us to be alone with Finnian, or for saying that Jake and Jared were good men. I'd have taken either.

"Jared said they'd tie things up with Chief Walden and arrange for the *Defender* to pick us up in the morning," Ash continued, pulling out the middle chair for me. I sat heavily before picking up Finnian's cool hand.

"We got the bastard, Dad. It was all pretty dramatic really," I said, unexpectedly smiling through my tears. "You would've been impressed. And they called me Lady Shae! Imagine that? I know you would've given me hell for that one."

I felt guilty that the last time we were together on

Lilania, I'd been annoyed with Finnian for not letting Francis come with us on our mission. But more than anything, I felt guilty for not saving him. I would never forgive myself. Big, fat tears rolled down my cheeks, falling on my beautiful velvet dress – which was ruined and ripped apart. The symbolism wasn't lost on me.

My heart ached in my chest, and I knew that was something my gift couldn't fix. The King's survival was cold comfort at that point.

It was late when we finally left Finnian. Dr Offenbach promised to keep him safe until we returned to collect him in the morning, and we thanked her for her kindness.

"You have a message from Captain Marcos," she added. "He asked that you not be disturbed, but that I give you this as you left." She handed a data-pad to Francis.

"The *Defender* will rendezvous with the *Athena* at zero-eight-hundred," he relayed. "The Captain asked if we want to join them in the Regency Bar for a drink." He looked at his com-pad. "They might still be there. What do you think?"

"I think I could do with a strong one," replied Ash. "There's nothing more we can do here tonight, and under the circumstances I don't think Finnian would object. Shae?"

"Thanks, but I'll give it a miss. It's late and I'm tired." And I didn't feel like being sociable. "You two go though, don't let me stop you."

"Perhaps you're right. Maybe I'll head back with you," said Ash.

"No, you won't. You'll go and have a drink with Francis. I'll be okay, I promise. Besides, I could really do with some alone time."

"Are you sure?" Francis asked.

"Yes." My tone was so final, neither of them attempted to argue further.

The suite was warm and quiet, but I'd have felt happier if Ash had been there. I would've gone to sleep in his arms, and he would've made everything seem better somehow – but I knew Francis also needed him. I stripped off the red velvet dress and deposited it on the bathroom floor with the other ruined outfit. Henrietta would pitch a fit if she saw what I'd done to her clothes. I didn't care.

I pulled on pyjamas and slipped into the large bed, leaving enough room on the other side for Ash. I'd planned to stay awake until he returned, but one minute I was wrapped in soft, warm sheets, the next I was back in the cold blackness of the maintenance tunnel.

Gabriel was tied and resting against the wall, exactly how it'd happened earlier, but in my dream, we were the only two there, and he was laughing. It was a loud, cruel bark, and his eyes were nasty and bright. He looked directly at me, no fear showing on his face.

Then everything changed and we were at the Royal Dinner, again as it happened before. Kraven had the knife to my throat and there was Jake, Jared and Francis to one side, and Ash and the King to the other. But this time Gabriel was there too, standing at the back, still laughing. The others seemed oblivious to him and I tried to tell them he was there, but Jared fired and Kraven and I were thrown backwards to the ground.

I tried to get up but Kraven's eyes shot open, and his hands closed around my neck. His grip wasn't the weak, dying hold it'd been before, it was strong, and I felt my throat tighten as air struggled to get to my lungs. I choked and fought, digging at his hands with my fingernails, but I couldn't loosen them. I became dizzy and unable to think straight.

Then Gabriel knelt on the ground by my side. "A new era will begin," he whispered. "We've played our parts."

That's when I woke, sweating and choking, and reaching for my throat. My heart raced, my body shook, and my eyes took a long time to focus. I reached out for Ash, but when he wasn't there I got upset, quickly getting out of bed to check the couch. He wasn't there either.

I headed for the bathroom and splashed water over my face, replaying the dream in my head, cold ripples of unease running over my skin. It was just a nightmare I kept telling myself. It was just a nightmare.

I returned to bed and tried to sleep but it was a waste of time – every time I shut my eyes, Gabriel's words repeated over and over again. The more I thought about them, the more I questioned what they meant.

I needed to talk to Ash.

It was a little after zero-one-hundred and I was surprised he wasn't back, but I decided it couldn't wait. I looked through the rest of the clothes bags for something to put on, but only found more fancy dresses and high heeled shoes. My slippers, robe, and pyjama combo wasn't particularly fitting attire for a bar, or for royalty, but they were decent enough. I made the decision to head out feeling comfortable, if not entirely appropriate.

I knew I'd found the bar by the ostentatious signage displaying the four House crests. The team occupied a table against the far wall, and as they hadn't noticed me enter, I detoured via the bar to get a beer before joining them. They were surprised to see me, or surprised to see me in my pyjamas, I wasn't sure which, but everyone was pleased I was there. It made me feel better.

Francis pulled up another chair and placed it between him and Jared, who lent sideways to kiss my cheek. "I'm so sorry," he said quietly, squeezing my hand briefly. I offered a sad, half-smile in appreciation.

"Nice pyjamas, Babe," said Jake, winking at me from the other side of the table, but the look in his eyes mirrored Jared's and I knew he cared more than he could show in front of the others.

"Couldn't sleep?" asked Ash.

"That's just it," I said, taking a large mouthful of cold beer, feeling it chill my insides all the way down to my stomach. "I went to sleep fine, but I had a dream... actually, I suppose you'd call it a nightmare. After that I couldn't get back off, so I thought I'd come find you guys."

"In your pyjamas?" asked Jake. "Not that I'm complaining, Babe."

"It was either these or another fancy dress, and I just couldn't face another dress tonight." I shivered in the coolness of the bar and within seconds Jared had draped his jacket over my shoulders. It was warm from his body, and as I pulled it around me I breathed in his scent.

"So what was your nightmare about?" Ash asked, trying to make his question sound like passing curiosity, when I knew he was far more interested than that.

"Actually, that's the main reason I came to come find you," I said, before telling them exactly what happened in my dream – right down to what Gabriel had whispered in my ear. "I'm probably just being nine kinds of crazy, and it means absolutely nothing… but I can't shake a nagging feeling that something isn't right." I caught a bunch of shared glances around the table. "What? I am being crazy, aren't I? I shouldn't have mentioned it; it's ridiculous."

"Maybe you're not so crazy, Shae," said Ash. "In fact, we've been talking about the same thing."

"Really?"

"Really," confirmed Jared, twisting his glass absentmindedly. "Something's definitely off, we just can't figure out what. We keep coming back to what Gabriel said: 'A new era will begin'. It doesn't make sense. If Kraven had killed Sebastian, Frederick would've taken the throne, and we all know he's a virtual copy of his father. Apart from the obvious immediate repercussions of losing its King, Sector Three would've continued almost as if nothing happened. ARRO wouldn't have changed a thing."

"So where's the new era in that?" asked Jake, more

thinking out loud than anything. "And they both seemed to be proud they'd played their part. But played their part in what exactly? It seems an odd thing to say when you know you've failed."

"Does anyone else have the feeling this thing isn't over?" I asked, but no one answered. We sat in reflective silence for a short while instead.

Eventually Ash said, "You realise what this means? If we're saying there's more to this than we initially thought, something else is coming. And we've no idea what, where, or when. We're right back to where we started, and…" he looked purposely around the group, "we could be wrong. The threat really could've been neutralised the moment we saved the King."

"True," I agreed. "But if we're right about this not being over and we don't do anything…"

"Kraven and Gabriel are dead," said Jake. "So even if we did want to look at this thing again, where do we start?"

"That's just it," Ash replied. "We start at the start. We go right back to where this all began and work through it again. We go back to the meeting we had with Nyan on Angel Ridge."

"We've done this before, Ash, and it got us nowhere," I moaned, closing my eyes and resting my forehead on the table. I pulled Jared's jacket closer around me, more for comfort than warmth, and felt Francis rub my back in slow gentle circles. It was nice and calming so I stayed like that, hoping he wouldn't stop.

"What do we lose? A few hours of our time?" I heard Ash continue. "If anyone has a better plan, I'm all ears."

"Okay, okay." I reluctantly sat up. "But all of our data-files are on the *Defender*."

"Then we go through what we can remember. We can do this." Ash seemed convinced. At least someone was.

"Fine, but I'm going to need something stronger than beer," I said. "Barkeep, Shatokian coffee all round, please.

And make it strong. Oh, and do you have any Carmichael's Chocamel ice-cream?" The barman nodded. "The biggest pot you've got and five spoons."

We worked our way carefully from our first meeting with Nyan all the way through to the point of Kraven's death. It was an in-depth and lengthy debrief, and by the time we got to the end it was nearly zero-four-hundred. Jared pushed back his chair and straightened his legs out. Francis stretched his arms above his head, one of his shoulders cracking loudly, and I stood up and paced for a bit, declining a fourth mug of coffee.

"This is fucking ridiculous," Jake grumbled. "Maybe we're just imagining monsters where there aren't any."

"One last time," said Ash, ignoring Jake's comment. "Let's go through it again, one last time." Jake groaned and rubbed his eyes vigorously with his fingers, but Ash was persistent. "Come on, guys. We've all been around the Galaxy a few times. When was the last time this many experienced people had a hunch about something that didn't turn out to be correct, at least in part?"

Jared sighed heavily, pulling his chair back under the table, and I returned to my seat next to him – even Jake shrugged his shoulders and re-engaged. We started at the Ridge and worked our way through events up to the shootout at the Water Terraces on Decerra. Fortunately, neither Jake nor Jared felt the need to discuss what went on in the *Veritas* after the Agent was killed. Instead they skipped over to the part where Peterson and Doctor Ford were apprehended.

"Doctor Ford?" Francis commented cryptically.

"What about him?" Jared asked.

"I may be missing something here, but what exactly is his involvement in all of this?"

"Unknown," I said. "His name was on Santiago's Kill List, so we know he's involved somehow, but does anyone really believe his theory about being on the List so he wouldn't be able to heal the King if needed?"

"It's bollocks, we just can't prove it," Jake said. "He's a lying bastard. I'd bet the *Veritas* on it."

As he spoke, a thought came together in my head. "It is crap," I said. "ARRO's plan was always to assassinate King Sebastian here on the *Athena* during the Summit, right? Never at the Palace of Palavaria?"

Jake's lips broke into a smile, and his eyes sparkled. "And Doc Ford was never on the guest list. He wouldn't have been here to help either way."

"Seems to me this Doc Ford character is the person we need to concentrate on. If we can figure out his part, we might get somewhere," reasoned Francis.

"Agreed," I said, "but I don't understand how he could be part of this when he hasn't even been in the Sector for the last few months."

"What do you mean?" asked Ash.

"He's been on some kind of Royal Physician exchange programme. I heard a medic and the King talking. Apparently, he's spent most of the last month or so in the other Sectors."

"You never mentioned this before."

"It was just a passing comment I heard. I didn't think about it until now." I was annoyed with myself for forgetting a piece of information, no matter how important or unimportant it was.

We carried on with the briefing but I couldn't let the Doc Ford thing go. Something nagged at the back of my brain – a thought that wouldn't quite form – and it drove me nuts. In the end I gave up and concentrated on Jake, who was talking through the transfer of Peterson and Ford to the *Veritas*.

As soon as I wasn't thinking about it, what was bothering me suddenly came into focus. "Wait," I interrupted. "I don't know if it means anything, and it's fairly tenuous, but we have a connection. Doc Ford was in each of the Four Sectors in the run up to the Summit… so was Frampton Edge."

"That's right," Jared concurred. "My techs managed to get that information after breaking the encrypted files on Edge's ship. But as you said, the link is tenuous."

"Do you know when Edge was in each Sector?" I asked.

"No. It didn't seem relevant at the time, so I didn't ask."

"Didn't you say something about there being a prostitute with him on those occasions?"

"Yes, but again, I don't see the relevance," Jared replied.

"It may be nothing, it may be something," Ash said. "Okay, let's concentrate on Edge for a moment. What else do we know about him?"

It was Jake's turn to talk. "The Wolfpack was investigating his part in the theft of Fleet munitions and terraforming kits – both of which could be sold for millions of credits on the black market. We had proof he was involved in the hijacking and transporting of them, but he was low level. We wanted the top dog, and that's why we were undercover in that stripper bar on GalaxyBase4."

"So we've got a trip to each of the Four Sectors with a prostitute, and involvement in the theft and smuggling of arms and terraforming equipment. What else? What about his ship? Was there anything onboard the *Hawkhurst* when you impounded her?" asked Francis.

"There wasn't a lot on the inventory." Jared tried to remember. "General items mostly. Wait… there were some narcotics hidden in a secret compartment. Can't remember what they were called though, I'd never heard of them. It'll be in the data-files."

"That's helpful, seeing as we don't have them," Jake muttered sarcastically.

"Pendoldine," I said suddenly, almost shouting.

"What? No, that wasn't it," Jared replied.

"I know that, Genius. A shipment of Pendoldine was stolen from Decerra. Don't you remember? Sergeant

Mollere told us about it, but he reckoned it was taken to sell on the black market. We've got two coincidences now: location and drugs. But what's all this got to do with ARRO?"

"It's no good, we can't keep working blind," said Ash. "We need the data-files, and we need Edge and Ford. Jared, how long till the *Defender* gets here?"

Jared looked at his wrist. "It's zero-five-thirty now, which means she's due to rendezvous with the *Athena* in two and a half hours. If we can get an external com-link, I can get them to increase speed and be here in about an hour. They'll be able to send us the data-files to look at in the meantime."

"Then it's time to speak to Chief Walden," Ash decided.

There was a busy hum when we got to the Central Security Hub, but Walden was easy to locate – he was the one mobbed by staff, all vying for his attention. Our group hung back while Ash went to speak to him.

After a couple of minutes, the two of them headed to a desk in the furthest corner of the room and Ash signalled for us to join them.

"Sam," Chief Walden said to the young officer occupying the desk. "I want you to patch through a secure com-link to Captain Marcos's ship immediately. He'll give you the Ident codes you need. Once you're through, give them full security access to your station and report to me for reassignment."

"But… Sir?"

"That's an order, Officer Parks."

"Yes, sir." She looked embarrassed.

"Brother Asher," Walden continued. "I still have work I need to do before the Summit starts, but please keep me informed. Is there anything else I can arrange before I go?"

"That'll be all for now, Chief. We appreciate your help… and discretion."

Walden started to walk away, but I had a thought. "Chief, I don't suppose someone could find me a spare set of fatigues?"

"See to that," Walden ordered Sam before being mobbed once more by his staff.

Officer Parks surveyed our group like she had a bad smell under her nose, but she managed a smile for Jared as he gave her the Ident codes for the *Defender*.

After a cursory discussion with the Officer on Watch, the com-link was transferred to Commander Tel'an's personal quarters, where, quite sensibly for that time of the morning, she'd been in bed, asleep.

Tel'an appeared on the screen, wearing a plain robe and looking perfectly beautiful. Jared requested she stand by while he asked Officer Parks to give us security access to the workstation. She huffed as she inputted the relevant codes, tapping out each digit with much more force than actually required. When she was finally done, Jared thanked her and apologised again for the inconvenience we were causing. He laid on the charm in spades, giving her one of his brightest smiles, and by the time he'd finished, she was grinning like a schoolgirl and saying it was no problem at all.

Jared briefed Tel'an quickly, but when he got to the part where Finnian had been killed, she was saddened and expressed her deepest sympathy. I closed my eyes and my bottom lip began to quiver, but I felt Francis rubbing my back in small circles, like he'd done in the bar, and it gave me strength. Only when I opened my eyes, Francis stood on the other side of the station with Ash, and it was Jared who was next to me. His hand was back resting on the desk, but Jake still scowled at him.

"I need you to increase speed and get here as soon as possible. In the meantime, send us every data-file we have on the investigation," Jared concluded. "And as soon you arrive, I want Edge, Peterson and Doc Ford in a Warrior and brought to the *Athena.* We haven't got time for an *Athena* shuttle to come get you, so I'll deal with the security issue from this end. I also need you to get a communication to Decerra to find out exactly where Ford has been over the last few months, and when. Plus, get on to GalaxyBase4. Ask the local cops there to see if they can track down our mystery prostitute."

"Aye, Captain. I'll also wake up Doctor Anderson and get him to evaluate the Pendoldine and the other drug we found on the *Hawkhurst.* See if he comes up with anything."

"Excellent. One last thing: I know it's an hour until you arrive, but get Edge, Peterson and Ford awake and into interrogation cells. Make it look like something's happened, I want them as off guard as possible. Oh, and get Doc to check them for suicide pills – I don't want to lose any more prisoners today."

There was a short delay while we waited for the files to be sent over, but Officer Parks broke the wait by bringing me my clothes, and I almost hugged her when I saw the military fatigues. There was no way I was going to risk missing anything by leaving the Hub, and figured if I moved to the back of the workstation, I could pretty much get changed without anyone seeing.

Jared's jacket was so long on me it covered everything anyway, and I had my trousers and boots on before anyone realised what was happening. My shirt, however, was going to prove more difficult. I tried to get Ash's attention, only succeeding in getting Jared's, but decided he would have to do because I heard Jake say that the files were coming through.

"Here, hold this up," I said, passing him his jacket back. "Promise you won't look?"

"On my honour," he replied. That was good enough for me.

I'd just started to pull my pyjama top up when Jake hissed, "What the hell are you doing, Marcos?" I lowered my top and peeked over the collar of the jacket.

"Relax, Mitchell. I'm not looking," Jared whispered back.

"Damn right you're not. Get over there." Jake barged him out of the way with his shoulder, snatching the jacket – which he held up as if nothing had happened.

"Seriously?" I was angry.

"What?"

"The innocent routine doesn't wash, Jake. That was uncalled for."

"But—"

"But nothing. He promised not to look."

"Oh really?" His sarcasm was blatant. "And you believed him?"

I didn't have to think about it. Not even for a second. "Yes," I replied, taking off my pyjama top and switching it for the shirt. "Grow up," I added angrily as I moved around him to return to the workstation.

"There. That one. No… go back one," Jared said as Francis flicked through data on the plexi-screen. I went to stand next to him, just to piss Jake off. "Okay," he addressed us all. "This file shows the dates Edge was in each Sector, including this one." He put a finger on the screen and moved the information to the left. "This file has just come in from the House of Palavaria, listing Ford's locations over the last couple of months." He slid the data to the right. "Let's see what we've got. If they don't match then maybe Jake's right, we're seeing monsters where there aren't any."

I scanned the documents quickly. "I think those monsters might be real after all," I said, getting that sinking feeling in my chest.

# 22

I pointed at the screen and everyone crowded around, pushing me closer to Jared. "They all match," I said. "Every time Edge visited one of the other Sectors, Ford was there too. That's more than a coincidence."

"So Edge's more involved than he let on. That sneaky little fucker," said Jake.

"Or more involved than he realises," Ash corrected. "You saw Shae's interrogation with him. I still believe he told her everything he knew, but perhaps he knows more than he thinks. On each of those visits he had a prostitute with him, yes? For all he knew, that was his only reason for the trip – to deliver her to her client."

"Okay," said Francis. "But what has she got to do with anything? Unless Doctor Ford was her client?"

We were still debating whether Ford seemed like the kind of person who'd use the services of a prostitute, when Doctor Anderson appeared on the plexi-screen. "Good morning everyone," he said. "Rough night it seems."

"That it is, Doc. What've you got for us?" Jared asked.

"I'm not sure really. Ullincanth, the drug found on the *Hawkhurst*, is an anti-convulsant. It was commonly used on the outlying planets about forty years ago to treat miners suffering from DMT's."

"DMT's?" Ash asked.

"Deep Mining Tremors. It was phased out because better drugs came on the market, ones that didn't have the side effects."

"What side effects?" several of us chorused.

"Steady on." Doc laughed. "If taken to excess, Ullincanth caused cold sweats, swollen glands, extremely high temperatures, dark pink rash, trouble breathing… want me to go on?"

"Those sound like the symptoms of Thecian Moon Flu," I said. I guess I'd listened in some of my classes at school after all.

"What the hell's Thecian Moon Flu?" asked Jake.

"It's a nasty little disease," explained Doc. "Easily treatable nowadays, but the symptoms aren't too pleasant. And Shae's right, they're very similar."

"Let me get this straight… this Ullincanth, if given to someone in a high enough dose, would leave the victim with practically the same symptoms as this Moon Flu thing?" clarified Jake.

"Yes, I suppose that's about right."

"And the person would need to visit a doctor?"

"Oh yes, most definitely."

"So here's a theory," Jake continued. "Edge takes a hooker to each of the Four Sectors where she meets up with some client, slipping him enough Ullincanth to make him think he's got Moon Flu. Our victim, who's got to be a high-ranking member of a House to have access to the Royal Physician, then heads to the doctor's – which in each case just happens to be Ford."

"It's a good theory," agreed Anderson. "But why?"

Jake shrugged, massaging the back of his neck. "Fuck knows. That's where your guess is as good as mine."

"What about the Pendoldine?" I asked Doc.

"That's just as confusing. Pendoldine is a high-end medication. It's hugely expensive to make because of the rarity of the ingredients, and incredibly expensive to buy. It certainly fits with Sergeant Mollere's theory that it was stolen to sell on the black market… but I don't understand why they had any on Decerra in the first place – let alone the quantity that was stolen. Pendoldine treats a rare genetic disorder that mainly afflicts the inhabitants of Sector Four. As far as I'm aware, nobody in the House of Palavaria has it, though I'd have to check to be sure."

"Okay, thanks Doc," Jared said. "Keep looking into the drugs to see if there's anything else unusual about them, and check if there's anything strange about any other drugs Ford may have ordered. Also, contact Decerra. Find out if anyone's being treated for the genetic disorder."

"Will do." The com-link terminated.

"The *Defender* will arrive in ten minutes," continued Jared. "It's probably a ten to fifteen minute flight time to get the prisoners here, and I'd guess another ten to get them settled into interrogation rooms. There's not a lot we can do until then. I suggest we take the opportunity to have a breather, grab some coffee, whatever."

"Actually, I do need to pee," I shared. "All that coffee's gone straight through me… sorry, you didn't need to know that." I left quickly so they couldn't see my embarrassment.

"Wait up," called Jake, but I kept walking. He caught up quickly. "We've got to talk... about before."

"I can't do this now, Jake."

"Not now then, but we do need to talk. Yes?" he pushed. I nodded reluctantly.

I spent a long time in the restroom staring into the mirror, thinking again about how things had gone so wrong. My heart ached and I was angry and hurt, and I didn't like feeling so completely helpless. I splashed some cold water on my face, wiped my eyes, and pasted my game-face back on before heading out.

Jared sat on a lounge chair opposite the restrooms, but he got up and came over when he saw me. "Shae, I…" I was about to tell him exactly what I'd told Jake, but for some reason I couldn't. "Last night," he continued slowly, "I don't know what I'd have done if… When Kraven sliced your throat with that knife…"

I put my hand on his shoulder and he placed his own on top of it. I could tell he was struggling with his words, which was unusual, and I had a sudden urge to throw my arms around him. I took a step towards him, but we both heard Ash in our earpieces telling us that Tel'an was on the plexi. We headed straight back to the Hub, neither of us saying another word.

"Captain," Tel'an started as we arrived. "The security team on GalaxyBase4 knew exactly where to find the prostitute. Unfortunately, it's because she's in their morgue – single bullet to the forehead. Sound familiar?" She didn't wait for a reply. "We're currently in a Warrior heading to the *Athena*. I've done a pretty good job at shaking up Edge and Peterson, but Ford's still composed. We've arranged to meet the *Athena* Security when we land and they'll escort us to their Interrogation Suite. I'll let you know as soon as I have them settled in. Oh, and Doctor Anderson asked me to tell you that he was right – no one on Decerra is suffering from a genetic disorder. He said you'd understand."

"I do. Thank you, Commander. See you shortly." Turning to us, Jared added, "So that's another literal dead-end courtesy of our friendly Agent of Death. Okay, let's discuss next steps."

After much debate, we managed to agree that Peterson wasn't worth wasting any more time on, deciding he'd given us everything he knew, but Francis said he would give it a go. Just in case. Edge, however, would need to be re-interrogated to see if we could dig out anything new from him – something he hadn't thought important before. Ash suggested he and I take another run at him because we'd interviewed him the first time around, and that was one more thing everyone managed to agree on. Perhaps we were making progress after all.

The interrogation of Doctor Ford was the one we argued over. Jake wanted to go in hard, forcing the information out of him using Cruillian Truth Serum if necessary. And after what'd happened to Finnian, I actually liked his plan. In the end though, we managed to agree that Jared and Jake would both interrogate Ford, using the age-old good-guy-bad-guy routine. They would tell him they knew the assassination attempt on King Sebastian was not the final plan and bluff the rest. Personally, I didn't think it would work, but as I didn't have a better plan, I thought I should just keep my mouth shut.

Questioning Edge again was like interviewing an incoherent three-year old. Commander Tel'an had done an exceptional job at freaking him out, as per Jared's instructions, but that meant he was almost hysterical when Ash and I went in. It took us several valuable minutes to convince him he was safe and that there wasn't an Agent of Death about to leap out from under the table and tap one through his forehead.

When I finally believed he was calm enough to understand, I began. "Mr Edge, last night we were able to foil an assassination attempt on King Sebastian." His eyes grew wild, and it looked like I was going to lose him again, so I hurried on. "The thing is… we don't believe the plot against the King is the end of the threat. In fact, we believe there's something much bigger coming."

Predictably, he launched in to a vehement denial of any knowledge.

Ash took over. "Your ship's records show that you took a prostitute to locations in each of the Four Sectors. Tell us what you know about the woman, and what she was doing."

Edge fidgeted and chewed on his bottom lip. "I don't see what this has to do with anything," he said, frowning heavily.

"Humour us," replied Ash.

"Okay, well, firstly I guess I took the job from Cady," he explained, the deep frown lingering. "He booked me to take the woman to four separate locations and said it was on the down-low 'coz the men she was meeting were all high-ranking officials."

"And that's all he said about the job?" Ash asked.

"Yeah, that's all. Swears."

"Really?" I raised a sceptical eyebrow.

"All I needed to know. Don't ask, don't tell – that's my motto – and in my line of employment, it's best to stick to it. Anyway, on each job we stayed one night then returned to GalaxyBase4."

"And you didn't think it strange to go all that way for a one-night stay?" I asked.

"Hey, lady, trust me, that's not the strangest thing I've been asked to do." His eyes darted around the room, his pupils wide and black. "Okay, sure it was weird, the cost of fuel alone was phenomenal, but credit's credit, right? I just figured she musta been a really, really good lay, if you know what I mean." A smirk tugged up the corner of his lips. "If you ask me though, she wasn't all that. Not a patch on you in the looks stakes," he said, staring at me with a leer that lingered on his lips until I glowered at him.

"Is there anything else about her you can think of? Anything weird or unusual?"

Edge rubbed his forehead, thinking. "She had some drugs with her. I asked her what they were for and she said they made a good time even better. She left them on board after her last job so I hung on to them – thought I might be able to get something for them. That's it. Swears. I still get protection, right? You're still going to save me from the Agents of Death?"

He knew nothing more than we did, and we were wasting time when there were more important things to concentrate on. Ash and I stood to leave, and that was Edge's cue to tell us again how much he feared for his life, and that we had an obligation to protect him. He was still whimpering and moaning about being on a Kill List when we left.

I looked at my com-pad as we walked down the hallway to the Ops Centre, troubled by how much time we'd wasted with him. We found Tel'an and Francis watching the monitors. "Edge was a bust," I said, resting against one of the desks.

"We saw," said Francis tapping one of the plexi-screens in front of him. "And for info, Peterson was worse than useless. Even more so than Edge."

"Great," I huffed.

"How are Jake and Jared doing?" asked Ash.

Tel'an turned up the volume on one of the monitors and Ash and I moved around to the other side of the desk to watch. I noticed how nice Tel'an smelled. I swear she was perfect.

As interrogators go, Jake and Jared worked surprisingly well together. They bounced off each other, seemed to know where the other one was going with a line of questioning, and their difference in styles complemented perfectly. Unfortunately, Doctor Ford was as ice-cool as he'd been all the way through.

"They've got nothing so far," Tel'an confirmed. I wasn't surprised, but I was disappointed. "The only time he got even mildly ruffled was when he was told he'd been brought to the *Athena*. Before that, he just knew he'd been transported to another ship. I know the Captain's technique – he's moved away from the topic, but he'll work his way back round to it to try and catch him off guard again."

After a few minutes, as Tel'an had predicted, Jared slipped in another question about the *Athena*, and the

Doctor's body language shifted. His back stiffened, he crossed his arms, and when he spoke, his voice had a slight but perceptible hardness to its tone. "You're lying. I would've thought better of you, Captain," Ford sneered.

"Really? Why would I lie to you about something like that?"

"I really have no idea, but you are."

"How can you be so sure?"

"Because your Commander brought me to this ship on a Warrior. Security protocols for the *Athena* dictate that no external ships be allowed anywhere near, let alone dock. Delegates are always picked up by the *Athena's* own shuttles." As soon as the words were out of his mouth, Ford realised he'd said too much.

"Delegates to what?" Jake asked. For a moment, the Doctor's cool exterior cracked and he looked anxious, but within seconds the shutters had come down and he was back to composed.

"I'm not saying anything further," he said bluntly, his face resolute. I hoped Jake would punch him in the head, better still, I wanted to go in there and lamp him myself.

"Delegates to what?" Jake repeated. "You know the *Athena* is the meeting place for the Tetrad Summit, don't you? How do you know that? And how would you know their security protocols?" Silence. "Okay, let me tell you what we know… we know you were on the Agent's Kill List, we know you're involved, and we know you're lying. Tell us everything now and we'll be lenient on you."

Silence.

Jake and Jared continued the interrogation, but it was a waste of time. Ford had shut down. After a while they ended the interview and joined us at the Ops desk.

Jared slumped into a chair and rubbed his eyes vigorously. "So, what now? Any ideas?" he asked.

"Beat the crap out of him until he talks," I replied. I think I meant it as a joke, but it seemed to come out as a statement.

Jared raised his head. "You don't mean that."

"Don't I?"

"It's the grief talking."

He was right of course, but my anger at the situation was spilling over. I needed a way to vent, and Jared was the unlucky person who'd stepped right into the firing line. Fortunately, before I said something I'd regret, one of the security officers informed Jared that he had an incoming call from Doctor Anderson.

As soon as Doc's face filled the screen, we knew something was up.

"Captain, we have a problem."

"Add it to the list," Jake mumbled.

"I've contacted Doctor Offenbach and asked her to join you, she should be with you any moment," Doc said as the *Athena's* Chief Medical Officer arrived. "Ah, good, you're there Miriam. I've asked Doctor Offenbach to be present because I think she may be able to help. At the very least she'll be able to confirm my findings."

Jake was restless. "Help with what Doctor? You haven't told us anything yet."

"Yes, well… here goes. To be thorough, I did a search of all drugs and chemicals that'd been stolen or misplaced over the last few months – not just from Decerra, but from across the Sectors."

"And?" Jake asked, rolling his eyes.

"And it seems your team's already investigating the biggest theft, Colonel Mitchell."

"I don't understand," said Ash.

"Before being pulled into this current predicament," Doc continued, "the Wolfpack was investigating the theft of Fleet weapons and terraforming kits, correct Colonel?"

"Yup." Jake nodded. "But that's not exactly secret."

"I appreciate that, but the terraforming kits are the key," Doc explained. "I don't know how much you all know about them, but they contain everything necessary to modify a planet or moon to support Human habitation. Engineers prefer to alter dead planets because they have a blank canvas to start with, but extremely rarely, and only after a Combined Sector Ethical Committee has agreed it, a location which already has indigenous plant and unintelligent life is chosen. Normally due to it being in a strategic military location. Anyway, in those cases the planet is targeted with an Omega missile – which contains enough chemical defoliants and bio-toxins to lay waste to the planet. Wiping out a planet has complex social and ethical ramifications, so as I said, it's extremely rare. So rare in fact, that terraforming kits don't contain the Omega missile as standard."

"That's all very interesting, but is there a point in there, Doc?" Jake complained.

"Yes, Colonel, there is. The stolen shipment of terraforming kits included one going to a remote planet in the outer belt – one which currently has indigenous plant and animal habitation. That particular kit included an Omega missile. An Omega missile that's now missing."

"You think someone's going to target the *Athena* with an Omega missile?" I asked, fear and confusion fluttering indecipherably in my chest.

"No, you misunderstand. If it was only that simple," said Doc, shaking his head wearily. "Look, this is all about chemistry. That's why I asked Doctor Offenbach to be there – because of her expertise in biochemistry. Let me try to explain… amongst other things, the Omega missile contains Flintoxin."

"I'm sorry, what?" Ash asked.

"Flintoxin," repeated Doctor Offenbach. "It's a manmade exogenous neurotoxin, and once ingested, it's a hundred percent fatal. It's highly regulated though, I'm surprised the REF isn't doing everything in their power to get it back."

Jake ran his fingers through tangled hair. "Well that explains why my Spec Ops team was put on a Fleet theft case. It wasn't the weapons they were after, it was the Omega missile. It all makes sense now. I knew there must've been more to it."

"That's not the worst of it," said Anderson. "I believe, though I might be wrong, that ARRO plans to use a modified version of the Flintoxin to wipe out everyone attending the Tetrad Summit."

"You can't be serious," I choked out before anyone else had a chance to.

"I know it sounds crazy—"

"It's not crazy, it's impossible!" Offenbach was part appalled, part indignant. "The *Athena's* security bio-scans would stop a toxin like that getting on board. Neurotoxins, poisons, chemical weapons – our tests cover them all. They even pick up the common Earth cold, for goodness sake. There's no way anyone would get something like that aboard."

"They might… if it'd been chemically altered to appear non-threatening."

"I don't understand, Philip. It's simply not possible," decided Offenbach.

"I thought so too, Miriam, but... the main active ingredient in the Ullincanth from Edge's ship is Linca 4, however there's also a stabiliser called ST-39-SC. The Pendoldine, used to treat the genetic disorder, has an inhibitor ingredient extracted from a rare plant called Gann C12. You take a person who has the ST-39-SC stabiliser already in their system, administer a microscopic amount of Flintoxin mixed with the Gann C12, and the altered toxin will sit in the host's body, completely harmless. And totally undetectable by your scans, Miriam."

"My God!" cried Offenbach. "You're right… in principle."

"What do you mean, 'in principle'?" Jared asked.

"Technically, Doctor Anderson's correct. If you administered the chemicals in that order, at exactly the right dose, the Flintoxin would become harmless. The thing is, no one could know what the correct doses are. The only way to identify the exact mix would be by trial and error, and as even a fraction out on any one of the ingredients would kill the patient, I don't see it's possible. It would be virtually unachievable for Ford to do what you're suggesting without killing the host."

"I agree, Miriam, but Ford was a bio-chemist before he turned to medicine and became the Palavarian Royal Physician. What if he's worked it out?" Anderson said. "Can we afford to ignore this, however improbable it may seem?"

The rest of us watched in dumbfounded silence as the discussion continued between the two doctors. Eventually, Jared asked, "So, hypothetically, what happens to the host, given they survive this procedure?"

"Well, nothing," replied Offenbach. "As long as the procedure goes correctly, the newly altered toxin would just sit in the body, completely harmless. In fact, they wouldn't even know they have it in their system. But eventually, over time, it would seep into every part of the host's body: blood, organs, skin, sweat… the lot."

Jake revisited he previous theory. "Just say my hypothesis earlier was right: our hooker gives her mark Ullincanth, leaving ST-39-SC in his blood. He goes to the infirmary thinking he has Moon Flu, only for Ford to inject him with a mixture of Gann C12 and Flintoxin. Assuming he survives the procedure, we now have an individual with an inert form of Flintoxin in his system. I'm with you until that point, but if the toxin has been altered so much that it's now considered harmless by the *Athena's* scans, where's the problem?"

"I don't have an answer for you," said Offenbach, shaking her head, her face pale and blotchy.

"I do," Anderson said grimly. "Captain, remember you asked me to review the drugs that Doctor Ford had ordered? To see if there was anything that seemed out of order? Well, there is. A little under a month ago, he took a huge, and I mean huge, delivery of Nollam-b."

"Whoa, whoa, whoa!" Offenbach held her arms up in front of her as if trying to ward off something evil. "My God!" I looked at her and my fear levels spiked as I saw the terror in her normally steady eyes. "Nollam-b is a widely used and common drug for migraines," she explained. "There's nothing dangerous or offensive about it, so someone could've brought as much of it on board as they wanted without setting our scans off. But one of the ingredients is… well, you don't need to know the science. The important thing is… you expose one of your hosts to concentrated Nollam-b, and the resulting chemical reaction would revert the Flintoxin back to its lethal state."

"But how will that kill everyone in the Summit?" Francis asked from behind the workstation.

"You don't get it," Offenbach explained. "Once the Flintoxin is reactivated, every breath the host lets out will release deadly toxins. The poison will be in the sweat evaporating from their skin, hell, even the skin cells themselves. You can't smell it, taste it, or see it, but effectively the host will become a walking, talking, bio-weapon. And there's no antidote."

To hammer it home, Doc Anderson added, "Any contact is one hundred percent fatal within a matter of minutes. Let me be totally clear about this… if even one host is reactivated, everyone at the Summit will be dead within five to ten minutes from the point of exposure."

So that was it.

That was the event that would see in a new era.

In just ten minutes, the Royal Families, high level Administrators and Officials, representatives from ruling planets, high ranking military personnel and prominent members of the Brotherhood – from all four Sectors – would be annihilated. ARRO would be able to step in and take over with no resistance whatsoever.

We stood in stunned silence until Ash's clear, rational voice brought us back to reality. "Okay, so we know the plan. Now we need to focus on filling in the bits we don't know – like who the hosts are, and how and when the drugs will be mixed."

"I've got a theory on that," said Chief Walden, who'd been standing so quietly behind us I couldn't have told you how long he'd been there. "Every single member of the Summit is required to attend the first opening session. Which, by my com-pad," he looked at his wrist, "starts in thirty minutes. After that, people come and go depending on the session and what's being discussed. Once a session starts, however, the Summit room is sealed, and no-one's allowed to enter or leave. If ARRO wants to get everyone, I predict they'll do it sometime in that first session."

"How long is the sitting," Ash asked.

"Zero-nine-hundred till eleven-thirty. And if you can place any logic to this, I would also suggest that your second drug, the Nollam-b, would be most effectively distributed through the air filtration systems. There are two: one supports the *Athena*, the other supports the Summit room only. It's a closed system to protect the delegates in case anything happens elsewhere on the ship. I may be simplifying things, but why don't we just cancel the first Summit meeting?"

"I don't think it would make a difference," Doctor Anderson said. "I believe whoever planned this will have made preparations for that happening. I wouldn't rule out the Nollam-b being introduced to both systems simultaneously. By my calculations, they have enough of it. The hosts will be reactivated wherever they are and the toxin will spread regardless. Plus, the chaos that will ensue if you cancel will be unprecedented, especially after last night's events. Even if we do identify who the hosts are, we would need to find them in all the disorder. If you continue with the first session, at least you'll know the hosts are in that room."

Jared rubbed his chin. "The Doctor's logic is sound, but surely if they've got enough to cover the whole ship, they could release it at any time. It doesn't need to be during a closed Summit Meeting."

"True," agreed Ash. "Maybe there's symbolism in killing everyone together?"

"If ARRO releases the Nollam-b during a meeting, everyone will be in one place, trapped by the locked doors," Doc explained. "Death will be almost instantaneous in such closed quarters. If the hosts are loose on the rest of the ship, it will take time for the toxins to spread – maybe even enough time for people to get to escape pods."

"We should assume the chemicals could be released as soon as the Summit starts and the doors are sealed. That only gives us half an hour to stop this," Jared said, looking urgently around our group. "Chief, I need you to get all of your people combing the air filtration units from source to the Summit room. Concentrate on the closed system. If the room is sealed and the hosts are inside, it won't matter if the chemical is released anywhere else in the ship."

"I'll get them on it immediately, Captain, but that system's vast. There are miles of primary and secondary pipe-work, not to mention hundreds of junctions and equipment boxes." The Chief looked doubtful. "I'm just saying we can't rely on finding the second chemical before it is due to be released."

"I understand, but we have to try," replied Jared. "No offence, Chief, but Jake has more experience in dealing with this kind of threat. Perhaps it would be better if he coordinated your people? You okay with that?" Chief Walden nodded and I thought I saw a flicker of relief cross his eyes. "Jake?"

"I'm on it. What are you going to do?"

"I'm going to find out who the hosts are."

Doctor Offenbach, who'd been exceptionally quiet, stepped forward. "Captain, I might, and I reiterate, might, be able to come up with something to alter the chemical composition currently in the host."

"What good would that do?"

"The second chemical will only re-activate the Flintoxin from its current state, but if I can alter that current state enough, the second chemical won't be able to convert it back, keeping it harmless. I'll do my best, but don't count on it."

"You best get on it then," Jared said. He turned to Tel'an. "Commander, contact the medical centres for each of the Four Sectors. We need to know who's been treated for Moon Flu symptoms in the last couple of months, and I don't care about medical confidentiality. Use my security credentials if you need to, and make it clear to them that time's of the essence." She nodded and headed to a separate workstation.

"There's nothing more the three of us can do here," said Ash, indicating him, Francis and me. "We'll assist in the search of the air filtration system."

Searching the pipes was necessary, I got that, but we all knew the chances of finding and deactivating the chemical release mechanism was slim to impossible. We did, however, have someone in custody who had all the information we needed. The only problem was, he wasn't talking.

"I've had enough of his bullshit," I said, marching off in the direction of Ford's interrogation room, but Jared stepped in front of me, blocking my way.

"Give me a second before you go rushing in there," Jared pleaded. "Are you all right?"

"I'm peachy," I said sarcastically. After all, what kind of a stupid, dumb-arse question was that? I'd gone through anger into that weird, scary-calm thing again. "Are you coming?"

"Sure. Shae? You're not going to do anything stupid, are you?"

I couldn't answer, because right at that moment, I truly didn't know what the answer would be.

# 23

Jared and I sat opposite Ford, and I felt the loathing for him rise in my throat like vomit. He stared at us with about as much distaste.

"Back I see, only this time you've brought a friend with you. How nice." Ford smiled, reminding me of the cruel smirk on Gabriel's face in my dream. "How many times do I have to tell you I'm innocent? I don't know anything about an assassination attempt, or anything else for that matter. So what if I know the Tetrad Summit is held on the *Athena*? I'm the King's Personal Physician – it's not inconceivable that he, or his family, or any other member of his Senior Staff for that matter, might've let it slip at some point." His casual smile widened and he revelled in his self-superiority.

"So you know about the Tetrad Summit and the *Athena*. Big deal. I don't care," I said. The Doctor eyed me carefully, his smile slipping slightly. "And I don't care how many times you tell us you're not involved. Truth is I don't care for you at all. There are only three things I do care about right now: who the Flintoxin hosts are, how the Nollam-b will be introduced to the Summit room's air conditioning system, and when it will happen."

His breath faltered, and when he got it back it was shallow and irregular. His neck blotched scarlet, but he remained silent.

Jared took over. "You see, Ford, we know almost everything about ARRO's plan: the Flintoxin from the Omega missile, the ST-39-SC stabiliser, the Nollam-b… shall I go on? We've all the evidence we need to convict you of multiple crimes, including terrorism and treason – which I'm sure you're aware carries the death sentence. But as Shae said, what we don't know is who the Flintoxin hosts are and how the Nollam-b is going to be introduced. You tell us that and I'll cut you a deal: life in a medium security prison instead of termination. It's a good deal, but you need to tell us everything ARRO has planned, right now."

"You consider that a deal?" Ford barked out a dry laugh. "I'd rather be dead. At least I would have the honour of dying for a righteous cause."

"Honour? What do you know about honour?" I challenged.

"More than you know," he replied coldly.

"I seriously doubt that."

Jared continued trying to negotiate a deal, but I wasn't paying attention to his words any more. I studied Ford's face, and he looked resolute and unyielding. He believed unreservedly in ARRO's cause, and I believed he would absolutely choose a painless lethal injection over telling us what we wanted to know.

I looked at the time as an idea took hold. It was a bluff, and I'd no idea whether it would work, but we were out of options. I had to try, and I hoped Jared would understand and play along.

"How many different ways can I tell you the same thing?" continued Ford. "I won't talk – I'd rather die."

"That's fine with us. In fact, we can arrange it for you right now," I said, trying to sound calm and rational even though my insides twisted. Ford opened his mouth to say something but couldn't find the words. I got out of my chair, ignoring him. "Captain, I need your cuffs."

A groove settled between Jared's eyebrows, but he stood and handed them over.

"Get up," I ordered Ford. He didn't move. "Get up!" I repeated, hauling him from his chair and pulling his arms behind his back so I could cuff him. When they were secure, I turned him around to face me so I knew he was paying attention. "The thing is, Ford, a High Court trial is both time-consuming and costly. Isn't that right, Captain?"

"That it is," confirmed Jared.

"And we already know with the evidence we have, the outcome will be termination, right?" I asked Jared again. He nodded, the frown lingering. "And you seem so very keen to die anyway… so I say why waste the credits and time? Why wait?" I hoped Jared would back me up on the next bit. "Captain, I'm going to take Doctor Ford to the Summit room. The doors aren't sealed for another ten minutes, so I think I can get him there in time."

Jared's forehead smoothed and he smiled. I was glad he got it. Ford, on the other hand, had blanched ghost-white.

"You can't do this," he spluttered.

"What's the matter, Doctor?" I said calmly. "I thought you wanted to die. Though it's not so much fun when it's from Flintoxin, I bet. Gasping and panting for breath as your lungs feel like they are on fire. The excruciating pain as every organ in your body turns to mush. What? Not so keen on it anymore? Move!"

"The REF would never sanction this. Captain?" he pleaded, but Jared shrugged and took a step backwards.

I pushed Ford heavily against the wall, the back of his head cracking against the metal. "Because of you, my father's dead," I growled. "Do you really think I give a crap about what happens to you? Besides," I pulled the medallion from around my neck and showed it to him, "I'm

Brotherhood. I don't answer to the REF"

Ford looked desperately at Jared. "You have to stop this," he begged.

"No, I don't," Jared replied. "In fact, I've got other things I really should be doing – like finding chemicals and Flintoxin hosts. I think I'll leave you in Shae's capable hands."

The doctor tried to protest as Jared turned to leave the room, but I ignored him, pulling on his jacket to move him towards the door. "Stop. Stop! Okay, I'll tell you what I know about ARRO… just don't take me to the Summit room."

We had him. I pushed Ford back into his chair, leaving the cuffs on.

"We're running out of time so talk fast," Jared ordered.

"I don't know where the Nollam-b is being introduced to the air filtration system. I had nothing to do with that part of the plan." I stood up, making to grab him again, but he continued quickly. "It's true, all information is compartmentalised, but I do know it's being released at nine-thirty." I sat again.

"What about the hosts? Who are they? How many are there?" Jared asked.

"Four – one from each Sector. I can't tell you who they are though because I don't know."

"What?" I said incredulously. "You expect us to believe that you treated them and don't even know who they are?"

"It's true," he replied, his voice conceding. "I made a point of not knowing their names."

"Not knowing the names of the people you were condemning to death?" Jared was disgusted. "You're a coward, Ford. And you haven't given us much of anything," he added accusingly.

"That's the whole point. Compartmentalised information, remember? None of us involved knew everything – for this very reason. I doubt even Gabriel knew the whole plan."

"Gabriel?" I said, my blood suddenly cold. "Then it wasn't him who organised this?" Ford looked startled. "Of course it wasn't," I carried on, thinking out loud. "It was logical that Gabriel, Head of Sector Three's ARRO chapter, was the orchestrator when we thought the plan was to assassinate Sebastian, but now we know it's much, much bigger…"

"Who's behind this?" asked Jared. "And you better have an answer this time." Ford remained silent, but his head shot up when Jared slammed his fists on the table. Even I jumped.

"I can't…"

"Maybe that trip to the Summit Room will jog your memory," I said, reaching for him.

"Colderon! It was Maximilian Colderon – let me go," whimpered Ford.

"I don't believe you," Jared growled, pacing angrily. "For starters, as Master of Ceremonies, he'd be in the Summit room – exposed to the same neurotoxin as everyone else. You're lying."

"I'm not," Ford grunted. "My life depends on it. Why would I lie? I promise, he's in charge of everything."

"Wait a minute, are you saying Colderon is Head of ARRO?" I asked.

"No… yes… maybe," Ford mumbled. "I don't know. All I know is that Gabriel got his orders from him. I don't know any more than that."

I'm not sure why, but I believed him.

Jared filled the others in over the com-link as we returned to the Ops Centre. "Tel'an, tell me you have something," he said when we arrived.

"I've spoken to all Sectors, but everyone said they needed to verify your security credentials before they'd even look for the information we need. I took the liberty of contacting Commodore Northfield to fill him in on the situation. He's adding his authorisation to our request." Tel'an looked harassed for the first time since I'd met her.

"Good call, Commander. Ford confirmed that he treated the hosts, and while he may not know who they are by name, he should be able to recognise them," said Jared. "Get someone in to him with pictures of every single summit attendee to see if he can pick them out."

"Aye, sir, I'll—" Tel'an was cut off by Doctor Offenbach, who rushed into the room wearing a stained lab coat, her hair wild and frizzy.

"Captain, in theory this should change the current chemical composition within the host so that the Nollam-b won't convert it back to the deadly toxin." She held out four hyposprays.

"In theory? I'm really beginning to dislike those words," he replied.

"Like I said, I can't guarantee anything without any tests. I only had enough of the necessary chemicals to make four doses, so I suggest you keep your fingers crossed there aren't more hosts than that."

"Ford says there are only four, but it won't matter a damn if we don't get those names." Jared said it loudly so Tel'an got the point.

"Captain, there's something else," Offenbach continued. "You have to administer the drug at least ten minutes before the Nollam-b is released. It needs time to act on the body."

"Great! Anything else we need to know?" Offenbach shook her head. "Tel'an?"

"Still nothing, sir."

"Keep on it. Forward host names, photos, and allocated seat numbers to all of our data-pads as soon as you get them," he said before opening a com-link. "Jake, Ash, drop what you're doing and meet us at Sector Two's entrance to the Summit room."

Jared and I double-timed it to the Summit room, getting

there seconds before Jake and Ash. Jared handed each of us a hypospray.

"This has got to be administered by twenty past nine at the absolute latest." He tapped his com-pad and a synchronised countdown clock appeared on all of ours. Somehow, seeing the numbers counting down made everything even more real. "If we don't get all four hosts by the time these hit zero, it's game over. Shae, you take this door. Ash, take Sector One's, Jake, take Three's, and I'll take Four's. I know the doors are sealed, but get Security to let you in – don't take no for an answer. Stay at the back, and try not to draw attention to yourselves. When Tel'an gives you the name of the person in your Sector, find them, inject them, and get them out as quickly and quietly as you can. The last thing we need is a panic in there. Got it? Go."

The three men sprinted off and I turned to the security contingent at my gate. As they'd heard everything that'd been said, they opened the door without question and I slipped in quietly. In front of me, steps ran all the way down to a centre stage, where the four ruling monarchs sat at a square table. I quickly surveyed the area for anything weird or unusual.

Around the Royals was an arena, a few rows of seats at the same level as the centre table, and just behind King Sebastian, sat Phina and Frederick with a few Senior House Officials. Nothing weird about that, but what was strange was that I couldn't see Maximillian Colderon. I continued scanning.

Each side sloped up towards the back of the room, starting with more senior delegates nearer the stage and lesser administrators at the back. Every seat was like a luxury armchair, and stewards meandered between rows offering drinks and snacks. Still no Colderon.

As I got my bearings, I noticed Ash appear through the door to my right and I nodded to him in acknowledgement. A moment later, Jake appeared in the doorway to my left, and the team was completed when Jared entered the gate directly across from me.

"Sector One's host's in," Tel'an said over coms. "Transferring details now." That was Ash's area.

I looked at the time counting down on my wrist: 00:09:58. Just less than ten minutes before the deadline.

I checked the picture and location of the first host on my mini data-pad and watched Ash make his way towards the front of the stalls. When he got to the third row up from the bottom, he carefully picked his way along the line until he bent down and spoke briefly to someone. I couldn't see him inject the host, but he confirmed over the com-link that it was done.

I continued watching as Ash said something else to the man, who reluctantly rose and allowed himself to be guided out. When they got to the top of the stairs, the door opened, and Ash pushed the man out before stepping back into the room. The door sealed again. What was he doing? There was no reason for him to stay in here, it was too dangerous.

I tried to indicate with my arms that he should leave, but he either didn't understand my bizarre form of semaphore, or he was ignoring me. It was probably the latter.

00:07:17

Coms were silent.

I turned towards Jake. His eyes skimmed the room, but as I caught his attention, he shrugged his shoulders.

00:06:01

"Tel'an, we're running out of time," Jared said, the desperation I felt mirrored in his voice.

"I don't have anything to give you. I'm sorry, Captain," Tel'an replied. In comparison, her voice was quiet and hopeless.

00:04:19

"I've got another one," she said suddenly, her voice stronger. "Sector Two's host is in. Sending now." That was my area. I looked at the information on the data-pad and moved down the stairs, grateful that he was sat near the end of one of the rows and was easy to find.

00:03:54

I was almost to my target when Tel'an said they'd identified the next host. It was Jake's area and I glanced over to see him start down the stairs.

When I got to my man, I confirmed his identity and injected him in the leg before he had the opportunity to object. He looked startled as I informed the others it was done, but I explained quickly that it was for his own good. He didn't want to leave the Summit, so I told him the hooker had given him a disease that would leave him impotent if he wasn't treated immediately. He agreed to follow me without further protest after that.

We were halfway up the stairs when Jake confirmed he'd administered his injection, but there was something in his voice that made me turn to look at him.

His host had stood but was reluctant to leave. A ripple of whispers spread from their location, the people nearest getting out of their seats to get a better view. Jake made to grab the man, but he pushed him away, and I watched helplessly as Jake then punched him so hard he knocked him unconscious. He hoisted him over his shoulder and carried him towards the stairs.

Panic spread like wildfire throughout the auditorium.

00:02:17

Cold sweat trickled down my back. We were so close – only one host left – but people all across the room were on their feet, pushing and shoving as they headed towards the exits.

00:01:57

"Sector Four's host's in. Coming over now," Tel'an spluttered through my earpiece. I looked across the room, taking a moment to locate Jared in the melee. He tried to force his way down the stairs, but was impeded by the tide of panicked guests heading in the opposite direction. I glanced at my data-pad for the host's allocated seat number and attempted to locate it, but after Jake's last-resort tactics, delegates had scattered throughout the auditorium. The chair was obscured by a crowd of people, but finally they moved out the way.

00:01:38

"Jared, the seat's empty!" I said over the com-link. His head snapped up to look at me. "Everyone search for the last host," I ordered as the room spiralled into chaos. I scanned the area, but it was impossible to see faces as people bunched up on the stairs, trying to get out through doors that were still sealed.

00:01:12

"Jared," Ash shouted. "There! Over there." He pointed and I followed his gaze, identifying the last host. Jared had already started towards him, but he was still hampered by a solid, scared wall of people. Jake was next closest, but he was fending off a couple of burly officials, who'd obviously mistaken him as the threat.

00:01:02

I left my host and headed for Jared's, cursing the no-gun rule yet again. A surge of delegates knocked me sideways and I slipped, falling heavily over one of the chairs. Picking myself up, I continued towards the front stage, but in those precious moments, I'd lost sight of my target.

"Shit! Where is he?"

"There," yelled Ash, pointing. The host was heading across the arena towards the stairs, so I ran to the centre stage and clambered on top of the table.

"Throw me the hypospray," I yelled to Jared.

"Don't miss it."

"I won't," I promised. He lifted his arm above the crowd and pitched the serum towards me. I stretched up, my fingers closing safely around the metal and glass. I jumped off the table, crossed the arena, and grabbed the final host by the back of his jacket, wheeling him around.

00:00:38

"Is this you?" I said as he tried to pull away from me. "Is this you? Are you Martin Drewer?" I showed him my data-pad, but he looked confused and scared.

"Yes. Yes, I am," he muttered. He stopped resisting and I let go of his jacket.

"Don't be frightened," I said, but as I raised the hypospray, I was barged out the way by a rotund official. I lost my balance, landing heavily, and my knuckles cracked on the hard floor.

00:00:29

Ignoring the pain, I tightened my fingers around the glass tube, securing it, but Martin took the opportunity to flee. I grabbed the bottom of his trouser leg, his momentum dragging me along the floor. I struggled to keep hold of him as he tried harder to pull away, but finally I managed to get in a position where I could reach forward and inject him in the calf. He stopped dead and stared at me, eyes wide, as if I'd just stabbed him with a knife.

"It's done," I said, standing up and dusting myself off. "The last host's been injected. You," I added to Martin. "Sit there. Do not move. Understand?" He sat obligingly, too scared to do anything else.

That was singularly the most nerve-wracking thing I'd

ever done in my life. The hosts were alive, everyone at the Summit was alive, and the four of us were alive. I started laughing – a relieved, slightly crazed, laughter.

Jared appeared out of nowhere, pulling me into a tight hold. I flung my arms around his neck and hugged him back, and when he let go I was still laughing. His eyes sparkled as he smiled, and I was reminded how beautiful they were, about how beautiful he was. I was about to pull him into another hug when Jake swept me off my feet.

He spun me around several times before kissing me passionately, and when he put me down, I was dizzy and breathless – though I'm not sure whether that was from the spinning or the kiss. He held my face in his hands and looked in to my eyes with such energy and excitement it was impossible not respond in the same way.

It was as if all the tension of the last few days had suddenly lifted, and I felt giddy with relief. Jake let go of me long enough to congratulate the others, but as soon as he was done, he slipped his arm back around my waist.

"Captain," Tel'an said over the com-link. "I'm patching through Doctor Offenbach."

"Hello everyone. Congratulations on finding all the hosts," Offenbach said, her voice apprehensive. "I hate to be the voice of reason, but we don't know for certain that my serum will work. I suggest you keep your fingers crossed and pray for a miracle. Another one."

My smile faded, but Jake pulled closer as he looked at his com-pad. "Zero-nine-twenty-six," he told us. "I presume the Chief's people didn't find the Nollam-b?"

"I'm afraid not," Tel'an answered.

"How quickly will we know if your serum worked, Doctor Offenbach?" asked Ash.

"Depends how close you are to a host," she said. We all turned to look at Martin, who was still sat on a chair next to us. He jumped and began to shake.

"Just say, for example's sake, we're right next to a host.

How quickly would we know we were safe?" Ash pushed.

"Chief Walden got one of the engineers to calculate it. It will take a maximum of ninety-seven seconds for the Nollam-b to make its way through the air filtration system. If the Flintoxin is reactivated, and you're next to a host, you'll know within seconds."

"Great," said Jake.

"We'll get back to you in a few minutes… if we're still alive," Jared added before cutting the link.

By the time zero-nine-thirty-five came, none of us were gasping for air, hacking our lungs up, or breathing our last, so we agreed the Doc was officially a genius. I felt Ash take my hand, his utter relief almost overwhelming as it surged through the Link, and I was so happy I hugged everyone all over again. After that, we escorted Martin to the Infirmary to thank Doctor Offenbach personally.

When we got there, she confirmed the Flintoxin had remained in its harmless state, even though it had been subjected to the Nollam-b. She also told us the hosts had been placed in decontamination units for safe measure until they could figure out what to do with them.

It really was over.

The Doc opened her bottom drawer and produced a bottle of Santian Vodka. "For special occasions," she assured us. Hell, I didn't care what it was for, it was nice to just sit and relax. I didn't even care that I hated Santian Vodka, I drank it, and it burnt the inside of my throat as I listened to Jake toast our success.

About an hour later, when I felt able to breathe properly for the first time in days, we were summoned to a gathering with the Tetrarchy of Souls. We'd turned their Summit into pandemonium, and the four ruling monarchs wanted to know why.

I couldn't blame them.

# 24

It was the first time I'd met the Tetrarchy as a group. All the way there my stomach vibrated with nervous excitement, but when we finally came face-to-face, I felt shy and awkward – sticking to Ash's side for support. I couldn't quite believe I was in the company of the most powerful people in the Four Sectors.

Once the introductions were over and everyone was settled, Ash explained everything from the moment we'd met Nyan, to the point Doctor Offenbach had confirmed the all-clear on the hosts. The doctor chipped in occasionally with information about the Flintoxin and other drugs, but mostly everyone sat in rapt silence.

I watched the reactions of the monarchs, but I found my gaze drawn to Queen Sophia from the House of Washington, Sector One. Her long, thick hair was completely straight, and china-white like the chalk cliffs on the western continent of Lilania. Her wide-set, deep green eyes sparkled as they caught the soft light from the lamp on the table beside her, a bright contrast against her skin – which was even paler than mine. She was a petite lady, elegant and feminine, and she wore a white and silver gown adorned with clear crystals and shimmering grey pearls. She looked enchanting, virtually ethereal, and I could hardly draw my eyes from her.

"There's something I don't understand," she said in a quiet voice that immediately had the attention of the entire room. "Why would Maximilian do something like this? He's always proven himself devoted and loyal to the Crowns. How could he possibly be ARRO?"

"We don't have the answer to that question yet, Your Majesty," said Walden. "But we'll get the answers when our people interrogate him."

"You have him in custody?" Sebastian asked, a note of surprise catching in his voice.

"Yes, sire."

"Perhaps you could've lead with that particular piece of information, Chief."

"Yes, sire." Walden shifted in his seat. "The information came through my earpiece as Brother Asher was mid-explanation. I thought it best not to interrupt. My apologies."

"Well… do you want to fill us in?" the King pressed.

"Of course, sire. According to gate security, Colderon feigned illness at the last moment to avoid going into the first session. A medical team were called when he complained of chest pain and shortness of breath, and he was taken to the infirmary where I'm guessing he planned to stay until everyone was dead. He could then come forward as the sole survivor, having had a miraculous recovery. As soon as we had confirmation from Ford that Colderon was responsible, I took a team to apprehend him, but he'd already disappeared."

"I'm afraid that was probably my fault," said Offenbach. "I was making the antidote serum for the Flintoxin in my lab. He must've realised his plan wasn't going the way he'd expected."

"I knew someone as meticulous as Colderon would have

an exit plan," continued Walden. "Which on a ship like this, could only mean one thing."

"To get off it," said Jake.

"Exactly. I gave the order to lock down all escape modules, and dispatched officers to every hanger. He had a shuttle fuelled and prepped for an emergency take-off in one of the auxiliary hangars, but my men got to him before he could launch. He put up some resistance, small-arms fire, but he was out-manned and out-gunned – plus he was wounded during the fire-fight."

"Badly?" Sebastian asked.

"A bullet to the shoulder, sire. It'll hurt like hell, but he'll live."

"You might want to check him for a suicide pill if you want to keep him alive," suggested Jake. "Just a suggestion."

"Already checked," replied Walden. "He didn't have one. Guess he's not as prepared to be a martyr to the cause as the people who worked for him. Anyway, he's in custody and on his way to the brig right now."

"No," said Queen Sophia, her quiet voice cutting through the room. "Have him brought here."

"Here?" Walden echoed. "With all due respect, Your Majesty, are you sure that's a wise idea? I mean, do you really want to put him in the same room with Tetrarchy? The same people he's just tried to kill?"

"That's precisely why I want him brought here, Chief," she replied. "I want to hear what he has to say for himself. I appreciate your concern, however I think we can risk it, don't you?" She looked at all the people in the room. "Fleet, Marines, Warrior Caste… you. How much better protected could we be?"

"Of course, I'll see to it personally," Walden replied before leaving.

Sebastian poured himself a glass of something orange then sat on the arm of a chair. "Notwithstanding what has happened to get us to this point," he sipped from his drink, "taking Colderon alive is a big win for us. Whether he's head of ARRO is debatable, but even if he's not, he's most certainly high up in their ranks. I'm confident we'll be able extract everything he knows about the organisation."

"With luck, we'll be able to finally neutralise the terrorist threat once and for all," added Queen Isabella, head of the House of Santona, Sector Four.

Sebastian sipped at the orange liquid again, creases spreading across his forehead.

"What is it, Bastian," Sophia asked.

"Something doesn't seem right," he replied, moving to sit next to her on the couch. "If ARRO's plan was to kill us all during the first session of the Summit, why try to kill me during the Royal Welcome Dinner?"

"I think I can answer that, sire," said Jared, surprising me. "While we were waiting to identify hosts, I had Commander Tel'an interrogating Doctor Ford. She asked him the same question, and according to him, the Agent of Death reported to Colderon that he'd been unable to neutralise his target on Angel Ridge before he'd spoken to the Brotherhood."

"Nyan," I said quietly.

"Right," continued Jared. "Nyan overheard part of the meeting on the Planet of Souls, but apparently Colderon hadn't given those people details of the final plan at that point – all part of the compartmentalisation of information ARRO employs. Anyway, Colderon told Ford he knew Nyan couldn't have given the Brotherhood much information to go on, but he also knew that the Brotherhood wouldn't give up without a full investigation." He smiled at Ash and me. "So, he concocted King Sebastian's assassination attempt as a ruse to keep everyone busy and off the trail of the real plan."

"And it almost worked," said Sebastian.

"But it didn't – thanks to the tenacity and instincts of a

remarkable group of individuals," said Queen Sophia. The monarchs were supposed to be equal, but it was clear from the way the rest deferred to Sophia that she was, for lack of a better word, Alpha-Royal. "I don't think I've ever heard of representatives from the Brotherhood, our Royal Fleet, and the Royal Marines, working together so closely and so effectively."

While we waited for Walden to return with Colderon, the Tetrarchy asked more questions about our mission. King Alexander from the House of Mercia, Sector Two, seemed particularly interested in the science behind the Flintoxin hosts, and he and Offenbach had an animated debate about the upgrading of the bio-scans on the *Athena*. I'd managed to keep up with most of their discussion, but I was glad of the distraction provided by Walden's return.

"You're Majesties," he said. "Maximillian Colderon, as requested."

Colderon shuffled in behind him, his hands and feet shackled, the left shoulder of his robes dark with blood. Two officers stood at his side, but Jake and Jared replaced them quickly, forcing Colderon to his knees. I noticed Jake squeeze his bloodied shoulder, and even though the pain was clear from the grimace on his face, he didn't cry out.

Queen Sophia took a couple of steps forward, giving Sebastian an almost undetectable glance as he opened his mouth – almost daring him to object. He nodded briefly then sat back down.

"I have just one question for you," she said to Colderon. "Maximillian, please look at me when I'm talking to you." For a moment he continued to stare at the shackles on his wrists, then slowly he raised his head and his cold eyes locked on hers. "Why?" she asked.

Colderon smiled and sighed. "Why what?" he replied. "Why do ARRO want you dead? Or why do I want you dead?"

"Either," grunted Alexander, but Colderon barely

acknowledged him, talking only to Sophia.

"Let me ask you a question first. Why did you promote Bellamy, my apprentice, over me, when the role of Lord High Steward should've been mine?"

"Now we're getting somewhere," said Sebastian. "All this because you feel slighted?"

Colderon laughed. "You stupid, arrogant bastard. As always, you've completely misunderstood the point. You… all of you," he looked at each of the Tetrarchy with equal disgust, "gave Bellamy the position over me because his blood-line was better than mine. It had nothing to do with whether he would make a better Lord High Steward. You…" he looked around the group again, "are the problem. You ask, 'Why did I do this', when everyone else is asking, 'Why should you have all the power?'"

"I've heard enough of this," said Alexander, signalling for the guards, but Sophia raised her hand and they stopped in their tracks.

"You see that?" Colderon laughed again before looking at Alexander. "Even you're deluded – can't you see? You think the four of you are equal? Look at her." He pointed to Sophia. "Equality is an illusion! Do you really think any of you could do anything she hasn't already agreed to?"

"That's enough," grunted Jake, squeezing Colderon's shoulder. He buckled to the side, but didn't stop staring at Sophia.

"You think your blood-line gives you the right to power, but true power comes from the people. ARRO has proved that, and they will continue their campaign to rid the Four Sectors of everyone who is unworthy – starting with the Tetrarchy. Royal rule is over. Democracy is the fair way forward, and if the only way to achieve this is through violent revolution, then so be it. You may have stopped our plans this time, but there is nothing but time ahead of us. You cannot stop the people – the revolution will—"

Sophia raised her hand again and the guards grabbed

Colderon, cutting him off mid-sentence. "I think we've got the picture, Chief," she said. "You can take him away now."

I could still hear Colderon shouting about the unfairness of Royal Leadership as they dragged him down the hall, until the door slid shut and silence fell.

"What will happen to him now?" asked Ash.

"We'll keep him here until the end of the summit then he'll come with me back to Earth," Sophia said. "I have people who'll find out everything he knows about ARRO, and then he'll be charged with treason, amongst many other things. He will also be held accountable for the death of Primus Finnian."

"That's much appreciated," replied Ash.

"Well, now that's Colderon taken care of, on to other business," Sophia continued. Her tone lifted. "On behalf of the Four Sectors, I would like to thank each and every one of you in this room for the respective parts you have played in saving many lives here today. That said, Captain Marcos, Colonel Mitchell, Brother Asher, Shae," she looked at each of us individually, "the four of you have been determined and unrelenting throughout this whole affair, and it is quite clear to me – to us – that without you, things would've turned out very differently today. Our special gratitude to you." She blinked her green eyes and carefully swished her chalky hair over one shoulder to reveal a slender neck. She turned her attention back to the whole group. "As you can imagine, the Tetrarchy has much to discuss, and I'm sure you all have things you need to do. We won't keep you any longer." We stood to leave, but Sophia touched Ash's arm and we both turned to look at her. "Not you two," she said, indicating for us to sit back down. "Colonel, Captain, if you would remain also?" She directed them to the empty seats by the side of me.

When the last person had left, and the door had closed, the Queen nodded delicately to King Alexander. Out of the corner of my eye I saw Jared and Jake share an interested glance, but I remained focussed on Alexander. He wasn't quite as imposing as Sebastian, but nonetheless he had my attention. I crossed my legs and tried not to fidget.

Alexander rose and poured himself a drink. "For a while now we've been in confidential talks with the Supreme Primus of the Brotherhood, the Field Marshal, and the Admiral of the Fleet, regarding the security and safety of the Royal Houses. ARRO has just proved how vulnerable we are, and they are only one of many threats we face throughout the Sectors. As you may know, it was a security incident that forced us to move the Tetrad Summit from Sector Two to Sector Three in the first place." He paused and turned to face us. "Despite the Constantine Agreement, which clearly separates the jurisdiction of the REF and the Brotherhood, Supreme Primus Isaiah has agreed that there are particular situations when a… how should I put it… a union of the two, would lead to a more expedient and successful outcome – especially in circumstances involving a member of the Tetrarchy or one of the Four Families. Our plan is to set up a small collection of elite, covert teams called 'Guardians of the Four', who will report directly to us when needed."

"The idea is quite simple," Queen Isabella added. "A Guardian will be selected because they're the best in whichever discipline they're in, whether that's Marines, Brotherhood or Fleet, and they'll have excelled themselves – gone above and beyond what's expected of them to the extreme. Guardians will continue in whatever jobs they were doing before they were selected. They'll carry on their day-to-day activities, and continue to report to their Commanding Officer or Primus. Life as normal. But occasionally they'll be called together with the rest of their team to complete a mission of the utmost importance to the Four Crowns. To be selected will be a great honour."

"The truth is we haven't finalised the details," said Sophia. "However, we talked before you arrived, and we unanimously agree that you will become our first Guardians. And, as you so clearly work well together, you'll also be our first team."

My head spun. After everything else that'd happened, I was a Guardian of the Four? It didn't seem real, and I must've looked stunned because Queen Sophia lent forward and put her hand gently on my knee, smiling kindly.

"It's an honour to protect the Four Houses," said Jared.

"In any capacity," added Jake.

Ash nodded briefly. "I know I speak for Shae when I say, our lives are your lives."

"Thank you all," Sophia said. Then, in a voice that cut through the reverence thickening in the room, she added, "As we have current matters that require our attention, we'll talk further after the Summit. I request you keep our discussion confidential until we finalise all necessary details."

And that was it – the conversation was back to reviewing the activities of the previous few hours, as if the Guardian's conversation had never happened.

After more discussion, the Royals seemed content that they knew everything of relevance, and that the threat had been contained. Before we left them to reconvene their Summit, each of them expressed their individual gratitude, and their sincere sadness for Finnian's sacrifice.

As I made to leave, I felt a cool, dainty hand on my shoulder, and found myself looking down into the pale rose lips and high cheekbones of Queen Sophia.

"My dearest child, I know you have pain in your heart. It will diminish in time, you'll see. You're an extraordinarily special young lady, more than you realise, and you have to stay strong – not just for yourself, but for others as well. We have so much more we need to discuss… but now is not the time. We'll talk more when we meet again." She took my hand, smiling, and her familiarity surprised me, then she turned her attention back to the Tetrarchy and the moment was over.

When my wits came back to me, I turned and followed the others out of the room, still thinking about her words.

"What did the Queen say?" asked Ash.

"I… I'm not really sure," I mumbled. "She told me to stay strong and that we had other things to talk about. Guess she was referring to Guardian stuff," I added, shrugging my shoulders.

"Guess so," Ash replied, but I got the tiniest hit of something I couldn't recognise through the Link.

"So what now?" I asked.

"Now we pack up and get the hell off this tub," Jake replied.

Ash and I returned to our suite to gather up our belongings, while Jake and Jared went to find Walden to formally transfer the prisoners to his custody.

"Leave them," Ash said as I half-heartedly stuffed fancy dresses into bags. "Someone else can take care of the clothes, just take any personal belongings."

"Ash, do you think… do you think if we'd done things differently, Finnian would still be…?" I couldn't say the word.

"You mustn't think like that, Shae."

"It's hard not to."

"I know, but Finnian made his own choices. He was a stubborn as a mule at times – even if you'd been there with him, he would've done the same thing if he thought it was the right thing to do."

"My head knows you're right, but my heart says I should've done more."

"There was nothing more any of us could've done. You shouldn't torture yourself."

"But—"

There was a knock on the door and Francis entered. "Are you set?" he asked. "The infirmary is ready for us."

I picked up a small bag, all I needed to fit what actually

belonged to me, and we headed to the infirmary to collect Finnian. When we got there, I was surprised to see Jake and Jared waiting for us.

"We understand this is Brotherhood business," said Jake, "but out of respect for the Primus, and for you all, Jared and I would be honoured if we could join you in escorting Finnian's body to the *Nakomo*."

"Thank you, Colonel," Ash replied. "I think we would appreciate that."

"Ash, I know the location of your monastery is confidential," added Jared, "but my crew and I would be privileged if we could take Primus Finnian on part of his final journey. Perhaps you could give us coordinates to a closer, secondary location. That way, you, Francis, and Shae, can rest before leaving again, and the position of your home remains secure. It's been a tough few days; everyone's exhausted."

Ash looked to Francis, who nodded wearily, then to me.

"That's a very thoughtful offer, Jared. Thank you," I said.

"Then it's agreed," added Ash.

I wanted to help transfer my father's body, but as tears started to fall, Jared and Jake assisted Francis and Ash in carrying the stretcher, while I walked silently beside it.

I was tired and sad when I walked down the *Nakomo's* ramp into the *Defender's* pristine hangar, but my spirits lifted when I saw Jake and Jared waiting – just like they had in the infirmary. I didn't really want to hand Finnian's body over to the med-techs, but they said they would take good care of him until we were ready to leave. I couldn't move until they'd left, and the doors had closed behind them.

"Well, this has certainly been one hell of a week," said Jake. "I need a drink. "Anyone want to join me?"

"I don't think—" Jared started.

"Come on," Jake pushed. "It's just what we need. We'll drink to a successful mission… to new friends…" he grinned at me, but then became serious, "to absent friends. It's tradition, Jared. We honour our fallen."

Jared deferred to Ash. "It's your call," he said. "I don't want you to do anything you're uncomfortable with."

"Actually, I appreciate the sentiment," Ash replied. "Perhaps it would be good for us. Shae?"

"I'm not sure…" I said, glancing back at the *Nakomo*. Ash didn't push, he simply slipped his hand into mine, and I looked up into his sad, grey eyes. "Okay," I conceded.

Malcolm, the distinguished looking barman I'd met only days earlier, was on duty again, and he waved happily as we entered the Queen's Tap. A few officers sat at the bar, but they diplomatically moved out of the way when they saw our party, and the five of us settled ourselves on the green padded stools.

Francis sat on the far left, then Ash, Jared, me, and Jake to my right. All my boys together. Safe.

"Six Fire Whisky's please, Malcolm," Jared said.

"Six?" he replied, mentally counting our group.

"Yes please."

"Okay then." Malcolm poured six shots and set them up on the bar in front of us. We each picked one up, leaving the sixth where it sat.

"To Finnian, may he rest in peace," said Ash.

"To Finnian," we chorused, before downing the shot in one. My throat burned and tears welled.

"Another round please, Malcolm. On second thoughts… leave the bottle," Jared added. "I have a feeling we're going to need it."

# ABOUT THE AUTHOR

British author, S.M.Tidball, has been writing since her teens, starting with poetry before moving on to short stories. Despite the challenges of being diagnosed with dyslexia, she has continued follow her passion, and now shares her epic vision of secrets, danger, and rebellion in the Helyan Series.

**Books available in the Helyan Series:**

Part One: Guardians of the Four
Part Two: Fallen Star

**Don't miss out:**

**Follow** on twitter: @SarahTidball

**Like** on Facebook: @SMTidball

**Follow** on Instagram: @SMTidball

Printed in Great Britain
by Amazon

38471102R00229